PUBLIC LIBRARY
OCT 2 6 2012
ORILLIA, ON

W9-BRR-562

PRAISE FOR *FORBIDDEN*

"The novel's surprises continue to the very end, and the secondary characters are well developed. . . . Most of all, though, it's Lochan's and Maya's alternating first-person, present-tense narratives, both tender and heartbreaking, that will stay with readers." —*Booklist*

"Ms. Suzuma's ability to dig so deeply into the various layers of human need and desire across several strata—physical, emotional, situational—renders a cringe-worthy premise another human experience to evaluate. The poignant and shocking ending will leave the reader pondering this story long after the final page is turned." —*New York Journal of Books*

"There is nothing about this novel that is easy, but readers who snag the book for the controversy will stick around for the polished writing and compelling character development." —*BCCB*

"It's a credit to the author that she is able to create genuine compassion for characters involved in this cultural taboo." —*SLJ*

An Amazon.com Best of the Month selection

OCT 20 20

FORBIDDEN

Tabitha Suzuma

SIMON PULSE

NEW YORK   LONDON   TORONTO   SYDNEY   NEW DELHI

This book is a work of fiction. Any references to historical events,
real people, or real locales are used fictitiously. Other names, characters, places,
and incidents are the product of the author's imagination, and any resemblance
to actual events or locales or persons, living or dead, is entirely coincidental.

SIMON PULSE

An imprint of Simon & Schuster Children's Publishing Division
1230 Avenue of the Americas, New York, NY 10020
First Simon Pulse paperback edition June 2012
Copyright © 2010 by Tabitha Suzuma
Originally published in 2010 in Great Britain by Random House UK.
Published by arrangement with Random House UK.
All rights reserved, including the right of reproduction
in whole or in part in any form.
SIMON PULSE and colophon are registered trademarks
of Simon & Schuster, Inc.
For information about special discounts for bulk purchases,
please contact Simon & Schuster Special Sales at 1-866-506-1949
or business@simonandschuster.com.
The Simon & Schuster Speakers Bureau can bring authors to your live event.
For more information or to book an event contact the Simon & Schuster Speakers
Bureau at 1-866-248-3049 or visit our website at www.simonspeakers.com.
Designed by Mike Rosamilia
The text of this book was set in Perpetua.
Manufactured in the United States of America
2 4 6 8 10 9 7 5 3 1
Library of Congress Cataloging-in-Publication Data
Suzuma, Tabitha, 1975-
Forbidden / by Tabitha Suzuma. — 1st Simon Pulse hardcover ed.
p. cm.
Summary: Sixteen-year-old Maya and seventeen-year-old Lochan tell,
in their separate voices, of their confusion and longing as they fall in
love with one another after years of functioning as parents to three
younger siblings due to their alcoholic mother's neglect.
[1. Brothers and sisters—Fiction. 2. Family problems—Fiction.
3. Alcoholism—Fiction. 4. Incest—Fiction. 5. England—Fiction.]
I. Title. PZ7.S96918For 2011 [Fic]—dc22 2010027433
ISBN 978-1-4424-1995-7 (hardcover)
ISBN 978-1-4424-2754-9 (eBook)
ISBN 978-1-4424-1996-4 (pbk)

For Akiko, with love

ACKNOWLEDGMENTS

I wish I could say writing this book was easy. It wasn't. In fact, it was possibly the hardest thing I've ever done in my life. . . . Therefore, I owe an enormous thank-you to all those who helped and supported me during this tough time. First of all, this book never would have existed had it not been for the passion and unwavering faith of my editor, Charlie Sheppard, who not only fought for this book's creation, but continued to fight, during the many times I wanted to give up, to keep the book alive. I also want to offer my heartfelt thanks to Annie Eaton, who has been so encouraging and has kept believing in me and in this book so strongly. Editors Sarah Dudman and Ruth Knowles worked extremely hard, and I am very grateful for their patience, expertise, and commitment. My thanks also extend to Sophie Nelson and to the design team for their invaluable contribution.

I am especially grateful for the incredible support of my family. My mother not only tirelessly proofreads my books at every stage, but also helps me find the time and energy to write them. Tansy Roekaerts offers me constructive feedback on all my books and always seems to know how to help me when I am stuck. Tiggy Suzuma is the pride of my life and somehow manages to make me laugh during the bad times and not take it all too seriously. Thalia Suzuma gives me invaluable feedback, too, along with practical help and professional advice. Finally, I am so lucky to have as my best friend Akiko Hart, who not only helps me to write, but, more importantly, to live.

You can close your eyes to the things you do not want to see, but you cannot close your heart to the things you do not want to feel.

—Anonymous

instincts keep it going until it is physically capable of no more, or does it eventually learn after one crash too many that there is no way out? At what point do you decide that enough is enough?

I turn my eyes away from the tiny carcasses and try to focus on the mass of quadratic equations on the board. A thin film of sweat coats my skin, trapping wisps of hair against my forehead, clinging to my school shirt. The sun has been pouring through the industrial-size windows all afternoon and I am foolishly sitting in full glare, half blinded by the powerful rays. The ridge of the plastic chair digs painfully into my back as I sit semi-reclined, one leg stretched out, heel propped up against the low radiator along the wall. My shirt cuffs hang loose around my wrists, stained with ink and grime. The empty page stares up at me, painfully white, as I work out equations in lethargic, barely legible handwriting. The pen slips and slides in my clammy fingers. I peel my tongue off my palate and try to swallow; I can't. I have been sitting like this for the best part of an hour, but I know that trying to find a more comfortable position is useless. I linger over the sums, tilting the nib of my pen so that it catches on the paper and makes a faint scratching sound—if I finish too soon, I will have nothing to do but look at dead flies again. My head hurts. The air stands heavy, pregnant with the perspiration of thirty-two teenagers crammed into an overheated classroom. There is a weight on my chest that makes it difficult to breathe. It is far more than this arid room, this stale air. The weight descended on Tuesday, the moment I stepped through the school gates, back to face another school year. The week has not yet ended and already I feel as if I have been here for all eternity. Between these school walls, time flows like cement. Nothing has changed. The people are still the same: vacuous faces, contemptuous smiles. My eyes slide past theirs as I enter the classrooms and they gaze past me, through me. I am here but not here. The teachers tick me off in the register but no one sees me, for I have long perfected the art of being invisible.

There is a new English teacher—Miss Azley. Some bright young thing from Down Under: huge frizzy hair held back by a rainbow-colored head scarf, tanned skin, and massive gold hoops in her ears. She looks alarmingly out of place in a school full of tired middle-aged teachers, faces etched with lines of bitterness and disappointment. No doubt once, like this plump, chirpy Aussie, they entered the profession full of hope and vigor, determined to make a difference, to heed Gandhi and be the change they wanted to see in the world. Now, after decades of policies, intraschool red tape, and crowd control, most have given up and are awaiting early retirement, custard creams and tea in the staff room the highlight of their day. But the new teacher hasn't had the benefit of time. In fact, she doesn't look much older than some of the pupils in the room. A bunch of guys erupt into a cacophony of wolf whistles until she swings round to face them, disdainfully staring them down so that they start to look uncomfortable and glance away. Nonetheless, a stampede ensues when she commands everyone to arrange the desks in a semicircle, and with all the jostling, play fighting, desk slamming, and chair sliding, she is lucky nobody gets injured. Despite the mayhem, Miss Azley appears unperturbed—when everyone finally settles down, she gazes around the scraggly circle and beams.

"That's better. Now I can see you all properly and you can all see me. I'll expect you to have the classroom set up before I arrive in the future, and don't forget that all the desks need to be returned to their places at the end of the lesson. Anyone caught leaving before having done his or her bit will take sole responsibility for the furniture arrangements for a week. Do I make myself clear?" Her voice is firm but there appears to be no malice. Her grin suggests she might even have a sense of humor. The grumbles and complaints from the usual trouble-makers are surprisingly muted.

She then announces that we are going to take turns introducing ourselves. After expounding on her love of travel, her new dog, and her previous career in advertising, she turns to the girl on her right. Surreptitiously I slide my watch round to

 TABITHA SUZUMA

the inside of my wrist and train my eyes on the seconds flashing past. All day I have been waiting for this—final period—and now that it is here I can hardly bear it. All day I've been counting down the hours, the lessons, until this one. Now all that's left is the minutes, yet they seem interminable. I am doing sums in my head, calculating the number of seconds before the last bell. With a start I realize that Rafi, the dickhead to my left, is blabbering on about astrology again—almost all the kids in the room have had their turn now. When Rafi finally shuts up about stellar constellations, there is sudden silence. I look up to find Miss Azley staring directly at me.

"Pass." I examine my thumbnail and automatically mumble my usual response without looking up.

But to my horror, she doesn't take the hint. Has she not read my file? She is still looking at me. "Few activities in my lessons are optional, I'm afraid," she informs me.

There are sniggers from Jed's group. "We'll be here all day, then."

"Didn't anyone tell you? He don't speak English—"

"Or any other language." Laughter.

"Martian, maybe!"

The teacher silences them with a look. "I'm afraid that's not how things work in my lessons."

Another long silence follows. I fiddle with the corner

of my notepad, the eyes of the class scorching my face. The steady tick of the wall clock is drowned out by the pounding of my heart.

"Why don't you start off by telling me your name?" Her voice has softened slightly. It takes me a moment to figure out why. Then I realize that my left hand has stopped fiddling with the notepad and is now vibrating against the empty page. I hurriedly slide my hand beneath the desk, mumble my name, and glance meaningfully at my neighbor. He launches eagerly into his monologue without giving the teacher time to protest, but I can see she has backed down. She knows now. The pain in my chest fades to a dull ache and my burning cheeks cool. The rest of the hour is taken up with a lively debate about the merits of studying Shakespeare. Miss Azley does not invite me to participate again.

When the last bell finally shrieks its way through the building, the class dissolves into chaos. I slam my textbook shut, stuff it into my bag, get up, and exit the room rapidly, diving into the home-time fray. All along the main corridor overexcited pupils are streaming out of doors to join the thick current of people; I am bumped and buffeted by shoulders, elbows, bags, feet. . . . I make it down one staircase, then the next, and am almost across the main hall before I feel a hand on my arm.

"Whitely. A word."

Freeland, my form tutor. I feel my lungs deflate.

The silver-haired teacher with the hollow, lined face leads me into an empty classroom, indicates a seat, then perches awkwardly on the corner of a wooden desk.

"Lochan, as I'm sure you are aware, this is a particularly important year for you."

The A-level lecture again. I give a slight nod, forcing myself to meet my tutor's gaze.

"It's also the start of a new academic year!" Freeland announces brightly, as if I needed reminding of that fact. "New beginnings. A fresh start . . . Lochan, we know you don't always find things easy, but we're hoping for great things from you this term. You've always excelled in written work, and that's wonderful, but now that you're in your final year, we expect you to show us what you're capable of in other areas."

Another nod. An involuntary glance toward the door. I'm not sure I like where this conversation is heading. Mr. Freeland gives a heavy sigh. "Lochan, if you want to get into UCL, you know it's vital you start taking a more active role in class. . . ."

I nod again.

"Do you understand what I'm saying here?"

I clear my throat. "Yes."

"Class participation. Joining in group discussions. Contributing to the lessons. Actually replying when asked a question. Putting your hand up once in a while. That's all we ask. Your grades have always been impeccable. No complaints there."

Silence.

My head is hurting again. How much longer is this going to take?

"You seem distracted. Are you taking in what I'm saying?"

"Yes."

"Good. Look, you have great potential and we would hate to see that go to waste. If you need help again, you know we can arrange that. . . ."

I feel the heat rise to my cheeks. "N-no. It's okay. Really. Thanks anyway." I pick up my bag, sling the strap over my head and across my chest, and head for the door.

"Lochan," Mr. Freeland calls after me as I walk out. "Just think about it."

At last. I am heading toward Bexham, school rapidly fading behind me. It is barely four o'clock and the sun is still beating down, the bright white light bouncing off the sides of cars, which reflect it in disjointed rays, the heat shimmering off the tarmac. The high street is all traffic, exhaust fumes, braying horns, schoolkids, and noise. I have been waiting for this moment since being jolted awake this morning, but now that it is finally here I feel strangely empty. Like being a child again, clattering down the stairs to find that Santa has forgotten to fill up our stockings; that Santa, in fact, is just the drunk on the couch in the front room, lying comatose with three of her friends. I have been focusing so hard on actually getting out of school that I seem to have forgotten what to do now that I've escaped. The elation I was expecting does not materialize and I feel lost, naked, as if I'd been anticipating something wonderful but suddenly forgot what it was. Walking down the street, weaving in and out of the crowds, I try to think of something—anything—to look forward to.

In an effort to shake myself out of my strange mood, I jog across the cracked paving stones past the litter-lined gutters, the balmy September breeze lifting the hair from the nape of my neck, my thin-soled sneakers moving soundlessly over the sidewalk. I loosen my tie, pulling the knot halfway down my chest, and undo my top shirt buttons. It's always good to stretch my legs at the end of a long, dull day at Belmont, to dodge, skim, and leap over the smeared fruit and squashed veg left behind by the market stalls. I turn the corner onto the familiar narrow road with its two long rows of small, run-down brick houses stretching gradually uphill.

It's the street I've lived on for the past five years. We only moved into the council house after our father took himself off to Australia with his new wife and the child support stopped.

Before then, home had been a dilapidated rented house on the other side of town, but in one of the nicer areas. We were never well-off, not with a poet for a father, but nonetheless, things were easier in so many ways. But that was a long, long time ago. Home now is number sixty-two Bexham Road: a two-story, three-bedroom, gray stucco cube, thickly sandwiched in a long line of others, with Coke bottles and beer cans sprouting among the weeds between the broken gate and the faded orange door.

The road is so narrow that the cars, with their boarded-up windows or dented fenders, have to park with two wheels on the curb, making it easier to walk down the center of the street than on the sidewalk. Kicking a crushed plastic bottle out of the gutter, I dribble it along, the slap of my shoes and the grate of plastic against tarmac echoing around me, soon joined by the cacophony of a yapping dog, shouts from a children's soccer game, and reggae blasting out of an open window. My bag bounces and rattles against my thigh and I feel some of my malaise begin to dissipate. As I jog past the soccer players, a familiar figure overshoots the goalpost markers and I exchange the plastic bottle for the ball, easily dodging the pint-size boys in their oversize Arsenal T-shirts as they follow me up the road, yelping in protest. The blond firework dives toward me, a towheaded little hippie with hair down to his shoulders, his

 TABITHA SUZUMA

once-white school shirt now streaked with dirt and hanging over torn gray trousers. He manages to get ahead of me, running backward as fast as he can, shouting frantically, "To me, Loch, to me, Loch. Pass it to me!"

With a laugh I do, and whooping in triumph, my eight-year-old brother grabs the ball and runs back to his mates, yelling, "I got it off him, I got it off him! Did you see?"

I slam into the relative cool of the house and sag back against the front door to catch my breath, brushing the damp hair off my forehead. Straightening up, I pick my way down the hallway, my feet automatically nudging aside the assortment of discarded blazers, book bags, and school shoes that litter the narrow corridor. In the kitchen I find Willa up on the counter, trying to reach a box of Frosted Cheerios in the cupboard. She freezes when she sees me, one hand on the box, her blue eyes wide with guilt beneath her fringe. "Maya forgot my snack today!"

I lunge toward her with a growl, grabbing her round the waist with one arm and swinging her upside down as she squeals with a mixture of terror and delight, her long golden hair fanning out beneath her. Then I dump her unceremoniously onto a kitchen chair and slap down the cereal box, milk bottle, bowl, and spoon.

"Half a bowlful, no more," I warn her with a raised finger.

"We're having an early dinner tonight—I've got a ton of home-work to do."

"When?" Willa sounds unconvinced, scattering sugar-coated hoops across the chipped oak table that is the center-piece of our messy kitchen. Despite the revised set of house rules that Maya taped to the fridge door, it is clear that Tiffin hasn't touched the overflowing trash bins in days, that Kit hasn't even begun washing the breakfast dishes piled up in the sink, and that Willa has once again mislaid her miniature broom and has only succeeded in adding to the crumbs lit-tering the floor.

"Where's Mum?" I ask.

"Getting ready."

I empty my lungs with a sigh and leave the kitchen, taking the narrow wooden stairs two at a time, ignoring Mum's greet-ing, searching for the only person I really feel like talking to. But when I spot the open door to her empty room, I remem-ber that she is stuck at some after-school thing tonight and my chest deflates. Instead I return to the familiar sound of Magic FM blasting out of the open bathroom door.

My mother is leaning over the basin toward the smeared, cracked mirror, putting the finishing touches on her mascara and brushing invisible lint off the front of her tight silver dress. The air is thick with the stench of hair spray and perfume. As

TABITHA SUZUMA

she sees me appear behind her reflection, her brightly painted lips lift and part in a smile of apparent delight. "Hey, beautiful boy!"

She turns down the radio, swings round to face me, and holds out an arm for a kiss. Without moving from the doorway, I kiss the air, an involuntary scowl etched between my brows.

She begins to laugh. "Look at you—back in your uniform and almost as scruffy as the kiddies! You need a haircut, sweetie. Oh dear, what's with the stormy look?"

I sag against the door frame, trailing my blazer on the floor. "It's the third time this week, Mum," I protest wearily.

"I know, I know, but I couldn't possibly miss this. Davey finally signed the contract for the new restaurant and wants to go out and celebrate!" She opens her mouth in an exclamation of delight and, when my expression fails to thaw, swiftly changes the subject. "How was your day, sweetie pie?"

I manage a wry smile. "Great, Mum. As usual."

"Wonderful!" she exclaims, choosing to ignore the sarcasm in my voice. If there's one thing my mother excels at, it's minding her own business. "Only a year now—not even that—and you'll be free of school and all that silliness." Her smile broadens. "Soon you'll finally turn eighteen and really will be the man of the house!"

I lean my head back against the doorjamb. *The man of the*

house. She's been calling me that since I was twelve, ever since Dad left.

Turning back to the mirror, she presses her breasts together beneath the top of her low-cut dress. "How do I look? I got paid today and treated myself to a shopping spree." She flashes me a mischievous grin as if we were conspirators in this little extravagance. "Look at these gold sandals. Aren't they darling?"

I am unable to return the smile. I wonder how much of her monthly wage has already been spent. Retail therapy has been an addiction for years now. Mum is desperate to cling on to her youth, a time when her beauty turned heads in the street, but her looks are rapidly fading, face prematurely aged by years of hard living.

"You look great," I answer robotically.

Her smile fades a little. "Lochan, come on, don't be like this. I need your help tonight. Dave is taking me somewhere really special—you know the place that's just opened on Stratton Road opposite the movie theater?"

"Okay, okay. It's fine—have fun." With considerable effort I erase the frown and manage to keep the resentment out of my voice. There is nothing particularly wrong with Dave. Of the long string of men my mother has been involved with ever since Dad left her for one of his colleagues, Dave has been the most benign. Nine years her junior and the owner of the restaurant where she now works as head waitress, he is currently separated from his wife. But like each of Mum's flings, he appears to possess the same strange power all men have over her, the ability to transform her into a giggling, flirting, fawning girl, desperate to spend her hard-earned cash on unnecessary presents for her "man" and tight-fitting, revealing outfits for herself. Tonight it is barely five o'clock and already her face is flushed with anticipation as she tarts herself up for this dinner, no doubt having spent the last hour fretting over what to wear. Pulling back her freshly highlighted blond perm, she is now experimenting with some exotic hairdo and asking me to fasten her fake diamond necklace—a present from Dave—that she swears is real. Her curvy figure barely fits into a dress her sixteen-year-old daughter wouldn't be seen dead in, and the comment "mutton dressed as lamb," regularly overheard from neighbors' front gardens, echoes in my ears.

I close my bedroom door behind me and lean against it for a few moments, relishing this small patch of carpet that is my own. It never used to be a bedroom, just a small storage room with a bare window, but I managed to squeeze a camp bed in here three years ago when I realized that sharing a bunk bed with siblings had some serious drawbacks. It is one of the few places where I can be completely alone: no pupils with knowing eyes and mocking smirks; no teachers firing questions at me; no shouting, jostling bodies. And there is still a small oasis of time before our mother goes out on her date and dinner has to get under way and the arguments over food and homework and bedtime begin.

I drop my bag and blazer on the floor, kick off my shoes, and sit down on the bed with my back against the wall, knees drawn up in front of me. My usually tidy space bears all the frantic signs of a slept-through alarm: clock knocked to the floor, bed unmade, chair covered with discarded clothes, floor littered with books and papers, spilled from the piles on my desk. The flaking walls are bare, save for a small snapshot of the seven of us, taken during our final annual holiday in Blackpool two months before Dad left. Willa, still a baby, is on Mum's lap, Tiffin's face is smeared with chocolate ice cream, Kit is hanging upside down off the bench, and Maya is trying to yank him back up. The only faces clearly visible are Dad's and mine—we have our arms slung across each other's shoulders, grinning broadly at the camera. I rarely look at the photo, despite having rescued it from Mum's bonfire. But I like the feel of it being close by: a reminder that those happier times were not simply a figment of my imagination.

TABITHA SUZUMA

CHAPTER TWO

Maya

My key jams in the lock again. I curse, then kick the door in
my usual manner. The moment I step out of the late afternoon
sunshine and into the darkened hallway, I sense that things are
already a little wild. Predictably, the front room is a tip—crisp
packets, book bags, school letters, and abandoned homework
strewn across the carpet. Kit is eating Cheerios straight from
the box, trying to throw the odd one across the room into
Willa's open mouth.

"Maya, Maya, look what Kit can do!" Willa calls excitedly
to me as I shed my blazer and tie in the doorway. "He can get
them into my mouth all the way from over there!"

Despite the mess of cereal trampled into the carpet, I can't help smiling. My little sister is the cutest five-year-old in history. Her dimpled cheeks, flushed pink with exertion, are still gently rounded with baby chubbiness, her face lit with a soft innocence. Since losing her front teeth she has taken to poking the tip of her tongue through the gap when she smiles. Her waist-length hair hangs down her back, straight and fine like gold silk, the color matched by the tiny studs in her ears. Beneath overgrown bangs, her large eyes wear a permanently startled look, the color of deep water. She has exchanged her uniform for a flowery pink summer dress, her current favorite, and is hopping from foot to foot, delighted by her teenage brother's antics.

I turn to Kit with a grin. "Looks like the two of you have been having a very productive afternoon. I hope you remember where we keep the vacuum cleaner."

Kit responds by throwing a handful of cereal in Willa's direction. For a moment I think he is just going to ignore me, but then he declares, "It's not a game, it's target practice. Mum won't care—she's out with Lover Boy again tonight, and by the time she makes it home she'll be too wasted to notice."

I open my mouth to object to Kit's choice of words, but Willa is egging him on, and seeing that he is neither sulking nor arguing, I decide to let it pass and collapse on the couch.

My thirteen-year-old brother has changed in recent months: a summer growth spurt has accentuated his already skinny frame, his sandy hair has been cut short to show off the fake diamond stud in his ear, and his hazel eyes have hardened. Something has shifted in his manner, too. The child is still there but buried beneath an unfamiliar toughness; the change around the eyes, the defiant set of the jaw, the harsh, mirthless laugh all give him an alien, jagged edge. Yet during brief, genuine moments like these, when he is just having fun, the mask slips a little and I see my kid brother again.

"Is Lochan doing dinner tonight?" I ask.

"Obviously."

"Dinner . . ." Willa's hand flies to her mouth in alarm. "Lochie said one last warning."

"He was bluffing—" Kit tries to forestall her, but she is off down the corridor to the kitchen at a gallop, always anxious to please. I sit up on the couch, yawning, and Kit starts flicking cereal at my forehead.

"Watch it. That's all we've got for the morning and I don't see you eating it off the floor." I stand up. "Come on. Let's go see what Lochan's cooked up."

"Fucking pasta—what else does he ever make?" Kit tosses the open cereal box onto the armchair, spilling half its contents across the cushions, his good mood evaporating in a heartbeat.

"Well, perhaps you could start learning how to cook. Then we could all three take turns."

Kit shoots me a condescending look and stalks ahead of me into the kitchen.

"Out, Tiffin. I said, get the ball out of the room." Lochan has a boiling saucepan in one hand and is trying to manhandle Tiffin through the door with the other.

"Goal!" Tiffin yells, shooting the ball under the table. I catch it, toss it into the corridor, and grab Tiffin as he tries to dive past me.

"Help, help, she's strangling me!" he yells, miming asphyxiation.

I maneuver him onto his chair. "Sit!"

At the sight of food he complies, grabbing his knife and fork and beating out a drumroll on the table. Willa laughs and picks up her cutlery to copy.

"Don't . . ." I warn her.

Her smile fades, and for a moment she looks chastened. I feel a pang of guilt. Willa is loving and biddable, whereas Tiffin is always bursting with energy and mischief. As a consequence she is always witnessing her brother get away with murder. Moving quickly round the kitchen, I set out the plates, pour the water, return the cooking ingredients to their respective homes.

"Okay, tuck in, everyone." Lochan has dished up. Four plates, one pink Barbie bowl. Pasta with cheese, pasta with cheese and sauce, pasta with sauce but no cheese, broccoli—which neither Kit nor Tiffin will touch—craftily hidden round the sides.

"Hello, you." I catch his sleeve before he heads back to the cooker and smile. "You okay?"

"I've been home two hours and they've already gone crazy." He shoots me a look of exaggerated despair and I laugh.

"Mum left already?"

He nods. "Did you remember the milk?"

"Yeah, but we need to do a proper shop."

"I'll go after school tomorrow." Lochan spins round in time to catch Tiffin leaping for the door. "Oi!"

"I'm done, I'm done! I'm not hungry anymore!"

"Tiffin, would you just sit down at the table like a normal person and eat your meal?" Lochan's voice begins to rise.

"But Ben and Jamie are only allowed out for another half hour!" Tiffin yells in protest, his face scarlet beneath his mop of tow-colored hair.

"It's six thirty! You're not going back outside tonight!"

Tiffin throws himself back into his chair in fury, arms folded, knees drawn up. "That's so not fair! I hate you!"

Lochan wisely ignores Tiffin's antics and instead turns his

attention to Willa, who has given up trying to use a fork and is eating the spaghetti with her fingers, tilting back her head and sucking in each strand from the bottom. "Look." Lochan shows her. "You wind it round like this. . . ."

"But it keeps falling off!"

"Just try a bit at a time."

"I can't," she moans. "Lochie, cut it up for me?"

"Willa, you need to learn—"

"But fingers is easier!"

Kit's place remains empty as he works his way round the kitchen, opening and slamming cupboard doors.

"Let me save you some time—the only food we've got left is on the table," Lochan says, picking up his fork. "And I haven't put any arsenic in it, so it's unlikely to kill you."

"Great, so she's forgotten to leave us any money for market again? Well, of course, it's all right for her—Lover Boy's taking her to the Ritz."

"His name's Dave," Lochan points out from behind a forkful of food. "Calling him that doesn't make you sound in any way cool."

Swallowing my mouthful, I manage to catch Lochan's eye and give a barely perceptible shake of the head. I sense Kit is gearing up for an argument, and Lochan, usually so adept at sidestepping confrontation, looks tired and on edge and seems

TABITHA SUZUMA

to be steering blindly for a head-on collision tonight.

Kit slams the last cupboard with such force that everyone jumps. "What makes you think I'm trying to sound cool? I'm not the one stuck in an apron because his mother is too busy spreading her legs for—"

Lochan is out of his chair in a flash. I lunge for him and miss. He launches himself at Kit and grabs him by the collar, slamming him up against the fridge. "You speak like that in front of the little ones again and I'll—"

"You'll what?" Kit has his older brother's hand round his throat, and despite the cocky smirk, I recognize a glimmer of fear in his eyes. Lochan has never threatened him physically before, but in recent months their relationship has deteriorated. Kit has begun to resent Lochan more and more deeply for reasons I struggle to understand. Yet despite his initial shock, he somehow manages to retain the upper hand with the mocking expression, the look of condescension for the brother nearly five years his senior.

Suddenly Lochan seems to realize what he is doing. He lets go of Kit and springs back, stunned by his own outburst.

Kit straightens up, a slow sneer creeping onto his lips. "Yeah, that's what I thought. Gutless. Just like at school."

He has gone too far. Tiffin is silent, munching slowly, his eyes wary. Willa is gazing anxiously at Lochan, tugging nervously at her ear, her meal forgotten. Lochan is staring at the now empty doorway through which Kit has just departed. He wipes his hands on his jeans and takes a long, steadying breath before turning round to face Tiffin and Willa. "Hey, come on, guys, let's finish up." His voice quavers with false cheer.

Tiffin eyes him dubiously. "Were you gonna punch him?"

"No!" Lochan looks deeply shocked. "No, of course not, Tiff. I'd never hurt Kit. I'd never hurt any of you. Jeez!"

Tiffin returns to his meal, unconvinced. Willa says nothing, solemnly sucking each finger clean, silent resentment radiating from her eyes.

Lochan doesn't return to his seat. Instead he appears at a loss, chewing the corner of his lip, his face working. I lean back in my chair and reach for his arm. "He was just trying to wind you up as usual. . . ."

He doesn't respond. Instead, he takes another deep breath before glancing at me and saying, "D'you mind finishing this up?"

"Course not."

"Thanks." He forces a reassuring smile before leaving the room. Moments later I hear his bedroom door close.

I manage to persuade Tiffin and Willa to finish their food and then put Lochan's barely touched plate in the fridge. Kit can have the stale bread on the counter for all I care. I give

  TABITHA SUZUMA

Willa a bath and force a protesting Tiffin to take a shower. After vacuuming the front room, I decide that an early bedtime would do them no harm and studiously ignore Tiffin's furious protests about the lingering evening sunlight. As I kiss them in their bunks, Willa puts her arms round my neck and holds me close for a moment.

"Why does Kit hate Lochie?" she whispers.

I draw back a little in order to look into her eyes. "Sweetheart, Kit doesn't hate Lochie," I say carefully. "Kit's just in a bad mood these days."

Her deep blue eyes flood with relief. "So they love each other really?"

"Of course they do. And everybody loves you." I kiss her again on the forehead. "Nighty-night."

I confiscate Tiffin's DS and leave the two of them listening to an audio book, then make my way down to the far end of the corridor, where a ladder leads up to the box-size attic, and shout up at Kit to turn the music down. Last year, after one pitiful complaint after another about having to share a room with his younger siblings, Kit was helped by Lochan to clear the previously unused tiny attic of all the junk left there by former owners. Even though the space is too small to stand up in properly, it is Kit's lair, the private den where he spends most of his time when at home. Its sloping walls painted black and plastered with rock chicks, the dry, creaking floorboards covered with a Persian rug Lochan unearthed from some charity shop. Cut off from the rest of the house by a steep ladder that Tiffin and Willa have been strictly forbidden to climb, it is the perfect hideaway for someone like Kit. The music fades to a monotonous bass thud as I finally close the door to my room and start my homework.

The house is quiet at last. I hear the audio book come to an end and the air falls silent. My alarm clock reads twenty past eight, and the golden dusk of the Indian summer is fading rapidly. Night is falling, the street lamps coming on one after the other, casting a funereal light on the workbook in front of me. I finish off a comprehension exercise and find myself staring at my own reflection in the darkened window. On an impulse I stand up and walk out onto the landing.

My knock is tentative. Had it been me, I'd have probably stalked out of the house, but Lochan isn't like that. He's far too mature, far too sensible. Never once in all the nights since Dad left has he stormed out—not even when Tiffin plastered his hair down with treacle and then refused to have a bath, or when Willa sobbed for hours on end because someone had given her doll a Mohawk.

However, things have been going rapidly downhill lately. Even before his adolescent metamorphosis, Kit was prone to

 TABITHA SUZUMA

throwing a tantrum whenever Mum went out for the evening. The school counselor claims that he blames himself for Dad's leaving, that he still harbors the hope that Dad might return and therefore feels deeply threatened by anyone trying to take his father's place. Personally, I have always suspected it is something far simpler: Kit doesn't like the little ones getting all the attention for being small and cute, and Lochan and me telling everyone what to do, while he's stuck in no-man's-land, the archetypal middle child with no partner in crime. Now that Kit has gained the necessary respect at school by joining a gang who sneaks out of the gates to smoke weed in the local park at lunchtime, he bitterly resents the fact that at home he is still considered just one of the children. When Mum's out, which is increasingly more often, Lochan is the one in charge, the way it's always been—Lochan, the one she dumps on whenever she has to work overtime or fancies a night out with Dave or the girls.

There is no answer to my knock, and when I wander downstairs, I find Lochan asleep on the couch in the front room. A thick textbook rests against his chest, its pages splayed, and sheets of scrawled, spidery calculations litter the carpet. Uncurling his fingers from the book, I gather his things into a pile on the coffee table, pull the blanket off the back of the couch, and lay it over him. Then I sit in the armchair and draw up my legs, resting my chin on my knees, watching him sleep beneath the soft orange glow of the street lamps falling through the curtainless window.

Before there was anything, there was Lochan. When I look back on my life, all sixteen and a half years of it, Lochan was always there. Walking to school by my side, propelling me in a shopping trolley across an empty car park at breakneck speed, coming to my rescue in the playground after I'd caused a class uprising by calling Little Miss Popular "stupid." I still remember him standing there, fists clenched, an unusually fierce look on his face, challenging all the boys to a fight despite being vastly outnumbered. And I suddenly realized that, so long as I had Lochan, nothing and no one could ever harm me. But I was eight then. I've grown up since those days. Now I know that Lochan won't always be here, won't be able to protect me forever. Although he's applying to study at University College, London, and says he will continue to live at home, he could still change his mind and see that this is his chance to escape. Never before have I imagined my life without him—like this house, he is my only point of reference in this difficult existence, this unstable and frightening world. The thought of his leaving home fills me with a terror so strong, it takes my breath away. I feel like one of those seagulls covered in oil from a spill, drowning in a black tar of fear.

Asleep, Lochan looks like a boy again—ink-stained fingers, creased gray T-shirt, scuffed jeans, and bare feet. People say there is a strong family resemblance—I don't see it. For a start he is the only one of us with bright green eyes, as clear as cut glass. His shaggy hair is tar black, covering the nape of his neck and reaching his eyes. His arms are still tanned from summer, and even in the half light I can make out the faint outline of his biceps. He is beginning to develop an athletic look. He hit puberty late, and for a while even I was taller than he was, something I teased him about mercilessly, calling him "my little brother," back when I thought that kind of thing funny. He took it all on the chin, of course, the way he does everything.

But recently things have begun to change. Despite the fact that he is painfully shy, most of the girls in my year fancy him—filling me with a conflicting mixture of annoyance and pride. Yet he is still unable to talk to his peers, rarely smiles outside these walls, and always, always wears the same distant, haunted look, a hint of sadness in his eyes. At home, however, when the little ones aren't being too difficult or when we are joking together and he feels relaxed, he sometimes displays an entirely different side: a love of mischief, a dimple-cheeked grin, a self-deprecating sense of humor. But even during these brief moments, I feel he is hiding a darker, unhappier part of himself, the part that struggles to cope at school, in the outside world—a world where for some reason he has never felt at peace.

A car backfires across the street, jolting me out of my thoughts. Lochan lets out a small cry and struggles up, disoriented.

"You fell asleep," I inform him with a smile. "I think we could market trigonometry as a new treatment for insomnia."

"Shit. What time is it?" He appears panicked for a moment, pushing back the blanket and swinging his feet to the floor, running his fingers through his hair.

"Just gone nine."

"What about—"

"Tiffin and Willa are fast asleep and Kit's busy being an angry teenager in his room."

"Oh." He relaxes slightly, rubbing his eyes with the heels of his hands and blinking sleepily down at the floor.

"You look whacked. Perhaps you should forget homework for tonight and go to bed."

"No, I'm okay." He gestures toward the pile of books on the coffee table. "Anyway, gotta finish reviewing that lot before the test tomorrow." He reaches out to switch on the lamp, casting a small circle of light on the floor.

"You should have told me you had a test. I'd have done dinner!"

"Well, you did everything else." There is an awkward pause. "Thanks for . . . for sorting them out."

"No problem." I yawn, shifting sideways in the armchair to hang my legs over the armrest, and comb the hair away from my face. "Perhaps from now on we should just leave Kit's meal on a tray at the bottom of the ladder. We can call it room service. Then we might all get a bit of peace."

The hint of a smile touches his lips, but then he turns away to stare out the blank window and silence descends.

I take a sharp breath. "He was being a little shit tonight, Loch. That stuff about school . . ."

He seems to freeze. I can almost see the muscles tighten beneath his T-shirt as he sits sideways on the couch, an arm slung over the back, one foot on the ground, the other tucked beneath him. "I'd better finish this. . . ."

I recognize my cue. I want to say something to him, something along the lines of *It's all an act.* Everyone else is pretending anyway. Kit may have surrounded himself with a group of kids who spit in the face of authority, but they're just as scared as everyone else. They make fun of others and pick on loners just so they can belong. And I'm not much better. I might appear confident and chatty, but I spend most of my time laughing at jokes I don't find funny, saying things I don't really mean—because at the end of the day that's what we're all trying to do: fit in, one way or another, desperately trying to pretend we're all the same.

"Good night, then. Don't work too late."

"Night, Maya." He smiles suddenly, dimples forming at the corners of his mouth. But when I pause in the doorway, looking back at him, he is flicking through a textbook, his teeth chafing at the permanent, painfully red sore beneath his bottom lip.

You think no one else understands, I want to tell him, *but you're wrong. I do. You're not alone.*

TABITHA SUZUMA

CHAPTER THREE

Lochan

Our mother looks raddled in the harsh gray morning light. She nurses a mug of coffee in one hand, a cigarette in the other. Her bleached hair is a tangled mess, and smudged eyeliner has leaked into black half moons beneath her bloodshot eyes. Her pink silk robe is knotted over a skimpy nightdress— her disheveled appearance a clear sign that Dave did not stay over last night. In fact, I don't even remember hearing them come in. On the rare occasions they come back to this house, there is the bang of the front door, muffled laughter, keys being dropped on the doorstep, loud shushes and more thuds, followed by cackling laughter as he attempts to give her a piggyback up the stairs. The others have learned to sleep through it, but I have always been a light sleeper and their slurred voices force me to acknowledge consciousness, even as I press my eyelids closed and try to ignore the grunts and squeals and the rhythmic squeak of bedsprings from the main bedroom.

Friday is Mum's day off, which means that for once she gets to sort out breakfast and take the little ones to school. But it's already quarter to eight, Kit has yet to appear, Tiffin is eating breakfast in his underwear, and Willa has no clean socks and is bemoaning that fact to anyone who will listen. I fetch Tiffin's uniform and force him to get dressed at the table since Mum seems unable to do much more than sip coffee and chain-smoke at the window. Maya goes off in search of Willa's socks, and I hear her pound on Kit's door and yell something about the consequences of getting another late slip. Mum finishes her last cigarette and comes to sit with us at the table, talking about plans for the weekend that I know will never materialize. Both Willa and Tiffin start chatting away at once, delighted by the attention, their breakfast forgotten, and I feel my muscles tense.

"You've gotta be out of the house in five minutes and that breakfast needs to be eaten before then."

Mum catches me by the wrist as I pass. "Lochie-Loch, sit

down for a moment. I never get a chance to talk to you. We never sit down like this—as a family."

With a monumental effort I swallow my frustration. "Mum, we've got to be at school in fifteen minutes and I have a math test first thing."

"Oh, so serious!" She pulls me down into the chair beside her and cups my chin in her hand. "Look at you, so pale and stressy—always studying. When I was your age, I was the most beautiful girl at school—all the guys wanted to go out with me. I used to cut class and spend all day in the park with one of my boyfriends!" She winks conspiratorially at Tiffin and Willa, who both burst into paroxysms of giggles.

"Did you kiss your boyfriend on the mouth?" Tiffin inquires with an evil snicker.

"Oh, yes, and not just on the mouth." She winks at me, running her fingers through her tangled hair with a girlish smile.

"Yuck!" Willa swings her legs violently under the table, throwing back her head in disgust.

"Did you lick his tongue," Tiffin persists, "like they do on TV?"

"Tiffin!" I snap. "Stop being disgusting and finish your breakfast."

Tiffin reluctantly picks up his spoon, but his face breaks into a grin as Mum quickly nods her head at him with a mischievous smile.

"Aargh, that's gross!" He starts making gagging noises just as Maya comes in, trying to coax Kit through the doorway.

"What's gross?" she inquires as Kit slinks grumpily into his chair and drops his head to the table with a thud.

"You don't want to know," I begin quickly, but Tiffin fills her in anyway.

Maya pulls a face. "Mum!"

"Yeah, well, that little story really kick-started my appetite," Kit snaps irritably.

"You've got to eat something," Maya insists. "You're still growing."

"No, he's not—he's shrinking!" Tiffin guffaws.

"Shut up, you little shit."

"Loch! Kit called me a little shit!"

"Sit down, Maya," Mum says with a gooey smile. "Ah, look at all of you, so smart in your uniforms. And here we are having breakfast all together as a family!"

Maya gives her a tight smile as she butters toast and places it on Kit's plate. I feel my pulse begin to rise. I can't leave until they're all ready or there's a good chance that Kit will cut school again and Mum will keep Tiffin and Willa at home until midmorning. And I can't be late. Not because of the test . . . because I can't be the last one to walk into the classroom.

"We've got to go," I inform Maya, who is still trying to

persuade breakfast into Kit as he remains slumped with his head on his arms.

"Oh, why are my bunnies in such a rush this morning!" Mum exclaims. "Maya, will you get your brother to relax? Look at him. . . ." She rubs my shoulder, her hand like a burn through the fabric of my shirt. "So tense."

"Loch's got a test and we really are going to be late if we don't make a move," Maya informs her gently.

Mum still has her other hand clenched tightly round my wrist, preventing me from getting up to grab my usual cup of coffee. "You're not honestly nervous about a stupid test, are you, Loch? Because there are far more important things in life, you know. The last thing you want to do is turn into a nerd like your father, nose always buried in a book, living like a tramp just to get one of those useless PhD thingies. And look where his posh Cambridge education got him—a flipping poet, for chrissakes! He'd have earned more money sweeping the streets!" She gives a derisive snort.

Raising his head suddenly, Kit asks sneeringly, "When's Lochan ever failed a test? He's just afraid of coming in late and—"

Maya threatens to stuff the toast down his throat. I disengage myself from Mum's clasp and rattle through the front room, collecting blazer, wallet, keys, bag. I bump into Maya in the hallway and she tells me to go ahead, she'll make sure Mum leaves on time with the little ones and Kit gets to school. I squeeze her arm in thanks and then I'm off, running down the empty street.

I reach school with seconds to spare. The huge concrete building rises up before me, spreading its tentacles outward, sucking in the other ugly, smaller blocks with barren walkways and endless tunnels. I make it to the math room just before the teacher shuffles in and starts handing out the papers. After my half-mile sprint I can hardly see—red blotches pulsate before my eyes. Mr. Morris stops by my desk and my breath catches in my throat.

"Are you all right, Lochan? You look as if you've just run a marathon."

I nod quickly and take the paper from him without looking up.

The test begins and silence descends. I love tests. I have always loved tests and exams of any kind. As long as they are written. As long as they take up the whole lesson. As long as I don't have to speak or look up from my paper until the bell goes.

I don't know when it started—this thing—but it's growing, muffling me, suffocating me like poison ivy. I grew into it. It grew into me. We blurred at the edges, became an amorphous seeping, crawling thing. Sometimes I manage to distract myself, trick myself out of dwelling on it, convince myself that I'm okay. At home, for instance, with my family, I can be myself, be normal again. Until last night. Until the inevitable happened—until news finally filtered down the Belmont grapevine that Lochan Whitely is a socially inept weirdo. Even though Kit and I never really got along, the realization that he is ashamed of me takes hold: a horrible, clutching, sinking feeling in my chest. Just thinking about it makes the floor tilt beneath my chair. I feel as if I am on a slippery slope and all I can do is plummet downward. I know all about being ashamed of a family member—the number of times I've wished my mother would act her age in public, if not in private. It's horrible, being ashamed of someone you care about; it eats away at you. And if you let it get to you, if you give up the fight and surrender, eventually that shame turns to hate.

I don't want Kit to be ashamed of me. I don't want him to hate me, even if I feel like I hate him sometimes. But that little messed-up kid full of anger and resentment is still my brother; he's still family. Family: the most important thing of all. My siblings may drive me crazy at times but they are my blood. They're all I've known. My family is me. They are my life. Without them I walk the planet alone.

The rest are all outsiders, strangers. They never metamorphose into friends. And even if they did, even if I found, by some miracle, a way of connecting to someone outside my family—how could they possibly compare to those who speak my language and know who I am without having to be told? Even if I were able to meet their eyes, even if I were able to speak without the words cluttering up my throat, unable to surface, even if their gaze didn't burn holes in my skin and make me want to run a million miles away, how would I ever be able to care about them the way I care about my brothers and sisters?

The bell goes and I am one of the first out of my seat. As I pass the rows and rows of pupils, they all seem to look up at me. I see myself configured in their eyes: the guy who always buries himself at the very back of every class, who never speaks, always sits alone in one of the outdoor stairwells during break, hunched over a book. The guy who doesn't know how to talk to people, who shakes his head when picked on in class, who is absent whenever there is some kind of presentation to do. Over the years they have learned just to let me be. When I first arrived here, there was plenty of ribbing, plenty of pushing around, but eventually they grew bored. Occasionally a new pupil has tried to strike up a conversation. And I've tried, I really have. But when you can only come up with one-word answers, when your voice fails you altogether, what more can you do? What more can they? The girls are the worst, especially these days. They try harder, are more tenacious. Some even

ask me why I never speak—as if I can answer that. They flirt, try and get me to smile. They mean well, but what they don't understand is that their mere presence makes me want to die.

But today, mercifully, I am left alone. I speak to no one for the whole morning. I catch sight of Maya across the lunch hall, and she glances at the usual girl gabbing away at her side and then rolls her eyes. I smile. As I fork my way through mouthfuls of watery shepherd's pie, I watch her pretend to listen to her friend Francie, but she keeps glancing over at me, pulling faces to crack me up. Her white school shirt, several sizes too big, hangs over her gray skirt, several inches too short. She is wearing her white gym lace-ups because she has misplaced her school shoes. She is without socks, and a large bandage, surrounded by a multitude of bruises, covers a scraped knee. Her auburn hair reaches her waist, long and straight like Willa's. Freckles smatter her cheekbones, accentuating the natural pallor of her skin. Even when she is serious, her deep blue eyes always hold a glimmer that suggests she is about to smile. Over the last year she has turned from pretty to beautiful in an unusual, delicate, unnerving way. Boys chat her up endlessly—alarmingly.

After lunch I take my class copy of *Romeo and Juliet,* which I actually read years ago, and ensconce myself on the fourth step down of the north stairwell outside the science block, the one least frequently used. This is how my wasted hours

CHAPTER FOUR

Maya

"Are you going to introduce him to me?" Francie asks me mournfully. From our usual position on the low brick wall at the far end of the playground, she has followed my gaze to the lone figure sitting hunched on the steps outside the science building. "Is he still single?"

"I told you a million times: He doesn't like people," I reply tersely. I look at her. She exudes a kind of restless energy, the zest for life that comes naturally with being an extrovert. Trying to imagine her going out with my brother is almost impossible. "How d'you know you'll even like him?"

"Because he's fucking hot!" Francie exclaims with feeling.

I shake my head with a smile. "But the two of you have nothing in common."

"What's that supposed to mean?" She looks hurt suddenly.

"He doesn't have anything in common with anyone," I reassure her quickly. "He's just different. He—he doesn't really speak to people."

Francie tosses back her hair. "Yeah, so I've heard. Taciturn as hell. Is it depression?"

"No." I play with a strand of hair. "The school made him see a counselor last year but that was just a waste of time. He speaks at home. It's just with people he doesn't know, people outside the family."

"So what? He's just shy."

I sigh doubtfully. "That's a bit of an understatement."

"What's he got to be shy about?" Francie asks. "I mean, has he looked in a mirror recently?"

"He's not just like that around girls," I try to explain. "He's like that with everyone. He won't even answer questions in class—it's like a phobia."

Francie whistles in disbelief. "God, has he always been like that?"

"I don't know." I stop playing with my hair for a moment and think. "When we were young, we were like twins. We were born thirteen months apart, so everyone thought we were twins anyway. We did everything together. I mean, everything. One day he had tonsillitis and couldn't go to school. Dad made me go and I cried all day. We had our own secret language. Sometimes, when Mum and Dad were at each other's throats, we pretended we couldn't speak English, so we spoke to no one but each other for the whole day. We started getting into trouble at school. They said that we refused to mix, that we had no friends. But they were wrong. We had each other. He was my best friend in the world. He still is."

I come home to a house full of silence. The hall is empty of bags and blazers. *Maybe she's taken them to the park,* I think hopefully. Then I almost laugh out loud. When was the last time that happened? I go into the kitchen—cold coffee mugs, overflowing ashtrays and cereal congealing at the bottom of bowls. Milk, bread, and butter still left out on the table, Kit's hardened uneaten toast staring accusingly up at me. Tiffin's forgotten book bag on the floor. Willa's abandoned tie . . . A sound from the front room prompts me to spin on my heel. I walk back down the hall, noticing the dappled sunlight highlighting the dusty surfaces.

I find Mum looking dolefully up at me from beneath Willa's duvet on the couch, a wet cloth covering her forehead.

I gape at her. "What happened?"

"I think I've got stomach flu, sweetie. I've got this pounding headache and I've been throwing up all day."

"The kids—" I begin.

Her face dims and then reignites again, like a flickering match in the dark. "They're at school, sweetie pie, don't worry. I took them in this morning—I was all right then. It was only after lunch that I started—"

"Mum . . ." I feel my voice begin to rise. "It's four thirty!"

"I know, sweetie. I'll get up in a minute."

"You were supposed to pick them up!" I am shouting now. "They finish school at half past three, remember?"

My mother looks at me, a horrible, bottomless look. "But isn't it you or Lochan today?"

"Today's Friday! It's your day off! You always fetch them on your day off!"

Mum closes her eyes and lets out a little moan, modulated to elicit pity. I want to hit her. Instead I lunge for the phone. She has turned the ringer off but the answering machine's little red light flashes accusingly. Four messages from St. Luke's, the last one terse and angry, suggesting that this isn't the first time Ms. Whitely has been extremely late. I instantly press the callback button, rage thudding against my ribs. Tiffin and Willa will be terrified. They will think they have been abandoned, that she has walked out, as she keeps threatening to do when she's been drinking.

I get through to the school secretary and start blurting out my apologies. She cuts me off with a swift "Isn't your mother the one who should be calling, dear?"

"Our mother isn't well," I say quickly. "But I'm leaving right now and I'll be at the school in ten minutes. Please tell Willa and Tiffin I'm coming. Please, please just tell them that Mum's fine and Maya's on her way."

"Well, I'm afraid they're not here anymore." The secretary sounds a little put out. "They were eventually picked up by the babysitter half an hour ago."

My legs buckle. I sink down onto the arm of the couch. My body has gone so limp, I nearly drop the phone. "We don't have a babysitter."

"Oh—"

"Who was it? What did she look like? She must have given a name!"

"Miss Pierce will know who it was. The teachers don't let the children go off with just anyone, you know." Again the prim voice, coupled now with a defensive edge.

"I need to speak to Miss Pierce." My voice shakes with barely controlled calm.

"I'm afraid Miss Pierce left when the children were finally picked up. I can try to reach her on her mobile. . . ."

I can hardly breathe. "Please ask her to come straight back to the school. I'll meet her there."

I hang up and I am literally shaking. Mum lifts the flannel from her face and says, "Sweetie, you sound upset. Is every-thing all right?"

I am racing through the hall, shoving on shoes, grabbing keys, mobile phone, pressing speed dial one as I slam out of the house. He answers on the third ring.

"What's happened?"

I can hear laughter and jeering in the background, fading as he leaves his after-school review class. We both keep our phones on at all times. He knows I'd call during school hours only in an emergency.

I blurt out the events of the past five minutes. "I'm on my way to their school now." A juggernaut brays its horn at me as I streak across the main road.

"Meet you there," he says.

When I arrive at St. Luke's, I find the gates closed. I start to shove and kick at them until the caretaker takes pity on me and comes over to unlock them. "Easy," he says. "What's all the panic?"

Ignoring him, I run to the school doors and pound on them. I am buzzed through and lurch along the fluorescent-lit corridor that, stripped of the chaos of children, seems eerie and surreal. I spot Lochan at the far end, talking to the school secretary. He must have run all the way too. Thank God, thank God. Lochan will know what to do.

He hasn't noticed my arrival and so I slow to a dignified walk, straighten my clothes, take deep breaths, and try to calm myself down. I've learned the hard way, through the various dealings I've had with figures of authority, that if you start getting upset or angry, they treat you like a child and demand to speak to your parents. Lochan has worked hard at the art of appearing calm and articulate in these circumstances, but I'm all too aware what a terrible struggle it is for him. As I approach, I notice that his hands are shaking uncontrollably by his sides.

"Miss P-Pierce was the only person to see them leave?" he is asking. I can tell he's having to force himself to meet the secretary's gaze.

"That's right," says the horrible platinum blonde I've always despised. "And Miss Pierce would have never—"

"But surely—surely there's another number she can be reached on?" His voice is clear and firm. No one but I could detect the subtle tremor.

"I told you—I tried. Her mobile's switched off. But like I said, I left a message on her home line—"

"Please could you just keep trying her phone?"

The secretary mutters something and disappears back inside her office. I touch Lochan's hand. He jumps as if he has been shot, and beneath the calm exterior I see that he is crumbling too.

"She keeps talking about a babysitter," he says to me raggedly, backing out into the corridor and grabbing my hand. "Did Mum ever say anything to you about paying someone to fetch them?"

"No!"

"Where is she now?"

"Lying on the couch with a flannel on her face," I whisper. "When I asked her where Tiffin and Willa were, she said she thought it was our turn to pick them up!"

Lochan is breathing hard. I can see the rapid rise and fall of his chest beneath his school shirt. His bag and blazer are nowhere to be seen and he has removed his tie. It takes me a moment to realize he is trying to disguise the fact that he is still just a schoolboy.

"I'm sure it's some kind of misunderstanding," he says, desperate optimism creeping into his voice. "Another parent must have come in late and picked them up. It's all right. We're going to get this sorted out, Maya. Okay?" He squeezes my hands and gives me a tense smile.

I nod, forcing myself to breathe. "Okay."

"I'd better go back and speak to the—"

"D'you want me to?" I ask quietly.

The heat immediately springs to his cheeks. "Of course not! I can—I can sort this—"

"I know," I backpedal quickly. "I know you can."

He leaves my side to cross the office threshold and takes an audible breath. "Still—still no luck?"

"Nope. She could have got stuck in traffic, I s'pose. She could be anywhere, really."

I hear Lochan exhale in exasperation. "Look, I'm sure the teacher wouldn't have wilfully let them go with a stranger. B-but you've got to understand that, right now, these children are missing. So I think it would be best if you called the principal or the deputy or—or someone who can help. We're going to have to notify the police, and they're probably going to want to speak to the people who run this school."

In the corridor, out of sight of Platinum Blonde, I sag against the wall and press the back of my hand against my mouth. *Police* means the authorities. *The authorities* means social services. Lochan really must think that Tiffin and Willa have been kidnapped if he is willing to risk getting social services involved.

I am beginning to feel increasingly wobbly, so I go and sit

down on the stairs. I don't understand how Lochan can stand there being so controlled and sensible until I notice the damp patch of sweat on the back of his shirt, the increasing tremor in his hands. I want to get up and squeeze them, tell him it's going to be all right. Except I don't know that it is.

The principal, a stout, graying man, arrives at the same time as Miss Pierce, Willa's teacher. It transpires that she waited for over half an hour with both children before a lady, Sandra someone, showed up, apparently under instructions to fetch them.

"But surely you must have got a last name?" Lochan is saying for the second time.

"Naturally we have a record of each child's parent or guardian or babysitter. But the only contact information we were ever given for Tiffin and Willa was the mother's name and a home number," Miss Pierce, a pinched, pink-cheeked young woman, is saying. "And despite all our attempts, we couldn't get through. So when this lady arrived saying she was a family friend and had been asked to pick up the children, we had no reason to disbelieve her."

I see Lochan's hands clench into fists behind his back. "Surely checking who the children go home with is part of your job!" He's beginning to lose it now; the cracks are starting to show.

"I would have thought it part of the parent's job to pick up their children on time," Miss Pierce retorts, piqued, and suddenly I want to take her head and smash it against Platinum Blonde's and scream, *Don't you realize that while you stand there acting all self-righteous and arguing over who is to blame, a pedophile might be speeding off with my little brother and sister?*

"Where are the parents in all this?" the principal interrupts. "Why have we only got the siblings here?"

I feel the breath catch in my throat.

"Our mother is ill right now," Lochan says, and even as he comes out with this well-practiced line, I can tell that he is struggling to keep his voice calm.

"Too ill to come down the road and find out what has happened to her children?" Miss Pierce asks.

There is a silence. Lochan is staring at the teacher, his shoulders rising and falling rapidly. *Don't react,* I beg him silently, pressing my knuckles against my lips.

"Well, look, I think we should alert the authorities," the principal is now saying. "I'm sure it's a false alarm, but obviously we need to be on the safe side."

Lochan is backing away now, tugging at his hair in a characteristic gesture of extreme distress. "Okay. Yes, of course. But can you just give us a minute?"

He moves away from the office door and rushes over. "Maya,

they want to call the police—" His voice is shaking and his face glistens with sweat. "They'll come to the house. Mum—she'll have to be involved. . . . Was she sober?"

"I don't know. She's definitely hungover!"

"Maybe—maybe I should stay here and wait for the police while you go home and try to get her together. Hide any bottles and open all the windows." He is gripping the tops of my arms so hard they hurt. "Do whatever you can to get rid of the smell. Tell her to cry or—or something, so that she appears hysterical instead of—"

"Lochan, I've got it, I can do it. Go ahead and call the police. I'll make sure they never know—"

"They'll take the kids away and separate us—" His voice is fragmenting.

"No, they won't. Lochie, call the police—this is more important!"

Drawing back, he cups his hands over his nose and mouth, his eyes wide, and nods at me. I've never seen him look so afraid. Then he turns and walks back across the hallway and into the office.

I break into a run, heading toward the heavy double doors at the end of the corridor. The black and white linoleum disappears rhythmically beneath my feet. The bright colors on the walls seem to swim. . . . The sudden shout from behind me rips like a bullet through my chest. "They've found Sandra's number!"

One hand on the door, I stop. Lochan's face is alight with relief.

When they finally come through the school doors after another agonizing ten-minute wait, Tiffin is blowing pink bubbles, his mouth full of gum, and Willa is brandishing a lollipop. "Look what I got!"

I hug Willa so tight I can feel her heart beat against mine. Her lemon-scented hair is in my face, and all I can do is squeeze her and kiss her and try and keep her in my arms. Lochan has one arm round Tiffin as he wriggles and giggles in his grasp.

It's clear that neither of them has a clue that anything was amiss, so I bite my tongue to stop myself from crying. Sandra turns out to be nothing more sinister than an elderly lady, babysitter to one of the boys in another class. According to her, Lily Whitely rang just after four this afternoon, explaining that she was too ill to leave the house and asking whether she could do her a favor and pick up the children. Sandra had kindly returned to the school, collected Willa and Tiffin, and tried to drop them back home. Getting no reply when she rang the bell, she dropped a note through the door and took them back to her own charge's house, awaiting Lily's phone call.

As we cross the playground, I hold Tiffin and Willa tightly with each hand and try my best to engage in the prattle about their unexpected "playdate." I overhear Lochan thanking Sandra and see him scribble down his mobile number, telling her to call him should Lily ever ask her for a "favor" of this kind again. As soon as we leave the school, Tiffin tries to disengage himself from my grasp, looking for something in the gutter to kick and dribble down the road. I tell him I'll play Battleship with him for half an hour if he holds my hand all the way home. Surprisingly, he agrees, bounding up and down like a yo-yo on the end of my arm, threatening to dislocate it from its socket, but I don't care. As long as he keeps hold of my hand, I really don't care.

We follow Lochan all the way home. He strides ahead, and something prevents me from trying to catch up with him. Tiffin and Willa don't seem to mind; they are still full of stories about the new PlayStation they got to try out. I start a spiel on stranger danger, but it emerges that they have already been picked up by Callum's babysitter several times before.

As soon as we get in, Tiffin and Willa spot Mum, still half passed out on the couch. With a whoop they run over to her, delighted to find her home for a change, their anecdotes pouring out all over again. Mum uncovers her face, sits up, and laughs, hugging them tightly. "My little bunnies," she says. "Did you have a good time? I missed you all day, you know."

TABITHA SUZUMA

I stand in the doorway, the sharp edge of the frame cutting into my shoulder, watching this little scene unfold in silence. Tiffin is showing off his juggling skills with some old tennis balls and Willa is trying to interest Mum in a game of Guess Who? It takes me a moment to realize that Lochan disappeared upstairs the moment we entered the house. I turn away from the front room, utterly spent, and slowly climb the stairs. Music blasting from the attic above reassures me that at least the third child made it home without incident. I go into my room, shed my blazer and tie, kick off my shoes, and flop down on my bed in an exhausted heap.

I must have dozed off, for when I hear Tiffin shout "Dinner!" I sit up in bed with a start to discover a bluish dusk filling the small room. Combing the hair out of my eyes with my fingers, I pad sleepily downstairs.

The atmosphere in the kitchen is jarring. Mum has mutated into a butterfly—all wispy skirts and trailing sleeves and bright, patterned colors. She has showered and washed her hair, having apparently recovered from her earlier bout of flu. The heavy makeup gives her away—clearly she isn't staying in to watch *EastEnders* tonight. She has cooked up some kind of baked beans and sausage dish that Kit is prodding disdainfully with his fork. Tiffin and Willa sit side by side, swinging their legs and trying to kick each other under the table, telltale signs of chocolate round their mouths, ignoring the unappetizing mixture laid out before them.

"This isn't food." Head propped up on his hand, Kit scowls down at his plate, flicking the pieces of sausage around his plate. "Can I go out?"

"Just shut up and eat," Lochan snaps uncharacteristically, reaching into the cupboard for glasses. Kit is about to retort, then appears to decide against it and starts prodding at his food again. The tone of Lochan's voice suggests that this is no time to argue.

"Well, get started, everyone," Mum says with a nervous giggle. "I know I'm not the world's best cook, but I can assure you this tastes a lot better than it looks."

Kit snorts and mutters something inaudible. Willa lances a single baked bean with the prong of her fork and brings it reluctantly to her mouth, licking it gingerly with the tip of her tongue. With a long-suffering air, Tiffin takes a mouthful of sausage and then pulls a face, his eyes watering, ready to either gag or spit it out. I quickly bring over the water jug and fill the glasses. Finally Lochan sits down. He smells of school and sweat, and his tousled black hair contrasts sharply with his wan face. I notice the clench of his jaw, the stormy look in his eyes, and feel the tension radiate from his body like white heat.

"Are you going out again tonight, Mum?" Willa asks, taking delicate bird bites out of a piece of sausage.

TABITHA SUZUMA

"No, she's not," Lochan says quietly without looking up. Beneath the table, I press my foot against his in warning.

Mum turns to him in surprise. "Davey's picking me up at seven," she protests. "It's okay, bunnies. I'll tuck you in before I go."

"Forget about it," Tiffin mumbles angrily.

"Seven o'clock is a very early bedtime," Willa comments with a sigh, spearing a second bean.

"You're not going out again tonight," Lochan mutters at her.

There is a stunned silence.

"Told you he thinks he rules the place!" Kit looks up from his plate, delighted at his chance to chip in. "Are you gonna let him boss you around like this, Mum?"

I shoot Kit a warning look and shake my head. His face instantly darkens again. "What—I'm not even allowed to talk now?"

"Oh, I won't be late—" Mum says with a benign smile.

"You're not going out!" Lochan shouts suddenly, slamming his hand down on the table. The crockery rattles and everyone jumps. I feel a familiar tension headache grip my temples.

Mum claps a hand to her throat and lets out a high-pitched exclamation of surprise, a kind of shrill laugh. "Oh, listen to the big man of the house, telling his mummy what to do!"

"See how the other half live," Kit mutters.

Lochan throws down his fork, his face puce, the cords standing out in his neck. "Two hours ago you were too damn hungover to make it down the street to fetch your own children from school, and you couldn't even remember you'd asked someone else to pick them up!"

Mum opens her eyes wide. "But, darling, aren't you pleased I'm feeling so much better?"

"That's not going to last if you go out for another night on the piss!" Lochan yells, gripping the edge of the table with both hands, his knuckles white. "We nearly had to involve the police today. Nobody had any idea where the kids were. Anything could have happened to them, and you'd have been too out of it to notice!"

"Lochie!" Mum's voice quivers like a little girl's. "I had food poisoning. I couldn't stop throwing up. I didn't want to disturb you and Maya at school. What else was I supposed to do?"

"Food poisoning, my ass!" Lochan leaps up so violently, he sends his chair crashing back against the tiles. "When are you going to face reality and accept you've got an alcohol problem?"

"Oh, I've got a problem?" Mum's eyes flash suddenly, the little-girl act tossed aside. "I'm not a conventional mother—so sue me. I've had a hard life! I've finally met someone great and I want to go out and have some fun! Fun—something you

might want to try experiencing, Lochan, instead of living your life with your head in a book like your father. Where are your friends, hey? When do you ever go out—or bring someone home, for that matter?"

Kit has rocked back in his chair, watching the scene with relish.

"Mum, please don't—" I reach out for her but she swats me away. I smell fresh alcohol on her breath—in this state she is capable of saying anything, doing anything. Especially since Lochan has mentioned the unmentionable.

Lochan has turned to stone, one hand gripping the sideboard for support. Tiffin has his hands clamped over his ears and Willa is looking from one face to the other, her eyes wide and staring.

"Come on." I get up and pull them after me into the corridor. "Go up to your room and entertain yourselves for a while. I'll bring you some sandwiches in a minute."

Willa scampers fearfully up the stairs; Tiffin scowls, trailing in her wake. "We should have stayed at Callum's," I hear him mutter, and his words make my throat ache.

With no choice but to return to the kitchen in an attempt at damage control, I find Mum still shouting, her eyes narrowed under the weight of her lids. "Don't look at me like that—you know exactly what I'm talking about. You've never had a proper girlfriend, never even managed to make a single friend, for chrissakes! What does being top of the class matter when the school keeps telling me you need to see a psychologist because you're so shy you can't even speak to anyone! The only person who's got a problem is you!"

Lochan hasn't moved; he's staring at her with a look of sick horror. His lack of response only serves to spur Mum on as she starts trying to justify her outburst by fueling her own rage. "You take after him in every way—thinking you're better than everyone else with your long words and your top grades. You have absolutely no respect for your own mother!" she shrieks, her face mottled with fury. "How dare you speak to me like that in front of my children!"

I position myself in front of her and start maneuvering her out of the kitchen. "Just go out with Dave," I beg her. "Go and meet him early or something. Surprise him! Go, Mum, just go."

"You always take his side!"

"I'm not taking anyone's side, Mum. I just think you're getting yourself into a state, which isn't a very good idea considering you haven't been feeling very well." I manage to get her into the hallway. She grabs her handbag, but not without one last barb thrown over her shoulder. "Lochan, you can accuse me of not being a normal mother the day you start acting like a normal teenager!"

I propel her out the door, and it is an effort not to slam it hard behind her. Instead I lean against it, afraid she might unlock it and come storming back in. I close my eyes for a moment. When I open them again, I notice a figure sitting at the top of the stairs.

"Tiffin, haven't you got homework to do?"

"She said she was gonna tuck us in." There's a tremor in his voice.

"I know," I say quickly, straightening up. "And she meant it. But I said I would do it instead because she was running late—"

"I don't want you to do it. I want Mum!" Tiffin shouts, and jumping up, he runs into his room, slamming the door behind him.

Back in the kitchen, Kit has his feet on the table, shaking with silent laughter. "God, what a fucked-up family this is!"

"Just go upstairs. You're not helping," I tell him quietly.

He opens his mouth to protest, then launches himself angrily to his feet, his chair screeching against the tiles. Grabbing Tiffin and Willa's dinner money from the hall table, he makes for the front door.

"Where are you going?" I shout after him.

"Out to get some fucking food!"

Lochan is pacing the kitchen floor. He seems somehow dismantled, confused. His face is variegated with lines of crimson, giving his skin a curious raw look.

"I'm sorry, I shouldn't have started it—" He sounds like he is being shaken. I try to touch his arm but he jumps away from me as if stung. His pain is almost tangible: the hurt, the resentment, the fury, all filling the small room.

"Lochie, you had every right to lose your temper. What Mum did today was inexcusable. But listen to me. . . ." I position myself in front of him and try to touch him again. "Lochie, listen. That stuff she said was just her way of lashing out. You mentioned her drinking and she just can't deal with the truth. So she tried to find the most hurtful thing she could to throw back at you—"

"She meant it, she meant every word." He tugs at his hair, rubs his cheeks. "And she's right. I'm not—I'm not normal. There's something wrong with me and—"

"Lochie, don't worry about that right now, okay? It's something you can work on—it's something that's going to get better with time!"

Pulling away from me, he continues to pace, as if the continuous movement will stop him from falling apart. "But she's like Kit. She's—she's—" He can't bring himself to say the word. "Ashamed," he whispers finally.

"Lochie, stop for a minute. Look at me."

I grab him by the arms and hold him still. I can feel him trembling beneath my touch.

"It's all right. The kids are all right and that's all that matters. Don't listen to her. Never, ever listen to her. She's just a bitter old cow who never grew up. But she's not ashamed of you. No one's ashamed of you, Lochie. God, how could anyone be? We all know that without you this family would fall apart."

He drops his head in defeat. I can feel the clenched muscles in his shoulders beneath my fingers.

"It is falling apart."

I give him a small, desperate shake. "Lochan, it's not. Willa and Tiffin are fine. I'm fine! Kit is your standard screwed-up teenager. We're all together—all those years since Dad left—since Mum's problem started. We haven't been taken into care, and that's entirely thanks to you."

There is a long silence. All I can see is the top of Lochan's head. He leans toward me slightly. I reach up and put my arms around him and hold him tight. I lower my voice to a whisper. "You're not just my brother, you're my best friend."

CHAPTER FIVE

Lochan

I replay that sentence over and over during the next few days. It is a way of blotting out everything else—the awful incident with Tiffin and Willa, the row with my mother, the constant hell that is school. Every time I decline to answer a question in class, each moment I spend alone bent over a book, I am reminded of what my family thinks of me. Pathetic. A socially inept weirdo. A teenage son who can't get a friend, let alone a girlfriend. I try, I really try—small things, like asking my neighbor for the time. He has to lean across the aisle to ask me to repeat my question. I can't even hear the sound of my own voice. I still don't fully understand it—I managed to talk to the school staff the afternoon Tiffin and Willa disappeared. But that was an emergency, and the horror of the situation overrode any inhibitions I might have had. Talking to adults is bearable; it's talking to people my age that's impossible. So I keep replaying Maya's words in my head. Maybe there is someone who isn't ashamed of me after all. Perhaps there is one member of my family whom I haven't totally let down.

But the void yawns open like a cavern inside my chest. I feel so damn lonely all the time. Even though I'm surrounded by pupils, there is this invisible screen between us, and behind the glass wall I am screaming—screaming in my own silence, screaming to be noticed, to be befriended, to be liked. And yet when a friendly-looking girl from my math class comes up to me in the canteen and says "Mind if I sit here?" I just give a quick nod and turn away, hoping to God she won't try to engage me in conversation. And at home it's hardly as if I'm alone, either. The house is never silent—but Kit is still going through his evil phase, Tiffin is only interested in his DS and his soccer friends, and Willa is sweet but still just a baby. I play Twister and hide-and-seek with the little ones, help them with their homework, feed them, bathe them, read them goodnight stories, but all the while I have to stay upbeat for them, put on the damn mask, and sometimes I fear it will crack. Only with Maya can I really be myself. We share the

burden together and she is always on my side, by my side. I
don't want to need her, to depend on her, but I do, I really do.

At lunch break I am sitting in my usual place during the tired
afternoon, watching the cold light slowly move across the
empty stairwell beneath me, when footsteps from above startle
me. I lower my eyes to my book. Behind me, the feet slow and
I feel my pulse rate rise. Someone passes me on the steps. I feel
a leg brush against my shirtsleeve and I concentrate on the page
of blurred print before me. To my horror, just below me, the
footsteps stop altogether.

"Hi!" a girl's voice exclaims.

I flinch. Force myself to look up. I meet the brown-eyed
gaze of someone I vaguely recognize. It takes me several seconds to place her. It's the girl Maya always hangs around with. I
can't even remember her name. And she is looking at me with
a wide, toothy grin.

"Hi," she says again.

I clear my throat. "Hi," I mumble.

I'm not sure she can even hear me. Her gaze is unflinching
and she seems to be waiting for something more.

"The Hours," she comments, glancing down at my book.
"Isn't that a movie?"

I nod.

"Any good?" Her determination to make conversation is impressive. I nod again and return to the page. "I'm Francie," she says, still grinning broadly.

"Lochan," I reply.

She raises her eyebrows meaningfully. "I know."

I can feel my fingers making damp indentations in the pages of the book.

"Maya talks about you all the time."

There is nothing subtle about this girl. Her frizzy hair and dark skin contrast sharply with her blood-red lipstick, and she is wearing an obscenely short skirt and huge silver hoops in her ears.

"You know who I am, right? You've seen me hanging around with your sister?"

Another nod, the words evaporating as soon as they reach my throat. I start chewing my lip.

Francie looks at me pensively with a little smile. "You don't talk much, do you?"

My face starts to burn. If she hadn't been a friend of Maya's, I would be pushing past her down the stairs by now. But Francie seems more curious than amused.

"People say I never stop talking," she continues breezily. "It pisses them off."

You're telling me.

"I have a message for you," Francie declares suddenly. "From your sister."

I feel myself tense. "W-what is it?"

"Nothing serious," she says quickly. "Just that your mum is taking your brothers and sister out to McDonald's tonight so there's no need to rush home. Maya wants you to meet her at the mailbox at the end of the street after school."

"M-Maya asked you to c-come here and tell me that?" I ask, waiting for her to smirk at my stammer.

"Well, not exactly. She was trying to send you a text, but then she was kept in to finish off some course work, so I figured I might as well tell you myself."

"Thanks," I mumble.

"And . . . I also wanted to invite you to have a drink at Smileys with Maya and me, since the two of you don't have to go rushing off for once."

I stare at her, mute.

"Is that a yes?" She eyes me hopefully.

My mind has gone blank. I can't for the life of me think of an excuse. "Uh, well—okay."

"Cool!" Her face lights up. "I'll see you at the mailbox after school!"

She is gone as suddenly as she arrived.

 TABITHA SUZUMA

At the final bell I pack my bag with unsteady hands; I am the last to trail out of the classroom. I make a dive for the toilets and lock myself in a cubicle. Sitting on the closed lid after peeing, I try to pull myself together. On the way out, I stop in front of the mirrors. In the afternoon light the pale face staring back at me has the glittering green eyes of some alien creature. Leaning over the basin, I cup icy water in my hands and bring it up to my face, pressing my cheeks into the shallow puddles. I want to hide out here forever, but someone else bangs in through the door and I have no choice but to leave.

Maya and Francie are standing side by side by the mailbox at the end of the street, talking in rapid fire to each other, their eyes scanning the crowds. It takes all the will in the world to stop me from doubling back, but the look of expectation on Maya's face forces me forward. Her face breaks into a smile of delight as she catches sight of me.

"Thought you were going to do a no-show!" she whispers.

I smile and nod, words running through my mind like a stream of effervescent bubbles.

"Well, come on, guys!" Francie exclaims after a moment's awkward silence. "Are we going to Smileys or not?"

"Absolutely," Maya says, and as she turns to follow her friend, her hand brushes against mine in a gesture of reassurance—or perhaps it is thanks.

Smileys is still mercifully empty at this time. We take a small round table by the window and I hide behind the menu, my tongue rubbing the rough skin beneath my lip.

"Are you guys getting food?" Francie wants to know.

Maya glances at me and I give a subtle shake of the head.

"Shall we share some garlic bread?" Francie suggests. "I'm dying for a Coke."

Maya leans back in her seat to try to catch the waiter, and Francie turns to me. "So, are you looking forward to getting the hell out of Belmont?"

I put down the menu and nod, forcing a smile.

"You're so lucky," Francie continues. "Just another nine months and you'll be free of this hellhole."

Maya finishes ordering and returns to the one-sided conversation, which even Francie is struggling to maintain. "Lochan's going to UCL," Maya announces proudly.

"Well, no, I—I'm applying—"

"It's a dead cert."

"Shit, you must really be smart!" Francie exclaims.

"He is," Maya informs her. "He's been predicted four As."

"Fuck!"

I wince and catch Maya's eye, pleading with her to back off. I want to object, play it down, but I can feel the heat rushing to my face and the words evaporating from my mind

 TABITHA SUZUMA

the moment I conjure them up.

Maya elbows me gently. "Francie's no fool either," she says. "She is actually the only person I know who can touch the tip of her nose with her tongue."

We all laugh. I breathe again.

"You think I'm kidding?" Francie challenges me.

"No . . ."

"He's just being polite," Maya tells her. "I think he's gonna need proof."

Francie is all too keen to oblige. She sits up straight, extends her tongue as far as it will go, curls it upward, and touches the very tip to her nose. The cross-eyed look completes the picture.

Maya falls against me with mirth and I find myself laughing too. Francie's okay. As long as this doesn't last too long, I think I'm going to survive.

Suddenly there is a commotion in the doorway. Francie spins round in her seat and I identify a group of Belmont pupils by their uniforms.

"Hey, guys!" Francie shouts. "Over here!"

They clatter over, and through blurred vision I recognize a couple of girls from Maya's class, a guy from one of the other year groups, and Rafi, a guy from English. There are greetings and backslaps, and two tables are pushed together and more chairs drawn up.

"Whitely!" Rafi exclaims in astonishment. "What the hell are you doing here?"

"Just, uh, my sister—"

"He's hanging out with us!" Francie exclaims. "Is that a crime? He's Maya's brother—didn't you know?"

"Yeah, I just never thought I'd see him in a place like this!" There is no malice in Rafi's laughter, just genuine surprise, but now everybody's looking at me and the two other girls are talking.

Maya is doing the introductions, but although I can hear the voices, I can no longer make sense of what is being said. Emma, who has been going out of her way to bump into me since last spring, is determined to engage me in conversation. Their sudden intrusion just as I was beginning to relax, combined with the fact that they all know me as the class weirdo, is suddenly all too much, and I feel like the prey in some claustrophobic nightmare. Their words are like hammers, pounding my skull. I give in to the tide and feel myself beginning to drown. Their mouths move under water, opening and closing; I read the question marks on their faces—most of their questions are directed at me—but panic has caused my senses to shut down. I cannot distinguish one sentence from another; it has all turned into a blanket of noise. Abruptly I scrape back my chair and get to my feet, grabbing my bag and blazer. I mumble something about having left my mobile at school, raise my hand in good-bye, and lunge for the door.

I head down one street, then another. I'm not even sure where I'm going. I suddenly feel stupidly close to tears. I drape my blazer over my schoolbag and hook the strap over my shoulder, walking as fast as I can, the air rasping in my lungs, the sound of traffic drowned out by the frantic thud of my heart. I hear the smack of shoes on the sidewalk behind me and instinctively move aside to let the jogger past, but it's Maya, grabbing me by the arm.

"Slow down, Lochie, please—I've got a really bad stitch. . . ."

"Maya, what the hell are you doing? Go back to your friends."

She catches hold of my hand. "Lochie, wait—"

I stop and pull away from her suddenly, stepping back. "Look, I appreciate the effort, but I'd rather you just left me alone, okay?" My voice begins to rise. "I didn't ask you for help, did I?"

"Hey, hey!" She steps toward me, holding out her hand. "I wasn't trying to do anything, Loch. It was all Francie's idea. I only went along with it because she told me you'd agreed."

I run my hands through my hair. "Jesus, this was such a fucking mistake. Now I've gone and embarrassed you in front of your friends. . . ."

"Are you insane?" She laughs, grabs my hand, and swings my arm as we start walking again. "I'm glad you left! Gave me an excuse to get out too."

I check my watch, feeling myself relax slightly. "You know, since Mum's looking after the kids for once, we have the whole evening free." I raise a tentative eyebrow.

Maya flicks back her hair and a smile lights up her face, her eyes widening in animation. "Ooh, were you thinking of fleeing the country?"

I grin. "Tempting . . . but maybe something more along the lines of catching a movie?"

She tilts her face up to the sky. "But the sun's shining. It still feels like summer!"

"Okay then, you choose."

"Let's just walk," she says.

"Walk?"

"Yes. Let's catch a bus over to Chelsea Harbour. Let's ogle the houses of the rich and famous and wander down by the river."

CHAPTER SIX

Maya

As we walk along Chelsea Embankment, I stuff my blazer and tie into my bag and the warm evening breeze brushes my skirt against my bare thighs. The sun is just beginning to turn orange, sprinkling drops of gold across the water's scaly surface, muscled like the back of a serpent. This is my favorite time of day, the afternoon barely ended, the evening not yet begun; the languid hours of sunshine stretch out ahead of us before fading into dusky twilight. High above us the bridges are heavy with congested traffic—overloaded buses and impatient cars and reckless cyclists, men and women sweating in suits, desperate to get home—ferries and tugboats passing below. Gravel crunches underfoot as we cross the large, empty expanses between the glass office buildings, past the luxury apartments that stack their way high into the sky. It is so sunny that the world feels like a blank of light, a still whiteness. I toss Lochan my bag, take a running step, skip and hop, and do a cartwheel, the grainy path rough against my palms. The sun momentarily disappears and we are plunged into cool blue shade as we pass beneath the bridge, our footsteps suddenly magnified, bouncing off the smooth arch of the supports, startling a pigeon up into the sky. A few paces to my left, keeping a safe distance from my antics, Lochan strides along, hands in his pockets, shirtsleeves rolled up to the elbows. A light thread of veins is visible on his temples, and the shadows beneath his eyes lend him a haunted look. He glances at me with his bright green gaze and gives one of his trademark lopsided smiles. I grin and do another cartwheel, and Lochan lengthens his stride to match mine, appearing faintly amused. But when his gaze shifts away, the smile fades and the lip biting starts up again. Despite his loping presence at my side, I feel there is a space between us, an indefinable distance. Even when his eyes are on me, I sense that he doesn't quite see me, his thoughts somewhere else, out of reach. I lose my footing coming out of a forward walkover and stumble against him, almost relieved to feel him solid and alive. He laughs briefly and steadies me but quickly goes back to sucking his lip, his teeth chafing the sore.

When we were young, I could do something silly and break the spell, pull him out of it, but now it's harder. I know there are things he doesn't tell me. Things he has on his mind.

When we reach the shops, we buy pizza and Coke from a takeaway and head toward Battersea Park. Inside the gates, we wander out into the middle of the vast expanse of greenery, away from the trees, aligning ourselves with the sun, now lying westward and losing its brilliance. Cross-legged, I examine a bruise on my shin, while Lochan kneels in the grass, opening the pizza box and handing me a slice. I take it and stretch out my legs, lifting my chin to feel the sun on my face.

"This is a million times nicer than hanging out with those dorks from school," I inform him. "That was a good move, leaving when you did."

Munching solidly, he shoots me a penetrating look, and I can tell he is trying to read my mind, seeking the motive behind my words. I meet his gaze full on, and the corner of his mouth twitches upward as he realizes I am being completely honest.

I give up on the food before he does and lean back on my elbows, watching him eat. He's clearly starving. I open my mouth to tell him he has tomato sauce on his chin, then change my mind. My smile, however, doesn't go unnoticed.

"What?" he asks with a brief laugh, swallowing his last mouthful and wiping his hands on the grass.

"Nothing." I try to reel in the smile, but with his red-streaked chin, tousled hair, untucked shirt, and grubby cuffs flapping loosely against his hands, he looks like a taller, dark-haired version of Tiffin at the end of a busy school day.

"Why are you looking at me like that?" he persists, regarding me quizzically, a touch self-conscious now.

"Nothing. I was just thinking of what Francie says about you."

A hint of wariness touches his eyes. "Oh, not that again . . ."

"Your dimples are apparently very cute." I bite back a grin.

"Ha ha." A little smile and he is looking down, pulling at the grass, a flush creeping up his neck.

"And you have arresting eyes—whatever that means."

A grimace of embarrassment. "Piss off, Maya. You just made that up."

"I didn't. I'm telling you—she says things like that. What else . . . Oh, yes: Your mouth is apparently very snoggable."

He chokes, showering me with Coke. "Maya!"

"I'm not kidding! Those were her exact words!"

He is blushing hard now, peering intently into the Coke can. "Can I finish this or are you still thirsty?"

"Stop trying to change the subject." I laugh.

He shoots me an evil look and swigs down the dregs.

"She even said she caught sight of you through the open door of the boys' changing rooms and you looked really—"

TABITHA SUZUMA

He kicks out at me. He is still half joking but it hurt.

I feel confused. Beneath the jokey exterior, he suddenly seems upset. I appear to have inadvertently crossed some invisible line.

"Okay." I raise my hands in surrender. "But you get the idea, right?"

"Yeah, thanks a lot." He gives another wry smile to show he isn't angry and then turns his face away into the breeze. There is a long silence and I close my eyes, feeling the last of the summer sun on my face. The tranquility is unnerving. Muted playground shrieks reach us from what seems like a million miles away. Somewhere among the trees, a dog lets out a couple of short, sharp yaps. I roll over onto my stomach and prop my chin on my hands. Lochan hasn't realized I'm watching him, and all signs of laughter have been completely erased from his face. Elbows resting on drawn-up knees, he gazes out across the park, and I can feel his mind working. Scrutinizing his face for lingering signs of annoyance, I find none. Only sadness.

"You okay?"

"Yeah." He doesn't turn.

"Really?"

He's about to say something but then remains silent. Instead he starts rubbing at his sore with the side of his thumb.

I sit up. Reaching out, I gently pull his hand down from his face. His eyes dart to meet mine. "Maya, I'm not going to go out with Francie."

"I know. That's okay. It doesn't matter," I say quickly. "She'll get over it."

"Why are you so keen to set us up?"

I feel awkward suddenly. "I dunno. I guess—I guess I thought if you went out with a friend of mine, at least I'd still get to see you. You wouldn't—you'd be less likely to go away."

He frowns, uncomprehending.

"It's just that if you meet somebody next year at university—" A small pain rises in the back of my throat. I cannot finish the sentence. "I mean, of course I want you to, but I don't—I'm scared. . . ."

He gives me a long, steady look. "Maya, surely you know I'd never leave you—you or the others."

I force a smile and look down, tugging at the blades of grass. *But one day you will,* I can't help thinking. One day we'll all leave each other to forge families of our own. Because that's the way the world works.

"To be honest, I doubt if I'm ever going to go out with anyone," Lochan says quietly.

I look up in surprise. He glances at me and then away, an uncomfortable silence hanging between us.

I can't help smiling. "That's silly, Loch. You're the best-

looking guy at Belmont. Every girl in my class has a crush on you."

Silence.

"Are you saying you're gay?"

The corners of his mouth twitch in amusement. "If there's one thing I do know, it's that I'm not!"

I sigh. "That's a pity. I always thought it would be pretty cool to have a gay brother."

Lochan laughs. "Don't lose hope yet. There's still Kit and Tiffin."

"Kit? Yeah, right! Rumor has it he's already got a girlfriend. Francie swears she saw him snogging a girl from the year above in an empty classroom."

"Let's just hope he doesn't get her pregnant," Lochan says acerbically.

I wince and try to banish the thought from my mind. I don't even want to think of Kit with a girl. He's only thirteen, for chrissakes.

I sigh. "I've never even kissed anyone—unlike most of the girls in my class," I confess quietly, running my fingers through the long grass.

He turns to me. "So?" he says gently. "You're only sixteen."

I pick at the stems and pout. "Sweet sixteen and never

been kissed . . . What about you—have you ever—" I break off abruptly, suddenly realizing the absurdity of my question. I try to think of a way of turning it around, but it's too late; Lochan is already picking at the ground with his fingernails, the color high in his cheeks.

"Yeah, right!" He gives a derisive snort, avoiding my gaze, intent on the small hole he is digging in the earth. "Like—like that's ever going to happen!" With a short laugh, he glances at me as if imploring me to join in, and through the embarrassment I see the pain in his eyes.

Instinctively I move closer, stopping myself from reaching out and squeezing his hand, hating myself for my moment of thoughtlessness. "Loch, it's not always going to be like this," I tell him gently. "One day—"

"Yeah, one day." He smiles with forced nonchalance and gives a brief, dismissive shrug. "I know."

A long silence stretches out between us. I look up at him in the scattered light of the afternoon, now nearing its end. "Do you ever think about it?"

He hesitates, the blood still hot in his cheeks, and for a moment I think he isn't going to reply. He continues picking at the earth, still studiously avoiding my gaze. "Course." It's so quiet that for a moment I think I might have imagined it.

I look at him sharply. "Who?"

TABITHA SUZUMA

"There's never really been anyone. . . ." He still refuses to look up, but even though he's increasingly uncomfortable, he isn't trying to get out of the conversation. "I just think that somewhere there must be—" He shakes his head, as if suddenly aware he has said too much.

"Hey, me too!" I exclaim. "Somewhere in my head I have this idea of a perfect guy. But I don't think he even exists."

"Sometimes—" Lochan begins, then breaks off.

I wait for him to continue. "Sometimes . . ." I prompt gently.

"I wish things were different." He takes a deep breath. "I wish everything wasn't so damn hard."

"I know," I say quietly. "Me too."

CHAPTER SEVEN

Lochan

Summer gives way to autumn. The air turns sharper, the days grow shorter, gray clouds and persistent drizzle alternating with cold blue skies and bracing winds. Willa loses her third tooth, Tiffin attempts to cut his own hair when a supply teacher mistakes him for a girl, Kit is suspended for three days for smoking weed. Mum starts spending her days off with Dave and, even when she's working, frequently stays over at his flat above the restaurant to avoid the daily commute. On the few occasions she's home, she's rarely sober for long, and Tiffin and Willa have given up asking her to play with them or tuck them in. I make regular recycling trips to the bottle bank after dark.

is deafening: music, shouting, cheering. As we're already in the small hours of the morning, her speech is slurred and the fact that her son has gone missing barely seems to register. Laughing and breaking off every few words to talk to Dave, she informs me I need to learn to relax, that Kit is a young man now and should have some fun. I am about to point out he could be lying facedown in a gutter when I suddenly realize I'm wasting my breath. With Dave she can pretend she is young again, free of the restrictions and responsibilities of motherhood. She never wanted to grow up—I remember our father citing this as a reason for leaving. He accused her of being a bad mother, but then, the only reason they got married was because she accidentally fell pregnant with me—a fact she likes to remind me of whenever we have an argument. And now that I am just a few months away from being legally classed an adult, she feels freer than she has in years. Dave already has a young family of his own. He has made it very clear that he doesn't want to take on someone else's. And so she shrewdly keeps him away, only bringing him back to the house when everyone is asleep or out at school. With Dave she has reinvented herself—a young woman caught up in a passionate romance. She dresses like a teenager, spends all her money on clothes and beauty treatments, lies about her age, and drinks, drinks, drinks—to forget that youth and beauty are behind her, to forget that Dave has no intention of marrying her, to forget that at the end of the day she is just a forty-five-year-old divorcée in a dead-end job with five unwanted children. Yet understanding the reasons behind her behavior does little to stem the hate.

It is now half past two and I am beginning to panic. Seated on the sofa, strategically positioned so that the weak light of the naked bulb falls directly on my books, I have been straining to read through my notes for at least three hours, the scrawled words bleeding into each other, dancing about the page. Maya came to say good night over an hour ago, purple shadows beneath her eyes, her freckles contrasting starkly with the pallor of her skin. I am still in my uniform, the usual ink-stained cuffs pushed up, shirt half unbuttoned. From deep within my skull, a metallic shaft of pain bores its way through my right temple. Once again I glance up at the clock and my insides knot in fear and rage. I stare at my ghostly reflection in the darkened windowpane. My eyes hurt; my whole body throbs with stress and exhaustion. I have not the slightest idea what to do.

Part of me simply wants to blot the whole thing out—go to bed and just pray Kit is back by the time I wake up in the morning. But another part of me is forced to remember that he is little more than a child. An unhappy, self-destructive child who has got in with the wrong crowd because they provide him with the company and admiration his family does not. He could have been in a fight, he could be mainlining heroin, he could be breaking the law and screwing up his life before it has even begun. Worse still, he could be the victim of a mugger or some rival gang—his behavior has begun to earn him quite a reputation in the area. He could be lying bleeding somewhere, knifed or shot. He may hate me, he may resent me, he may blame me for everything that's wrong in his life, but if I give up on him, then he has no one left at all. His hatred of me will have been completely justified. Yet what can I possibly do? He refuses to share any part of his life with me, so I don't know any of his friends or where he hangs out. I don't even have a bike to go combing the streets with.

The clock now reads a quarter to three, nearly five hours after Kit's weekend curfew. He never actually comes home before ten but rarely stays out much past eleven. What places around here are even open at this time? Nightclubs require ID—he has a fake one but even an idiot couldn't mistake him for an eighteen-year-old. He has never been anywhere near as late as this before.

Fear snakes into my mind. It curls around itself, its body pressing against the walls of my skull. This is not rebellion; something has happened. Kit is in trouble and no one is there to help him. I feel clammy and shivery with sweat. I have no choice but to go out and walk the streets, searching for an open bar, a nightclub—anything. But first I need to wake Maya so she can call me if Kit returns. My mind flashes back to the exhaustion imprinted on her face, and the thought of dragging her out of bed sickens me, but I have no choice.

My first knock is far too soft—I'm afraid of waking the little ones. But if Kit is hurt or in trouble, there is no time to lose. I turn the handle and push the door open. Lamplight falls through the gap in the curtains, illuminating her sleeping face, her tawny hair fanned out over the pillow. She has kicked back the sheet and is sleeping facedown, splayed out like a starfish, knickers in full view.

I bend down and gently shake her. "Maya?"

"Mmm . . ." She rolls away from me in protest.

I try again. "Maya, wake up, it's me."

"Huh?" Rolling onto her side, she props herself up on her elbow, looking up at me groggily, blinking beneath a curtain of hair.

"Maya, I need your help." The words come out louder than I intended, the mounting panic catching in my throat.

"What?" She is suddenly alert, struggling to sit up, brushing the hair away from her face. She flicks on the bedside light and squints at me, wincing. "What's going on?"

"It's Kit—he hasn't come home and it's almost three. I—I think I should go and look for him. I think something must have happened."

She squeezes her eyes shut and then opens them wide again, as if trying to gather her thoughts. "Kit's still out?"

"Yes!"

"Have you tried his mobile?"

I recount my futile attempts at getting through to both Kit and Mum. Maya stumbles out of bed and follows me down into the hallway as I hunt for my keys. "But, Lochie, d'you have any idea where he could be?"

"No, I'll just have to look. . . ." I rummage through my jacket pockets and then through the pile of junk mail and unopened bills on the hall table, sending them flying. My hands have started shaking. "Jesus, where the fuck are my keys?"

"Lochie, you're never going to find him by combing the streets. He could be on the other side of London!"

I spin round to face her. "What the hell d'you suggest I do, then?"

I startle myself with the force of my voice. Maya takes a step back.

I stop and heave a deep breath, cupping my hands over my mouth, then running them through my hair. "Sorry. I just— I just don't know what to do. Mum was incoherent on the phone. I couldn't even persuade the bitch to come home!" I choke on the word "bitch" and find myself with barely enough breath to finish speaking.

"Okay," Maya says quickly. "Okay, Lochie. I'll stay down here and wait. And I'll call you the moment he turns up. Have you got your phone?"

I feel the pockets of my trousers. "No—shit—and my keys—"

"Here . . ." Maya reaches for her coat on the peg and digs out her phone and keys. Grabbing them, I wrench open the door.

"Wait!" She throws me my jacket.

I pull it on as I stride out into the cold night air.

It's dark, the houses all sleeping, save for a few still illuminated with the flickering blue light of television screens. The silence is eerie—I can hear the juggernauts shifting their loads miles away on the ridge of the motorway. I walk rapidly down to the end of our road and turn onto the high street. The place has a deserted, haunted look, the shop shutters battened down over their dark interiors. Trash from the market stalls still litters the street, a drunk staggers out of the all-night bodega, and two skimpily clad young women weave their way across the sidewalk arm in arm, shrill voices crisscrossing the still night air. Suddenly a car, pulsating with music, accelerates down the road, narrowly missing the drunk, its tires screeching as it takes a corner. I spot a group of guys hanging around a closed pub. They are all dressed the same: gray hoodies, baggy jeans sliding down their hips, white trainers. But as I cross the road and head toward them, I realize they are far too old to be part of Kit's lot. I quickly turn my head away again, but one of them shouts out: "Hey, what the fuck you lookin' at?"

I ignore them and keep on going, hands deep in my pockets, fighting the instinct to lengthen my stride. Like wolves, they follow the scent of fear. For a moment I think they're going to come after me, but it's only their laughter and obscenities that float in my wake.

My heart continues to pound as I reach the end of the high street and cross the junction, my mind running at full tilt. This is exactly why a thirteen-year-old boy should not be roaming the streets at this time of night. Those guys were bored, drunk or high or both, and just looking for a fight. At least one would have had a weapon of some sort—a broken bottle, if not a knife. Gone are the days of simple fistfights, especially round here. And what chance would a hothead like Kit stand against a gang?

It is beginning to drizzle and the headlights of passing taxis splinter the dark, illuminating the wet tarmac. I cross the junction blindly and get honked at by an irritable cabbie. I wipe the sweat from my face with my shirtsleeve, adrenaline coursing through my body. The sudden wail of a police car makes me start violently; the sound fades into the distance and I jump again as a cacophony of demented yaps explodes from my pocket. When I pull out Maya's phone, my hands are shaking. "What?" I shout.

"He's back, Lochie. He's home."

"What?"

"Kit's back. He came through the door just this second. So you can come home. Where are you, anyway?"

"Bentham Junction. I'll see you in a minute."

I return the phone to my pocket and turn round. Chest heaving, my breath coming in gasps, I watch the late-night cars flash by. *Right—calm down,* I tell myself. He's home. He's fine. But I can feel the sweat running down my back and there is this pressure in my chest like a balloon that's about to burst.

I am walking too fast, breathing too fast, thinking too fast. There's a stabbing pain in my side and my heart is pounding against my rib cage. *He's home,* I keep telling myself. *He's okay*—but I don't know why I don't feel more relieved. In fact, I feel physically sick. I was so sure something bad had happened to him. Why else would he have failed to answer his phone, to call?

As I near the house, the street lamps blur and dance, and everything feels strangely unreal. My hands are shaking so hard, I can't unlock the door; the metal keys keep slipping in my clammy fingers. I end up dropping them and lean one hand against the door to steady myself as I bend down to search. When the door suddenly opens, I stumble blindly into the brightly lit hall.

"Hey, watch out." Maya's hand steadies me.

"Where is he?"

The sound of canned laughter belts out of the front room and I push past. Kit is lying back, one arm behind his head, feet up on the couch, chuckling at something on TV. He reeks of cigarettes and booze and weed.

Suddenly the compressed anger of so many months explodes through my body like molten rock. "Where the hell have you been?"

Spinning the remote round and round in his hand, he takes a moment before flicking his eyes briefly away from the screen. "Absolutely none of your business." His gaze returns to the television and he starts chuckling again, turning up the volume, preemptively drowning out any further attempts at conversation.

I lunge for the remote and snatch it from his hand, catching him unawares.

"Give that back, you asshole!" He is on his feet in an instant, grabbing my arm and twisting it.

"It's four in the morning! What the fuck have you been doing?"

I grapple with him, trying to push him off, but he is surprisingly strong. A bolt of pain shoots up my arm from my hand to my shoulder, and the remote falls to the floor. As Kit makes a dive for it, I grab his shoulders and yank him back. He hurls himself round, and there is a blinding crack of pain as his fist makes contact with my jaw. I launch myself at him, grabbing him by the collar, losing my balance and dragging him down to the floor. My head hits the coffee table and for a moment the lights seem to go out, but then I resurface and I've got my hands round his throat and his face is crimson, his eyes wide and bulging. He kicks me in the stomach, again and again, but I don't let go, I can't let go, even when he knees me in the groin. There is someone else pulling at my hands, someone else in the way, someone shouting at me, screaming in my ear: "Stop it, Lochie, stop it! You're going to kill him!"

I've let go; he's got away, doubled over on hands and knees, coughing and retching, strings of saliva hanging from his mouth. Someone is restraining me from behind, pinning my arms to my sides, but all the strength has suddenly left me and I can barely sit up. I hear gasping sounds from Kit as he lurches to his feet, and suddenly he is towering over me.

"You ever touch me again and I'll kill you." His voice is hoarse and rasping. I hear him leave, hear him thunder up the wooden stairs, hear the sound of a wailing child. I seem to be falling, except the carpet is solid beneath me and the cold hard wall presses against my back. Through a dim haze I see Willa wrap her legs around Maya's waist as Maya lifts her into a hug and murmurs, "It's all right, it's all right, my love—they just had a silly argument. Everything's fine now. Let's go back upstairs and tuck you into bed, okay?"

They leave the room and the wails fade but continue above me, on and on and on.

My legs are unsteady as I make my way to my room. Safely inside, I sit down on the edge of the bed, elbows on knees, cupping my hands over my nose and mouth, trying to stop hyperventilating, the pain in my stomach sending small after-shocks through my body. I feel sweat running down the sides of my face and I cannot stop trembling. The halo round the lightbulb above me expands and retracts, creating dancing spots of light. The full horror of what happened is only just starting to hit me. I have never got into any kind of physical fight with Kit before, yet tonight I provoked one, I almost wanted one; once I got my hands round his throat, I honestly didn't want to let go. I don't understand what's happening to me—I seem to be unraveling. So Kit came home a few hours late—what teenager hasn't? Parents get angry with their children, sure—they shout, threaten, swear at them, maybe, but they don't try to strangle them.

The knock on the door sends another jolt through my body. But it's only Maya, looking completely wiped out as she sags against the door frame.

"Are you all right?"

Hands still covering my mouth, I nod, desperate for her to leave but unable to speak. She observes me soberly in the gloom, hesitates for a moment, then comes in.

I take my hands away from my face, clenching them into fists to stop them from shaking. "I'm fine," I say, my voice raw and ragged. "We should all just go to bed."

"You don't look fine." She closes the door and leans against it, her eyes huge, her expression unreadable. I can't tell if she's angry, horrified, disgusted . . .

"Maya, I'm sorry. I—I just lost it. . . ." A jagged pain runs through me.

"I know, Loch, I know."

I want to tell her just how sorry I am. I want to ask her whether Willa is okay. I want to ask her to check on Kit, make sure he's not packing his bags and planning to run away, reassure me that I haven't hurt him, even though I know I have. But I can't get the words out. Only the sound of my heaving breaths fills the air. I press my hands against my nose and mouth to try to muffle the sound, push my elbows down hard against my knees in an effort to stop shaking, and find myself rocking back and forth without knowing why.

Peeling herself off the door, Maya moves toward me, taking a seat beside me on the bed.

Instinctively my arm flies up to ward her off. "Maya, d-don't—I don't need—"

She takes my outstretched hand and gently pulls it onto her lap, rubbing my palm in circular motions with her thumb. "Try to relax." Her voice is gentle—too gentle. "It's all right. Everyone's okay. Willa's gone back to sleep and Kit's fine."

I shift away from her, struggling to disengage my hand from hers. "I—I just need some sleep. . . ."

"I know you do, but you have to calm down first."

"I'm trying!"

Her face is pinched with concern and I'm aware that the sight of me in this state is doing little to reassure her. Her fingers are warm on my wrist, moving up to stroke the inside of my arm, the touch of her hand somehow comforting. "Lochie, it wasn't your fault."

I bite down hard and turn away.

"It wasn't your fault," she says again. "Lochie, you know that. Kit's been trying to provoke you into something like this for ages. Anyone would have snapped."

There is a mounting pain at the back of my throat, a warning pressure behind my eyes.

"You can't keep blaming yourself for everything, just because you're the eldest. None of this is your fault—Mum's drinking, Dad leaving, Kit turning out the way he has. There's nothing more you could have done."

I don't know how she's figured all this out. I don't understand how she is able to read my mind like this. I turn to face the wall, shaking my head to tell her she's wrong. I pull my hand away from hers and rub the side of my face, trying to shield it from view.

"Lochie . . ."

No. I can't take this anymore. I can't, I can't. I'm not even going to get her out of the room before it's too late. My eyes pulsate with a rising ache. If I move, if I speak, if I so much as blink, I'm going to lose this battle.

Her hand touches my shoulder, strokes my back. "It's not always going to be like this."

A tear skims the side of my cheek. I put my hand up to my eyes to stop the next one. My fingers are suddenly wet. I take a deep breath and try to hold it, but a small sound escapes.

"Oh—Loch, no. Don't—not over this!" Maya sounds softly desperate.

I move closer to the wall, wishing I could disappear into it. I press my fist hard against my mouth. Then the bottled breath explodes from my lungs with a violent choking sound.

"Hey, hey . . ." Despite her reassuring tone, I recognize the note of panic. "Lochie, please, listen to me. Just listen. Tonight was hideous, but it's not the end of the world. I know things have been really, really tough recently, but it's all right, it's all right. Kit's fine. You're only human. These things happen. . . ."

I try to dry my eyes on my shirtsleeve, but the tears keep coming and I can't understand why I am so utterly powerless to stop them.

"Shh, come here—" Maya tries to pull me round to face her, but I push her roughly away. She tries again. Frenziedly I fend her off with one arm.

"Don't! Maya, stop it, for chrissakes—please! Please! I can't—I can't—" The sobs burst out with each word. I can't breathe, I'm terrified, I'm falling apart.

"Lochie, calm down. I just want to hold you, that's all. Just let me hold you." Her voice adopts the soothing tone she uses when Tiffin or Willa is upset. She's not going to give up.

I scrape the fingernails of one hand against the wall, violent sobs running in shock waves through my body, tears soaking my sleeve. "Help," I find myself gasping. "I don't understand what's wrong with me!"

Maya slides into the space between me and the wall, and suddenly there is nowhere for me to hide anymore. As she puts

 TABITHA SUZUMA

her arms around me and pulls me close, I try to resist one final time, but I am drained of all strength. Her body is warm against mine—alive, familiar, reassuring. I press my face against the curve of her neck, my hands clutching at the back of her nightdress as if she might suddenly disappear.

"I—I didn't mean to—I didn't mean to—Maya, I didn't mean to!"

"I know you didn't mean to, Lochie. I know that, I know."

She is talking to me softly now, almost whispering, one arm wrapped tightly around me, the other stroking the back of my head, rocking me gently back and forth. I cling to her as the sobs rack my body with such force, I think I will never be able to stop.

CHAPTER EIGHT

Maya

I open my eyes and find myself staring up at an unfamiliar ceiling. My head feels fuzzy with sleep, and it isn't until I find myself blinking over at a desk laden with A-level textbooks, a chair covered in discarded shirts and trousers, that I remember where I am. There is a distinctive smell, too—not unpleasant, but unmistakably Lochan. A slight weight on my chest prompts me to look down, and with a start I see an arm slung over my rib cage, bitten-down fingernails, a large black digital watch secured around the wrist. Lochan is fast asleep by my side, stretched out on his front, pressed up against the wall, his arm draped over me.

My mind flashes back to the previous night and I remember

the fight, remember coming up and finding him in a really bad way, the shock of seeing him on the verge of tears, the feeling of horror and helplessness as he broke down and sobbed—the first time since the day Dad left. Seeing him like that sucked me back through the years, back to the day Dad came to the house for that "special good-bye" before catching the flight that was to take him and his new wife to the other side of the world. There were presents, and photos of the new house with the pool, and promises of school holidays with him there, and assurances that he would be back regularly. The others had naturally bought into the whole charade—they were still so young—but somehow Lochan and I sensed that that was it, we would not be seeing our dad again—ever. And it wasn't long before we were proved right.

The weekly phone calls became monthly, then only on special occasions, then stopped altogether. When Mum told us his new wife had just given birth, we knew it was only a matter of time before even the birthday presents ceased. And cease they did. Everything ceased. Even Mum's child support. We older two had expected it—just never guessed he would erase us all from his life quite so fast. I clearly remember that moment after the final good-bye, after the front door had closed and the sound of Dad's car faded down the street. Huddled up against the pillows with my new cuddly dog and the picture of the house I knew I'd never get to visit, I was suddenly overcome by a huge surge of rage and hatred for a father who had once claimed to love me so much. But to my surprise and annoyance, Lochan had seemed to go along with it all, rejoicing with the others at the idea of us all jetting off to Australia someday soon. I actually thought he was stupid. I sulked and ignored him all day while he forced himself through his charade. Only later that night, once he thought I was asleep, did he break down—softly sobbing into his pillow in the bunk above mine. He had been inconsolable then, too—fighting me off when I attempted to give him a hug before finally giving in, letting me snuggle under the duvet and cry with him. We'd promised each other then that even when we grew up, we would always stay together. Finally, exhausted and all cried out, we'd fallen asleep. And now here we are, five years on, and so much has changed, and yet so little.

It feels strange, lying here in Lochan's bed with him sleeping beside me. Willa used to climb into bed with me whenever she had nightmares—in the morning I'd wake up to find her small body pressed against mine. This is Lochan, though: my brother, my protector. Seeing his arm slung so casually across me makes me smile—he would be very quick to remove it if he woke. I don't want him to wake up just yet, though. His leg is pressed against mine, squashing it slightly. He is still in his

 TABITHA SUZUMA

school clothes, his shoulder heavy against my arm, pinning it to the bed. I am well and truly wedged in—in fact, we both are: His other arm has disappeared down the narrow crack between the mattress and the wall. I turn my head gingerly to see if he looks as if he might wake up anytime soon. He doesn't. He is sound asleep, taking those long, deep, rhythmical breaths, his face turned toward me. It's not often that I have him so near—not since we were young. It is strange to observe him at such close range; I see things I've barely noticed before. The way his hair, drenched in a shaft of sunlight slanting through the curtains, is not quite jet-black but actually contains streaks of golden brown. I can make out a pattern in the fine tracing of veins beneath the skin of his temples, even distinguish the individual hairs of his eyebrows. The faint white scar above his left eye from a childhood fall has not completely faded, and his eyelids are fringed with surprisingly long dark lashes. My eyes follow the smooth ridge of his nose down to the bow of his upper lip, so clearly defined now that his mouth is relaxed. His skin is smooth, almost translucent, the only blemish a self-inflicted sore beneath his mouth where his teeth have repeatedly rubbed, chafed, and scraped at the skin to leave a small crimson wound: a reminder of his ongoing battle with the world around him. I want to stroke it away, erase the hurt, the stress, the loneliness.

I find myself thinking back to Francie's comment. A kissable mouth . . . What does that mean, exactly? At the time I thought it was funny; I don't anymore. I wouldn't want Francie to kiss Lochan's mouth. I wouldn't want anyone to. He is my brother, my best friend. The idea of anyone seeing him like this, so close, so exposed, is suddenly unbearable. What if they hurt him, broke his heart? I don't want him to fall in love with some girl—I want him to stay here, loving us. Loving me.

He shifts slightly, his arm sliding up my rib cage. I can feel his sweaty warmth against my side. The way his nostrils contract slightly each time he inhales reminds me of the tenuous, precarious hold we all have on life. Asleep, he looks so vulnerable that it frightens me.

There are shouts, yelps from downstairs. Thundering feet on the stairs. A loud bang against the door. Tiffin's unmistakable, overexcited voice yelling, "Homey! Homey!"

Lochan's arm contracts and he opens his eyes with a start. For a long moment he just stares at me, emerald irises flecked with blue, his face very still. Then his expression begins to change.

"What—what's going on?"

I smile at the blurriness of his speech. "Nothing. I'm stuck."

He glances down at his arm, still slung across my chest, and retracts it quickly, struggling to sit up.

"Why are you—? What on earth are you doing here?" He

looks disoriented and slightly panicked for a moment, tousled hair hanging in his eyes, face hazy with sleep. The imprint of the pillow has left scarlet indentations across his cheek.

"We were talking late last night, remember?" I don't want to mention the fight or its aftermath. "I guess we both just crashed." I pull myself up against the headboard, curl my legs beneath me, and stretch. "I haven't been able to move for the past fifteen minutes because you were half crushing me."

He has retreated to the far end of the bed, leaning against the wall, dropping his head back with a thud. He closes his eyes for a moment. "I feel rough," he murmurs as if to himself, hugging his knees, his torso limp and yielding.

Concern grips me: It's not like Lochan to complain. "Where does it hurt?"

He releases his breath with a ghost of a smile. "Everywhere."

The smile fades when I don't return it and he holds me with his gaze, eyes heavy with sadness. "Today's Saturday, right?"

"Yes, but everything's fine. Mum's up—I heard her voice a few minutes ago. And Kit's up too. It sounds like they're all downstairs having breakfast or brunch or something."

"Oh. Okay. Good." Lochan sighs in relief and closes his eyes again. I don't like the way he is talking, sitting, behaving. He seems helpless somehow, in pain and utterly defeated. There is a long silence. He doesn't open his eyes.

"Lochie?" I venture softly.

"Yeah." He looks at me with a start and blinks rapidly, as if attempting to engage his brain.

"Stay here while I get you some coffee and painkillers, okay?"

"No, no . . ." He catches me by the wrist to restrain me. "I'm fine. I'll wake up properly once I've had a shower."

"Okay. There's Tylenol in the bathroom cabinet."

He gazes blankly at me. "Right," he says dully.

Nothing happens. He doesn't move. I begin to feel uneasy.

"You're not looking too good, you know," I inform him gently. "How about you get back into bed for a bit and I'll bring you breakfast?"

He turns his head to look at me again. "No—seriously, Maya, I'm fine. Just give me a minute, okay?"

The unspoken rule in our family is that Lochan is never ill. Even last winter, when he had the flu and a high fever, he insisted he was well enough to do the school run.

"Then I'm going to get you some coffee," I declare abruptly, jumping up from the bed. "Go and have a hot shower and—"

He stops me, catching my hand before I reach the door. "Maya . . ."

I turn, tightening my fingers around his. "What?"

His jaw tenses and I see him swallow. His eyes seem to be searching mine, hoping for something—a sign of understanding, perhaps. "I can't—I really don't think I can—" He breaks off, breathing deeply. I wait. "I don't think I've got the energy to do the whole family meal thing today." He pulls an apologetic face.

"Well, of course I'll do it, you silly!" I think for a moment and begin to smile. "Hey, I've got an even better idea."

"What?" He looks hopeful suddenly.

I grin. "I'll get rid of them all—you'll see."

I stand in the doorway for a moment, soaking up the chaos. They are seated around the kitchen table, a mess of Coco Pops, Coke cans, Jaffa Cakes, and crisps strewn out in front of them. Mum must have sent Tiffin to the corner shop when she discovered only muesli and brown bread for breakfast. But at least she's up before noon, albeit still in her sleazy pink dressing gown, her blond hair uncombed, great bags beneath her bloodshot eyes. Judging by the ashtray, she has already been through half a packet of cigarettes, but despite her appearance, she seems surprisingly spry and perky, helped no doubt by the shot of whiskey I can smell in her coffee.

"Princess!" She holds out her arms. "You look like an angel in that dress."

"Mum, this is the same nightie I've been wearing for the past four years," I inform her with a sigh.

Mum just smiles complacently, my words barely registering, but Kit chuckles through a mouthful of Coco Pops, showering the table. I'm relieved to see that he looks none the worse for his run-in with Lochan last night. Beside him, Tiffin is trying to juggle three oranges from the fruit bowl, his sugar levels clearly sky-high. Willa is talking rapidly and indistinctly, her mouth crammed to capacity, chocolate smeared across her chin. I make some coffee, retrieve the muesli from the cupboard, and start slicing the bread on the sideboard.

"Wanna Mars bar?" Tiffin offers me generously.

"No thanks, Tiff. And I think you've probably had enough chocolate for today. Remember what happens when you have too much sugar?"

"I get sent to the head," Tiffin responds automatically. "But I ain't at school now."

"I'm not at school now," I correct him. "Hey, guess what, I've had a really good idea for a family day out!"

"Oh, how lovely!" Mum exclaims eagerly. "Where are you going to take them?"

"Actually, I was thinking of a day out with the whole family," I continue jovially, careful to keep the edge out of my voice. "And we'd definitely want you to come too, Mum!"

Kit glances up at me with dark, mistrustful eyes, snorting

in derision. "Yeah, let's go to the seaside or something and have a fucking picnic and pretend we're just one big happy family."

"Where, where?" Tiffin shouts.

"Well, I was thinking we could all go to—"

"The zoo, the zoo!" Willa cries, practically falling off her chair in excitement.

"No, the park!" Tiffin counters. "We can play three-a-side soccer."

"How about the bowling alley?" Kit suggests unexpectedly. "They have arcade games there."

I smile indulgently. "We might be able to do all three. There's a massive fairground that's just opened in Battersea Park—there's a zoo on the other side of the park, and I think the fairground even has arcade games, Kit."

A flicker of interest registers in his eyes.

"Mum, will you buy me cotton candy?" Tiffin yells.

"And me, and me!" Willa shrieks.

Mum smiles wanly. "A day out with all my bunnies. How lovely."

"But you'll all have to get ready double-quick," I warn. "It's almost noon."

"Mum, come on!" Tiffin yells at her. "You gotta put on all your makeup and get dressed right now!"

"Just one last ciggie . . ."

But Tiffin and Willa have already gone tearing out of the room to put on their coats and shoes. Even Kit has swung his feet off the table.

"Is Lochan coming on this little jaunt?" Mum asks me, dragging heavily on her cigarette. I notice Kit's eyes sharpen suddenly.

"No, he's got a ton of homework to catch up on." I stop clearing the table suddenly and slap a hand to my forehead. "Oh no. Damn!"

"What's the matter, sweetie?"

"I completely forgot. I can't come today. I promised I'd babysit the Davidsons' new baby this afternoon."

Mum looks alarmed. "Well, can't you just cancel and say you're ill or something?"

"No, they're going to a wedding and I told them I'd do it ages ago." I can't believe what a good liar I am. "Besides," I add pointedly, "we could do with the money."

Tiffin and Willa return to the kitchen, bundled up in their coats, and stop, instantly sensing the change in atmosphere.

"Clever Maya's just realized we can't go after all," Kit informs them.

"We'll go tomorrow instead!" Mum exclaims brightly.

"Nooo!" Tiffin's howl is one of despair. Willa looks up at me accusingly, her blue eyes stricken.

"But you can still go with Mum," I say casually, carefully avoiding her gaze.

Tiffin and Willa turn to look at her, their eyes pleading. "Mum! Mum, pleeeease!"

"Oh, all right, all right." She sighs, shooting me a pained, almost angry look. "Anything for my babies."

As Mum goes upstairs to get dressed and Tiffin and Willa tear about the house in a sugar-induced frenzy, Kit returns his feet to the table and starts idly flicking through a comic. "Well, look how that turned out," he mutters without looking up.

I feel myself tense but continue to clear the table. "What difference does it make?" I retort quietly. "Tiffin and Willa get to go out and have fun and you get five times your usual pocket money to spend on arcades."

"I'm not complaining," he says. "I just think it's touching the way you fabricate this whole complicated lie just cuz Lochan's too ashamed to face the fact that he's a violent bastard."

I stop cleaning the table, squeezing the sponge so hard that the warm, soapy water runs through the cracks between my fingers.

"Lochan doesn't know anything about this, okay?" I snap, my voice low with repressed anger. "It was my idea. Because frankly, Kit, it's the weekend, Tiffin and Willa deserve to have a bit of fun, and Lochan and I are completely shattered from running the house all week."

"I bet he is—after trying to kill me last night." He glares up at me now, his dark eyes as hard as pebbles.

I find myself gripping the edge of the table. "From what I remember, it was a two-way deal. And Lochan's so bashed up, he can hardly move."

A slow grin of triumph spreads across Kit's face. "Yeah, well, I can't say I'm surprised. If he didn't spend his days hiding in stairwells and actually learned to fight like a real—"

I slam my fist down on the table. "Don't give me your macho gang bullshit," I hiss in a furious whisper. "Last night wasn't some kind of sick competition! Lochan's really upset about what happened. He never wanted to hurt you."

"How very considerate of him," Kit replies, voice dripping with sarcasm, still flicking infuriatingly through his magazine. "But kind of hard to believe when just a few hours ago he had his hands around my neck."

"You played a part in this too, you know. You punched him first!" I glance nervously at the closed kitchen door. "Look, I'm not going to get into an argument with you about who started what. As far as the fight's concerned, you're both as guilty as each other. But just ask yourself this: Why the hell d'you think Lochan was so upset in the first place? How many of your friends have a brother who would stay up half the night waiting for them to return? How many of them have a brother who

 TABITHA SUZUMA

would go scouring the streets at three in the morning because he was afraid something terrible might have happened? How many have brothers who shop for them, cook for them, attend parent–teacher meetings, and stick up for them when they're suspended from school? Don't you get it, Kit? Lochan lost it last night because he cares about you—because he loves you!"

Kit throws the magazine across the table, making me jump, his eyes igniting in anger. "Did I ask him to do any of those things? D'you think I like having to depend on my fucking brother for every little thing? No, you're right, my mates don't have older brothers like that. They have brothers who hang out with them, get pissed with them, help them get fake IDs and sneak them into nightclubs and stuff. Whereas I've got a brother who tells me what time I've got to be home and then beats me up if I'm late! He's not my father! He may pretend to care, but it's only because he's on some sick power trip! He doesn't love me like Dad did, but he sure as hell thinks he can tell me what to do every second of the day!"

"You're right," I say quietly. "He doesn't love us the way Dad did. Dad buggered off halfway round the world with his new family the moment things got tough. Lochan could have left school last year, got himself a job, and moved out. He could choose to run off next year to a university at the other end of the country. But no, he's only applying to ones in London, even though his teachers were desperate for him to try for Oxbridge. He's staying in London so he can live here and look after us and make sure we're all right."

Kit manages to pull off a sardonic laugh. "You're deluded, Maya. You know why he isn't going anywhere? Cuz he's too damn scared, that's why. You've seen him—he can't even talk to his classmates without stammering like some kind of retard. And he certainly isn't staying here because of me. He's staying because he's power drunk—he gets his kicks from bossing Tiff and Willa around, cuz it makes him feel better about the fact he can't even articulate a single word at school. And he's staying here because he adores you, because you always take his side in everything, you think he's some kind of god, and his sister's the only friend he's got in the world." He shakes his head. "How pathetic is that?"

I stare at Kit, stare at the anger in his face, the color in his cheeks, but most of all at the sadness in his eyes. It pains me to see him still hurting so much about Dad, and I keep reminding myself he's only thirteen. But I just can't find a way to make him step out of his own self-centered circle, even for a second, and see the situation from any other view-point than his own.

Finally, in desperation, I say, "Kit, I understand why you resent Lochan's position of authority, I really do. But it's not

 TABITHA SUZUMA

his fault that Dad left and it's not his fault that Mum's the way she is. He's just trying to look out for us because there's no one else. I promise you, Kit, Lochan would much rather have remained your brother and friend. But just think—under the circumstances, what else could he possibly have done? What choice did he ever have?"

When the front door finally slams shut and the excited voices fade down the street, I heave a sigh of relief and glance at the kitchen clock. How many hours do we have until Tiffin and Willa start to bicker, Kit starts arguing about money, and Mum decides she has done more than enough to make up for her absence all week? Factoring in travel time, we can expect three hours—four if we're lucky. I feel as if I should immediately start making the most of it, try out all those things that I'm forever planning to do but putting off because there is always something more pressing at hand. . . . But suddenly it feels absurdly luxurious just to be sitting here in the silent kitchen, the dappled sunlight falling through the kitchen window and warming my face—not thinking, not moving, not worrying about homework or arguing with Kit or trying to control Tiffin or entertaining Willa. Just being. I feel I could stay here forever in the sunny, empty afternoon, slung sideways on a wooden chair, my arms folded against the smooth curve of its back, watching the sunbeams dance through the leaves, the branches peering in through the window, creating swaying shadows on the tiled floor. The sound of silence fills the air like a beautiful smell: no raised voices, no slamming doors, no pounding feet, no deafening music or babbling cartoons. I close my eyes, warm sun caressing my face and neck, filling my eyelids with a bright pink haze, and rest my head on my folded arms.

I must have fallen asleep, for time suddenly seems to have leaped forward and I find myself sitting up in a shaft of bright white light, wincing and massaging a crick in my neck. I stretch and stand up stiffly, moving over to the kettle and filling it. Padding out into the corridor with two steaming mugs and heading for the stairs, I hear the rustle of paper behind me and turn. Lochan has ensconced himself in the front room, binders, textbooks, and copious notes spread out over the coffee table and carpet around him as he sits on the floor against the edge of the couch, one leg stretched out beneath the table, the other drawn up to prop open a hefty tome. He is looking a lot better—much more relaxed in his favorite green T-shirt and faded jeans, barefoot, his hair still wet from the shower.

"Thanks!" Sliding the textbook off his lap, he takes the mug from me. He leans back against the couch, blowing on his coffee as I sit down on the carpet against the opposite wall, yawning and rubbing my eyes.

"I've never seen anyone sleep with their head hanging off the back of a wooden chair before—was the couch not comfortable enough for you?" His face lights up with a rare smile. "So tell me—how the hell did you get rid of the whole lot of them?"

I tell him about my fairground suggestion, my lie about the babysitting.

"And you managed to persuade Kit to accompany them on this little family outing?"

"I told him there were arcade games at the fair."

"Are there?"

"No idea."

We both laugh. But Lochan's amusement is quick to fade. "Did Kit seem . . . Was he . . ."

"Absolutely fine. In true antagonistic form."

Lochan nods but his eyes remain troubled.

"Honestly, Lochan. He's fine. How's the studying going?" I ask quickly.

Shoving the huge textbook away from him in disgust, he emits a labored sigh. "I don't understand this stuff. And if Mr. Parris understood it, at least I wouldn't have to be teaching myself from some library book."

I groan inwardly. I was hoping we'd go out and do something this afternoon—take a long walk in the park or have a hot chocolate at Joe's or even treat ourselves to the movies—but Lochan's exams are only three months away, and trying to study over the Christmas break with the kids at home all day will be a nightmare. I can't say I'm particularly bothered about my AS-levels—unlike Lochan I'm just sticking to the subjects I find easiest. My strange brother, on the other hand, has decided, for reasons best known only to himself, to take on his two most challenging subjects, further math and physics, as well as English and history, the two big essay ones. My sympathy is limited: Just like our ex-father, he's a natural academic.

Absentmindedly sipping his coffee, he picks up his pen again and starts sketching some complex diagram on the nearest scrap of paper, labeling the various shapes and symbols with illegible code. Closing his eyes for a moment, he proceeds to pick up the scrap and compare it to the diagram in the book. Crumpling up the sheet, he tosses it across the room in disgust and starts chewing his lip.

"Perhaps you need a break," I suggest, looking up from the newspaper spread out at my side.

"Why the hell can't I get this to stick?" He gazes at me imploringly, as if hoping I will magically conjure up the answer.

TABITHA SUZUMA

I look at his pale face, the shadows beneath his eyes, and think: *because you're exhausted.*

"D'you want me to test you?"

"Yeah, cheers. Just give me a minute."

As he returns to his textbook and his diagrams and scribbles, his eyes narrow in concentration and he continues to gnaw at his lip. I flick idly through the paper, my mind flitting briefly to the French homework buried at the bottom of my bag, before deciding it can wait. I reach the sports section without finding a single article of interest and, suddenly bored, stretch out on my stomach and pull one of Lochan's folders off the coffee table. Leafing through it, I glance enviously at the pages and pages of essays, invariably accompanied by nothing but ticks and exclamations of praise. Nothing but As and A pluses—I wonder if next year I could get away with passing off some of Lochan's work as my own. They'd think I'd morphed into a genius overnight. A recent piece of creative writing makes me pause: an essay, written less than a week ago, its usual list of superlatives in the margins. But it's the teacher's comment at the end that catches my attention:

An extremely evocative, powerful depiction of a young man's inner turmoil, Lochan. This is a beautifully crafted story about suffering and the human psyche.

Beneath this panegyric, in large letters, the teacher has added: *Please at least consider reading this out loud in class. It would*

really inspire the others and would be good practice for you ahead of your presentation.

My curiosity aroused, I leaf back through the pages and start reading Lochan's essay. It's about a young man, an undergraduate, returning to university in the summer break to find out whether he has got his degree. Joining the throngs that crowd the display boards, the guy discovers to his astonishment that he has received a first, the only one in his department. But instead of elation, he feels only a sense of emptiness, and as he moves away from the crowds of students hugging distressed friends or celebrating with others, nobody seems to notice him—no one even looks in his direction. He receives not one single word of congratulation. My first thought is that this is some kind of ghost story—that this guy, at some point between sitting for finals and coming back to find out his results, has died in an accident or something—but an eventual greeting from one of his professors, who manages to mispronounce his name, proves me wrong. The guy is very much alive. Yet as he turns his back on the department and crosses the quad, he looks up at the tall buildings that surround him, trying to gauge which one will guarantee him a fatal fall.

The story ends and I raise my head from the page, stunned and shaken, blown away by the strength of the prose and suddenly close to tears. I glance across at Lochan, who is drumming his fingers on the carpet, eyes closed, chanting some

TABITHA SUZUMA

physics formula under his breath. I try to imagine him writing this tragically poignant piece and fail. Who could think up such a story? Who would be able to write about something like this so vividly unless they had experienced such pain, such desperation, such alienation, themselves . . .

Lochan opens his eyes and looks right at me. "The force per unit length between long parallel straight current-carrying conductors: F equals mu to the power of zero, iota to the power of one, iota to the power of two over two pi r. . . . Oh, for chrissakes, let it be right!"

"Your story is incredible."

He blinks at me. "What?"

"The English essay you wrote last week." I glance down at the pages in my hand. "'Buildings.'"

Lochan's eyes sharpen suddenly and I see him tense. "What are you doing?"

"I was flicking through your English file and I found this." I hold it aloft.

"Did you read it?"

"Yes. It's bloody good."

He looks away, appearing acutely uncomfortable. "It was just taken from something I saw on TV. Could you test me on this now?"

"Wait . . ." I refuse to let him brush this aside so easily.

"Why did you write this? Who's the story about?"

"Nobody. It's just a story, okay?" He sounds angry suddenly, his eyes darting away from mine.

The essay still in my hand, I don't move, giving him a long, hard look.

"You think it's about me? It's not about me." His voice rises defensively.

"Okay, Lochan. Okay." I realize I have no choice but to back off.

He is chewing his lip hard, aware that I'm not convinced. "Well, you know, sometimes you take a few things from your own life, change them, exaggerate parts," he concedes, turning away.

I take a deep breath. "Have you ever . . . Do you sometimes feel like this?"

I brace myself for another angry reaction. But instead he just gazes blankly at the opposite wall. "I think—I think maybe everyone does . . . now and again."

I realize this is the closest I'm going to get to an admission, and his words make my throat ache. "But you know—you do know you'll never ever find yourself alone like the guy in your story, right?" I say in a rush.

"Yeah, yeah, of course." He gives a quick shrug.

"Because, Lochan, you'll always have someone who loves

you—just you—more than anybody in the world."

We are silent for a moment and Lochan goes back to his formula, but the color is still high in his cheeks and I can tell he's not really taking anything in. I glance back down at the teacher's scrawled message at the end.

"So, hey—did you ever read this out loud in class?" I ask brightly.

He looks up at me with a labored sigh. "Maya, you know I'm crap at stuff like that."

"But this is so good!"

He pulls a face. "Thanks, but even if that were true, it wouldn't make any difference."

"Oh, Lochie . . ."

Drawing up his knees, he leans back against the couch, turning his head to gaze out of the window. "I've got to give this damn presentation soon," he says quietly. "I don't know—I really don't know what the hell to do." He seems to be asking me for help.

"Did you ask if you could hand it in as a written assignment?"

"Yes, but it's that crazy Aussie. I'm telling you, she's got it in for me."

"From the comments and the grades she's been giving you, it's clear she thinks pretty highly of you," I point out gently.

"It's not that. She wants—she wants to turn me into some kind of orator." He gives a strained laugh.

"Maybe it's time you allowed yourself to be converted," I suggest tentatively. "Just a little bit. Just enough to give it a go."

A long silence. "Maya, you know I can't." He turns away suddenly, looking out of the window at two boys on bikes doing stunts in the street. "It—it feels like people are burning me with their stares. Like there's no air left in my body. I get the stupid shakes, my heart pounds, and the words just—they just disappear. My mind goes completely blank and I can't even make out the writing on the page. I can't speak loud enough for people to hear me, and I know that everyone's just waiting—waiting for me to fall apart so they can laugh. They all know—they all know I can't do it—" He breaks off, the laughter gone from his eyes, his breathing shallow and rapid, as if aware he has already said too much. His thumb rubs back and forth over the sore. "Jesus, I know it's not normal. I know it's something I've got to sort out. And—and I will, I'm sure I will. I have to. How else can I ever get a job? I'll find a way. I'm not always going to be like this. . . ." He takes a deep breath, tugging at his hair.

"Of course you're not," I reassure him quickly. "Once you're free of Belmont, the whole stupid school system—"

"But I'll still have to find a way to get through uni—and

work, after that. . . ." His voice quavers suddenly and I see desperation in his eyes.

"Have you talked to this English teacher about it?" I ask. "She doesn't sound too bad, you know. Maybe she could help. Give you some tips. Better than that useless counselor they forced on you—the one who made you do breathing exercises and asked whether you were breast-fed as a baby!"

He starts laughing before I do. "Oh God, I'd almost forgotten about her—she really was a nutcase!" He sobers suddenly. "But the thing is—the thing is, I can't—I really can't."

"You keep saying that," I point out gently. "But you massively underestimate yourself, Lochie. I know you could read something out loud in class. Maybe not start off with a whole presentation, but perhaps you could agree to read one of your essays. Something shorter, a bit less personal. You know, it's like with anything: once you take that first step, the next is a whole lot easier." I break off with a smile. "You know who first told me that?"

He shakes his head and rolls his eyes. "No clue. Martin Luther?"

"You, Lochie. When you were trying to teach me to swim."

He smiles briefly at the memory, then exhales slowly. "Okay. Maybe I could try. . . ." He shoots me a teasing grin. "The wise Maya has spoken."

"Indeed!" I suddenly jump to my feet, deciding that on our

rare day off, a bit of fun is called for. "And in return for all this wisdom, I want you to do something for me!"

"Uh-oh."

I turn on the radio, tuning in to the first pop station I find. I turn to Lochan and hold out my arms. He groans, dropping his head back against the cushions. "Oh, Maya, please be kidding!"

"How am I supposed to practice without a partner?" I protest.

"I thought you'd given up salsa dancing!"

"Only because they moved the lunchtime club to after school. Anyway, I've learned loads of new moves from Francie." I push the coffee table out of the way, pile up the papers and books, and reach down to grab his hand. "On your feet, partner!"

With a dramatic show of reluctance, he obeys, muttering crossly about his unfinished homework.

"It'll restore the blood flow to your brain," I tell him.

Trying not to look embarrassed and failing, Lochan stands in the middle of the room with his hands in his pockets. I raise the volume a couple of decibels, place one hand in his and the other on his shoulder. We begin with a few easy steps. Even though he constantly looks down at his feet, he isn't a bad dancer. He has a good sense of rhythm and picks up new moves more quickly than I do. I show him the new steps Francie taught me. Once he's got it, we're on a roll. He treads on my toes a few times, but since we're both barefoot, it just makes us laugh. After a while I start to improvise. Lochan twirls me around and nearly sends me into the wall. Finding this highly amusing, he tries to do it again and again. The sun is on his face; the dust particles swirl about him in the golden light of the afternoon. Relaxed and happy, he suddenly, for a brief moment, seems at peace with the world.

Soon we are breathless, sweaty and laughing. After a while the style of the music changes—a crooner with a slow beat—but it doesn't matter because I am too dizzy from spinning round and laughing to continue. I hook my arms about Lochan's neck and collapse against him. I notice the damp hair sticking to his neck and inhale the smell of fresh sweat. I expect him to pull away and return to his physics now that our moment of silliness is over, but to my surprise he just puts his arms around me and we sway from side to side. Pressed up against him, I can feel the thud of his heart against mine, his rib cage expanding and contracting rapidly against my chest, the warm whisper of his breath tickling the side of my neck, the brush of his leg against my thigh. Resting my arms on his shoulders, I pull back a little to get a look at his face. But he isn't smiling anymore.

CHAPTER NINE

Lochan

The room is plunged in golden light. Maya is still smiling at me, her face bright with laughter, tawny wisps of hair hanging in her eyes and down her back, tickling my hands clasped around her waist. Her face glows like an old-fashioned street lamp, lit from the inside, and everything else in the room disappears as if into a dark fog. We are still dancing, swaying slightly to the crooning voice, and Maya feels warm and alive in my arms. Just standing here, moving gently from side to side, I realize I don't want this moment to end.

I find myself marveling at how pretty she is, standing here, leaning against me in her short-sleeved nightgown, bare arms warm and smooth against my neck. Her top buttons are undone, revealing the curve of her collarbone, the expanse of smooth white skin beneath. Her gown stops well above her knees and I'm aware of her bare legs brushing against the thin, worn fabric of my jeans. The sun highlights her auburn hair, catches in her blue eyes. I drink in every tiny detail, from her soft breaths to the touch of each finger on the back of my neck. And I find myself filled with a mixture of excitement and euphoria so strong that I don't want the moment to ever end. . . . And then, out of nowhere, I am aware of another sensation—a tingling surge across my whole body, a familiar pressure against my groin. Abruptly I let go of her, shove her away from me, and stride over to the radio to cut the music.

Heart slamming against my ribs, I withdraw to the couch, coiling into myself, groping for the nearest textbook to pull across my lap. Still standing where I left her, Maya looks at me, a bemused expression on her face.

"They're going to be back any minute," I tell her by way of explanation, my voice rushed and ragged. "I've—I've got to finish this."

Seemingly unperturbed, she sighs, still smiling, and flops down onto the couch beside me. Her leg touches my thigh and I recoil violently. I need an excuse to leave the room but

I can't seem to think straight, my mind a mess of jumbled thoughts and emotions. I feel flushed and breathless, my heart hammering so loudly that I'm afraid she will hear it. I need to get as far away from her as possible. Pressing the textbook against my thighs, I ask her if she could make me some more coffee, and she obliges, picking up the two used mugs and heading off to the kitchen.

The moment I hear the rattle of crockery in the sink, I dash upstairs, trying to make as little noise as possible. I lock myself in the bathroom and lean against the door as if to reinforce it. I pull off all my clothes, almost tearing at them in my haste, and, careful not to look down at myself, step under an icy shower, heaving with shock. The water is so cold it hurts, but I don't care: It's a relief. I have to stop this . . . this—this madness. After just standing there for a while, eyes tightly closed, I start to go numb and my nerve endings deaden, erasing all signs of my earlier arousal. It stills the racing thoughts, relieves the pressure of the madness that had begun crushing my mind. I lean forward against the wall, letting the frigid water lash my body, until all I can do is shiver violently.

I don't want to think—so long as I don't think or feel, I will be fine and everything will return to normal. Seated at my bedroom desk in a clean T-shirt and jogging bottoms, wet hair sending cold rivulets down the back of my neck,

I pore over quadratic equations, grappling to keep the figures in my head, fighting to make sense of the numbers and symbols. I barely nod at Maya when she brings me my coffee a few minutes later. I repeat the formulas under my breath, cover page after page with calculations, and every time I sense a crack in my self-imposed armor, a chink of light entering my brain, I force myself to work harder, faster, obliterating all other thoughts. I am dimly aware of the others returning, of their raised voices in the hall, of the clatter of plates from the kitchen beneath me. I concentrate on tuning it all out. When Willa comes in to say they've ordered pizza, I tell her I'm not hungry; I must finish this chapter by tonight, I must work my way through every exercise at top speed, I have no time to stop and think. All I can do is work or I will go crazy.

The sounds of the house wash over me like white noise, the evening routine for once unfolding without me. An argument, a door slamming, Mum shouting—I don't care. They can sort themselves out—they have to sort themselves out. I must concentrate on this until it's so late that all I can do is collapse into bed, and then it will be morning and none of this will have happened. Everything will be back to normal—but what am I on about? Everything is normal! I just forgot, for one insane moment, that Maya was my sister.

*   *   *

For the remainder of the weekend I keep myself closeted in my room, buried in schoolwork, and leave Maya in charge. In class on Monday I struggle to sit still, jittery and restless. My mind has become strangely diffuse—I am possessed by myriad different sensations at once. There is a light flashing in my brain, like the headlight of a train in the dark. A vise is slowly tightening around my head, gripping my temples.

When Maya came into my room yesterday to say good night, informing me she had left my dinner in the fridge, I couldn't even turn round to look at her. This morning I shouted at Willa during breakfast and made her cry, dragged Tiffin out the door, allegedly causing him grievous bodily harm, completely ignored Kit, and snapped at Maya when she asked me for the third time what was wrong. I am a person coming undone. I am so disgusted with myself that I want to crawl out of my own skin. My mind keeps pulling me back to that dance: Maya, her face, her touch, that feeling. I keep telling myself these things happen—I'm sure they are not all that uncommon. After all, I'm a seventeen-year-old guy—anything can set us off. Just because it happened while I was dancing with Maya doesn't mean a thing. But the words do little to reassure me. I'm desperate to escape myself because the truth of the matter is that the feeling is still there—perhaps it always has been—and now that I've acknowledged it, I am terrified

TABITHA SUZUMA

that however much I may want to, I will never be able to turn things back.

No, that's ridiculous. My problem is that I need someone to focus my attention on, some object of desire, some girl to fantasize about. I look around the class but there is no one. Attractive girls—yes. A girl that I care about—no. She can't just be a face, a body; there has to be more than that, some kind of connection. And I can't connect, don't want to connect, with anyone.

I send Maya a text asking her to pick up Tiffin and Willa, then skip last period, go home to change into my running gear, and drag myself round the sodden periphery of the local park. After a glorious weekend, the day is gray, wet, and miserable: bare trees, dying leaves, and slippery mud underfoot. The air is tepid and damp; a fine veil of drizzle speckles my face. I run as far and as hard as I can, until the ground seems to shimmer beneath my feet and the world around me expands and retracts, blood-red blotches puncturing the air in front of me. Eventually pain courses through my body, forcing me to stop, and I return home to another freezing shower and work until the others return and the evening chores begin.

Over half term I play soccer out in the street with Tiffin, attempt to strike up conversations with Kit, and play endless games of hide-and-seek and Guess Who? with Willa. At night, after my mind shuts down from information overload, I rearrange kitchen drawers and cupboards. I go through Tiffin and Willa's bedroom, collecting outgrown clothes and discarded toys, and haul them off to the charity shop. I am either entertaining or tidying or cooking or studying; I comb through study notes late into the night, pore over my books until the small hours of the morning, until there is nothing else to do but collapse on my bed and fall into a short, deep, and dreamless sleep. Maya comments on my boundless energy but I feel numb, utterly drained from trying to keep myself occupied at all times. From now on, I will just do and not think.

Back at school, Maya is busy with course work. If she notices a difference in my behavior toward her, she doesn't mention it. Perhaps she, too, feels uncomfortable about that afternoon. Perhaps she, too, realizes that there needs to be more distance between us. We negotiate each other with the caution of a bare foot avoiding shards of glass, confining our brief exchanges to practicalities: the school run, the weekly shop, ways to persuade Kit to take over the laundry, the likelihood of Mum turning up sober on parents' evening, weekend activities for Tiffin and Willa, dental appointments, figuring out how to stop the fridge from leaking. We are never alone together. Mum is increasingly absent from family life, the pressure of balancing schoolwork and housework intensifies, and I welcome the endless chores; they literally leave me with no

time to think. Things are beginning to improve—I'm starting to return to a state of normality—until late one night there is a knock on my bedroom door.

The sound is like a bomb exploding in an open field.

"What?" I am horribly jumpy from an overdose of caffeine. My daily coffee consumption has reached new heights, as it's the only way to keep up my energy levels through the days and late into the sleepless nights. There is no reply but I hear the door open and close behind me. I turn from my desk, my pen still pressed against the indentations in my fingers, my borrowed school laptop anchored amid a sea of scribbled notes. She is in that nightdress again—the white one that she has long outgrown and that barely reaches her thighs. How I wish she wouldn't walk around in that thing; how I wish her copper hair wasn't so long and shiny; how I wish she didn't have those eyes, that she wouldn't just wander in uninvited. How I wish the sight of her didn't fill me with such unease, twisting my insides, tensing every muscle in my body, setting my pulse thrumming.

"Hi," she says. The sound of her voice pains me. With that single word she manages to exude both tenderness and concern. With just one word she conveys so much, her voice calling to me from outside a nightmare.

I try to swallow, my throat dry, a bitter taste trapped in my mouth. "Hi."

"Am I disturbing you?"

I want to tell her she is. I want to ask her to leave. I want her presence, her delicate, soapy smell, to evaporate from this room. But when I fail to reply, she sits down on the end of my bed, inches away from me, one bare foot tucked beneath her, leaning forward.

"Math?" she asks, glancing down at my sheaves of paper.

"Yeah." I return my gaze to the textbook, pen poised.

"Hey—" She reaches out for me, making me flinch. Her hand misses mine as I jerk away and comes to rest, loose and empty, against the desk's surface. I train my eyes back on my computer screen, the blood hurting my cheeks, heart paining my chest. I am still aware of her hair, falling like a curtain around her face, and there is nothing between us but torturous silence.

"Tell me," she says simply, her words piercing the fragile membrane that surrounds me.

I feel my breathing quicken. She can't do this to me. I lift my eyes to stare out the window, but all I see is my own reflection, this small room, Maya's soft innocence by my side.

"Something's happened, hasn't it?" Her voice continues to puncture the silence like an unwanted dream.

I push my chair away from her and rub my head. "I'm just tired." My voice grates against the back of my throat. I sound alien, even to my own ears.

"I've noticed," Maya continues. "Which is why I'm wondering why you carry on running yourself into the ground."

"I've got a lot of work to do."

Silence tightens the air. I sense she is not going to be brushed off so easily. "What happened, Lochie? Was it something at school? The presentation?"

I can't tell you. I can't tell you, of all people. Throughout my life you were the one person I could turn to. The one person I could always count on to understand. And now that I've lost you, I've lost everything.

"Are you just generally feeling down about things?"

I bite down on my lip until I recognize the metallic taste of blood. Maya notices and her questions stop, leaving in their place a muddy silence.

"Lochie, say something. You're frightening me. I can't bear seeing you like this." She reaches again for my hand and this time makes contact.

"Stop it! Just go to bed and leave me the fuck alone!" The words fire from my mouth like bullets, ricocheting off the walls before I can even register what I am saying. I see Maya's expression change, her face freeze in a look of incredulous surprise, her eyes wide with incomprehension. No sooner have my words slammed into her than she is moving away, flicking her head to hide the tears pooling in her eyes, the door clicking shut behind her.

CHAPTER TEN

Maya

"Oh my God, oh my God, you'll never guess what happened this morning!" Francie's eyes are burning with excitement, the corners of her cherry-red lips drawn up into a grin.

I drop my bag on the floor and collapse on the seat behind her, my head still echoing with Tiffin's yells as he had to be dragged to school this morning after a furious row with Kit over a plastic Transformer at the bottom of a cereal packet. I close my eyes.

"Nico DiMarco was talking to Matt and—"

I force my eyes open to cut her off. "I thought you were going on a date with Daniel Spencer."

"Maya, I may have decided to give Danny a chance while I wait for your brother to come to his senses, but this has nothing to do with that. Nico was talking to Matt this morning, and guess what he said. . . . Guess!" Her voice spikes with excitement and Mr. McIntyre stops screeching his pen against the whiteboard for a moment to turn and give us a long-suffering sigh. "Girls, if you could at least pretend to pay attention."

Francie flashes him her toothy smile and then turns back round in her seat to face me. "Guess!"

"I have no idea. His ego got so big, it exploded and now he needs surgery?"

"Nooo!" Francie clatters her nonregulation school shoes against the linoleum in a tap dance of excitement. "I overheard him telling Matt Delaney he was going to ask you out after school today!" She opens her mouth so wide that I can actually make out her tonsils.

I gaze at her numbly.

"Well?" Francie shakes me brutally by the arm. "Isn't this huge? Everyone's been after him since he broke up with Anorexic Annie, and he's gone and picked you! And you're the only girl in the class who doesn't wear makeup!"

"I'm so flattered."

Francie throws back her head dramatically and groans. "Aargh! What the hell's the matter with you these days? At the beginning of the term you were telling me he was the only guy at Belmont you'd ever consider snogging!"

I heave a sigh. "Yeah, yeah. So he's hot. But he knows it. I might fancy him just like everyone else, but I never said I wanted to go out with the guy."

Francie shakes her head in disbelief. "D'you know how many girls would kill for a date with Nico? I think I'd even put Lochan on hold for a chance to snog Mister Latino."

"Oh God, Francie. Then you go out with him."

"I went over to find out if he was serious and he asked me if I thought you'd be interested! So of course I said yes!"

"Francie! Tell him to forget it. Tell him at morning break."

"Why?"

"I'm not interested!"

"Maya, d'you realize what you're doing here? I mean, he may not give you a second chance!"

I drag myself through the rest of the day. Francie isn't talking to me because I accused her of being a meddling cow when she refused to go back and tell Nico I wasn't interested. But I honestly don't care if she never speaks to me again. A cold slab of despair presses down on my chest, making it difficult to catch my breath. My eyes ache with suppressed tears. By midafternoon even Francie is worried, breaking her vow of silence and offering to accompany me to see the nurse. *What could the school nurse offer me?* I wonder. A pill to make the loneliness disappear? A tablet that would get Lochan to speak to me again? Or perhaps a capsule to turn back time, rewinding the days so I could break away from Lochan when we'd finished dancing the salsa, instead of remaining in his arms, swaying to the gentle crooning of Katie Melua. Is he angry with me because he thinks I planned it somehow? That the salsa was just a ruse to get him to slow dance with me, our bodies pressed up against each other, the heat of his soaking into mine? I didn't mean to stroke the back of his neck—it just happened. My thigh rubbing against the inside of his was just an accident. I never meant any of it to happen. I had no idea that something like slow dancing could get a guy aroused. But when I felt it, pressing against my hip, when I suddenly realized what it was, I felt this crazy head rush. I didn't want to stop dancing. I didn't pull away.

I can't bear to think I might have lost our closeness, our friendship, our trust. He was always so much more than just a brother. He is my soul mate, my fresh air, the reason I look forward to getting up every morning. I always knew I love him more than anyone else in the world—and not just in a brotherly way, the way I feel about Kit and Tiffin. Yet somehow it never crossed my mind there could be a whole step beyond. . . .

But I know it's ridiculous, too stupid to even think about. We're not like that. We're not sick. We're just a brother and sister who also happen to be best friends. That's the way it's always been between us. I can't lose that or I will not survive.

By the end of the day Francie is pestering me about Nico DiMarco again. She seems to think I'm depressed and that having a boyfriend—especially one of the hottest guys in school—will help snap me out of my funk. Perhaps she's right. Perhaps I need a distraction. And what better way to show Lochan that what happened the other day was just an accident, a bit of fun? If I have a boyfriend, then he'll realize that none of that stuff meant anything. And Nico is very cute. His hair is the same color as Lochan's. His eyes are kind of greenish, too. Although Francie is way off beam when she claims they are in the same league. No way. Lochan is ferociously bright, emotionally intelligent, the kindest, most selfless person I know. Lochan has a soul. Nico might be the same age, but he is just a boy in comparison—a spoiled little rich boy, expelled from his posh private school for smoking weed, a pretty face with an arrogant swagger, a charm as carefully crafted as his clothes and hairstyle. But yes, I suppose the idea of dating him—kissing him, even—isn't totally repellent.

After the last bell, as we are crossing the playground toward

 TABITHA SUZUMA

the gates, I see him heading toward us. He's been waiting, that much is clear. Francie gives a half-strangled squawk and elbows me in the ribs so hard that I am momentarily winded, before she swerves away. Nico is coming straight for me. As if drawn toward each other by an invisible cord, we walk and walk. He has removed his tie even though it's enough to earn him a detention this side of the school exit.

"Maya, hi!" His smile broadens. He's very smooth, very confident; he's been doing this for years. He stops close to me, too close, and I have to take a step back. "How're you doing? I haven't had a chance to speak to you for ages!"

He is acting like a long-lost friend, despite the fact that we have barely exchanged more than a few words until now. I force myself to meet his gaze and smile. I was wrong: His eyes are nothing like Lochan's—the green is muddied with brown. His hair is brown too. I don't know why I ever saw any similarities.

"Are you in a hurry," he asks, "or d'you have time for a drink at Smileys?"

Jesus, he doesn't waste any time. "I have to pick up my little brother and sister," I answer truthfully.

"Listen, I'm gonna be straight with you." He places his schoolbag between his feet as if to indicate that this has turned into a proper conversation and tosses the hair out of his eyes.

"You're a great girl, you know. I've always had—you know—a kind of thing for you. I didn't think it was reciprocated so I haven't said anything until now. But hell, you know, carpe diem and all that."

Does he think he's going to impress me with his command of Latin?

"I've always considered you a good friend, but you know what? I think it could be even stronger than that, you know. All I'm saying is—perhaps we could get to know each other a little better, you know?"

If he says "you know" one more time, I swear I'm going to scream.

"I'd be really honored if you'd let me take you out to dinner one night. Is there even the remotest possibility I could get you to agree to that?" He flashes his teeth at me again in what could almost pass for a wistful smile. Oh, he's good at this, all right.

I pretend to consider it for a moment. His smile doesn't falter. I'm impressed. "Okay, I suppose. . . ."

His smile broadens. "That's great. Really great. How would Friday suit you?"

"Friday's fine."

"Cool. What kind of food do you like? Japanese, Thai, Mexican, Lebanese?"

"Pizza's good for me."

TABITHA SUZUMA

His eyes light up. "I know this great restaurant—serves the best Italian food round here. I'll drive by to pick you up at, say, seven?"

I am about to protest that it would be easier to meet him there when it dawns on me that having him come to the house might be no bad thing.

"All right. Seven o'clock on Friday." I smile again. My cheeks are beginning to ache.

He cocks his head and raises his eyebrows. "You'll have to give me your address!"

He produces a pen while I rummage through my pockets and find a crumpled receipt. I write down my address and number and hand it back to him. As I do so, he holds on to my fingers for a moment and flashes another of his high-wattage smiles. "I look forward to it."

I'm beginning to think this might be quite fun, even if it's just to laugh about him the next day with Francie. I manage a genuine smile this time and say, "Yeah, me too." Nico walks away, holding his hand up to say good-bye.

I start walking through the gates, and Francie leaps out from behind the phone booth at the end of the street. "Oh my God, oh my God, tell me everything!"

I wince and bring my hand up to my ear. "Aargh! Jesus— try to give me a heart attack, why don't you?"

"You're blushing! Oh my God, you said yes, didn't you?"

I briefly recount the conversation. Francie grabs me by the shoulders, shakes me brutally, and starts to shriek. A woman looks round in alarm.

"Calm down." I laugh. "Francie, he's a complete twat!"

"So? Tell me you don't fancy him!"

"Okay, maybe I find him slightly attractive—"

"I knew it! You were complaining just the other week you'd never kissed a guy! As of Friday, you'll be able to cross that off your list."

"Maybe . . . Listen, I've got to run. I'm late for Tiffin and Willa."

Francie grins at me as I begin to move off. "You're gonna tell me everything, Maya Whitely. Every little detail. You owe me that much!"

I have to confess that the prospect of a date with Nico does make me feel fractionally better. Fractionally less abnormal, at least, and that's quite something. That evening, as I sit at the kitchen table helping Tiffin and Willa with their homework, my mind keeps flicking back to the flirtatious exchange, the way he smiled at me. It's not a lot—not nearly enough to fill the gaping void inside me—but it's something. It's always nice being fancied. It's always nice being wanted. Even if it's by the wrong person.

I'd let it slip to Tiffin and Willa. I was ten minutes late picking them up, and when Tiffin demanded to know why, in my stupidity, still a little dazed, I told him that I was talking to a boy from school. I thought this would be the end of it, but I'd forgotten Tiffin is eight. "Maya's got a boyfriend, a boyfriend, a boyfriend!" he sang all the way home.

Willa looked worried. "Does that mean you're going to go away and get married?"

"No, of course not." I laughed, trying to reassure her. "It just means I've got a friend who's a boy and maybe I'll go and see him once in a while."

"Like Mum and Dave?"

"No! Nothing like Mum and Dave. I'll probably only ever go out with him once or twice. And if I do go out with him more than that, it'll still be hardly ever. And of course it will only be when Lochie's at home to look after you."

"Maya's got a boyfriend!" Tiffin announces as Kit slams through the door and executes a whirlwind tour of the kitchen, hunting for snacks.

"Great. I hope the two of you will have lots of babies and be very happy together."

By dinnertime Tiffin has other things on his mind—namely, the soccer game his friends are playing loudly and unhelpfully right outside the house while he is stuck inside, simultaneously being force-fed runner beans and grilled on his times tables by Lochan. Willa is studying "materials" at school and wants to know what everything is made of: the plates, the cutlery, the water jug. Kit, bored, is in one of his most dangerous moods, trying to wind everyone up so that he can sit in the eye of the storm and laugh at the chaos he has created all around him.

"Four sevens?" Lochan picks up Tiffin's fork and spears two runner beans before handing it back to him. Tiffin looks down at it and grimaces. "Come on. Four sevens. You've got to be quicker than that."

"I'm thinking!"

"Do it like I told you. Go through it in your head. One seven's seven, two sevens are . . ."

"Thirty-three," Kit chips in.

"Thirty-three?" Tiffin echoes optimistically.

"Tiff, you've got to think for yourself."

"Why did you put two beans on my fork? It'll make me choke! I hate runner beans!" Tiffin exclaims angrily.

"What are runner beans made of?" Willa asks.

"Snake poo," Kit informs her.

Willa drops her fork and looks down at her plate in horror.

"One seven's seven," Lochan continues doggedly. "Two sevens are . . ."

 TABITHA SUZUMA

"Lochie, I don't like runner beans too!" Willa protests.

For the first time in my life I don't feel the slightest bit inclined to help out. Lochan has said exactly five words to me since coming home two hours ago: *Have they done their homework?*

"Tiffin, you must know what two sevens are! Just add them together, for chrissakes!"

"I can't eat all this—you've given me too much!"

"Hey"—Kit cocks his head—"did you hear those shouts, Tiff? Sounds like Jamie just scored another goal."

"That's my soccer ball they're playing with!"

"Kit, just leave him alone, will you?" Lochan snaps.

"I've finished." Willa pushes her plate as far away as possible, knocking over Kit's glass in the process.

"Willa, watch what you're doing!" Kit yells.

"How come she gets to leave all her beans?" Tiffin begins to shout.

"Willa, just eat your beans! Tiffin, if you don't know what four sevens are, you're going to fail your test tomorrow!" Lochan is losing his cool. It gives me a perverse sort of pleasure.

"Maya, do I have to eat my beans?" Willa turns to me plaintively.

"Ask Lochan—he's the cook."

"I think you're being a bit free and loose with the word 'cook' there," Kit remarks, chuckling to himself.

"The boss, then," I substitute.

"Yeah, that's the one!"

Lochan flashes me a look that says, *What have I done to you?* Again, I'm aware of a fleeting sense of satisfaction.

"Willa, for fuck sake, clean up this mess—you've got water all over the table!" Kit protests.

"I can't!"

"Stop being a baby and get the sponge!"

"Lochie, Kit said the F word."

"I'm not eating any more!"Tiffin roars. "And I'm not doing no more tables, neither!"

"Do you want to fail your math test?" Lochan shouts back.

"I don't care! I don't care! I don't care!"

"Lochie, Kit said the F word!"Willa wails, angry now.

"Fuck-a-doodle-do," Kit sings.

"Will you all just shut up! What the hell's the matter with you!" Lochan slams his fist down on the table.

Tiffin, seizing on this distraction, leaps up, grabs his soccer gloves, and races out of the house. Willa bursts into noisy tears, slides off her chair, and stamps her way up to her room. Kit tips three plates of uneaten runner beans back into the saucepan and says, "Look, now you can feed us the same old shit tomorrow."

With a groan, Lochan puts his head in his hands.

Suddenly I feel awful. I don't know what I was trying to prove. That Lochan needs me, perhaps? Or was I just trying to get him back for the silent treatment? Either way, I feel lousy. It would have cost me nothing to chip in and diffuse the situation. I do it all the time, without even having to think about it. I could have prevented Lochan's stress levels going through the roof, stopped him from feeling like a failure as yet another family meal ended in mayhem. But I didn't. And the worst thing is, I actually enjoyed watching everything fall apart.

Looking exhausted, Lochan rubs his eyes with a wry smile. Glancing at all the leftover food, he tries to make a joke of it. "Maya, more runner beans? Don't be shy!"

He has every right to be angry with the lot of us, but instead he is so forgiving that it makes me ache. I want to say something, do something to take it all back, but I can't think of a thing. Chewing his lip, Lochan gets up and starts clearing dishes, and I suddenly notice that lately his sore has got bigger, that he has been gnawing at it more and more. It looks so painful, so raw, that to see him bite at it like that makes my eyes water. Getting up to help him clear the table, I remind Kit that it's his turn to do the washing up and, without thinking, touch Lochan's hand to get his attention—but this time, to my surprise, he doesn't pull away.

"Ouch, your poor lip," I say gently. "You're going to make it worse."

"Sorry." He stops chewing and presses the back of his hand self-consciously against his mouth.

"Yeah, God, that thing has become really gross." Kit seizes the opportunity to chip in, his voice loud and brash as, with a crash, he drops a pile of plates unceremoniously into the sink. "The guys at school were asking me if it was some kind of disease."

"Kit, that's rubbish—" I begin.

"What? I'm just agreeing with you. That thing's gross, and if he keeps on biting it, he's gonna end up disfigured."

I try giving him one of my warning looks but he studiously avoids my eye, crashing the crockery around in the sink. Lochan leans one shoulder against the wall, waiting for the kettle to boil, staring out the darkened window. I decide to give Kit a hand with the washing up—Lochan seems to have ground to a halt and I don't want to leave the two of them alone together while Kit still has the bit between his teeth.

"So you've finally managed to nail yourself a boyfriend," Kit remarks scathingly as I join him at the sink. "Who the hell is it?"

I feel my insides clench. Instinctively my gaze flies over to Lochan, who drops his hand from his mouth, his head jolting back in surprise.

"He's not a boyfriend," I correct Kit quickly. "Just—just some random guy from school who asked me out for—uh—" I break off. Lochan is staring at me.

"For—uh—sex?" Kit suggests.

"Don't be so childish. He asked me out for dinner."

"Whoa—no introductory drink at Smileys, then? Straight in there, wining and dining you." Kit is clearly enjoying watching me squirm. "What guy at Belmont can possibly afford to take a girl out for dinner? Don't tell me it's one of your teachers!" His eyes light up in delight.

"Stop being ridiculous. It's a guy in the year above called Nico. You don't even know him."

"Nico DiMarco?" But of course Lochan does. Shit.

"Yeah." I force myself to meet his look of astonishment over the top of Kit's head. "I—he asked me out for Friday. Is that— can you—is that all right?" I don't know why I'm suddenly finding it so hard to speak.

"Uh-oh, you should have asked permission first!" Kit crows. "You're gonna have to stick to the curfew, remember. Tell you what, I'll give you my last condom—"

"Okay, Kit, that's enough!" I shout, slamming a plate down on the counter. "Go and bring Tiffin inside and then do your homework!" I'm the one losing it now.

"Fine! Excuse me for breathing!" Kit throws the washing-up

brush into the sink with a splash and stalks out of the room.

Lochan hasn't moved from his position by the window, scraping at the sore with his thumbnail. His face looks hot, his eyes deeply troubled. "Nico? D'you know him? I mean, the guy's pretty, uh—you know. He's kind of got a rep. . . ."

I keep my head down, scrubbing the plates hard. "Yeah, well, it's only a date. We'll see how it goes."

Lochan takes a step toward me and then changes his mind and moves back again. "Do you—do you—I mean, do you like him?"

I feel the heat rush to my face and suddenly I am angry again. How dare Lochan give me the third degree when I agreed to the date for us—for him?

"Yes, as a matter of fact, I do, okay?" I stop scrubbing and force my eyes to meet his. "He's the hottest guy in school. I've fancied him for ages. I can't wait to go out with him."

beyond her years; she'll be careful, and maybe it will work out. He won't hurt her—not intentionally, at least. No, I'm sure he won't hurt her—he wouldn't. She is such a lovely person; she is so precious—he'll see that; he must. He'll know he can never break her heart, never harm her. He wouldn't. He couldn't. So, fine—I'm going to be able to sleep at last. I don't need to think about this anymore. What I do desperately need is sleep. Otherwise I'll fall apart. I'm going to fall apart. I am falling apart.

The first rays of dawn begin to touch the edge of the rooftops. I sit on my bed and watch the pale light dilute the inky blackness, a thin wash of color slowly diffusing the eastern sky. The air is chilled as it blows through the cracks in the window frame, and sparse flecks of rain spatter the pane as the birds begin to wake. A golden patch of sunlight slants across the wall, slowly widening like a spreading stain. *What is the point of it all?* I wonder—this endless cycle. I haven't slept all night and my muscles ache from remaining immobile so long. I'm cold but I can't find the energy to move or even pull the duvet up around me. Now and then my head, as though succumbing to a narcotic, begins to drop, and my eyes close and then reopen with a start. As the light begins to intensify, so does my misery, and I wonder how it is possible to hurt so much when nothing is wrong. A swelling despair presses outward from the center of my chest, threatening to shatter my ribs. I fill my lungs with the cold air and then drain them, running my hands gently back and forth over the rough cotton sheets as if anchoring myself to this bed, to this house, to this life—in an attempt to forget my utter solitude. The sore beneath my lip throbs with a pulse and it's a struggle just to let it alone, not chafe it in an attempt to annihilate the agony inside my mind. I continue stroking the covers, the rhythmical movement soothing me, reminding me that, even if I am breaking up inside, all around me things remain the same, solid and real, bringing me the hope that perhaps one day I, too, will feel real again.

A single day encompasses so much. The frantic morning routine: trying to make sure everyone eats breakfast, Tiffin's high-pitched voice jarring my ears, Willa's continuous chatter fraying my nerves, Kit relentlessly reinforcing my guilt with his every gesture, and Maya . . . it's best if I don't think about Maya. But perversely I want to. I must chafe at the wound, scrape back the scab, pick at the damaged skin. I cannot leave the thought of her alone. Like last night at dinner, she is here but not here; her heart and mind have left this dingy house, the annoying siblings, the socially inept brother, the alcoholic mother. Her thoughts are with Nico now, racing ahead to her date this evening. However long the day may seem, the evening will arrive and Maya will go. And from that moment, part of her life, part of herself, will be severed from me forever. Yet, even as I wait for this to happen, there is so much to do: coax Kit out of his lair, get Tiffin and Willa to school on time, remember to test Tiffin on his tables as he tries to run ahead down the road. Make it through my own school gates, check without being seen that Kit's in class, sit through a whole morning of lessons, find new ways of deflecting attention should a teacher press me to participate, survive lunch, make sure I avoid DiMarco, explain to the teacher why I can't give a presentation, make it to the last bell without falling apart. And finally pick up Willa and Tiffin, keep them entertained for the evening, remind Kit of his curfew without prompting a row—and all the time, all the while, try to purge every thought of Maya from my mind. And the hands of the kitchen clock will continue moving forward, reaching midnight before starting all over again, as though the day that just ended never began.

I was once so strong. I used to be able to get through all the small things, all the details, the treadmill routine, day after day. But I never realized that Maya was the one who gave me that strength. It was because she was there that I could manage, the two of us at the helm, propping each other up when one of us was down. We may have spent the bulk of our time looking after the little ones, but beneath the surface we were really

TABITHA SUZUMA

looking after each other, and that made everything bearable—more than just bearable. It brought us together in an existence only we could understand. Together we were safe—different but safe—from the outside world. . . . Now all I have is myself, my responsibilities, my duties, my never-ending list of things to do . . . and my loneliness, always my loneliness—that airless bubble of despair that is slowly stifling me.

Maya leaves for school ahead of me, dragging Kit with her. She seems annoyed with me for some reason. Willa dawdles, picking up twigs and crisp curled-up leaves along the way. Tiffin abandons us as he spots Jamie at the end of the road, and I haven't the strength to call him back, despite the busy junction in front of the school. It is a monumental effort not to snap at Willa—to tell her to hurry, to ask her why she seems so intent on making us both late. As soon as we reach the school gates, she spots a friend and breaks into a stumbling run, her coat flapping and flying out behind her. For a moment I just stand and watch her go, her fine golden hair streaming behind her in the wind. Her gray pinafore is stained with yesterday's lunch, her school coat is missing its hood, her book bag is falling apart, her red tights have a large hole behind the knee, but she never complains. Even though she is surrounded by mums and dads hugging their children good-bye, even though she hasn't seen her mother for two weeks now, even though she has no memory of ever having a father. She is only five, yet already she has learned that there is no point in asking her mother for a bedtime story, that inviting friends over is something only other children can do, that new toys are a rare luxury, that at home Kit and Tiffin are the only ones who get their own way. At the age of five she has already come to terms with one of life's harshest lessons: that the world isn't fair. . . . Halfway up the school steps, best friend in tow, she suddenly remembers she has forgotten to say good-bye and turns, scanning the emptying playground for my face. When she spots it, her face breaks into a radiant, plump-cheeked smile, the tip of her tongue poking out through the gap of her missing front teeth. Raising a small hand, she waves. I wave back, my arms fanning the sky.

Entering my own school building, I am hit by a wall of artificial heat—radiators turned up too high. But it isn't until the afternoon when I walk into the English room and come face-to-face with Miss Azley that I remember. She smiles at me, a thinly disguised attempt at encouragement. "Are you going to be needing the projector?"

I freeze at her desk, a horrible, clutching, sinking feeling in my chest, and say in a rush, "Actually—actually I thought it might work better as a written assignment—there was too much information to condense into just—just a half hour. . . ."

Her smile fades. "But this wasn't a written assignment,

TABITHA SUZUMA

Lochan. The presentation is part of your course work. I can't mark you on this." She takes my file and flicks through it. "Well, you've certainly got a lot of material here, so I suppose you could just read it out."

I look at her, a cold hand of horror wrapping itself around my throat. "Well, the thing is—" I can barely speak. My voice is suddenly no more than a whisper.

She gives a puzzled frown. "The thing is?"

"It's—it's not really going to make much sense if I just read it—"

"Why don't you just give it a try?" Her voice is suddenly gentle—too gentle. "The first time is always the hardest."

I feel the burn in my face. "It won't work. I—I'm sorry." I take back the folder from her outstretched hand. "I'll make sure I make up for the failed grade with—with the rest of my course work."

Turning quickly, I find a seat, crimson waves crashing through me. To my relief she does not summon me back.

Nor does she bring up the subject of the presentation during the lesson. Instead she covers the gap left by my lack of a contribution by talking to us about the lives of Sylvia Plath and Virginia Woolf, and a heated debate arises about the link between mental illness and the artistic temperament. Normally this is a subject I'd find fascinating, but today the words just wash over me. Outside, the sky disgorges rain, which drums against the dirty windows, washing them with tears. I look at the clock and see there are only five more hours to go until Maya's date. Perhaps DiMarco broke his leg playing soccer. Perhaps he is in the sick bay right now with food poisoning. Perhaps he suddenly found some other girl to pull. Any girl other than my sister. He had the whole school to choose from. Why Maya? Why the one person who matters the most to me in the world?

"Lochan Whitely?" The raised voice jolts through me as I head for the door amid the chaos of exiting pupils. I turn my head long enough to see Miss Azley beckoning me over to her desk and realize I have no choice but to fight my way back through the fray.

"Lochan, I think we need to have a little chat."

Christ, no. Not this, not today. "Um—I'm sorry. I—I actually have math," I say in a rush.

"This won't take long. I'll give you a note." She indicates a chair in front of her desk. "Have a seat."

Lifting the strap of my bag over my head, I take the proffered seat, realizing there is no way out. Miss Azley crosses over to the door and closes it with a harsh metallic thud that sounds like a prison gate.

She comes back toward me and takes the chair by my side,

turning to me with a reassuring smile. "There's no need to look so worried. I'm sure by now you know my bark is worse than my bite!"

I force myself to look at her, hoping she will reel off the spiel about the importance of class participation more quickly if I appear cooperative. But instead she chooses the roundabout route. "What happened to your lip?"

Aware that I'm biting it again, I force myself to stop, my fingers flying to it in surprise. "Nothing—it's—it's nothing."

"You should put some Vaseline on it and take up pen chewing instead." She reaches over to her desk for a couple of gnawed pens. "Less painful and does the job just as well." She gives me another smile.

With all the will in the world, I cannot return it. The pally small talk is throwing me off balance. Something in her eyes tells me she isn't about to give me a lecture on the importance of class participation, teamwork, and all the usual shit. Her look is not one of admonishment, but of genuine concern.

"You know why I've kept you back, don't you?"

I reply with a quick nod, my teeth automatically scraping my lip again. *Look, this isn't a good day,* I want to tell her. I could grit my teeth and nod my way through a heart-to-heart with an overzealous teacher another time, but not today. Not today.

"What is it about speaking out in front of your peers that frightens you so much, Lochan?"

She has caught me off guard. I don't like the way she used the word "frightens." I don't like the way she seems to know so much about me.

"I'm not—I don't—" My voice is dangerously unsteady. The air circulates slowly in the room. I am breathing too fast. She has cornered me. I'm aware of sweat breaking out across my back, heat radiating from my face.

"Hey, it's all right." She leans forward, her concern almost tangible. "I'm not having a go at you, Lochan, okay? But I know you're bright enough to understand why you need to be able to speak in public from time to time—not just for the sake of your academic future but also your personal one."

I wish I could just get up and walk out.

"Is it just a problem at school or is it all the time?"

Why the hell is she doing this? Principal, detention, expulsion—I don't care. Anything but this. I want to tune her out but I can't. It's that damn concern, cutting through my consciousness like a knife.

"It's all the time, isn't it?" Her voice is too gentle.

I feel the heat rush to my face. Taking a panicked breath, I let my eyes scour the classroom, as if seeking a place to hide.

TABITHA SUZUMA

"It's nothing to be ashamed of, Lochan. It's just perhaps something worth tackling now."

Face thrumming, I start chewing my lip again, the sharp pain a welcome relief.

"Like any phobia, social anxiety is something that can be overcome. I was thinking maybe we could devise an action plan together to set you on track for next year at university."

I can hear the sound of my breathing, sharp and rapid. I reply with a barely perceptible nod.

"We'd take it very slowly. One small step at a time. Perhaps you could aim to put your hand up and answer just one question each lesson. That would be a good start, don't you think? Once you can comfortably volunteer one answer, you'll find it much easier to answer two, and then three—and, well, you get the idea." She laughs and I sense she is trying to lighten the atmosphere. "Then, before you know it, you'll be answering every question and no one else will have a chance in hell!"

I try to return her smile but it doesn't work. *Take one small step at a time. . . .* I used to have someone helping me do just that. Someone who introduced me to her friend, encouraged me to read out my essay in class, someone who was subtly trying to help me with my whole problem, yet I never realized. And now I've lost her—lost her to Nico DiMarco. One evening with him, and Maya will realize what a loser I've become, start feeling the same way toward me as Kit and my mother do. . . .

"I've noticed you've been looking quite stressed recently," Miss Azley remarks suddenly. "Which is perfectly understandable—it's a tough year. But your grades are as good as ever and you excel at written exams. So you'll sail through your A-levels; there's nothing to worry about there."

I give a tense nod.

"Are things difficult at home?"

I look at her then, unable to disguise my shock.

"I have two children to look after," she says with a little smile. "I gather you have four?"

My heart stutters and almost stops. I stare at her. Who the hell has she been talking to?

"N-no! I'm seventeen. I do have two brothers and—and two sisters, but we live with our mother, and she—"

"I know that, Lochan. It's all right." It isn't until she cuts me off that I realize I'm not speaking in particularly measured tones.

For God's sake, try to keep it cool! I beg myself. *Don't go and react as if you've got something to hide!*

"What I meant was, you have younger siblings to help take care of," Miss Azley continues. "That can't be easy, on top of all your schoolwork."

TABITHA SUZUMA

"But I don't—I don't take care of them. They're—they're just a bunch of annoying brats. They certainly drive my mother round the bend. . . ." My laugh sounds painfully artificial.

Another strained silence stretches out between us. I glance desperately at the door. Why is she talking to me about this? Whom has she been speaking to? What other information do they have in that damn file? Are they thinking of contacting social services? Did St. Luke's get in touch with Belmont when the kids went missing?

"I'm not trying to meddle, Lochan," she says suddenly. "I just want to make sure you know that you don't have to carry the burden alone. Your social anxiety, the responsibilities at home . . . it's a lot to have to deal with at your age."

Out of nowhere a pain rises through my chest and into my throat. I find myself biting down on my lip to stop it from trembling.

I see her face change and she leans toward me. "Hey, hey, listen to me. There is lots of help available. There's the school counselor or any one of your teachers you can talk to—or outside help I can recommend if you don't want to involve the school. You don't have to carry all this on your own. . . ."

The pain in my throat intensifies. I'm going to lose it. "I—I really have to go. I'm sorry—"

"All right, that's all right. But, Lochan, I'm always here

if you want to talk, okay? You can make an appointment with the counselor at any time. And if there's any way I can make things easier in class . . . We'll forget the presentations for the moment. I'll just mark it as a written assignment as you suggested. And I'll leave answering questions up to you and stop pushing you to participate. I know it's not much, but would that help at all?"

I don't understand. Why can't she just be like the other teachers? Why does she have to care?

I nod wordlessly.

"Oh, love, the last thing I wanted was to make you feel worse! It's just that I think really highly of you and I'm worried. I wanted you to know there's help available. . . ."

It's only when I hear the defeat in her voice, see the look of shock on her face, that I realize my eyes have filled with tears.

"Thank you. C-can I go now?"

"Of course you can, Lochan. But would you just think about it—think about talking to someone?"

I nod, unable to utter another word, grab my bag, and run from the room.

"No, stupid. You're only supposed to lay four places." Tiffin yanks one of the plates off the table and returns it to the cupboard with a loud clatter.

172   TABITHA SUZUMA

"Why? Is Kit going to Burger King again?" Willa nibbles the end of her thumb nervously, her large eyes darting around the kitchen as if looking for signs of trouble.

"Tonight Maya's going on her date, stupid!"

I turn from the cooker. "Stop calling her stupid. She's younger than you, that's all. And how come she's done her job and you haven't even started yours?"

"I don't want Maya to go out on a date," Willa protests. "If Maya goes out and Kit goes out and Mum goes out, that means there's only three of us left in this family!"

"Actually it means there's two left cuz I'm going for a sleepover at Jamie's," Tiffin informs her.

"Oh, no, you're not," I intervene quickly. "That wasn't discussed, Jamie's mother never rang, and I've already told you to stop inviting yourself over to other people's houses—it's very rude."

"Fine, then!" Tiffin shouts. "I'll tell her to phone you! She invited me herself, so you'll see!" He stalks out of the kitchen just as I begin to dish up.

"Tiff, get back in here or no DS for a week!"

He arrives at ten past seven. Maya has been on edge ever since she got in. For the past hour she has been upstairs, vying with Mum for the bathroom. I even heard the two of them laughing together. Kit jumps up, banging his knee on the table leg in his haste to be the first to greet him. I let him go and quickly close the kitchen door behind him. I don't want to see the guy.

Fortunately Maya doesn't invite him in. I hear her feet pounding down the stairs, voices raised in greeting, followed by "I'll be with you in a minute."

Kit returns, looking impressed and exclaiming loudly, "Whoa, that guy's loaded. Have you seen his designer gear?"

Maya rushes in. "Thank you for doing this." She comes straight over to me and squeezes my hand in that annoying way she has. "I'll take them out all day tomorrow, I promise."

I pull away. "Don't be silly. Just have a good time."

She's wearing something I've never seen before. In fact, she looks totally different: burgundy lipstick, her long russet hair pinned up, a few stray wisps delicately framing her face. Small silver pendants hang from her ears. Her dress is short, black, and figure hugging, sexy in a sophisticated kind of way. She smells of something peachy.

"Kiss!" Willa cries, flinging up her arms.

I watch her hug Willa, kiss the top of Tiffin's head, give Kit a punch on the shoulder, and smile again at me. "Wish me luck!"

I manage to return the smile and give a small nod.

"Good luck!" Tiffin and Willa shout at the tops of their

TABITHA SUZUMA

voices. Maya cringes and laughs as she hurries out into the corridor.

There are slamming doors and then the sound of an engine starting. I turn to Kit. "He came by car?"

"Yeah, I told you, he's loaded! It wasn't exactly a Lamborghini, but jeez, he's got his own wheels at seventeen?"

"Eighteen," I correct him. "I hope he doesn't intend to drink."

"You should have seen him," Kit says. "That guy's got class."

"Maya looked like a princess!" Willa exclaims, her blue eyes wide. "She looked like a grown-up, too."

"Okay, who wants more potatoes?" I ask.

"Maybe she'll marry him and then she'll be rich," Tiffin chips in. "If Maya's rich and I'm her brother, does that mean I get to be rich as well?"

"No, it means she dumps you as a brother cuz you're an embarrassment—you don't even know your times tables," Kit replies.

Tiffin's mouth falls open and his eyes fill.

I turn to Kit. "You're not even funny, d'you realize that?"

"Never claimed I was a comedian, just a realist," Kit retorts.

Tiffin sniffs and wipes the back of his hand across his eyes. "Don't care what you say. Maya would never do that, and anyway, I'm her brother until I die."

"At which point you'll go to hell and never see anyone again," Kit shoots back.

"If there's a hell, Kit, believe me, you'll be in it." I can feel myself losing my cool. "Now, would you just shut up and finish your meal without tormenting anyone else?"

Kit tosses his knife and fork onto his half-finished plate with a clatter. "To hell with this. I'm going out."

"Ten o'clock and no later!" I shout after him.

"In your dreams, mate," he calls back from halfway up the stairs.

Our mother is next to come in, reeking of perfume and struggling to light a cigarette without smudging her freshly painted nails. The complete antithesis to Maya, she is all glitter and crimson lips, her ill-fitting red dress leaving little to the imagination. Soon she disappears again, already unsteady on her high heels, screeching up at Kit for having nicked her last packet of smokes.

I spend the rest of the evening watching TV with Tiffin and Willa, simply too exhausted and fed up to attempt anything more productive. When they start to bicker, I get them ready for bed. Willa cries because I get shampoo in her eyes, and Tiffin forgets to hang the shower curtain inside the bath and floods the floor. Teeth brushing seems to take hours; the kiddie toothpaste tube is almost empty so I use mine instead, which

makes Tiffin's eyes water and Willa gag into the basin. While Willa takes fifteen minutes to choose a story,. Tiffin sneaks downstairs to play on his DS and, when I object, gets unreasonably upset and claims Maya always lets him play while she reads to Willa. Once they are in bed, Willa is immediately hungry, Tiffin is thirsty by association, and by the time the clamoring finally stops, it is half past nine and I am shattered.

But once they are asleep, the house feels eerily empty. I know I should go to bed myself and try to get an early night, but I feel increasingly agitated and on edge. I tell myself I have to stay up to check that Kit comes home at some point, but deep down I know that it's only an excuse. I'm watching some stupid action movie but I've no idea what it's about or who is supposed to be chasing whom. I can't even focus on the special effects—all I can think of is DiMarco. It's past ten now—they must have finished dinner; they must have left the restaurant. His father is often away on business—or so Nico claims, and I have no reason to disbelieve him. Which means he has his mansion to himself . . . Has he taken her back there? Or are they in some dodgy car park, his hands and lips all over her? I begin to feel sick. Maybe it's because I haven't eaten all evening. I want to wait up and see for myself what kind of state she's in when she gets home. *If* she decides to come home. It suddenly strikes me that most sixteen-year-olds would have some kind of curfew. But I'm only thirteen months her senior, so I'm hardly in a position to impose one. I keep telling myself that Maya has always been so sensible, so responsible, so mature, but now I remember the flushed look on her face when she came into the kitchen to say good-bye, the sparkle in her smile, the fizz of excitement in her eyes. She is still only a teenager, I realize; she is not yet an adult, however much she may be forced to behave like one. She has a mother who thinks nothing of having sex on the floor of the front room while her children lie sleeping overhead, who brags to them about her teenage conquests, who goes out on the piss every week and staggers in at six in the morning with smudged makeup and torn clothes. What kind of role model has Maya ever had? For the first time in her life she is free. Am I so sure she won't be tempted to make the most of it?

It's stupid to think like that. Maya is old enough to make her own choices. Plenty of girls her age sleep with their boy-friends. If she doesn't this time, she will the next, or the time after, or the time after that. One way or another it's going to happen. One way or another I'm going to have to deal with it. Except I can't. I can't deal with it at all. The very idea makes me want to pound my head against the wall and smash things. The idea of DiMarco, or anyone, holding her, touching her, kissing her . . .

A deafening bang, a blinding crack, pain shooting up my arm before I realize I've punched the wall with all my might; pieces of paint and plaster are flaking away from the imprint of my knuckles above the couch. Bent over double, I clutch my right hand with my left, clenching my teeth to stop myself from making a sound. For a moment everything darkens and I think I'm going to pass out, but then the pain hits me repeatedly in shocking, terrifying waves. I actually don't know what hurts more, my hand or my head. The thing I have feared and railed against these past few weeks—the total loss of control over my mind—has set in, and I have no way to fight it anymore. I close my eyes and feel the coil of madness climb up my spine and creep into my brain. I watch it explode like the sun. So this is it, this is what it feels like after a long hard struggle—to lose the battle and finally go crazy.

CHAPTER TWELVE

Maya

He's lovely. I don't know why I ever thought he was some arrogant tosser. Just goes to show how flawed one's perception of others can be. He's considerate, he's courteous, he's polite; he actually seems genuinely interested in me. He tells me I look beautiful and then gives me a bashful smile. Once we are seated in the restaurant, he translates every single item on the menu for me and doesn't laugh or even look surprised when I tell him I've never tried artichokes before. He asks me lots of questions, but when I explain that my family situation is complicated, he appears to take the hint and backs off. He agrees that Belmont is a shit hole and admits he can't wait to get out. He asks about

Lochan and says he wishes he could get to know him better. He confides that his father is more interested in his business than in his only son and buys him ridiculous presents such as a car to assuage his guilt for being abroad half the year. Yes, he is rich and he is spoiled, yet he is as neglected as we are. A completely different set of circumstances, the same sad outcome.

We talk for a long time. As he drives me home, I find myself wondering if he is going to kiss me. At one point, as we both reach out to turn down the radio, our hands touch and his lingers on mine for a moment. It feels strange, his fingers unfamiliar.

"Shall I walk you to your door or would that be . . . awkward?" He looks at me hesitantly and smiles when I do. I envision small faces peering from upstairs windows and agree that it's probably best if I get out alone. Fortunately, in the darkness, he has overshot the front door by two houses so no one from home can see us.

"Thank you for dinner. I had a really good time," I say, surprised to find myself meaning it.

He smiles. "Me too. D'you think maybe we could do it again sometime?"

"Yeah, why not?"

His smile broadens. He leans toward me. "Good night, then."

"Good night." I hesitate, my fingers on the door handle.

"Good night," he says again with a smile, but this time he cups my chin in his hand. His face approaches mine and suddenly the realization hits me. I like Nico. I actually think he's a pretty decent person. He's good-looking and I'm attracted to him. But I don't want to kiss him. Not now. Not ever . . . I turn my head away just as his face meets mine and his kiss lands on my cheek instead.

As I draw back, he looks surprised. "Okay, well, till next time."

I take a deep breath, groping for my bag at my feet, grateful for the darkness that hides the blush spreading across my face. "I really like you as a friend, Nico," I say in a rush. "But I'm sorry—I don't think I can go out with you again."

"Oh." He sounds surprised and a little hurt now. "Well, look, just think about it, okay?"

"Okay. See you Monday." I get out of the car and slam the door behind me. I wave, and he is still wearing that look of perplexed amusement as he drives off, as if he thinks I am playing games.

I lean against a thick tree trunk, staring up through the drizzle at a moonless sky. I have never felt so embarrassed in all my life. Why did I spend the whole evening leading him on? Acting fascinated by his stories, confiding in him? Why did I agree to see him again ten seconds before telling him we could only be friends? Why did I turn down a guy who, as well as being hot, actually turned out to be nice? *Because you're crazy, Maya.* Because you are crazy and stupid and you want to spend the rest of your life as a social outcast. Because you so wanted this to work, you so desperately wanted this to work, that you actually kidded yourself into believing things were going really well. Until you realized that the idea of kissing Nico, or any guy you could think of, was not what you wanted at all.

What does this mean, then—I'm afraid? Scared of physical intimacy? No. I crave it; I dream about it. But for me there's no one. No one. Any guy, even imaginary, would just feel like second best. Second best to what? I don't even have an image of the perfect boyfriend. I just know he must exist. Because I have all these feelings—of love, longing, wanting to be touched, dreaming of being kissed—yet no one to focus them on. It makes me want to scream in frustration. It makes me feel like a freak. But worse than that, I feel so desperately disappointed. Because all evening I believed Nico was the one. And then, when he tried to kiss me in the car, I realized with total, earth-shattering certainty that it would never feel right.

I trail back up to the house. This stupid dress is so short and skimpy, I'm beginning to freeze. I feel so empty, so let down. Yet I have only let myself down. Why couldn't I have acted normal for a change? Why couldn't I have forced myself to kiss him? Maybe it wouldn't have been so terrible. Maybe I could have borne it. . . . The lights in the front room are still on. I check my watch: quarter to eleven. Oh please, not another argument between Kit and Lochan. I unlock the door and it sticks. I kick it with the stupid high heels I doubt I'll ever wear again. The house, like a giant tomb, makes no sound. I slide off my shoes and pad in stockinged feet down the hallway to switch off the light in the front room. All I want to do is go to bed and forget about this whole lousy, self-deluded evening.

A figure seated on the edge of the couch makes me jump. Lochan is hunched over, his head in his hands.

"I'm back."

Not even a flicker of acknowledgment.

"Is Kit still out?" I ask with trepidation, fearing another scene.

"He came in about twenty minutes ago." Lochan doesn't even look up. Charming.

"I had a great evening, by the way." My tone is caustic. But if he's feeling sorry for himself just because he had to put the children to bed on his own for once, I refuse to give him the satisfaction of knowing that my evening was crap too.

"You only went out for dinner?" Abruptly he lifts his head and favors me with a penetrating gaze. Self-conscious under his sudden scrutiny, I become aware that my hair is coming down, stray strands hanging over my face, damp from standing out in the drizzle.

"Yes," I answer slowly. "Why?"

"You went out at seven. It's nearly eleven."

I can't believe this is Lochan talking. "You're telling me I have to be home by a certain time?" My voice rises in outrage.

"Of course not," he snaps irritably. "I'm just surprised. Four hours is a hell of a long time to spend over dinner."

I close the front-room door behind me as I feel my blood pressure begin to rise. "It wasn't four hours. By the time we'd driven halfway across town, found a place to park, waited for a table . . . We just talked—a lot. Turns out he's a pretty interesting guy. He doesn't exactly have it easy, either."

As soon as the words are out of my mouth, Lochan leaps up, strides over to the window, then swings back wildly. "I don't give a damn about how poor little rich boy didn't get the exact car he wanted for his eighteenth—I've heard all about that at Belmont. What I'm having trouble understanding is why the hell you pretend to have just been out for dinner when you've been gone four hours!"

This can't be happening. Lochan has gone mad. He's never spoken to me like this in his life. I've never seen him so furious with me before.

"Are you saying I have to account for my every move?" I

challenge him, my eyes widening in disbelief. "You're actually asking me for a blow-by-blow account of what happened throughout the whole evening?" My voice continues to rise.

"No! I just don't want to be lied to!" Lochan starts to shout.

"What I do or don't do on a date is none of your damn business!" I yell in return.

"But why does it have to be secret? Can't you just be honest?"

"I am being honest! We went out for dinner, we talked, he drove me home. End of story!"

"Do you really think I'm that gullible?"

This is the last straw. A row with Lochan after weeks of being ignored: the perfect end to an evening of bitter disappointment that, had I allowed it, could have been so great. All I wanted to do when I came in was crawl into bed and try to put this wasted opportunity out of my mind. And instead I find myself subjected to this.

I start backing away toward the door, raising my hands in surrender. "Lochan, I don't know what the hell your problem is, but you're being an absolute bastard. What's happening to you? I come in expecting you to ask me if I had a nice time, and instead you give me the third degree and then accuse me of lying! Even if something had happened on this date, what on earth makes you think I'd want to tell you?" I turn for the door.

"So you did sleep with him," he says flatly. "Like mother, like daughter."

His words slice the air between us. My hand freezes around the cold metal knob. Slowly, painfully, I turn. "What?" The word escapes from me in a small puff of air, barely more than a whisper.

Time seems to be suspended. He is standing there in his green T-shirt and faded jeans, squeezing the knuckles of one hand with the palm of the other, his back to the giant slice of night. And I find myself facing a stranger. His face has a curious raw look, as if he's been crying, but the fire in his eyes scorches my face. How foolish I was to kid myself I knew him so well. He is my brother and yet, for the very first time, appears before me as a stranger.

"I can't believe you said that." My voice, a quiver of disbelief, emanates from a being I barely recognize—one that is crushed, hurt beyond repair. "I always thought of you as the one person"—a steadying breath—"the one person who would never, ever hurt me."

He looks stricken, his face mirroring the pain and disbelief I feel inside. "Maya, I'm not feeling well—that was unforgivable. I don't know what I'm saying anymore." His voice is shaking, as appalled as my own. Pressing his hands to his face, he swings away from me, pacing the room, gasping for breath, his eyes filled with a wild, almost manic look.

"I just need to know—please understand—I have to know, or otherwise I'm going to lose my mind!" He shuts his eyes tightly and inhales raggedly.

"Nothing happened!" I shout, my anger abruptly replaced by fear. "Nothing happened. Why won't you believe me?" I grab him by the shoulders. "Nothing happened, Lochie! Nothing happened—nothing, nothing, nothing!" I am practically screaming but I don't care. I don't understand what is happening to him. What is happening to me.

"But he kissed you." His voice is hollow, devoid of all emotion. Pulling away from me, he crouches down on his heels. "He kissed you, Maya; he kissed you." His eyes are half closed, his face expressionless now, as if he is so depleted, he no longer has the strength to react.

"He didn't kiss me!" I yell, grabbing his arms and trying to shake him back to life. "He tried to, okay, but I didn't let him! D'you know why? D'you want to know why? D'you really, really want to know why?" Still gripping him with both hands, I lean forward, gasping, as tears, hot and heavy, fall down my cheeks. "This is why. . . ." Crying, I kiss Lochan's cheek. "This is why. . . ." With a muffled sob, I kiss the corner of Lochan's lips. "This is why . . ." Closing my eyes, I kiss Lochan's mouth.

I'm falling, but I know I'm okay, because it's with him, it's with Lochie. My hands are on his burning cheeks, my hands

are in his damp hair, my hands are against his warm neck. He is kissing me back now, with strange little sounds that suggest he might be crying, too, kissing me so hard that he is shuddering, gripping the tops of my arms tightly and pulling me toward him. I taste his lips, his tongue, the sharp edges of his front teeth, the soft warmth inside his mouth. I slide up astride his lap, wanting to get even closer, wanting to disappear into him, blend my body with his. We come up briefly for air and I catch sight of his face. His eyes brim with unfallen tears. He emits a ragged sound; we kiss some more, soft and tender, then fierce and hard again, his hands grasping at the straps of my dress, twisting them, clenching the material in his fists as if fighting back pain. And I know how he feels—it's so good it hurts. I think I'm going to die from happiness. I think I'm going to die from pain. Time has stopped; time is racing. Lochie's lips are rough yet smooth, hard yet gentle. His fingers are strong; I feel them in my hair and on my neck and down my arms and against my back. And I never want him to let me go.

A sound explodes like a thunderclap above us; our bodies jolt in unison and suddenly we are not kissing anymore, although I cling to the collar of his T-shirt, his arms strong and tight around me. There is the sound of the toilet flushing, then the familiar creak of Kit's ladder. Neither of us seems able to move, even though the ensuing silence makes it clear

Kit has gone back to bed. My head against Lochan's chest, I hear the magnified sounds of his heart—very loud, very fast, very strong. I can hear his breathing, too: sharp jagged spikes piercing the frozen air.

He is the first to break the silence. "Maya, what the hell are we doing?" Although his voice is barely more than a whisper, he sounds close to tears. "I don't understand. Why—why the hell is this happening to us?"

I close my eyes and press against him, stroking his bare arm with my fingertips. "All I know right now is that I love you," I say in quiet desperation, the words spilling out of their own accord. "I love you far more than just as a brother. I . . . I love you in—in every kind of way."

"I feel like that too. . . ." His voice is shocked and raw. "It's—it's a feeling so big, I sometimes think it's going to swallow me. It's so strong, I feel it could kill me. It keeps growing and I can't—I don't know what to do to stop it. But—but we're not supposed to do this—to love each other like this!" His voice cracks.

"I know that, okay? I'm not stupid!" I'm angry suddenly because I don't want to hear it. I close my eyes because I just can't think about that now. I can't let myself think about what it means. I won't think about what it's called. I refuse to let labels from the outside world spoil the happiest day of my life. The

 TABITHA SUZUMA

day I kissed the boy I had always held in my dreams but never allowed myself to see. The day I finally ceased lying to myself, ceased pretending it was just one kind of love I felt for him when in reality it was every kind of love possible. The day we finally broke free of our restraints and gave way to the feelings we had so long denied just because we happened to be brother and sister.

"We've—oh God—we've done a terrible thing." Lochan's voice is shaking, hoarse and breathless with horror. "I—I've done a terrible thing to you!"

I wipe my cheeks and turn my head to look up at him. "We haven't done anything wrong! How can love like this be called terrible when we're not hurting anyone?"

He gazes down at me, his eyes glistening in the weak light. "I don't know," he whispers. "How can something so wrong feel so right?"

CHAPTER THIRTEEN

Lochan

I tell Maya that she needs to sleep but I know I can't—I'm too afraid to go upstairs and sit on my bed and go crazy in that tiny room, alone with my terrifying thoughts. She says she wants to stay with me; she's frightened that if she goes away, I'll disappear. She doesn't need to explain—I feel it too: the fear that if we part now, this incredible night will just vanish, evaporate like a dream, and we will wake in the morning back in our separate bodies, back in our ordinary lives. Yet here on the couch, my arms around her as she sits curled up against me, head resting against my chest, I still feel frightened—more frightened than I've ever been before. What just happened was unbelievable yet somehow completely natural, as if deep down I always knew this moment would come, even though I never once allowed myself to consciously think about it, to imagine it in any way. Now that it has arrived, I can only think of Maya, sitting right here against me, her breath warm against my bare arm.

It's as if there is a great wall preventing me from crossing to the other side, from casting my mind out into the external world, the world beyond the two of us. Nature's security valve is at work, preventing me from even contemplating the implications of what just happened, keeping me, for the moment, at least, safe from the horror of what I have done. It's as if my mind knows it cannot go there yet, knows that right now I'm not strong enough to deal with the outcome of these overwhelming feelings, these momentous actions. But the fear remains—the fear that in the cold light of day we will be forced to come to terms with what was, quite simply, an awful mistake; the fear that we will have no choice but to bury this night as if it never took place, a shameful secret to be filed away for the rest of our lives until, brittle with age, it crumbles to dust—a faint, distant memory, like the powder of a moth's wings on a windowpane, the specter of something that perhaps never occurred, existing solely in our imagination.

I cannot bear the thought of this being just one moment in time, over almost before it started, already retreating into the past. I must hold on to it with all my might. I cannot allow Maya to slip away because, for the first time in my life, my love for her feels whole, and everything that has led up to this point suddenly makes sense, as if all this was meant to be. But as I gaze down at her sleepy face, the freckled cheekbones, the white skin, the dark curl of her eyelashes, I feel an overwhelming ache, like acute homesickness—a longing for something I can never have. Sensing my eyes on her, she looks up and smiles, but it is a sad smile, as if she, too, knows how precarious our new love is, how dangerously threatened by the outside world. The ache inside me deepens, and all I can think of is what it felt like to kiss her, how brief that moment was and how desperately I want to live it once more.

She keeps on looking at me with that little wistful smile, as if waiting, as if she knows. And the blood is hot in my face, my heart racing, my breath quickening, and she notices that, too. Raising her head from my chest, she asks, "Do you want to kiss me again?"

I nod, mute, heart pounding anew.

She looks at me expectantly, hopefully. "Go on, then."

I close my eyes, my breathing labored, my chest filling with a mounting sense of despair. "I don't—I don't think I can."

TABITHA SUZUMA

"Why not?"

"Because I'm worried . . . Maya, what if we can't stop?"

"We don't have to. . . ."

I breathe deeply and turn away, the air around me thrumming with heat. "Don't even think like that!"

Her expression sobers and she brushes her fingers up and down the inside of my arm, her eyes heavy with sadness. Yet her touch fills me with longing. I never thought that the mere touch of a hand could stir so much.

"All right, Lochie, we'll stop."

"We have to stop. Promise me."

"I promise." She touches my cheek, turning me back toward her. I take her face in my hands and start to kiss her, gently at first; and as I do so, all the pain and worry and loneliness and fear start to evaporate until all I can think of is the taste of her lips, the warmth of her tongue, the smell of her skin, her touch, her caresses. And then I'm struggling to keep calm and her hands are pressing against the sides of my face, her breath hot and rapid against my cheek, her mouth warm and wet. My hands want to touch her all over, but I can't, I can't, and we're kissing so hard it hurts—it hurts that I can't do more, it hurts that however hard I kiss her I can't . . . I can't—

"Lochie . . ."

I don't care about the promise. I don't remember why

I even suggested it. I don't care about anything—anything except for—

"Easy, Lochie—"

I press my lips back down over her mouth, holding her tight to stop her from moving away.

"Lochie, stop." This time she pulls away and pushes me back, holding me at arm's length, her fingers gripping my shoulders. Her lips are red—she looks flushed and wild and exquisite.

I'm breathing too fast. Much too fast.

"You made me promise." She looks upset.

"I know—all right!" Jumping up, I start pacing the room. I wish there was an icy pool of water for me to dive into.

"Are you okay?"

No, I'm not. I've never felt like this before and it scares me. My body seems to have taken over. I'm so aroused I can hardly think. I've got to calm down. I've got to stay in control. I can't let this happen. I run my hands through my hair repeatedly and the air escapes from my lungs in a rush.

"I'm sorry. I should have said it sooner."

"No!" I spin round. "It's not your fault, for God's sake!"

"All right, all right! Why are you angry?"

"I'm not! I'm just—" I stop and lean my forehead against the wall, fighting the urge to head-butt it. "Oh, Jesus, what are we going to do?"

"Nobody would have to find out," she says softly, chewing the tip of her thumb.

"No!" I shout.

Storming into the kitchen, I rummage furiously through the freezer for ice cubes for a cold drink. Hot acid shoots through my veins and my heart is hammering so hard that I can hear it. It's not just the physical frustration—it's the impossibility of our situation, the horror of what we've got ourselves into, the despair of knowing that I will never be able to love Maya the way I want to.

"Lochie, for goodness' sake, calm down." Her hand touches my arm as I wrestle with the freezer drawer.

I knock it away. "Don't!"

She takes a step back.

"D'you know what we're doing here? Have you any idea at all? D'you know what they call this?" I slam the freezer shut and move round to the other side of the table.

"What's got into you?" she says breathlessly. "Why are you suddenly turning on me?"

I stop abruptly and stare at her. "We can't do this," I blurt out, aghast with the sudden realization. "We can't. If we start, how will we ever stop? How on earth will we be able to keep this a secret from everyone for the rest of our lives? We'll have no life—we'll be trapped, living in hiding, always having to pretend. . . ."

She stares back at me, her blue eyes wide with shock. "The kids . . ." she says softly, a new realization suddenly dawning. "The kids—if even one person found out, they'd be taken away!"

"Yes."

"So we can't do this? We really can't?" It's phrased as a question, but I can see by the stricken look on her face that she already knows the answer.

Shaking my head slowly, I swallow hard and turn to look out the kitchen window to hide the tears in my eyes. The sky is on fire and the night has ended.

TABITHA SUZUMA

CHAPTER FOURTEEN

Maya

I'm tired. So terribly tired. It crushes down on me like an invisible force, obliterating all rational thought, all other feeling. I'm tired of dragging myself through each day, wearing my mask, pretending everything is okay. Trying to take in what others are saying, trying to concentrate in class, trying to appear normal in front of Kit, Tiffin, and Willa. I'm tired of spending every minute of every hour of every day fighting back tears, swallowing repeatedly to try and ease the constant ache at the back of my throat. Even at night, as I lie there hugging my pillow, staring out through the open curtains, I don't allow myself to give in—because if I did, I would fall apart; I would fragment into a thousand pieces like shattered glass. People constantly ask me what's the matter and it makes me want to scream. Francie thinks it's because Nico dumped me and I let her—it's easier than coming up with another lie. Nico tries to talk to me a couple of times during break but I make it clear that I'm in no mood for conversation. He looks hurt, but I'm beyond caring. *If it weren't for you* . . . I find myself thinking. If it weren't for that date . . .

But how can I blame Nico for making me realize I'm in love with my brother? The feeling had been there for years, rising closer and closer to the surface with every passing day. It was only a matter of time before it broke through our fragile web of denial, forcing us to confront the truth and acknowledge who we are: two people in love—a love that nobody else could possibly understand. Do I really regret that night? That one moment of joy beyond compare—some people never experience it in a lifetime. But the downside to that taste of pure happiness is that, like a drug, a glimmer of paradise, it leaves you craving more. And after that moment, nothing can ever be the same again. Everything grays in comparison. The world becomes bland and vacuous; there seems little point to anything anymore. Going to school—for what? To pass exams, to get good marks, to go to university, to meet new people, to find a job, to move away? How will I be able to live a life apart from Lochan? Will I just see him a few times a year, like

TABITHA SUZUMA

Mum and Uncle Ryan? They grew up together; they were once close, too. But then he got married and moved to Glasgow. So what do Mum and Uncle Ryan have in common now? Separated by so much more than distance and lifestyle, even their memories of a shared childhood have faded from their minds. Is that what will happen to Lochan and me? And even if we both stay here in London, when he finds a girlfriend, when I find a boyfriend, how will we bear it? How will we be able to watch each other leading separate lives, knowing what could have been?

I try to shock myself out of the pain by thinking about the alternative. Having a physical relationship with one's brother? Nobody does that; it's disgusting; it would be like having Kit as my boyfriend. I shudder. I love Kit, but the idea of kissing him is beyond revolting. It would be horrendous; it would be repulsive—even the thought of him snogging that skinny American girl he's always hanging around with is bad enough. I don't want to know what he gets up to with his so-called girlfriend. When he's older, I hope he meets someone kind, I hope he falls in love, gets married, but I would never, ever want to even think about the intimate details, the physical side of things. That's his business. Why, then—why is it so different with Lochan? But the answer is simple: because Lochan has never felt like a brother. Neither an annoying younger one nor a bossy older one. He and I have always been equals. We've been best friends since we were toddlers. We've shared a bond closer than friendship all our lives. Together we've brought up Kit, Tiffin, and Willa. We've cried together and comforted each other. We've each seen the other at our most vulnerable. We've shared a burden inexplicable to the outside world. We've been there for each other—as friends, as partners. We've always loved each other, and now we want to be able to love each other in a physical way as well.

I want to explain all this to him, but I know I can't. I know that whatever the reasons for our feelings, however much I try to justify them, it doesn't change anything: Lochan cannot be my boyfriend. Out of the millions and millions of people that inhabit this planet, he is one of the tiny few I can never have. And this is something I must accept—even if, like acid on metal, it is slowly corroding me inside.

The term grinds on, gray, bleak, relentless. At home, the daily routine continues to follow its course, over and over. Autumn gives way to winter, the days growing noticeably shorter. Lochan behaves as if that night never happened. We both do. What alternative do we have? We speak together about mundane things, but our gazes rarely meet, and when they do, it is only a moment or two before they shrink nervously away. But I wonder what he is thinking. I suspect that, seeing it as something so wrong, he

 TABITHA SUZUMA

has pushed it right out of his head. And anyway, he has enough on his mind. His English teacher is still on a one-woman mission to get him to speak in front of the class and I know he dreads her lessons. Mum's behavior is increasingly erratic—she spends more and more time at Dave's and rarely comes home sober. Now and then she goes out on a shopping spree and returns with guilt-induced presents for everyone: flimsy toys that will get broken within days, more computer games to keep Kit glued to his screen, sweets that will get Tiffin hyper. I watch it all as if from a very great distance, incapable of engaging with anything anymore. Lochan, white-faced and tense, tries to keep some kind of order in the house, but I sense he, too, is close to his breaking point and I am unable to help him.

Sitting across from him at the kitchen table, watching him help Willa with her homework, I'm overcome with this terrible ache, this profound sense of loss. Stirring my long-cold tea, I watch all his familiar traits: the way he blows the hair out of his eyes every few minutes, chews on his lower lip whenever he feels tense. I look at his hands, with their bitten-down nails, resting on the tabletop, his lips, which once touched mine, now chapped and raw. The pain I feel when looking at him is more than I can bear but I force myself to keep watching, to soak in as much of him as I can, trying to recapture, in my mind, at least, all that I've lost.

"The boy went into the c-a-v-e." Willa sounds the letters

out. Kneeling up on the kitchen chair, she points at each letter in turn, her fine golden hair curtaining her face, the ends brushing the page of her book with a faint whispery sound.

"What word does that make?" Lochan prompts her.

Willa studies the picture. "Rock?" she says optimistically, glancing up at Lochan, her blue eyes wide and hopeful.

"No. Look at the word: c-a-v-e. Put the sounds together and say them quickly. What word does it make?"

"Kav?" She is restless and inattentive, desperate to go and play but pleased, nonetheless, by the attention.

"Nearly, but there's an *e* at the end. What do we call that *e*?"

"A capital *e*?"

Lochan's tongue darts out, rubbing his lip in impatience. "Look, this is a capital *e*." He flicks through the book in search of one, fails, and writes one himself on a piece of used paper towel.

"Ew. Tiffin blew his nose on that."

"Willa, are you looking? That's a capital *e*."

"A snotty capital *e*." Willa begins to laugh; she catches my eye and I feel myself smile too.

"Willa, this is very important. It's an easy word—I know you can read it if you try. This is a magic *e*. What does a magic *e* do?"

She frowns hard and leans over the book again, curling her tongue above her lip in concentration, her hair partially obscur-

ing the page. "It makes the vowel say its name!" she shouts out suddenly, punching the air triumphantly with her small fist.

"Good. So which one's the vowel?"

"Hmm . . ." She returns to the page with the same frown, the same curled tongue. "Hmm . . ." she says again, stalling for time. "The *a*?"

"Good girl. So the magic *e* turns the *a* sound into an—"

"Ay."

"Yes. So try to sound out the word again."

"K-ay-v. Cave! The boy went into the cave! Look, Lochie, I read it!"

"Clever girl! See, I knew you could do it!" He smiles, but there is something else in his eyes. A sadness that never fades.

Willa finishes reading her book and goes to join Tiffin in front of the TV. I pretend to sip my tea, watching Lochan over the rim of the mug. Probably too tired to move, he sits back, limp, bits of paper and scattered books and school letters and Willa's book bag spread out in front of him. A long silence stretches out between us, as taut as a rubber band.

"Are you okay?" I ask him eventually.

He gives a wry smile and appears to hesitate, gazing down at the littered table. "Not really," he replies at length, avoiding my gaze. "You?"

"No." With the rim of my mug I press my lip down against

my teeth in an attempt to stop the tears. "I miss you," I whisper.

"I miss you, too." He is still staring down at the cover of Willa's reading book. His eyes seem to catch the light. "Maybe—" His voice comes out unsteady so he tries again. "M-maybe you should give DiMarco another chance. Rumor has it he's—he's pretty crazy about you!" A forced laugh.

I stare at him in stunned silence. I feel like I've been dealt a blow to the head. "Is that what you want?" I ask with carefully controlled calm.

"No—no. That's not what I want at all. But maybe it would . . . help?" He glances up at me with a look of pure desperation.

I continue pressing my teeth into my lip until I'm sure I'm not going to start crying, swirling his outrageous proposition around in my head. "Help me or help you?"

His bottom lip quivers for a moment and he immediately bites down on it, apparently unaware that he is making a concertina out of the cover of Willa's reading book. "I don't know. Maybe both of us," he says in a rush.

"Then you should go out with Francie," I shoot back.

"Okay." He doesn't look up.

I am momentarily speechless. "You—but—I thought you didn't fancy her?" The horror in my voice resonates across the room.

TABITHA SUZUMA

"I don't, but we've got to do something. We've got to go out with other people. It's—it's the only way—"

"The only way to what?"

"To—to get over this. To survive."

I slam my mug down on the table, sloshing tea over my hand and shirt cuff. "You think I'm just going to get over this?" I shout, the blood pounding in my face.

Ducking his head and flinching as if I am about to deal him a blow, he raises a hand to ward me off. "Don't—I can't—please don't make it worse."

"How could I?" I gasp. "How could I possibly do anything to make this worse?"

"All I know is that we have to do something. I can't go on—I can't go on like this!" He inhales raggedly and turns away.

"I know." I lower my voice, forcing myself back into some semblance of calm. "Neither can I."

"What else can we do?" His eyes plead with mine.

"Fine." I shut down my thoughts, shut down my senses. "I'll tell Francie tomorrow. She'll be over the moon. But she's a decent person, Lochan. You can't just dump her after a week."

"I won't." He looks at me, his eyes full. "I'll stay with her for as long as she likes. I'll marry her, if that's what she wants. I mean, at the end of the day, what the hell does it matter who I end up with if it can't be you?"

*　*　*

Everything feels different today. The house is chilled and alien. Kit, Tiffin, and Willa seem like impersonators of their real selves. I can't even look at Lochan, the embodiment of my loss. The streets on the way to school seem to have changed overnight. I could be in some foreign town, in some far-flung country. The pedestrians around me don't feel quite alive. I don't feel alive. I'm not sure who I am anymore. The girl who existed before that night, before the kiss, has been erased from life. I am no longer who I was; I still don't know who I will become. The nervous honks of cars jar me, as do the sounds of feet on the sidewalk, buses going by, shops opening their shutters, the high-pitched chatter of children making their way to school.

The building is bigger than I remember—a stark, colorless concrete landscape. Pupils hurrying this way and that look like extras on a movie set. I must move in order to fit into all this activity, just as an electron must obey the current. I take the stairs very slowly, one at a time, as people shove and push past me. When I reach my homeroom, I see things I have never noticed before: the fingerprints on the walls; the speckled linoleum, cracked like a delicate eggshell, disappearing rhythmically beneath my feet. Far off, voices try to bump up against me, but I repel them. The sounds bounce off me without registering: the scraping of chairs, the laughs and the chatter, Francie's nattering, the history teacher's drone. Sunlight breaks through a blanket of cloud, slanting in through the great glass windows, across my desk, into my eyes. White spots form in the space in front of me, dancing bubbles of color and light that hold me captive until the bell goes. Francie is at my side, her mouth full of questions, her painted red lips forming and re-forming—lips that will soon touch Lochan's. I have to tell her now before it's too late, but my voice is gone and all that comes out is empty air.

I skip second period to escape her. Walk around the empty school, my giant prison cell, searching for answers that can never be found. My shoes tap against the steps as I go up and down and round and round each floor, searching for—what— some kind of absolution? The harsh winter light strengthens, flooding through the windows and bouncing off the walls. I feel the pressure of it against my body, burning holes into my skin. I am lost in this maze of corridors, staircases, floors stacked one above the other like a pile of cards. If I keep going, maybe I will find my way back—back to the person I used to be. I am moving more slowly now. Maybe even floating. I swim through space. The earth has lost its gravity; everything feels liquid around me. I reach another staircase, the treads melting down. The sole of my shoe peels off the landing and I step into nothingness.

CHAPTER FIFTEEN

Lochan

I stare at the back of Nico DiMarco's head. I fix on his dark, blunt-fingered hand resting on the edge of his desk, and the thought of those fingers touching Maya makes me feel physically sick. I can't stand by and watch anyone go out with my sister, any more than I myself can go out with Francie or any other girl and pretend she can replace her. I need to find Maya and hope to God it's not too late. I need to tell her the deal is off. Perhaps, with time, she will find someone she can be with. And I will be happy, if only for her. But for me there can never be anyone else. The absolute certainty of this fact suffocates me.

Above the board, the hands of the clock are moving. Second period is almost over. She wouldn't have told Francie yet, surely? She must be planning to wait until morning break. I feel spectacularly ill. Just because I can't go ahead with this doesn't mean she will feel the same way. It may have been my idea, but she proposed the exchange. Maybe she has made up her mind to give DiMarco a second chance. Maybe the agony of the past few weeks has made her realize what a relief a normal relationship would be.

The bell goes and I shoot out of my seat, grabbing my bag and blazer as I go, ignoring the teacher's shouts about homework. There is a massive jam on staircase five. I head for the stairs at the other end. Throngs of people have accumulated here, too. Except they are motionless. They have stopped in their tracks, an amoeba-like cluster, turning to one another to talk in urgent, excited tones. I push past them. Thick red tape strung across the top of the staircase brings me to a halt. As I duck underneath, I'm pulled back by a hand on my shoulder.

"You can't go down that way," a voice says. "There's been an accident."

I step back. *Oh, this is just great.*

"Some girl fell. They've only just moved her to the medical room. She was unconscious," someone else adds in a reverential tone.

I look at the tape, tempted just to duck underneath again.

"Who fell?" I hear another voice behind me ask.

"It was a girl from my class. Maya Whitely. I saw it happen—she didn't fall, she jumped."

"Hey!"

I dive under the tape and race down the two flights of stairs, the soles of my shoes screeching on the linoleum. The ground floor is crawling with pupils heading out to break, everyone moving in slow motion. I shove my way through the crowds, shoulders bruising shoulders, people jostling me from all angles, angry shouts following me as I force my way past.

"Hey, hey, hey—" Someone has me by the arm. I spin round, ready to shove them back, and find myself staring into the face of Miss Azley. "Lochan, you need to wait out here—the nurse is busy."

I wrench my arm out of her grasp and she moves to block the entrance.

"What's the matter?" she asks. "Are you feeling unwell? Sit here and let me see if I can help you."

I take an involuntary step backward. "Let me past," I gasp. "For God's sake, I need to—"

"You need to wait here. Someone's just had an accident and Mrs. Shah is dealing with that at the moment."

"It's Maya—"

TABITHA SUZUMA

"What?"

"My sister!"

Her face changes. "Oh, God. Lochan, listen, she's going to be fine. She just fainted. She didn't fall very far—"

"Please let me see her!"

"Sit down for a second and I'll ask the nurse."

Miss Azley disappears through the door. I sit on one of the plastic chairs and press my fist against my mouth, my lungs crying out for air.

Minutes later, Miss Azley comes out to tell me that Maya is fine, just a little shocked and bruised. She asks me for our mother's phone number—I tell her that she is away and that I will take Maya home. She looks concerned and informs me that Maya needs to be taken to the ER to be checked for a concussion. I insist I can deal with that, too.

Finally they let me see her. She is in the small white anteroom, sitting on a bed, sagging back against a cushion, a lime-green blanket pulled halfway across her lap. Her tie has been removed and her right sleeve rolled up, revealing a thin white arm with vivid pink bruising. A large bandage covers her elbow. Her shoes have been taken off too, and her bare legs hang off the side of the bed, a white crepe bandage enveloping one knee. Her copper hair, freed from its ponytail, hangs loose over her shoulders. Her face is drained of all color. Cracked, dried blood surrounds a small cut on her cheekbone, the crimson stain contrasting painfully with the rest of her face. Violet shadows underline pink-rimmed, empty eyes. She doesn't smile when she sees me; the light is gone from her face, a dull look of shocked resignation in its place.

As I take a step into the small space between the door and the bed, she seems to shrink away. Quickly I move back again, pressing my sweaty palms against the cold wall behind me.

"What—what happened?"

She blinks a couple of times and studies me wearily for a moment. "It's all right. I'm all right—"

"Just t-tell me what happened, Maya!" There is an edge to my voice that I can't conceal.

"I fainted while I was going down the stairs. I skipped breakfast and I was dehydrated, that's all."

"What did the nurse say?"

"That I'm fine. That I shouldn't miss meals. She wants me to go to the hospital to be checked out for a concussion but there's no need. My head doesn't hurt."

"They think you fainted because you missed breakfast?" My voice begins to rise. "But that's absurd! You've never fainted before and you hardly ever eat breakfast."

She closes her eyes as if my words are hurting her.

"Lochie, I'm fine. Really. Could you please just persuade the nurse to let me out of here?" She opens her eyes again and looks troubled for a moment. "Or—or have you got classes you can't miss?"

I gape at her. "Don't be ridiculous. I'm taking you home with me right now."

She gives me a little smile and I feel as if I'm falling. "Thank you."

Mrs. Shah calls a cab to take us to the local hospital, but as soon as we're outside the gates, Maya sends the driver away. She moves away from me along the sidewalk, her hand trailing the wall for balance. "Come on. I'm going home."

"The nurse said you might have a concussion! We've got to go to the hospital!"

"Don't be silly. I didn't even bump my head." She continues her unsteady path down the road, then half turns, holding out her hand. At first I just stare at it, uncomprehending.

"Can I lean on you a bit?" Her eyes are apologetic. "My legs feel kind of wobbly."

I rush to her and grab her hand, wrapping her arm round my waist, putting my arm around her. "Like this? Is—is this okay?"

"That's great, but you don't have to squeeze me so tightly. . . ."

I loosen my grip fractionally. "Better?"

"Much better." We move off down the road, her body, leaning against mine, as light and frail as a bird's.

"Hey, look at this," she says, a hint of amusement in her voice. "I got us both a whole day off school and it's not even"— she lifts my hand from her waist to get a look at my watch— "eleven o'clock." With a smile, she raises her head so that her eyes meet mine and the late morning sun washes across her colorless face.

I force an uneven breath into my lungs. "Crafty," I manage, swallowing hard.

We walk on for a few minutes in silence. Maya is holding on to me tightly. Now and again she slows to a halt and I ask her if she wants to sit down, but she shakes her head.

"I'm sorry," she says softly.

God. No. The air starts to shudder in my chest.

"It was my idea too," she adds.

I take a deep breath and hold it, turning my head away. If I bite my lip hard enough and force myself to meet the stares of curious passersby, I can keep myself together for a bit longer, just a bit longer. But she can tell. I feel her concern permeate my skin like a gentle warmth.

"Lochie?"

Stop. Don't speak. I can't bear it, Maya. I can't. Please understand.

TABITHA SUZUMA

She turns her face toward me. "Don't beat yourself up about it, Lochie. It wasn't your fault," she whispers against my shoulder.

Maya goes into the kitchen while I hang back, pretending to sort through the mail, trying to pull myself together. And then, suddenly, I'm aware of her silhouette in the doorway. She looks battered, with her tangled hair and crumpled clothes and bandaged knee. A burgundy stain is spreading beneath the skin of her cheekbone; in a couple of days it will have bloomed into a large bruise right across her cheek. *Maya, I'm so sorry*, I want to say. *I never ever meant to hurt you.*

"Would you mind making me a cup of coffee?" she asks with a tentative smile.

"Course . . ." I glance down unseeingly at the envelopes in my hand. "Of c-course . . ."

She smiles at me properly this time. "I think I might curl up on the couch in front of some crappy daytime TV."

There is a silence. I flick through some junk mail and take a moment to reply as a pain, like a sliver of glass, slowly pierces the back of my throat.

"Come and keep me company?" She is hesitating now, still waiting for my reply.

An invisible noose tightens round my neck. I cannot answer.

"Lochie?"

I don't move. If I do, I lose.

"Hey . . ." She takes a sudden step toward me and I immediately back up, banging my elbow against the front door.

"Lochie, I'm all right." Slowly she holds up her hands. "Look at me—I'm fine. You can see that, can't you? I just slipped, that's all. I was tired. Everything's all right."

But it's not, it's not, because I'm slowly being torn in two. You stand there, covered in cuts and bruises that I might as well have inflicted on you with my own hands. And I love you, so much that it's killing me, yet all I can do is push you away and hurt you until eventually your love will turn to hate.

The pain wells up in my chest, my breathing starts to fragment, and scalding tears force their way into my eyes. Abruptly I crumple up the glossy ads in my hands and lean heavily against the wall, pressing the shiny paper against my face.

There is a moment of shocked silence before I feel Maya by my side, gently pulling at my hands. "Don't, Lochie—it's all right. Look at me. I'm fine!"

I take an uneven breath. "I'm sorry—I'm just so sorry!"

"Sorry about what, Lochie? I don't understand!"

"The idea—last night—it was so awful, it was so stupid—"

"It doesn't matter about that now. It's finished, okay? We know we can't do it, so we're never going to think about

doing anything like that again." Her voice is firm, reassuring.

I throw down the paper and bang my head back against the wall, rubbing my arm savagely across my eyes. "I didn't know what else to do! I was desperate—I'm still desperate! I can't stop feeling like this!" I am shouting now, frantic. I feel as though I'm losing my mind.

"Listen . . ." She takes my hands and rubs them in an effort to calm me. "I never wanted Nico or anyone else. Just you."

I look at her, the sound of my breath rough and uneven in the sudden silence. "You can have me," I whisper shakily. "I'm here. I'll always be here."

Her expression floods with relief as her hands reach for my face. "We were stupid—we thought they could stop us." She strokes my hair, kisses my forehead, my cheeks, the edge of my lip. "They'll never stop us. Not as long as this is what we both want. But you've got to stop thinking it's wrong, Lochie. That's just what other people think; it's their problem, their stupid rules, their prejudices. They're the ones who are wrong, narrow-minded, cruel. . . ." She kisses my ear, my neck, my mouth.

"They're the ones who are wrong," she repeats. "Because they don't understand. I don't care if you happen biologically to be my brother. You've never just felt like a brother to me. You've always been my best friend, my soul mate, and now I've fallen in love with you, too. Why is that such a crime? I want to be able to hold you and kiss you and—and do all the things that people in love are allowed to do." She takes a deep breath. "I want to spend the rest of my life with you."

I close my eyes and press my hot face against her cheek. "We will. We'll find a way. Maya, we have to. . . ."

When I push open her bedroom door with my elbow, a glass of juice in one hand, a sandwich in the other, I find her fast asleep, sprawled out facedown on the bed, the duvet kicked back, arms circling her head on the pillow. She looks so vulnerable, so fragile. The bright midday light illuminates the side of her sleeping face, a strip of her crumpled, oversize school shirt, the edge of her white knickers, the top of her thigh. Navigating the discarded skirt, socks, and shoes strewn across the carpet, I place the plate and glass beside a stack of papers on her desk and straighten up slowly. I watch her for a long time. After a while my legs begin to ache and I slide down into a sitting position against the wall, arms resting on my knees. I'm afraid that if I leave, even for a moment, something might happen to her again; I'm afraid that if I leave, the black wall of fear will return. But here beside her, the sight of her sleeping face reminds me that nothing else matters, that in this I'm not alone. This is what Maya wants, this is what I want—fighting it is no use, can only hurt us both. The human body needs a constant flow of nourishment, air, and love to survive. Without Maya, I lose all three; apart, we will slowly die.

I must have drifted off, for the sound of her voice sends a jolt through my body and I straighten up, rubbing my neck. She blinks at me sleepily, her cheek resting on the edge of the mattress, russet hair brushing the floor. I don't know what she said to wake me, but now her arm is outstretched, her palm turned toward me. I take her hand and she smiles.

"I made you a sandwich," I tell her, glancing up at the desk. "How are you feeling?"

She doesn't reply, her eyes drawing me in. The warmth of her hand seeps into mine and her fingers tighten as she pulls me gently toward her. "Come here," she says in a voice still scratchy with sleep.

I stare back at her, feeling my pulse quicken. She releases my hand and moves back to the far side of the bed, leaving a space for me. I pull off my shoes and socks and stand up unsteadily as she holds out her arms.

As I lower my body onto the mattress beside her, I inhale her smell and feel her legs entwine with mine. She kisses me gently—soft, whispery kisses that make my face tingle and send tremors running through my body, creating instant arousal. I am acutely aware of her bare legs caught between mine—afraid she will feel, afraid she will know. I close my eyes and inhale deeply in an effort to keep calm, but she kisses my eyelids and her hair tickles my neck and face and I hear my breathing become shallow and rapid.

"It's all right," she says with a smile in her voice. "I love you."

I open my eyes and lift my head off the pillow and start kissing her back, gently at first, but then she puts her arm round my neck and pulls me closer, and our kisses begin to quicken, growing deeper and more urgent until it's difficult to find time to breathe. I cradle her head with one arm, clasping her hand with the other. Every kiss is becoming fiercer than the one before until I'm frightened I'm hurting her. I don't know where to go from here; I don't know what to do. I press my face into the hot curve of her neck with a strange sound and find myself stroking her breasts, the cotton shirt rough beneath my hands. I feel her fingertips running up and down my back, beneath my shirt, then traveling round beneath my arms to reach my chest, touching my nipples. Small electric shocks ricochet through my body. My mouth reaches for hers again and I'm gasping for air and she's making sounds that make my heart pound harder and harder. I feel swept up in some kind of burning whirl of madness, barraged by a million sensations at once—the heat of her lips, the pressure of her tongue, the taste of her mouth, the smell of her hair, the feel of her breasts—the buttons of her shirt scratching my palm as I slide my hand down them, the peaks of her ribs abruptly giving way to the soft inward curve of her stomach, the shock of reaching under her shirt and feeling taut, warm skin. Maya has one hand in my hair and the other on my stomach. My muscles convulse in response to her touch, pulling away yet desperate for her hand to follow, and I'm acutely aware of her fingers sliding under the top of my trousers, pressing against my stomach, hesitating at the waistband of my boxers; I have to break away from the kiss and press my face into the pillow to stop myself from begging her to keep going. I can't think of anything anymore except for this blind madness; I want to stop myself but I'm unable to hold still. I want to pretend that it's an accident, that I don't know what I'm doing, but I do. My hands claw at the sheet, twisting it into knots as I push myself toward her, rubbing myself against her, imperceptibly at first, in the hope she won't notice—but soon that, too, is out of my control as the pace and the pressure increase of their own accord, my crotch against her pelvic bone, the thin, soft material of our clothing all that is left between us. I wish I could feel her bare skin, yet even the feel of her body under her uniform is enough to send me into a whirl of longing and desire. I can hear the sound of my rasping breath, the friction between our two bodies. I know I should stop, I know I must stop now, because if I keep going, if I keep going, I know what will happen. . . . I have to stop, I must, I must. . . . Then her mouth finds mine—she kisses me deeply, and a crackling, spitting electric current shoots through my body, sending out red sparks of exquisite elation. And suddenly I'm shuddering hard against her, ecstasy exploding throughout my body like the sun. . . .

Maya rolls onto her side to face me and strokes the hair away from my face, looking startled, a touch of amusement on her lips. As her laughing eyes meet mine, I take a sharp breath and feel a strong wave of embarrassment wash over me.

"I got—I got a bit carried away." I pull a face to try and disguise my acute discomfort. Does she actually know what happened? Is she disgusted?

She raises her eyebrows and bites back a smile. "No kidding!"

She does. Fucking hell.

"Well, that's what happens when you—when you do stuff like that." My voice comes out louder than I intended—defensive, shaky, uneven.

"I know," she says quietly. "Wow."

"I couldn't—I couldn't stop." My heart is pounding. I feel frantic with embarrassment.

She kisses my cheek. "Lochie, it's okay—I didn't want you to stop!"

Relief floods through me and I pull her closer so that her hair is in my face. "Really?"

"Really!"

I close my eyes. "I love you."

"I love you, too."

A long moment passes, and then hot, spasmodic breaths blow against my cheek: silent laughter. "You've gone all sleepy!"

I force my eyes open and give an embarrassed laugh. It's true. I'm wiped out. My eyelids are dragged down by invisible weights and every ounce of energy has evaporated from my body. I have just experienced the most intense few minutes of my life and my whole body feels weak. I shift uncomfortably against the bed and pull an embarrassed face. "I think I need a shower. . . ."

I can't stop thinking about it—at night, but during the daytime, too. What have we done? What have we done? Even though we never took our clothes off, even though what we did isn't technically against the law, I know we have started on a dangerous slippery slope. Where it could eventually land us is both too terrifying and too fantastic to even think about. I try telling myself that it was nothing, that I was just trying to comfort her—but even I'm not self-deluded enough to believe my own ridiculous excuse. And now it's like a drug, and I cannot believe I have managed to live so long, in the daily presence of Maya, without this new level of closeness. . . .

CHAPTER SIXTEEN

Maya

At the end of the day, it's all about how much you can bear, how much you can endure. Being together, we harm nobody; being apart, we extinguish ourselves. I wanted to be strong—wanted to show Lochan that if he could walk away after that first night, then so could I; that if he could distract himself by going out with a girl, then I could do the same with a guy. My mind was set on the idea but the rest of me wouldn't obey. Rather than go through with our deal, my body chose to take a dangerous tumble down a flight of stairs.

Lochan is still Lochan, except he's not. When I look at him, he seems different to me now. My mind keeps flashing back to that afternoon on the bed—the taste of his hot mouth, the brush of his fingertips against my skin. I want to be with him all the time. I follow him from room to room, finding any excuse to be near him, to look at him, to touch him. I want to hold him, stroke him, kiss him, but of course, with the others always around, I can't. Loving him like this has become a deep physical ache. I am overcome by a kaleidoscope of conflicting emotions: on the one hand, fizzing with so much adrenaline and excitement that I find it difficult to eat; on the other, consumed with terror that Lochan is suddenly going to say we cannot do this because it's wrong. Or that someone may find out and force us apart. I will not listen to the ticking time bomb inside my head, will not think of the future, that gaping dark hole in which neither of us can exist, together or apart. . . . I refuse to allow my fears for the future to ruin the present. All that matters right now is that Lochan is here with me and that we love each other. I have never felt so happy in my life.

Lochan, too, seems more alive. The strained look of exhaustion and false cheer is erased from his face. He cracks up at Tiffin's jokes, tickles Willa and swings her round and round until I beg him to stop. He humors Kit and lets the usual inflammatory remarks go; he has even stopped chewing his lip. And every time his eyes meet mine, his face ignites with a smile.

On Friday morning, two whole weeks after we last held each other on the bed, I come up behind him as he stands alone at the sink with his back to the door, sipping his morning coffee and staring out the window. His raven hair is still tousled from the night, his white shirtsleeves rolled up to the elbows as usual. The skin on his arms looks so smooth, I long to stroke them. Unable to hold back, I slip my hand into his loose one. He turns to me with a smile of surprise but I recognize a hint of alarm in his eyes, accompanied by another emotion: a longing ache, a painful desperation.

"The others will be down in a minute," Lochan warns me softly.

I glance at the closed kitchen door, wishing it had a lock. Turning back, I stroke the inside of his palm with my fingertips. "I miss you," I whisper.

He smiles slightly but his eyes are sad. "We just have to—to wait for the right moment, Maya."

"There never is a right moment," I reply. "Between the kids and school and Kit up half the night, we're never alone."

He starts on his lip again, turning to stare out the window. I rest my head against the top of his arm.

"Don't!" he says hoarsely.

"But I was just—"

"Don't you get it? It makes it even harder. It makes it even

worse." He takes an unsteady breath. "I can't—I can't bear it when you . . ."

"When I what?"

He doesn't reply.

"Why are you tuning me out?"

"You don't understand." He turns to me almost angrily, his voice beginning to shake. "Seeing you, being with you every day but not being able to do anything—it's like cancer. It's like this cancer growing inside my body, inside my mind!"

"Okay. I know. I'm sorry." I try to disengage my hand but his fingers tighten round mine.

"Don't—"

I lean toward him and hold him tightly as he wraps his arms around me. The warmth of his body flows into mine like an electric current. His hot cheek brushes against my face; his lips touch mine, then pull away again; his breath is moist and urgent against my neck. I want him to kiss me so much, it hurts.

The door crashes open like the sound of a gunshot. We reel apart. Tiffin stands there, trailing his tie, his shirt untucked. His eyes are wide, flicking from my face to Lochan's.

"Wow, first one to be ready!" My voice comes out shrill with false cheer. "Come here and I'll do your tie. What d'you fancy for breakfast?"

He still doesn't move. "What happened?" he asks at length, his face worried.

"Nothing!" Lochan turns from making the coffee and gives him a reassuring smile. "Everything's fine. Now, muesli, toast, or both?"

Tiffin ignores Lochan's attempts at distraction. "Why were you cuddling Maya?" he asks instead.

"Because—because—Maya was feeling a bit upset about this test she's got today," Lochan replies raggedly. "She's feeling very nervous."

I nod in agreement, quickly erasing my false smile.

Unconvinced, Tiffin walks slowly over to his chair, forgetting his usual complaints as Lochan fills his bowl with muesli.

My heart is hammering. We only heard the door after it had swung open all the way and hit the corner of the sideboard. Did Tiffin see Lochan kiss my neck—notice my lips brush against his? Tiffin starts eating his muesli without further comment and I know he doesn't believe our story. I know he senses something isn't right. It's almost a relief when Kit and Willa arrive, loud and complaining, one protesting about the breakfast menu, the other about the loss of her sticker album. I glance nervously at Tiffin but he stays unusually silent.

Lochan is clearly shaken too. The color is high in his cheeks and he is gnawing at his lip. He knocks over Willa's juice and

TABITHA SUZUMA

spills cereal on the table. He downs coffee after coffee and tries to rush everyone through breakfast, even though it is not yet eight, and his eyes keep returning to Tiffin's face.

After dropping the kids off at school, I turn to him and say, "Tiffin couldn't have seen anything. There wasn't time."

"He just saw me give you a hug and now he's worried that you're upset about something more serious than a test. I should never have come up with that pathetic excuse. But by this evening he'll have forgotten all about it, or if he hasn't, he'll realize you're okay. Everything's fine."

I can still feel the knot of fear in my stomach. But I just nod and smile reassuringly.

In math, Francie chews gum and props her feet up on the empty chair in front, passing me notes about the way Salim Kumar is looking at me and speculating about what he would like to do with me. But all I can think is that something has got to change. Lochan and I have to find a way of being together without fear of interruption for at least a little while every day. I know that after what happened this morning, he isn't going to touch me again while the others are in the house, which is basically whenever we are. And I still don't understand why I can't even stand close to him, hold his hand, rest my head against his arm, while we are in an empty room. He says it makes it worse, but how could anything be worse than not touching him at all?

It's my turn to pick up Tiffin and Willa today because Lochan has a late class. On the way home, they charge ahead as usual, giving me a heart attack at every road crossing. When we get in, I sort out snacks and rummage through their book bags for teachers' notes and homework while they fight over the remote in the front room. I put in a load of laundry, clear away the breakfast things, and go upstairs to tidy their room. When I return to the front room, they have tired of TV, the DS isn't working properly, and Tiffin's neighborhood friends are all out at soccer club. They start to bicker, so I suggest a game of Cluedo. Exhausted from the long week, they agree, and so we set up the game on the carpet in the front room—Tiffin lying on his front with his head propped up on his hand, his blond mane hanging in his eyes; Willa cross-legged at the foot of the couch, an enormous new hole in her red school tights revealing part of an even larger bandage.

"What happened to you?" I ask, pointing.

"I fell!" she announces, her eyes lighting up in anticipatory relish as she begins her account of the drama. "It was very, very serious. My knee gashed open and there was blood all down my leg and the nurse said we was gonna have to go to the hospital to get stitches!" She glances at Tiffin to make sure she has a cap-

TABITHA SUZUMA

tive audience. "I hardly cried much at all. Only till the end of break time. The nurse said I was really brave."

"You had stitches!" I stare at her, appalled.

"No, cuz after a while the blood stopped gushing out, so the nurse said she thought it would be okay. She kept trying to call Mum, but I told her and told her it was the wrong number."

"What d'you mean, 'the wrong number'?"

"I kept telling her that she had to call you or Lochie instead, but she didn't listen, even when I told her I knew the numbers by heart. She just left a lot of messages on Mum's mobile. And she asked me if I had a granny or a grandpa who could come and pick me up instead."

"Oh God, let me see. Does it still hurt?"

"Only a bit. No—ow—don't take the bandage off, Maya! The nurse said I have to leave it on!"

"Okay, okay," I say quickly. "But next time, you tell the nurse she has to call me or Lochie. You say she has to, Willa, okay? She has to!" I suddenly find myself almost shouting.

Willa nods distractedly, intent on setting out the pieces of the game now that the account of her drama is over. But Tiffin is looking at me solemnly, his blue eyes narrowing.

"Why does school always have to call you or Lochan?" he asks quietly. "Are you secretly our real parents?"

Shock runs like icy water through my veins. I am unable

to draw breath for a moment. "No, of course not, Tiffin. We're just a lot older than you, that's all. What—what on earth made you think that?"

Tiffin continues to fix me with his penetrating stare and I find myself literally holding my breath, waiting for him to comment on what he witnessed this morning.

"Cuz Mum's never here no more. Even hardly on weekends. She's got a new family now at Dave's house. She lives there and she's even got new kids."

I stare at him, sadness seeping through me. "It's not her new family," I attempt at last in desperation. "They only stay over on the weekend and they're Dave's children, not hers. We're her children. She just spends lots of time there at the moment because she works so late—it's dangerous for her to come home in the middle of the night on her own."

My heart is beating too fast. I wish Lochan were here to say the right thing. I don't know how to explain it to them. I don't know how to explain it to myself.

"Then how come she's never even here on weekends anymore?" Tiffin asks, his voice suddenly sharp with anger. "How come she never takes us to school or picks us up like she used to on her day off?"

"Because—" My voice wavers. I know I'm going to have to lie here. "Because she now works on weekends, too, and doesn't take days off during the week anymore. It's just so she can earn more money to buy nice things for us."

Tiffin gives me a long hard look, and with a start I see the teenager he will be in a few years' time. "You're lying," he says in a low voice. "All of you are lying." He gets up and rushes off upstairs.

I sit there, paralyzed with fear, guilt, and horror. I know I should go up after him, but what can I possibly say? Willa is pulling at my sleeve, demanding to be played with, the conversation thankfully lost on her. And so I pick up the pieces with an unsteady hand and start to play.

As time passes, the morning when I fainted begins to feel like a dream, slowly evaporating from the coils of my mind. I don't try touching Lochan again. I keep telling myself that this is only temporary—just until things calm down with Tiffin and he starts to focus on other things and gets back to his usual cheeky self. It doesn't take him long, but I know the memory is still there, along with the doubt, and the hurt, and the confusion. And that is enough to keep me from reaching out to Lochan.

The Christmas nightmare begins: Nativity plays; costumes to be made from scratch; a disco for Lochan's grade, of which Lochan is the only pupil not to attend. Then everyone breaks up and Christmas is upon us, the house decorated with streamers and tinsel that Lochan nicked from school. It takes the combined efforts of all five of us to carry the tree home from the high street, and Willa gets a pine needle in her eye, and for a few dreadful moments we think we'll have to take her to the hospital, but Lochan finally manages to remove it. Tiffin and Willa adorn the tree with home- and school-made decorations, and even though the end result is a great lopsided, glittery mess, it cheers us all up tremendously. Even Kit deigns to join in with the preparations, although he spends most of his time trying to prove to Willa that Santa isn't real. Mum gives us our Christmas money and I go shopping for Willa while Lochan takes care of Tiffin—a system we devised one unfortunate year when I bought Tiffin a pair of soccer gloves with a pink stripe down the side. Kit only wants money, but Lochan and I get him the pair of ridiculously expensive designer sneakers he's been banging on about for ages. On Christmas Eve we wait till we hear him softly snoring before placing the wrapped box at the foot of his ladder with the words "From Santa" written on it for good measure.

Mum makes an appearance late Christmas morning, when the turkey is already in the oven. She has presents too—mostly secondhand stuff that Dave's children have grown tired of: Legos and toy cars for Tiffin, despite the fact that he stopped playing with such things some time ago; a second copy of

TABITHA SUZUMA

Bambi on DVD for Willa, along with a grubby Teletubby, which she gazes at with a mixture of confusion and horror. Kit gets some old video games that don't work with his console but that he reckons he can sell at school. I get a dress several sizes too big that looks as if it probably once belonged to Dave's ex-wife, and Lochan is the proud new owner of an encyclopedia, generously adorned with obscene drawings. We all make the appropriate exclamations of joy and surprise, and Mum sits back on the couch, pours herself a large glass of cheap wine, lights up a cigarette, and pulls Willa and Tiffin onto her lap, her face already flushed with alcohol.

Somehow we survive the day. Dave is spending the occasion with his family, and Mum passes out on the couch just before six. Tiffin and Willa are cajoled into bed early by being allowed to take their presents with them, and Kit disappears upstairs with his video games to start wheeling and dealing. Lochan offers to clean up the kitchen, and to my shame, I let him do it and collapse into bed, thankful that the day is at an end.

It is almost a relief when school starts up again. Lochan and I both have exams, and keeping Tiffin and Willa amused every day for two weeks has taken its toll. We return to school exhausted and admire the new iPods, mobiles, designer clothes, and laptops that surround us. At lunch, Lochan walks past my table. "Meet me on the stairs," he whispers. Francie lets out a loud wolf whistle as he moves away and I swing round in time to see his face turn crimson.

Up here the wind is almost a gale, cutting right through me like slivers of ice. I have no idea how Lochan can bear it, day after day. He is hugging himself against the cold, his teeth chattering, his lips tinged with blue.

"Where's your coat?" I reproach him.

"I forgot it in the usual morning rush."

"Lochan, you're going to catch pneumonia and die! Would you at least go read in the library, for God's sake?"

"I'm okay." He is so cold, he can barely talk. But on a day like this, half the school is crammed into the library.

"What's up? I thought you didn't like me coming up here. Has something happened?"

"No, no." He bites his lip in an attempt to hold back a smile. "I've got something for you."

I frown, confused. "What?"

He reaches into his blazer pocket and brings out a small silver box. "It's a late Christmas present. I wasn't able to get it till now. And I didn't want to give it to you at home because, you know . . ." His voice tails off awkwardly.

I take it from him slowly. "But we made a pact ages ago," I protest. "Christmas is for the kids. We don't waste any more money than we have to, remember?"

 TABITHA SUZUMA

"I wanted to break the pact this year." He looks excited, his eyes on the box, willing me to open it.

"But then you should have told me. I didn't get you anything!"

"I didn't want you to get me anything. I didn't tell you because I wanted it to be a surprise."

"But—"

He takes me by the shoulders and gives me a gentle shake, laughing. "Aargh! Would you just open it?"

I grin. "Okay, okay! But I still object to this pact breaking without my consent. . . ." I lift the lid. "Oh . . . God . . . Lochie . . ."

"Do you like it?" He is practically bouncing on his toes, grinning in delight, a glow of triumph shining from his eyes. "It's solid silver," he informs me proudly. "It should fit you perfectly. I took the measurement from the mark on your watch strap."

I continue to stare into the box, aware I haven't moved or spoken for several moments. The silver bracelet lying there against the black velvet is the most exquisite thing I have ever seen. Made up of intricate loops and swirls, it sparkles as it catches the white light of the winter sun.

"How did you pay for this?" My voice is a shocked whisper.

"Does it matter?"

"Yes!"

He hesitates for a moment; the glow fades and he lowers his eyes. "I've—I've been saving. I had a kind of job—"

I look up from the beautiful bracelet, incredulous. "A job? What? When?"

"Well, it wasn't a real job." The light has gone from his eyes and he sounds embarrassed now. "I offered to write some essays for a few people and it kind of caught on."

"You did people's homework for money?"

"Yeah. Well, essays, mostly." He looks down sheepishly.

"Since when?"

"Beginning of last term."

"You've been saving for this for four months?"

His shoes scuff at the ground and his eyes refuse to meet mine. "At first it was just extra money for—you know—household stuff. But then I thought about Christmas and how you hadn't had a present for—forever. . . ."

I'm finding it hard to catch my breath. It's a struggle to take all this in. "Lochan, we have to return this immediately and get your money back."

"We can't." His voice wavers.

"What d'you mean?"

He turns the bracelet over. On the inside are the words "Maya, love you forever. Lochan x."

I stare at the engraving, numb with shock, the silence

between us punctuated only by distant shouts from the play-ground.

Lochan says quietly, "I thought—it shouldn't be too loose, so no one will be able to see the engraving. And if you're wor-ried, you could always just keep it hidden at home. L-like a lucky charm or something. I mean, only—only if you like it, of course. . . ." His voice trails off into silence again.

I cannot move.

"It was probably a silly idea." He's talking very fast now, tripping over his words. "It's—it's probably not what you'd have picked out for yourself—guys have the worst taste in this kind of thing. I should have waited and asked you. I should have let you choose, or got something more useful like, um, like—like . . ."

I drag my eyes away from the bracelet again. Despite the cold, Lochan's cheeks look hot with embarrassment, his eyes radiating disappointment. "Maya, look, it really doesn't matter. You don't need to wear it or anything. You—you could just keep it hidden at home—for the engraving." He gives me an unsteady smile, desperate to shrug the whole thing off.

I shake my head slowly, swallow hard, and force myself to speak. "No, Lochie, no. It's—it's the most beautiful thing I've ever owned. It's the most incredible present I've ever been given. And the engraving . . . I'm going to wear it all my life. I just can't believe you did this. Just for me. All that work, night after night. I thought you were going crazy about exams or something. But it was all just to—just to give me—" I can't finish the sentence and, holding tightly on to the box, lean toward him, my face pressed against his chest.

I hear him exhale in relief. "Hey, you know, the polite thing to do is smile and say thank you!"

"Thank you," I whisper against him, but the words mean nothing compared to what I feel.

He takes the box and lifts my arm from my side. I feel him reach round me and push up the sleeve of my coat. After a few moments of fumbling, I feel the cool silver against my skin.

"Hey, how's that? Take a look at it," he says proudly.

I take a deep breath, blinking back tears. The intricate silver round my wrist gleams. Against my pulse point rest the words "love you forever." Yet I already know that he will.

I wear the bracelet all the time. I only ever take it off in the safety of my own room, resting it in the palm of my hand and gazing, enraptured, at the engraving. At night I sleep with the curtains partially opened so the moonlight catches against the metal, making it sparkle. In the dark I feel its indentations with my lips, as if kissing it brings me closer to Lochan.

On Saturday evening Mum surprises us by slamming into

TABITHA SUZUMA

the house, her makeup running, hair wet with rain. "Oh, you're all here," she says with a sigh, making no attempt to hide her disappointment, standing in the doorway of the front room in an oversize man's anorak, fishnet stockings, and tottery heels. Tiffin is practicing headstands on the couch, Willa is sprawled out on the carpet gazing dully at the TV, and I'm attempting to finish my history homework on the coffee table. Kit is already out with his mates and Lochan is upstairs, studying.

"Mummy!" Willa leaps up and runs over, holding up her arms for a hug. Mum pats her on the head without looking down, and Willa settles for hugging her legs instead.

"Mum, Mum, look what I can do!" Tiffin shouts triumphantly, launching himself into an aerial somersault and knocking my pile of books to the floor.

"How come you're not at Dave's?" I ask her acerbically.

"He had to go and rescue his ex-wife," she replies, her lip curling in disgust. "Apparently she's now an agoraphobic or something. More like a chronic attention seeker, if you ask me."

"Mummy, let's go out somewhere. Please!" Willa begs, hanging on to her leg.

"Not now, sweetie pie. It's raining and Mummy's very tired."

"You could take them to the movies," I suggest quickly. "*Superheroes* starts in fifteen minutes. I was going to take them, but since they haven't seen you in over two weeks . . ."

"Yeah, Mum! *Superheroes* sounds cool—you'll love it! Everyone in my class has seen it." Tiffin's face lights up.

"And popcorn!" Willa begs, jumping up and down. "I love popcorn! And Coke!"

Mum manages a tight smile. "Kids, I've got a splitting headache and I've only just got in."

"But you've been at Dave's for two whole weeks!" Tiffin suddenly shouts, his face puce.

She flinches slightly. "Okay, okay. Fine." She shoots me an angry look. "You do realize I've been working for the past two weeks, right?"

I stare back at her coldly. "So have we."

She turns on her heel, and after an argument over an umbrella, furious yells about a missing coat, and anguished wails about someone's foot being stepped on, the front door bangs shut. I drop my head back against the edge of the couch and close my eyes. After a moment I open them again and smile. They've gone. They've all gone. This is too good to be true. We finally have the house to ourselves.

I tiptoe upstairs, my heart rate picking up. I'm going to surprise him. Creep up behind him, slide onto his lap, and announce our unexpected window of freedom with a long, deep kiss. Poised outside his bedroom door, I hold my breath and gently turn the handle.

Slowly I push the door ajar. Then I stop. He is not at his desk, head bent over his book, as I expected. Instead he's by the window, one hand fiddling intently with the broken mobile he still thinks he can salvage, the other trying to pull off a sock as he wobbles precariously on one leg. He is half turned away from me, so he hasn't noticed me behind the door, and I watch him in amusement as he struggles to remove his other sock, eyes still fixed on the phone's cracked screen. Then, with a sigh of annoyance, he chucks it onto his bed and, grabbing his T-shirt, pulls it swiftly over his head, his hair emerging comically tousled. Spotting the towel slung over the back of his chair, I realize he is about to take a shower and start to draw back, when something stops me. I'm suddenly struck by how much his body has changed. Always on the skinny side, he has now become more muscular. A slight curve of the biceps, his chest smooth and hairless, not exactly a six-pack but the hint of definition in his stomach . . .

Sneaking up behind him, I slide my arms around his waist and feel him tense.

"She's taken them out," I whisper in his ear.

He turns in my arms and suddenly we are kissing hard, frantically—no one to stop us, no limit on our time. But instead of making us languorous, it adds a new element of excitement and urgency to the situation. Lochan's hands shake as he cups my face in them. Between kisses, he pants gently against my cheek and the pain of longing pulses through my whole body. He kisses every part of my face, my ears, my neck. I run my hands up and down the warmth of his bare chest, his arms, his shoulders. I want to feel every part of his body. I want to inhale him. I want him so much, it hurts. He is kissing me so fiercely now that he hardly gives me time to draw breath. His hands are in my hair, against my neck, beneath my collar. His bare skin tingles beneath my touch. But there are still too many clothes, too many obstacles, between our two bodies. I slip my hand under the top of his jeans. "Wait . . ." I whisper.

His breath shudders against my ear and he tries to kiss my neck, but I push him gently away. "Wait," I tell him. "Stop for a second. I have to concentrate."

As I lower my head, I feel his body tauten in frustration and surprise. I force myself to focus on what I'm doing, careful not to rush. I don't want to get this wrong, make a mistake, make a fool of myself, hurt him. . . .

Undoing the button is easy. Sliding down the zipper is less so—on the first try, it sticks and I have to draw it back up before sliding it down all the way. But suddenly Lochan is grabbing me by the wrists, wrenching back my hands.

"What are you doing?" He sounds incredulous, almost angry.

"Shh . . ." I return to his open trousers.

"Maya, no!" He is panting hard, a frantic edge to his voice. His hands are between mine now, trying to zip himself up again, but his fingers are fumbling, shaking in shock.

Pulling back the waistband of his boxers, I slide my fingers inside and feel a rush of elation as I make contact. It feels surprisingly warm and hard. With a small gasp, Lochan buckles forward, sucking in his breath, tensing and staring at me with a look of complete astonishment, as if he has forgotten who I am, the color flooding his cheeks, his breathing fast and shallow. Then, with a small cry, he grabs me by the shoulders and shoves me backward.

"What the hell are you doing?"

I recoil, speechless, as he grapples with his fly. He is yelling at the top of his voice, literally shaking with rage. "What the fuck's wrong with you? What the hell were you trying to do? You know we can never ever—"

"I'm sorry," I gasp. "I—I only—I only wanted to touch—"

"This whole thing's completely out of hand!" he screams at me, the cords standing out in his neck. "You're just sick, you know that? This whole thing's just sick!" He pushes past me, his face red, and slams into the bathroom. Moments later I hear the shower running.

Downstairs in the front room, I pace the floor, breathing hard, anger and guilt coursing through me in equal measures.

Anger at the way he just screamed at me. Guilt at not having stopped when he first told me to. Still, I don't understand; I just don't understand. I thought we'd decided not to bother with what other people thought. I thought we'd decided we would be together no matter what. I hadn't been trying to trick him into anything. I'd just suddenly felt the overwhelming urge to touch him everywhere, even there—especially there. But fear now tugs at my throat, my shoulders, my chest. Fear that I've ruined what I thought we had.

The sound of his feet pounding on the stairs makes me back into the farthest corner of the room. But from the hall I hear only the jangle of keys, the squeak of trainers, the zip of a jacket. And then the front door bangs.

I stand there stunned. Appalled. I was expecting a confrontation of some sort, the chance to offer an explanation at the very least. Instead he has just gone off and left me. I won't accept this; I won't. It's not like I've done anything so terrible.

I shove my feet into my shoes and grab my school coat. Without even bothering to stop for my keys, I run out of the house. I can just make out his figure disappearing into the wet darkness at the end of our street. I break into a run.

When the sound of my footsteps reaches him, he veers off across the road, lengthening his stride still further. Even as I draw level with him, straining for breath, he raises his arm and knocks away my outstretched hand.

"Just leave it, will you? Just go back and leave me the hell alone!"

"Why?" I shout back, gasping in icy air as the rain lances my hair and face with sharp, wet needles. "What on earth have I done that's so awful? I crept up to surprise you. I wanted to tell you that Mum had come back and I'd cornered her into taking the kids to the movies. When we started kissing, I just wanted to touch—"

"D'you realize how fucking stupid that was? How danger-ous? You can't just suddenly do stuff like that!"

"Lochie, I'm sorry. I thought we could at least touch each other. It doesn't mean we would have gone any further—"

"Oh, really? Well, you can forget your fucking fairy tale! Welcome to the real world!" He turns briefly—long enough for me to make out a face mottled with fury. "If I hadn't stopped it, d'you realize what would have happened? It's not just dis-gusting, Maya—it's fucking illegal!"

"Lochie, that's crazy! Just because we can't have sex doesn't mean we can't touch each other and—" I reach out for him but he shoves my arm away again. Abruptly he turns down the alley toward the cemetery, only to find a padlocked fence at the end. With nowhere to go, he still refuses to turn back toward me. Standing in the middle of the rain-soaked road, my hair whipping against my face, I watch him grab the wire-mesh fence, shake it dementedly, punch it with both hands, kick at it wildly.

"You're crazy, you know that?" I scream at him, my fear suddenly replaced with anger. "Why would this have been such a big deal? How would this have been any different from what happened that time on the bed?"

He whirls round, crashing violently back into the fence. "Well, maybe that was a fucking mistake too! But at least—at least then one of us wasn't half undressed! And I'd have never— I'd have never let it go any further—"

"I wasn't planning to this time!" I exclaim in astonishment.

He sags back against the netting suddenly, the fury dissipating into the night like the white breath from our mouths.

"I can't do this anymore," he says, his voice hoarse and broken, and abruptly my anger is joined by a cold rush of fear. "It's too painful; it's too dangerous. I'm terrified—I'm just terrified of what we might end up doing."

His despair feels almost tangible, draining the frozen air around us of every last shred of hope. I wrap my arms around myself and begin to shiver.

"So what are you saying?" My voice begins to rise. "If we can't have sex, you'd rather we did nothing at all?"

TABITHA SUZUMA

"I guess so." He stares at me, his green eyes suddenly hard in the lamplight. "Let's face it—this is all pretty sick. Maybe the rest of the world's right. Maybe we're just a couple of fucked-up, emotionally disturbed teenagers who just—"

He breaks off, pushing himself away from the fence as I slowly back away from him, pain and horror rushing through me like liquid ice.

"Maya, wait—I didn't mean that." His expression changes abruptly and he approaches me cautiously with his arm outstretched as if I'm a wild animal, ready to flee. "I—I didn't mean that. I—I'm not thinking straight. I got carried away. I need to calm down. Let's just go somewhere and talk. Please . . ."

I shake my head and move in a wide arc around him, suddenly breaking away and hurling myself through a gap at the edge of the mesh.

Once inside the cemetery, I turn into the bitter wind, heading up the darkened, cracked path littered with the usual beer bottles, cigarette stubs, and syringes. The glow of the street lamps reaches me from a great distance, the sound of traffic fading to a distant murmur, the outlines of abandoned, broken gravestones nothing more than amorphous shapes in the dark. I can't believe this is happening. I can't. I trusted him. I try to make sense of what just happened, to process Lochan's words without completely falling apart. To somehow accept that the magic of that one night when we first kissed and the afternoon in my room was, to him, simply a dreadful, perverted mistake, to be filed away at the back of our minds until we can eventually kid ourselves it never happened. I need to try to absorb Lochan's true feelings about the situation—the feelings he has been hiding from me since this first started. And I need to work out how to survive this sudden revelation. But how can anything hurt so much? How can just those few words make me want to curl up and die?

"Maya, come on." I hear his feet thudding on the path behind me and a scream begins to build in my throat. I have to be alone right now or I will lose my mind. I will.

"You know I didn't mean any of that stuff! I was just embarrassed that I—that I nearly . . . you know. I was just scared of my own feelings, of what we might have done!" He looks frantic and wild. "Please, just come back to the house. The others will be back in a minute and they'll be worried."

The fact that he thinks he can appeal to my sense of duty shows how little he understands the effect of his earlier words, the violence of the emotions coursing through me.

He tries to grab my arm.

"Get off me!" I scream, my voice magnified in the silence of the cemetery.

He recoils as if he's been shot, shielding his face from the hysteria in my voice. "Maya, just try to calm down," he begs me, his voice shaking. "If anyone hears us, they'll—"

"They'll what?" I interrupt aggressively, whipping round to face him.

"They'll think—"

"Think what?"

"They might think I'm attacking—"

"Oh, it's all about you!" I scream at him, sobs threatening to explode in my throat. "This whole thing—it's always been about you! What will people think? How will I look? How might I be judged? Whatever feelings once existed between us clearly mean nothing to you compared to your pathetic fear of other people's narrow-minded, bigoted, parochial prejudices that you once despised but now adopt as your own!"

"No!" he yells desperately, launching himself after me as I start striding off again. "It's not like that—it's got nothing to do with that! Maya, please listen to me. You don't understand! I just said those things because I feel like I'm going crazy—seeing you every day but never being able to—to hold you, to touch you, when anyone else is around. I just want to take your hand, kiss you, hug you, without having to hide it all the time. All those little things every other couple just takes for granted! I want to be free to do them without being terrified that some-one will catch us and force us apart, call the police, take the

kids away, destroy everything. I can't bear it, don't you understand? I want you to be my girlfriend; I want us to be free—"

"Fine!" I scream, tears springing from my eyes. "If it's all so
sick and twisted, if it's causing you so much grief, then you're
right, we should just end it, right here, right now! That way at
least you won't have to walk around with some awful guilty
conscience, thinking how disgusting we are for having these
feelings for each other!" Frantic now to get away, I break into
a stumbling run.

"For chrissakes!" he yells after me. "Didn't you hear what I
said? That's the last thing I want!"

He tries to grab me again, tries to force me to slow down,
but I can't—I'm going to fall apart, break down in tears, and I
refuse to have him or anyone else as my witness.

Spinning round, I slam my hands against his chest and push
him as hard as I can. "Just get away from me!" I scream. "Why
can't you just leave me alone for five minutes? Please go home!
You're right—we should never have started this! So get away
from me! Just give me some space and time to think!"

His eyes are frantic, his expression stricken. "But I was
wrong! Why won't you listen to me? What I said was bullshit—
I just lashed out in frustration. This is not what I want!"

"Well, it's what I want!" I shriek. "God forbid you should
stay with me out of pity! Everything you said is true: We're

TABITHA SUZUMA

sick, we're twisted, we're deranged, and we have to end this now! So what the hell are you still doing here? Go home to your normal, socially acceptable life and we'll pretend nothing ever happened!"

I've completely lost it. Hammers pound against my skull and red lights zigzag in the darkness. But I'm afraid that if I don't keep screaming at him in blind fury, I'm going to collapse in tears. And I don't want him to see that. The last thing I want is for him to feel sorry for me, to feel he has to pretend to be in love with me, to realize I can't live without him.

With a desperate cry, he moves toward me, reaching out for me again. I take a step back. "I mean it, Lochan! Go home! Don't touch me or I'll shout for help!"

He withdraws his outstretched arm and steps back in defeat. Tears fill his eyes. "Maya, what the hell d'you want me to do?"

I take an uneven breath. "Just go," I say softly.

"But don't you understand?" he says in quiet despair. "I want to be with you, no matter what. I love you—"

"But not enough."

We stare at each other. His hair is ruffled by the wind, his green eyes luminous in the darkness, the zip of his black jacket broken, revealing his gray T-shirt beneath. He shakes his head, his eyes scanning the dark cemetery around us as if searching for help. He looks back at me and a harsh sob escapes him. "Maya, that's not true!"

"You just called our love sick and disgusting, Lochan," I remind him quietly.

He claws at the sides of his face. "But I didn't mean it!" His chin starts to tremble.

A sharp pain rises through me, filling my lungs, my throat, my head—so sharp that I think I might collapse. "Then why would you say it? You meant it, and now so do I. You're right, Lochan. You've made me see this whole sordid mess for what it is. Just a terrible mistake. We were both just bored, disturbed, lonely, frustrated—whatever. We were never in love—"

"But we were!" His voice cracks. He screws up his eyes and presses his fist against his mouth to muffle a sob. "We are!"

I look at him, numb. "Then how come it's gone?"

He stares at me, aghast, tears wet on his cheeks. "W-what are you talking about?"

I take a steadying breath, bracing myself against an onslaught of tears. "I mean, Lochan, how come I don't love you anymore?"

CHAPTER SEVENTEEN

Lochan

Something inside me has broken. There are moments during the day when I just grind to a halt and simply cannot find the energy to draw another breath. I stand there immobile, in front of the cooker, or in class, or listening to Willa read, and all the air exits my lungs and I cannot muster the strength to fill them again. If I keep breathing, then I have to keep living, and if I keep living, then I have to keep hurting, and I can't—not like this. I try to divide the day up into sections, take it one hour at a time: get through first period, then second, then break, then third, then lunch. . . . At home the hours are broken down into housework, homework supervision, dinner, bedtime, studying, bed. It's the only time I've ever been grateful for the relentless routine. It keeps me going from one section to the next, and when I start to think too far ahead and feel myself crumble, I manage to reel myself in by telling myself, *Just one more section,* and then *Just one more after that.* Get through today—you can fall apart tomorrow. Get through tomorrow, you can fall apart the day after. . . .

When Maya told me she no longer loved me, I had no choice but to retreat, to retract. At first I told myself it was said in anger, a reaction to my own stupid words—my inane declaration that it had all been a sick mistake—but now I know differently. I play and replay that phrase in my head, wondering where on earth it came from when I never believed it for a single moment. It must have been the anger of the moment, my embarrassment and shame—shame at wanting more than I could ever have—that made me blurt out the most hurtful, hateful thing that came to mind. Instead of coping with my own misery and frustration, I'd turned on Maya, as if by blaming her I could absolve myself. . . .

But now, through my own stupidity and selfish cruelty, I have lost everything, degraded everything, even our friendship. Despite the sadness in her eyes, Maya has been very good at going back to normal, pretending everything is fine, being friendly while keeping her distance. No awkwardness that might alarm the others—in fact, she is almost cheerful. So cheerful that at times I even wonder whether she is not secretly relieved it's all over, whether she actually does believe it was all a sick mistake, an aberration, born out of physical need. She has stopped loving me; Maya has stopped loving me. . . . And this one thought is slowly eating away at my mind.

Concentrating at school has long become a thing of the past; now, to my horror, teachers notice me, and for all the wrong reasons. I barely manage half a page of trigonometry before realizing I have been sitting immobile, staring into space, for the best part of an hour. They ask me if I'm all right, if I need to see the nurse, what it is I don't understand. I shake my head and avoid meeting their eyes, but without the counterbalance of top grades, my reticence is no longer acceptable, and so they summon me to the front, demanding answers to questions on the board, afraid that I am falling behind, that I am going to let them down by failing to gain an A in their subject this spring. Summoned to the whiteboard in front of the whole class, I fumble my way through easy questions, make stupid mistakes, and watch the bewildered horror spread across the teachers' faces as I return to my desk amid jeers and laughter, all too conscious of the sniggers of satisfaction that Weirdo Whitely has finally lost the plot.

In English we are doing *Hamlet*. I've read it a number

of times, so I don't feel the need to even pretend to focus. Besides, Miss Azley and I have had a tacit agreement ever since her unfortunate pep talk: She does not pick on me in class so long as I volunteer an answer once in a while, usually to help her out when no one else can come up with even the most asinine response. But today I am not playing ball; the double lesson is well into its second hour and the now-familiar ache in my chest has morphed into a stabbing pain. I drop my pen and stare out the window, watching a length of broken TV cable twist and writhe in the wind.

". . . according to Freud, the personal crisis undergone by Hamlet awakens in him repressed incestuous desires." Miss Azley waves the book in the air and paces to and fro in front of the class, trying to keep everyone awake. I feel her gaze pause on the back of my head and I snap round from the window.

"Which brings us to the Oedipus complex, a term coined by Freud himself at the beginning of the twentieth century."

"You mean when a guy wants to have sex with his mum?" someone asks, voice sick with disgust.

Suddenly Miss Azley has the class's attention. Everyone is buzzing.

"But that's mental! Why would any guy want to fuck his own mum?"

"Yeah. You hear about it on the news and stuff, though.

Mums who fuck their sons, dads who fuck their daughters and their sons. Brothers and sisters who fuck each other—"

"Language, please!" Miss Azley protests.

"That's bullshit. Who would want to fuck—sorry, screw—their own parents?"

"It's called incest, man."

"That's when a guy rapes his sister, dickhead."

There is a light flashing in my brain, like the headlamp of a train in the dark.

"No, it's—"

"Okay, okay, we're getting off topic here! Now remember, this is only one interpretation and has been refuted by many critics." As she stops to perch on the edge of her desk, Miss Azley's eyes suddenly meet mine. "Lochan, nice to have you back with us. What do you think about Freud's assertion that the Oedipus complex was Hamlet's primary motive for killing his uncle?"

I stare at her. I'm suddenly deeply afraid. Through the instant silence, my face is scorched by an invisible flame. Gripped by panic bordering on hysteria, I worry, with a sickening lurch, that perhaps it is no coincidence Miss Azley has chosen me to open this discussion. When was the last time she picked on me to answer anything? When has the subject of incest ever come up before? Her eyes drill into mine, burning holes straight through to my brain. She isn't smiling. No, this is planned—contrived, premeditated, and deliberate. She is waiting for my reaction. . . . I suddenly recall how I ran into her outside the nurse's office after Maya's fall. She must have been there, helped bring her round, asked her questions. Maya hit her head, was possibly even suffering from a concussion. What reason did she give for her faint? How much time elapsed between her fall and my arrival? In her confused state, what might Maya have said?

The eyes of the class are upon me. Every single person has turned round in their seat to gape. They, too, appear to be in on it somehow. It is all one giant setup.

"Lochan?" Miss Azley has moved away from her desk. She is walking rapidly toward me, but for some extraordinary reason I cannot move. Time has stopped; time is racing. My desk rattles against me as if the ground is being shaken by an earthquake. My ears fill up with water and I focus on the humming in my head, the electric grid of my mind snapping and flashing with light. A strange sound fills the room. Everyone is frozen, staring, waiting to see what will happen next, what terrible fate awaits me. Perhaps social services is already in the school. The world outside swells and presses in at the walls, trying to reach me, trying to eat me alive. I can't believe it. I can't believe it's happening like this. . . .

"You need to come with me, Lochan, okay?" Miss Azley's

voice is firm but not unkind. Perhaps she even feels some degree of pity. I am, after all, sick. Sick as well as evil. Maya herself told me that's what our love was.

Miss Azley's hands cuff my wrists. "Can you stand? No? Okay, just sit where you are. Reggie, would you run and fetch Mrs. Shah and ask her to come immediately? The rest of you—library, right now, in silence please."

The requiem of scraping chairs and clattering feet drowns me. Flashes of blinding color and light. Miss Azley's face blurs and fades before me. She is summoning the nurse, the other person involved in rescuing Maya from her fall. But something else is happening too. Beneath my arm, my desk continues to rattle. I look around, and everything appears to be moving, the walls of the emptying classroom threatening to topple down on us like a pack of cards. My heart keeps stopping and starting every few seconds, knocking wildly against the cage of my chest. Each time it stops, I feel this terrifying emptiness before the contraction returns with a flutter, then a violent thud. Oxygen is being drained from the room: My frantic efforts to breathe and remain conscious are in vain; darkness is slowly closing in. My shirt clings wetly to my back, rivulets of sweat running down my body, my neck, my face.

"Lovey, it's all right, it's all right! Sit still—don't struggle; you're going to be fine. Try to sit forward a bit. That's it. Put your elbows on your knees and lean forward and it'll help your breathing. No, you're fine where you are—hold still, and don't try to get up. Wait, wait—all I'm doing is removing your tie and undoing your collar. Leila, what are you still doing here?"

"Oh, miss, is he gonna die?" The voice is high-pitched with panic.

"Of course not—don't be silly! We're just waiting for Mrs. Shah to come and check him out. Lochan, listen to me now—are you asthmatic? Allergic to anything? Look at me— just nod or shake your head. . . . Oh, Christ. Leila, quickly, go through his bag, will you? See if you can find an inhaler or tablets or something. Check his coat and blazer pockets. Look in his wallet—see if you can find any kind of medical card. . . ."

She is acting very strangely, Miss Azley, as if she's still pretending—pretending she doesn't know. But I no longer have the strength to care. I just want this to stop. It's too painful, these electric shots being fired through my chest and into my heart, all the muscles in my body spasming out of control, rocking the chair and shaking the desk, my body surrendering to some greater force.

"Miss, miss, I can't find no inhaler or nothing! But he's got a sister in the year below—maybe she'll know?"

Leila is making these odd whimpering noises, like a dog being beaten. Yet when she moves away, the sounds grow closer.

TABITHA SUZUMA

It can't be Miss Azley, so there must be some animal cowering in the corner. . . .

"Lochan, hold my hand. Listen to me, love, listen. The nurse will be here any second, okay? Help is on its way."

Only when the whimpers intensify do I realize they are actually coming from my own mouth. I am suddenly aware of the sound of my voice, scratching against the thin air like a saw.

"Leila, yes, his sister, good idea. See if you can find her, will you?"

Time hiccups; it is either later or sooner, I can't tell which. The nurse has arrived, but I'm not sure why—I'm confused about everything now. Maybe I was wrong. Maybe they are actually trying to help me. Mrs. Shah's got a stethoscope in her ears and is pulling open my shirt. I immediately lash out but Miss Azley grabs my arms and I am too weak to even push her away.

"It's all right, Lochan," she says, her voice low and soothing. "The nurse is just trying to help you. She's not going to hurt you. Okay?"

The sawing noise continues. I throw back my head and screw up my eyes and bite down to stop it. The pain in my chest is excruciating.

"Lochan, can we get you off this chair?" the nurse is asking.

"Can you lie down on the floor so I can take a proper look at you?"

I cling to the desk. No. They are not going to pin me down.

"Should I call an ambulance?" Miss Azley is asking.

"It's just a bad panic attack—he's had them before. He's hyperventilating and his pulse is well over two hundred."

She gives me a paper bag to breathe into. I twist and turn and try to push it away, but I haven't the strength. I have surrendered. I'm not even trying to struggle anymore, but even so, the nurse has to ask Miss Azley to hold the bag over my nose and mouth.

I watch it inflate and then crumple in front of me. Inflate and crumple, inflate and crumple, the crackling sound of paper filling the air. I try desperately to push it away—it feels like they're suffocating me; there is no more oxygen left in the bag—but I have a dim recollection of breathing into a bag like this before and it helping.

"Okay, Lochan, just listen to me now. You were breathing much too fast and taking in far too much oxygen, which is why your body is reacting like this. Keep breathing into the bag. That's it—you're doing much better already. Try to slow your breathing down. It's just a panic attack, okay? Nothing more serious than that. You're going to be fine. . . ."

Breathing into the bag lasts forever, or it takes less than a

TABITHA SUZUMA

minute, a second, a millisecond; it takes so little time that it does not happen at all. I'm holding on to the side of my desk with my head resting against my outstretched arm. Everything is still shaking around me, the desk vibrating beneath my cheek, but it's getting easier to breathe—I am concentrating on regulating my breaths carefully now and the paper bag lies discarded by my side. The electric shocks seem to be less frequent, and I'm beginning to see and hear and feel things around me more clearly. Miss Azley is sitting beside me, her hand rubbing the back of my damp shirt. The nurse is kneeling on the floor, her finger and thumb cold against my wrist, the stethoscope dangling from her ears. I notice her brown hair is graying at the roots. I can make out a sheet of my own scrawled handwriting beneath my cheek. The sawing noise has faded, replaced by short, sharp sounds like hiccups, similar to the ones Willa makes after a long crying jag. The pain in my chest is lifting. My heart is steadier now—an aching, rhythmical thud.

"What happened?"

The familiar voice startles me and I struggle to sit up, my hand grasping feebly at the edge of the desk to stop myself from pitching forward. The jagged breaths intensify and I start shaking again. She's standing right in front of me, between the nurse and the teacher, her hands cupped over her nose and mouth, blue eyes huge with fright. Relief at seeing her floods through me and I reach out for her frantically, afraid she will suddenly walk away.

"Hey, Lochie, it's all right, it's all right, it's all right." She takes my hand in hers, gripping it tightly.

"What on earth happened?" she asks the nurse again, panic threading her voice.

"Nothing to worry about, love, just a panic attack. You can help by keeping nice and calm yourself. Why don't you sit with him for a bit?" Mrs. Shah snaps her medical bag shut and moves out of sight, followed by Miss Azley.

Nurse and teacher fade to the other side of the classroom, talking softly and rapidly between themselves. Maya pulls up a chair and sits down opposite me, her knees touching mine. She is pale with shock, her eyes, sharp and questioning, boring into mine.

Elbows on thighs, I look up at her and manage an unsteady smile. I want to make some kind of joke but it's too much effort to breathe and talk simultaneously. I try to stop shaking for Maya's sake and press my right fist to my mouth to muffle the hiccupping sounds. My left hand grips hers with all my strength, afraid to let go.

Stroking my clammy cheek and taking my right hand in hers, she draws it gently away from my mouth.

TABITHA SUZUMA

"Listen, you," she says, her voice full of concern. "What brought all this on?"

I think back to Hamlet and my whole conspiracy theory and realize with a jolt how ridiculous I was being.

"N-nothing." Breath. "Being stupid." I have to concentrate hard to get each word out between gasps, one cluster at a time. I feel my throat constrict, so I shake my head with a wry smile. "So stupid. I'm sorry—" I bite down hard on my lip.

"Stop being sorry, you idiot." She gives me a reassuring smile and strokes the inside of my hand. I find myself involuntarily clutching at her sleeve, afraid she is a mirage and will suddenly evaporate before my eyes.

The bell sounds, startling us both.

I feel my pulse start to race again. "Maya, d-don't go! Don't go just yet—"

"Lochie, I've no intention of going anywhere."

It's the closest we've been all week, the first time she's touched me since that terrible night in the cemetery. I swallow hard and gnaw at my lip, aware of the other two in the room, terrified I'm going to break down.

Maya notices. "Loch, it's all right. This has happened before. When you first started at Belmont, just after Dad left, remember? You're going to be fine. . . ."

But I don't want to be fine, not if it means she's going to

let go of my hand—not if it means we're going to go back to being polite strangers.

After a while we go down to the nurse's room. Mrs. Shah checks my pulse and blood pressure, hands me a leaflet on panic attacks and mental health issues. Yet again there is talk of seeing the school counselor, mention of exam pressure, the danger of overwork, the importance of getting enough sleep. . . . Somehow I make all the right noises, nod and smile as convincingly as I can, all the while holding myself tight like a coiled spring.

We walk home in silence. Maya offers me her hand but I decline—my legs are steadier now. She asks me if there was some trigger, but when I shake my head, she takes the hint and backs off.

At home I sit at the end of the couch. Right now, alone and uninterrupted, would be the perfect time for that conversation—the one where I apologize to her for what I said that night, explain again the reason for my crazy outburst, try to find out if she is still angry with me, while somehow making it clear that this is in no way an attempt to coerce her back into any kind of abnormal relationship. But I can't find the words, and I don't trust myself to utter a single thing. The aftershocks of the panic attack coupled with Maya's gentle concern have thrown me, and I feel as if I'm teetering on the edge of a precipice.

Being brought juice and a peeled apple cut into quarters

 TABITHA SUZUMA

like for Tiffin or Willa threatens to tip me over. Maya watches me from the doorway as I switch on and mute the TV, pick at my shirt cuff, pull at a loose button. I can tell how anxious she is from the way she fiddles with her earlobe, a characteristic sign of worry she shares with Willa.

"How are you feeling?"

I attempt a bright, cheerful smile and the ache in my throat intensifies. "Fine! It was just a stupid panic attack."

I want to laugh it off, but instead I feel a sudden tremor in my chin. I pull a face to disguise it.

Her smile fades. "Perhaps I should leave you in peace for a little while—"

"No!" The word comes out louder than I intended. Heat rushing to my face, I force a desperate smile. "I just mean, now that we've got some time off, perhaps we should—you know—hang out together, l-like old times. Unless, of course, you've got homework to do or something . . ."

A hint of amusement touches her lips. "Yeah, right. I'm not about to waste an afternoon off school on homework, Lochan James Whitely!"

Closing the door behind her, she curls up in the armchair. "So, what are we watching?"

I grab the remote and fumble with the buttons. "Uh—well—surely there's something other than CBeebies. . . . How about this?" I stop channel flicking when I reach an old episode of *Friends* and look at Maya for approval.

She gives me another of her sad smiles. "Great."

Canned laughter fills the room but neither of us seems able to join in. The episode drags on and on. I am painfully aware that the two of us, alone together, have absolutely nothing to say to each other. Has our friendship truly been shattered too?

I want to ask her, beg her, to tell me what's going on inside her head. I want to try to explain what was going on in my head that night, why I reacted like such a bastard. But I can't even turn to look at her. I feel her eyes, full of worry, on my face. And I'm sinking in a quicksand of despair.

"D'you want to talk about it?" Her voice, soft with concern, makes me start. Suddenly I'm aware of the pain from biting my lip, the weight of the tears that have slowly been accumulating in my eyes.

With a panicked breath I quickly shake my head, raising a hand to my face. I press my fingers briefly against my eyes and shake my head again dismissively. "I'm just feeling a bit weird from before." Straining to keep my voice steady, I can still hear its jagged edge. Turning, I force myself to meet her stricken gaze with a desperate smile. "But I'm fine now. It's nothing. Really."

After a moment's hesitation she gets up and comes over to

sit on the opposite end of the couch, one foot tucked beneath her, auburn wisps framing her pale face.

"Come on, silly—it's not nothing if it's making you cry." The words hang in the air, her concern swelling the silence.

"I'm not—it's not—" I reply hotly, cheeks ablaze. "It's just—I'm just—" I take a deep breath, frantic to deflect her worry, to pull myself together. The last thing I want is for her to know how devastated I am at having lost her, for her to feel any pressure to resume a relationship that, in her mind, is fundamentally wrong.

She hasn't moved. "You're just what?" she asks gently.

I clear my throat and raise my eyes to the ceiling, forcing a short, painful laugh. I run my sleeve rapidly across my eyes as, to my horror, a tear glances off my cheek.

"Do you want to try to go to sleep for a bit?"

The concern in her voice is killing me. "No. I don't know. I think—I think . . . Oh, for fuck sake—" Another tear falls down my cheek and I swipe at it furiously. "Shit! What is this?"

"Lochie, tell me. What happened? What happened at school?" Sounding aghast, she leans toward me, reaching out to touch me.

I immediately raise my arm to deflect her. "Just give me a minute!" I can't halt this—there's nothing I can do. My chest shudders with repressed sobs. I cup my hands over my face and try holding my breath.

"Lochie, it's going to be all right. Please don't . . ." Her voice is softly imploring.

The air bursts from my lungs. "Goddamn it, I'm trying, okay? I can't—I j-just can't seem able to—" I'm out of control now and it terrifies me. I don't want Maya to witness this. But neither do I want her to go. I need to get off this couch, out of this house, but my legs won't obey me. I'm trapped. I can feel the blind panic descending again.

"Hey, hey, hey." Maya firmly takes my hand in one of hers and cups my cheek with the other. "Shh. It's okay, it's okay. Just a buildup of stress, Lochie, that's all. Look at me. Look at me. Was it the argument? Was it? Can we talk about that a little bit?"

I'm too tired to fight anymore. I feel my torso crumple, slowly tilting toward her until the side of my head rests against hers, my hand covering my face. She strokes my hair and, reaching for my other hand, starts kissing my fingers.

"In—in the cemetery," I choke, closing my eyes. "Please just tell me the truth. W-what you said, was it—was it true?" I breathe deeply, hot tears escaping from beneath my lashes.

"God, Lochie, no," she gasps. "Of course it wasn't! I was just angry and upset!"

Relief floods through me, so strong it almost hurts. "Maya, Jesus, I thought it was all over. I thought I'd ruined everything."

I straighten up, breathing hard, rubbing my face fiercely. "I'm so sorry! All that horrible stuff I said. I just totally freaked out. I thought you wanted to—I thought you were going to—"

"I just wanted to touch you," she says quietly. "I know we can never go all the way. I know it's illegal. I know the kids could be taken away if anyone found out. But I thought we could still touch each other, still love each other in other ways."

I take a frantic breath. "I know. Me too. Me too! But we have to be so careful. We can't get carried away. We can't—we can't risk . . . The kids . . ."

I see the sadness in her eyes. It makes me want to scream. It's so unfair, so horribly unfair.

"Maybe one day, hey?" Maya says softly with a smile. "One day, when they've grown up, we can run away. Start anew. As a real couple. No longer brother and sister. Free from these awful ties."

I nod, desperately trying to share in some of her hope for the future. "Maybe. Yes."

She gives a tired smile and wraps her arms around my neck, resting her cheek against my shoulder.

"And until then we can still be together. We can hold each other and touch each other and kiss each other and be with each other in every other way."

I nod and smile through the tears, suddenly realizing how much we do have. "As well as the most important thing of all," I whisper.

The corner of her mouth twitches. "What's that then?"

Still smiling, I blink rapidly. "We can love each other." I swallow hard to ease the constriction in my throat. "There are no laws, no boundaries, on feelings. We can love each other as much and as deeply as we want. No one, Maya, no one can ever take that away from us."

TABITHA SUZUMA

CHAPTER EIGHTEEN

Maya

"How come it's you today?"

"Because Lochan's not feeling very well."

"Did he throw up?" Willa flicks her long fair hair back behind her shoulders and the tiny gold studs in her ears sparkle in the fading afternoon sun. Remnants of custard dapple the front of her pinafore and she is without her cardigan again.

"No, no. Nothing serious like that."

"Throwing up isn't serious. Mummy does it all the time."

Ignoring this last comment, I turn my attention to her clothes. "Willa, will you do up your coat? It's freezing!"

"Can't. The buttons are gone."

"All of them? You should have told me!"

"I did. Miss Pierce says I'm not allowed Sellotape on my book bag, too. She says I have to get a new one." She takes my hand and we cross the playground to the soccer area, where Tiffin is tearing around half undressed with a dozen other boys. "We're not allowed holes in our tights. I got told off in front of the whole assembly."

"Tiff! Time to go!" I yell as soon as he shoots past us. The game pauses briefly for a free kick and I yell again.

He glances over angrily. "Five more minutes!"

"No. We're going now. It's freezing, and you can play soccer at home with Jamie."

"But we're in the middle of a match!"

The game resumes and I try to get closer, nervously skirting the running, darting, yelling boys, their cheeks ablaze, eyes fixed on the ball, shouts echoing across the darkening playground. As he races past, I make a valiant grab for Tiffin, missing by miles. Behind me, Willa stands pressed up against the fence, coat flapping open, shivering hard.

"Tiffin Whitely! Home, now!" I shout at the top of my voice, hoping to embarrass him into submission. Instead, he dives into a tackle, wrong-footing his opponent and dribbling the ball toward the other side of the pitch at lightning speed. He pauses for a moment as a boy twice his size comes hurtling straight for him. Then he draws back his leg and shoots, the ball skimming the inside edge of the goalpost.

"Goal!" His hands punch the air. Whoops and yells join his own as his teammates rush up to slap him on the back. I give him a moment before diving in and dragging him out by the arm.

"I'm not going!" he screams at me as the game resumes behind us. "My team was winning! I scored the first goal!"

"I saw that and it was a great goal but it's getting dark. Willa is freezing and you've both got homework to do."

"But we always have to go straight home! How come the others are allowed to play? I'm sick of stupid homework! I'm sick of always being at home!"

"Tiffin, for God's sake, act your age and stop making a scene—"

"It's not fair!" The tip of his shoe suddenly makes violent contact with my shin. "I never get to do anything fun. I hate you!"

By the time we locate Tiffin's missing schoolbag and I get them both out of the playground, it's almost dark and Willa is so cold that her lips are purple. Tiffin stalks on ahead, his face puce, blond hair wild, deliberately trailing his coat on the ground to annoy me, kicking at the tires of parked cars in rage. My leg throbs painfully. *Four bloody hours till bedtime,* I think ruefully. Another hour before they are actually asleep. Five. My God, almost the length of a new school day. All I want is to reach that moment when the house goes quiet, when Kit finally turns down the rap and Tiffin and Willa stop bombarding me with requests. That moment when rushed, half-finished homework is pushed aside and Lochan is there, his smile tentative, his eyes bright, and anything, almost anything seems possible . . .

". . . so I don't think she wants to be my friend anymore," Willa finishes mournfully, her icy hand buried in mine.

"Mmm, never mind, I'm sure Lucy will change her mind tomorrow—she always does."

The small hand is suddenly wrenched from my own. "Maya, you're not listening!"

"I am, I am!" I protest quickly. "You said that—uh—Lucy didn't want to be your friend because—"

"Not Lucy—Georgia!" Willa cries woefully. "I told you yesterday that Lucy and me broke up because she stole my favorite purple pen, the one with the blue hearts on it, and she wouldn't give it back even though Georgia saw her take it!"

"Oh, that's right," I fumble, frantically trying to recall the conversation. "Your pen."

"You always forget everything these days, just like Mum did when she used to live at home," she mutters.

We walk on for a few minutes in silence. Guilt coils itself around me, cold and unforgiving as a snake. I try in vain to recall the saga of the missing pen and fail.

"Bet you don't even know who's my best friend now,"Willa says, throwing down the gauntlet.

"Course I do," I answer quickly. "It's—it's Georgia."

Willa shakes her head at the sidewalk in a gesture of defeat. "Nope."

"Well, then, it's Lucy, really, because I'm sure once she gives you back your pen, the two of you will—"

"It's no one!" Willa shouts suddenly, her voice cutting through the sharp air. "I don't even have a best friend!"

I stop and stare at her in astonishment. Willa has never shouted at me with such fury before.

I try to put my arm around her. "Willa, come on, you've just had a bad day—"

She pulls away. "No, I haven't! Miss Pierce gave me three gold stars and I got all my spellings right. I told you about it but all you said was 'Mmm.' You never listen to me anymore!"

Wrenching herself away from me, she breaks into a run. I catch up with her just as she rounds the corner into our street. Forcing her to face me, I squat down and try to hold her still. She sobs quietly, rubbing her face angrily with the palms of her hands.

"Willa, I'm sorry—I'm sorry, my darling, I'm so sorry. You're right. I haven't been listening properly and that was really mean of me. It's not that I'm not interested—it's not that I don't care. It's just that I've been so busy studying for my exams and I've got so much work and I've been so tired—"

"That's not true!" She gives a muffled sob and tears spill over her fingers, running down between the cracks. "You don't . . . listen . . . or play with me . . . as much . . . as you did . . . before. . . ."

I clutch at a nearby railing for support. "Willa, no—it's not that—I don't . . ." But even fumbling for excuses, I'm forced to confront the truth behind her words.

"Come here," I say at last, wrapping my arms tightly around her. "You're my favorite girl in the whole world and I love you so, so much. You're right. I haven't been listening to you properly because Lochie and I are always trying to sort out all the household things. But that's all boring stuff. From now on, I'm going to start having fun with you again. Okay?"

She nods and sniffs and wipes her hair away from her face. I pick her up and she wraps her arms and legs around me like a baby monkey. But through the warmth of her arms round my neck, the heat of her cheek against mine, I sense my words have left her unconvinced.

*　*　*

Despite the loud slap of shoes against the concrete steps, he does not lower his book. I stop halfway up the flight of steps and lean against the rail, waiting, the sounds of the playground rising up from below me. Still he refuses to look up, no doubt hoping whoever it is will ignore him and continue on his or her way. When it becomes clear that this is not going to happen, he glances briefly over the top of the paperback before almost dropping it in surprise. His face lights up with a slow smile. "Hey!"

"Hey yourself!"

He closes his book and looks at me expectantly. I stand there watching him, fighting back a grin. He clears his throat, suddenly shy, a flush creeping into his cheeks.

"What—um—what are you doing here?"

"I came to say hi."

He reaches for my hand and begins to get up, ready to move farther up the staircase, out of sight of the pupils in the playground below.

"It's all right—I'm not staying," I inform him quickly.

He stops and the smile fades. Registering the schoolbag on my back, the gym uniform slung over my shoulder, he looks concerned. "Where are you going?"

"I'm taking the afternoon off."

His eyes sharpen and his expression sobers. "Maya—"

"It's just one afternoon. I've only got art and crap."

He gives a worried sigh, looking bothered. "Yeah, but if you get caught, you know there could be trouble. We can't risk drawing any more attention to ourselves now that Mum's never around."

"We won't. Not if you come with me and use your pass."

He eyes me with a mixture of uncertainty and surprise. "You want me to come too?"

"Yes, please."

"I could just give you my pass," he points out.

"But then I wouldn't have the pleasure of your company."

The flush rises again, but the corner of his mouth pulls upward. "Mum said something about popping home today to pick up some clothes—"

"I wasn't thinking of going home."

"You want to walk the streets till three thirty? I haven't got any money on me."

"No. I want to take you somewhere."

"Where?"

"It's a surprise. Not far."

I can see his curiosity is roused. "O-okay—"

"Great. Go get your stuff. I'll meet you by the main entrance."

I disappear back down into the playground before he has time to start worrying again and change his mind.

Lochan takes forever. By the time he arrives, break is almost over and I fear he'll be questioned for leaving the building just before the bell. But the security guard barely glances at his pass as I slip unnoticed ahead of him through the glass doors.

Out on the street, Lochan turns up his jacket collar against the cold and asks, "Now are you going to tell me what all this is about?"

I smile and shrug. "It's about having an afternoon off."

"We should have planned this. I've only got fifty pence on me."

"I'm not asking you to take me to the Ritz! We're just going to the park."

"The park?" He looks at me as if I'm crazy.

Ashmoore on a weekday in the middle of winter is predictably empty. The trees are mostly bare, their long spiked branches silhouetted against the pale sky, the large expanses of grass splashed with silver patches of ice. We follow the wide central path toward the wooded area on the far side, the hum of the city gradually fading behind us. A few damp benches dot the empty landscape, abandoned and redundant. In the distance, an old man is throwing sticks for his dog, the animal's sharp yaps breaking the still air. The park feels vast and desolate—a cold, forgotten island in the middle of a big city. Curled sandpaper leaves skim across the path, carried by a whisper of wind. A scatter of pigeons dart excitedly around some crumbs, their heads bobbing up and down, pecking feverishly at the ground. As we approach the trees, squirrels dash out boldly in front of us, turning their heads this way and that to eye us with shiny, big black beads, hoping for signs of food. High above us in an anemic sky, the white orb of the sun, like a giant spotlight, fixes the park with its hard wintry rays. We abandon the path and enter the small wood, dried foliage and twigs crackling and crunching against the frozen earth beneath our feet. The uneven ground slopes gently downward.

Lochan follows me silently. Neither of us has spoken since entering the park gates and abandoning the world behind us, as if we are trying to leave our daily selves behind in the noisy hubbub of dirty streets and jostling traffic. As the trees begin to thicken around us, I duck beneath a fallen log and then stop and smile. "This is it."

We are standing in a small hollow. The shallow dip in the ground is carpeted with leaves and surrounded by a few remaining green ferns and winter shrubs, enclosed in a circle of bare trees. The ground beneath us is a tapestry of russet and gold. Even in the depths of winter, my little piece of paradise is still beautiful.

Lochan looks around in bewilderment. "Are we here to bury a body or dig one up?"

I give him a long-suffering look, but just then a sudden gust of wind causes the branches overhead to sway, scattering the sun's icy rays like shards of glass into my corral, making it feel magical, mysterious.

"This is where I come when things get too much at home. When I want to be alone for a while," I tell him.

He looks at me in astonishment. "You come here by yourself?" He blinks in confusion, hands dug deep into his jacket pockets, still gazing around. "Why?"

"Because when Mum starts drinking at ten o'clock in the morning, when Tiffin and Willa are tearing around the house screaming, when Kit is trying to pick a row with everyone who crosses his path, when I wish I didn't have a family to look after, this place gives me peace. It gives me hope. In summer it's lovely here. It silences the roar that's constantly in my head. . . .

"Maybe, from time to time, this could be your place too," I suggest quietly. "Everyone needs time off, Lochan. Even you."

He nods again, still looking around, as if trying to imagine me here by myself. Then he turns back to me, the collar of his black jacket flapping against his untucked white shirt, tie loosened, the bottoms of his gray trousers muddied by the soft earth. His cheeks are pink from the long cold walk, hair tousled by the wind. However, we are sheltered here, the sun warm on our faces. A sudden flurry of birds alights on the topmost branch of a tree, and as he raises his head, the light is reflected in his eyes, turning them translucent, the color of green glass.

His gaze meets mine. "Thanks," he says.

We sit down in my grassy enclave and huddle together for warmth. Lochan wraps his arm around me and pulls me toward him, kissing the top of my head.

"I love you, Maya Whitely," he says softly.

I smile and tilt my face to look up at him. "How much?"

He doesn't answer, but I hear his breathing quicken; he lowers his mouth over mine and a strange hum fills the air.

We kiss for a long time, sliding our hands in between layers of clothing and absorbing each other's heat until I am warm, hot, even, my heart thumping hard, a sparkling, tingling feeling rushing through my veins. Birds continue to peck at the earth around us; somewhere in the distance a child's whoop breaks the air. Here, we are truly alone. Truly free. If anyone happened to walk by, all they would see is a girl and her boyfriend kissing. I feel the pressure of Lochan's lips strengthen as if he, too, realizes how priceless this little moment of freedom is. His hand slides beneath my school shirt and I press my hand up against his thigh.

Then, abruptly, he is pulling back, turning away, breathing hard. I look round in surprise, but only the trees surround us, like silent witnesses, unchanged and unmoved and undisturbed. Beside me, Lochan sits with arms circling his drawn-up knees, face turned away. "Sorry . . ." He gives a small, embarrassed laugh.

"About what?"

His breathing is fast and shallow. "I needed to stop."

Something tightens in my throat. "But that's fine, Lochie. You don't have to apologize."

He doesn't respond. There is something about his stillness that disturbs me.

I move over so that I'm pressed close to him and give him a gentle nudge. "Shall we go for a wander?"

He tilts away from me slightly. Raises a shoulder without turning. Doesn't reply.

"You okay?" I ask lightly.

He gives a brief nod.

A flutter of worry rises in my chest. I stroke the back of his head. "You sure?"

No reply.

"Perhaps we should set up camp here, away from the rest

of the world," I tease, but he doesn't respond. "I just thought it would be nice to have some time alone, just the two of us," I say softly. "Was it—was coming here a mistake?"

"No!"

I cover his hand with mine and stroke the back of it with my thumb. "What then?"

"Just—" His voice quavers. "I'm afraid that all this will one day be nothing more than a distant memory."

I swallow hard. "Don't say that, Lochie. It doesn't have to be."

"But us—this—it won't last. It won't, Maya—we both know that. At some point we'll have to stop—" He breaks off suddenly and holds his breath, shaking his head wordlessly.

"Lochie, of course it's going to last!" I exclaim, aghast. "They can't stop us. I won't let anyone stop us. . . ."

He takes my hand in his, starts to kiss it, his lips soft and warm. "But it's the whole world," he says, his voice an anguished whisper. "How—how can we make it against the whole world?"

I want Lochan to say he'll find a way. I need him to say we'll both find a way. Together we'll manage it. Together we're so strong. Together we brought up a whole family.

"People can't separate us!" I begin angrily. "They can't, they can't! Can they . . ." And suddenly I realize I've no idea. However careful we are, there is always the chance we could get caught. Just as, however much we cover up for Mum, the

 TABITHA SUZUMA

threat of someone finding out and alerting the authorities gets stronger every day. We have to be so careful; everything has to be hidden, kept secret. One slipup and the whole family could collapse like a house of cards. One slipup and we could all be torn apart. . . . Lochan's defeatist attitude terrifies me. It's as if he knows something I don't. "Lochie, tell me we can stay together!"

He reaches out for me and I crumple against him with a sob. Wrapping his arms around me, he holds me tightly. "I'll do everything," he whispers into my hair. "I give you my word. I'll do everything I can, Maya. We'll find a way to stay together. I'll figure it out; I will. Okay?"

I look up at him and he blinks back tears, giving me a bright, reassuring, hopeful smile.

I nod, smiling in return. "Together we're strong," I reply, my voice bolder than I feel.

He closes his eyes for a moment, as if in pain, then opens them again and lifts my face from his chest, kissing me gently. We hold each other tightly for a long, long time, warming each other, until the sun gradually begins to dip in the sky.

CHAPTER NINETEEN

Lochan

In the mornings I shower with the speed of lightning, throw
on my clothes, and as soon as I've got Tiffin and Willa settled
at the breakfast table, I run back upstairs with the excuse of a
forgotten blazer or watch or book to join Maya, who has the
unenviable task of trying to get Kit out of bed in the mornings.
She's usually tying back her hair or buttoning her shirt cuffs or
stuffing books into her bag, her bedroom door ajar, and pops
out sporadically to shout up at Kit to hurry; but she stops when
she sees me and, with a look of nervous excitement, takes my
outstretched hand. My heart pounding in anticipation, we shut
ourselves in my bedroom. With only a few precious minutes to

spare, my foot pressed firmly against the bottom corner of the door, one hand gripping the handle, I pull her gently toward me. Her eyes light up with a smile, hands either reaching for my face, my hair, or sometimes even pressing up against my chest, fingertips scraping against the thin fabric of my shirt. We kiss shyly at first, half afraid. I can taste whether she has used Colgate or just grabbed the pink kiddie stuff while supervising brushing to save time.

It always gives me a jolt, that moment when our lips first meet, and I have to remind myself to breathe. Her lips are soft and warm and smooth; mine feel harsh and rough against them. At the sound of Kit's slow, dragging footsteps just on the other side of the thin wall, Maya tries to pull back. However, as soon as the bathroom door slams, she gives in and slides round so her back is pushed up against the door. I dig my nails into the wood on either side of her head in an attempt to keep my hands under control as our kisses grow increasingly frantic; the longing inside me quells any fear of being caught as I feel the last precious seconds of ecstasy run through my fingers like sand. A shout from downstairs, the sound of Kit reemerging from the bathroom, feet pounding up the stairs—all signals that our time is up—and Maya pushes me firmly back, her cheeks aglow, mouth stained red with the flush of unfinished kisses. We stare at each other, our hot panting filling the air, but as I press in toward her again, my eyes begging for just one more second, she closes her eyes with a look of pain and turns her head away. She is usually the first to leave the bedroom, striding into the vacated bathroom to splash water on her face while I cross over to my bedroom window and throw it open, clutching at the edge of the sill and sucking in great lungfuls of cold air.

I don't understand, I don't understand. Surely this has happened before. Surely other brothers and sisters have fallen in love. Surely they have been allowed to express their love, physically as well as emotionally, without being vilified, ostracized, thrown into prison, even. But incest is illegal. By loving each other physically as well as emotionally, we are committing a crime. And I'm terrified. It is one thing hiding from the world, another to be hiding from the law. So I keep repeating to myself, *As long as we don't go all the way, it will be all right.* As long as we don't actually have sex, we're not technically having an incestuous relationship. As long as we don't cross that final line, our family will be safe, the kids won't be taken away, Maya and I won't be forced apart. All we have to do is be patient, enjoy what we have, until perhaps one day, when the others are grown up, we can move away and forge new identities and love each other freely.

I have to force myself to stop thinking about it or I can't

get anything done—schoolwork, studying, making dinner, the weekly shop, fetching Tiffin and Willa from school, helping them with homework, making sure they have clean clothes for the following day, playing with them when they are bored. Keeping an eye on Kit—checking that he does his schoolwork and makes the money he's been given last the week, cajoling him into having dinner with us instead of disappearing with his mates to McDonald's, making sure he doesn't skip school and he comes home at night. And of course, arguing with Mum over money, always money, as less and less comes our way and more and more gets spent on alcohol and new outfits to impress Dave. Meanwhile, Tiffin's clothes get smaller, Willa's uniform gets more ragged, Kit complains bitterly about the new gadgets his friends all have, and the bills keep flooding in. . . .

Whenever I'm apart from Maya, I feel incomplete . . . less than incomplete. I feel like I'm nothing, like I don't exist at all. I have no identity. I don't speak; I don't even look at people. Being around others is just as unbearable as ever—I am afraid that if they see me properly, they might guess my secret. I'm afraid that even if I do manage to speak or interact with people, I might give something away. At break times I watch Maya over the top of my book from my post on the staircase, willing her to come over to sit with me, to talk to me, to make me feel alive and real and loved, but even just talking is too risky. So she sits on the wall at the far end of the playground, chatting to Francie, careful not to glance up at me, as aware as I am of the danger of our situation.

In the evenings I seek her out as soon as Tiffin and Willa have been tucked in, too early for it to be safe. She turns from her desk, her hair skimming the page of her textbook, and points meaningfully at the door behind me to indicate that the little ones are not yet asleep. But by the time they are, Kit is roaming the house, looking for food or watching TV, and by the time he finally goes to bed, Maya is passed out in hers.

Half term brings little respite. It rains all week and, cooped up inside with no money for outings or even the movies, Tiffin and Willa bicker constantly while Kit sleeps all day and then disappears with his friends until the small hours of the morning. Late one night, restless and burning with relentless agitation, I pull on my running shoes and leave the sleeping house, jogging all the way to Ashmoore Park, climbing the railings under the light of the stars, running across the moonlit grass. Stumbling through the darkened woods, I eventually find Maya's oasis of peace, but it brings me none. I fall to my knees before the trunk of a huge oak tree and, making a fist, grate my knuckles up and down its harsh, jagged, unforgiving bark until they are bloody and raw.

 TABITHA SUZUMA

"Lochie needs a bandage," Willa announces the following evening to Maya, the family's first-aider, as she comes through the door looking spent. "A big one."

Maya drops her bag and blazer to the floor and gives a tired smile.

"Rough day?" I inquire.

"Three tests." She rolls her eyes. "And gym in the hailstorm."

"I'm helping Lochie make dinner," Willa says proudly, kneeling on a kitchen stool and arranging frozen french fries into patterns on the oven tray. "Wanna help, Maya?"

"I think we're doing pretty well just the two of us," I point out quickly as Maya flops into a chair, her tie askew, and pushes the straggly wisps of hair back from her face, blowing me a discreet kiss.

"Maya, look! I made my name in capital fries!" Willa pipes up, noting our exchanged looks, anxious to be included.

"Very clever." Maya gets up and lifts Willa onto her lap before settling down with her and leaning over the tray to try and create her own name. I watch them for a moment. Maya's long arms encircle Willa's shorter ones. Willa is full of chatter about her day while Maya is the attentive listener, asking all the right questions. Heads bent close, their long straight hair mingles: Maya's auburn against Willa's gold. They both have the same delicate, pale skin, the same clear blue gaze, the same smile.

On her lap, Willa is solid and alive, full of bubble and laughter. Maya somehow looks more delicate, more fragile, more ethereal. There is a sadness in her eyes, a weariness that never really leaves. For Maya, childhood ended years ago. As she sits with Willa on her lap, I think: *Sister and sister. Mother and child.*

"You can do the *M* like this," Willa declares importantly.

"You're good at this, Willa," Maya tells her. "Now, what were you saying about Lochan needing a bandage?"

I realize I have been chopping up the same bunch of spring onions ever since Maya first came in. I have a board full of green and white confetti.

"Lochie hurt his hand," Willa states matter-of-factly, her eyes still narrowed on the fries.

"With a knife?" Maya looks up at me sharply, her eyes registering alarm.

"No, it's just a graze," I reassure her with a dismissive shake of the head and an indulgent smile toward Willa.

Willa turns to look at Maya. "He's lying," she stage-whispers conspiratorially.

"Can I see?" Maya asks.

I flash her the back of my hand.

She flinches at the sight and instantly moves to get up, but then, anchored to her seat by Willa, is forced to sit down again. She reaches out. "Come here."

TABITHA SUZUMA

"I don't want to see it!" Willa lowers her head toward the tray. "It's all bleeding and sticky. Eek, yuck, gross!"

I let Maya take my hand in hers, just for the pleasure of touching her. "It's nothing."

She strokes the inside of my hand with her fingers. "Jesus, what happened? Surely not a fight——"

"Of course not. I just tripped and scraped it against the wall of the playground."

She gives me a long, disbelieving look. "We need to clean it properly," she insists.

"I have."

Ignoring my last comment, she gently slides Willa off her lap. "I'm going upstairs to sort Lochie's hand out," she says. "I'll be back in a minute."

In the small confines of the bathroom, I rummage around in the medicine cupboard for the antiseptic. "I appreciate the concern, but don't you think you girls are being a bit paranoid?"

Ignoring me, Maya perches on the edge of the bath and reaches out toward me. "It's only because we love you so much. Come here."

I oblige, leaning in and closing my eyes for a brief moment, savoring the touch, the taste of her soft lips against mine. Gently she pulls me closer and I turn away, waving the antiseptic bottle aloft. "I thought you wanted to play nurse!"

She looks at me with a mixture of uncertainty and surprise, as if trying to gauge whether I'm teasing.

"Much as I love dabbing up blood, it doesn't quite match up to grabbing a rare moment to kiss the guy I love."

I force a laugh. "Are you saying you'd rather let me bleed to death?"

She pretends to consider this for a moment. "Ah, well, that's a tough one."

I start uncapping the bottle. "Come on. Let's get this over and done with."

Cuffing my wrist gently with her fingers, she draws my hand toward her, inspecting the raw, bloody knuckles, the skin grated back from the wound: a jagged white rectangle surrounding the wet, crimson lacerations. She winces. "Christ, Lochan. You did this falling against a wall? It looks like you took a grater to the back of your hand!"

She gently dabs at my savaged knuckles. I take a deep breath and watch her face; her eyes are narrowed in concentration, her touch very gentle. I swallow painfully.

After bandaging it with gauze and putting everything away, she returns to the side of the bath and kisses me again, and as I pull back, she rubs my arm with an uncertain smile.

"Is it really hurting?"

"No, of course not!" I exclaim truthfully. "I don't know

why you girls get into such a panic at the merest drop of blood. Anyway, thank you, Miss Nightingale." I give her a quick kiss on the head, stand up, and reach for the door.

"Hey!" She reaches out a hand to stop me, a sparkle of mischief in her eyes. "Don't you think I deserve a bit more than that for my efforts?"

I pull a face and motion awkwardly toward the door. "Willa . . ."

"She'll be spaced out in front of the TV by now!"

I take a reluctant step forward. "Okay . . ."

But she stops me before I have time to reach her, hand on my chest, gently holding me at arm's length. Her expression is quizzical. "What's up with you today?"

I shake my head with a wry smile. "I dunno. I think I'm just a bit tired."

She gives me a long look, rubbing the tip of her tongue against her upper lip. "Loch, is everything okay?"

"Of course!" I smile brightly. "Now, shall we get out of here? This is not exactly the most romantic place!"

I can feel her bewilderment as strongly as if it were my own. Throughout dinner, I keep catching her watching me, her eyes rapidly flicking away as soon as they meet mine. She is distracted, that much is obvious, failing to notice Willa eating with her hands or Kit openly winding up the little ones by ignoring his meal and eating the Jaffa Cakes meant for dessert. I sense it is better to let them just do what the hell they want rather than object—for fear that if I start, I won't be able to stop and the cracks will begin to show. I just panicked in the bathroom. I was afraid, too afraid, that if I let her get that close, she would sense it, realize there was something wrong.

But at night I can't sleep, my mind plagued with fears. With constant course work and the day-to-day hassle of living to contend with, added to the fact that we can never, ever show any display of affection in public or even within our own family, the familiar suffocating shackles are tightening still further. *Will we ever be free to exist like a normal couple?* I wonder. To live together, hold hands in public, kiss on a street corner? Or will we be forever condemned to lead closeted lives, hidden away behind locked doors and drawn curtains? Or worse still, once our siblings are old enough, will we have no choice but to run away and leave them behind?

I keep telling myself to take one day at a time, but how is this really possible? I am about to leave school, start university, and therefore, by default, am forced to contemplate my future. What I'd really like to do is write—for a newspaper or magazine, perhaps—but I know that is nothing more than a ridiculous flight of fancy. What matters is money: It's imperative I aim for a job with a decent starting salary and good earn-

made her choice—but now that I'm about to turn eighteen and legally become an adult, I fear she may cut us off completely in a final bid to get that ring on her finger. Every time I force her to part with some money for the basics—food, bills, new clothes, school things—she starts yelling about how she left school and started work at sixteen, moved out and asked her parents for nothing. Reminding her that she didn't have three younger siblings to care for is her cue to go on about how she never wanted children in the first place, how she had us only to please our father, how he'd wanted another and another until, tiring of us all, he'd run off to start anew with someone else. I point out that our father's desertion does not somehow magically give her the right to desert us too. But this only provokes her further, prompting the cheap-shot reminder that she would never have married our father had she not accidentally got pregnant with me. I know she says this out of drunken fury, but I also know it's true; this is why she has continued resenting me, far more than the others, all my life. This then leads to the usual tirade about how she works fourteen-hour days just to keep a roof over our heads, that all she asks of me is that I look after my siblings for a few hours after school each day. If I try reminding her that although this was the initial setup when our father left, the reality now is very different, she starts screaming about her right to a life too. Finally I find myself reduced to blackmail: Only the threat of us all turning up at Dave's, suitcases

TABITHA SUZUMA

in hand, will force her to part with the cash. In many ways I am thankful she is finally gone from our lives, even if it means that thoughts about the future, our future, weigh heavily upon me.

Sleep evades me once more, so in the early hours of the morning I go down to the kitchen to tackle the pile of letters addressed to Mum that have been accumulating on the sideboard for weeks now. By the time I finish opening them all, the kitchen table is completely covered with bills, credit card statements, payment demands. . . . Maya touches the back of my neck, making me jump.

"Didn't mean to startle you." She takes the chair beside me, resting her bare feet on the edge of my seat, circling her knees with her arms. In her nightdress, her hair hanging loose and smooth, the color of autumn leaves, she looks up at me with eyes as wide and innocent as Willa's. Her beauty makes me ache.

"You look just like Tiffin when he's lost a match and is trying to put on a brave face," she comments, laughter in her eyes.

I manage a small laugh. Sometimes, being unable to hide my emotions from her is frustrating.

The laughter leaves an unsettling silence.

Maya tugs gently at my hand. "Tell me."

I take a sharp, shallow breath and shake my head at the floor. "Just, you know, the future and stuff."

Although she keeps smiling, I see her eyes change and sense

she has been thinking about this too. "That's a big topic for three o'clock in the morning. Any part of it in particular?"

I force my eyes to meet hers. "Roughly from here up until the part where Willa goes off to university or starts work."

"I think you're jumping the gun a bit!" Maya exclaims, clearly determined to snap me out of my mood. "Willa is destined for greater things. The other day I had to take her to Belmont with me to pick up some homework I'd forgotten and everyone turned to mush! My art teacher said we should get her signed up with a children's modeling agency. So I reckon we just invest in her, and by the time she's eighteen, she'll be on the catwalk and supporting us! Then there's Tiffin. Rumor has it, Coach Simmons has never seen so much talent in one so young! And you know what they pay soccer players!" She laughs, frantic in her efforts to cheer me up.

"Good point. Exactly . . ." I try to imagine Willa on a cat-walk in the hope it will prompt a genuine smile. "That's a great idea! You can be her, um, stylist and I can be her manager."

But the silence descends again. It's clear from her expression that Maya is aware her tactics haven't worked. She skims her nails over the palm of my hand, her expression sobering. "Listen, you. First of all, we don't know what's going to happen with Mum and the whole financial situation. Even if she does marry Dave and tries to cut us off financially, we could just

 TABITHA SUZUMA

threaten to take her to court and sue her for neglect—she's too stupid to realize we'd never go through with it because of social services. And by our mere existence, we'll always have the potential to mess up her relationship—the threats about turning up at Dave's in order to get her to pay the bills have worked so far, haven't they? Thirdly, by the time you finish uni, a lot will almost have changed. Willa will be nearly nine; Tiffin will almost be a teenager. They'll be going to school by themselves, will be responsible for their own homework. Kit may have grown a conscience by then, but even if he hasn't, we'll insist he either goes out and gets a job or takes over his fair share of the chores—even if we have to resort to blackmail." She smiles, raising my hand to her mouth to kiss it. "The toughest part is happening right now, Lochie—with Mum suddenly out of the picture and Tiffin and Willa still so young. But it's only going to get easier; things will get better for all of us, and you and I will have more and more time together. Trust me, my love. I've been thinking about it too, and I'm not just saying all this to try to cheer you up."

I raise my eyes to meet hers and feel some of the weight lift from my chest. "I hadn't thought of it like that. . . ."

"That's because you're always busy thinking of the worst-case scenario! And because you always do your worrying alone." She gives me a teasing smile and shakes her head. "Also you always forget about the most important thing!"

I manage to match her smile. "What's that then?"

"Me," she declares with a flourish, flinging out her arm and knocking over the milk carton in the process. Fortunately it is almost empty.

"You and your ability to send things flying."

"Well, exactly," she concurs. "And the very important fact that I'm here to worry with you and go through all of this— every little bit of it—by your side, even your worst-case sce- nario, should it somehow come to that. You wouldn't be doing any of it alone." Her voice drops and she looks down at our hands, fingers entwined, resting on her lap. "Whatever hap- pens, there will always be us."

I nod, suddenly unable to speak. I want to tell her that I can't pull her down. I want to tell her that she has to let go of my hand in order to swim. I want to tell her that she must live her own life. But I sense she already knows that these options are open to her. And that she, too, has made her choice.

CHAPTER TWENTY

Maya

"Fifteen minutes," Francie begs. "Oh, come on, then—ten. Lochan knows you had a late class, so surely an extra ten minutes isn't going to make much difference!"

I look at my friend's pleading, hopeful face and a moment of temptation flickers through me. An ice-cold Coke and maybe a muffin at Smileys with Francie while she tries to get herself noticed by the new young waiter she has discovered there—postponing the hectic evening routine of homework, dinner, baths, and bed—suddenly feels like an absurd luxury. . . .

"Just give Lochan a call now," Francie persists as we cross the playground, bags slung over our shoulders, heads foggy and bodies restless after the long, stale school day. "Why on earth would he mind?"

He wouldn't—that's the whole point. In fact, he would urge me to go, and that knowledge weighs me down with guilt. Leaving him to make dinner and supervise homework and deal with Kit when his school day has been nearly as long as mine and undoubtedly more painful. But more to the point, I ache to see him even if it entails spending another evening struggling against the painful urge to hold him, touch him, kiss him. I miss him after a whole day apart—I really miss him. And even if it means diving straight from a deathly history lesson into the manic home fray, I can't wait to do it just to see his eyes light up at the sight of me, the smile of delight that greets me whenever I step through the front door—even when he is juggling saucepans in the kitchen, trying to persuade Tiffin to set the table and stop Willa from stuffing herself with cereal.

"I just can't. I'm sorry," I tell Francie. "There's just so much stuff to do."

But for once she displays no sympathy. Instead she sucks on her lower lip, leaning her shoulder against the outer wall of the school playground, the place at which we normally part. "I thought I was your best friend," she says suddenly, hurt and disappointment resonating in her voice.

 TABITHA SUZUMA

I flinch in surprise. "You are—you know you are—it's got nothing to do with—"

"I know what's going on, Maya," she interrupts, her words slicing the air between us.

My pulse begins to quicken. "What on earth are you talking about?"

"You've met someone, haven't you." She phrases it as a statement, folding her arms across her chest and turning to press her back against the wall, looking away from me, her jaw set.

I am momentarily lost for words. "No!" The word is no more than an astonished little gasp. "I haven't. I promise. Why did you . . . What made you think . . . "

"I don't believe you." She shakes her head, still staring angrily into the distance. "I know you, Maya, and you've changed. When you talk, you always seem to be thinking about something else. It's like you're daydreaming or something. And you seem weirdly happy these days. And you're always rushing off at the last bell. I know you've got all that shit to deal with at home, but it's as if you're looking forward to it now, as if you can't wait to get away—"

"Francie, I really haven't got some secret boyfriend!" I protest desperately. "You know you'd be the first to know if I had!" The words sound so sincere as they leave my lips that I feel slightly ashamed. But he's not just a boyfriend, I tell myself. He's so much more.

Francie scrutinizes my face as she continues to quiz me, but after a few moments she begins to calm down, appearing to believe me. I have to make up some crush on a boy in the next grade to explain the daydreaming, but fortunately I have the presence of mind to choose one who already has a steady girlfriend so Francie won't try to match-make. But the conversation leaves me shaken. I'm going to have to be more careful, I realize. I'm even going to have to watch the way I behave when I'm away from him. Just the tiniest slip could give us away. . . .

I arrive home to find Kit and Tiffin in the front room watching TV, which surprises me. Not so much the fact that they are watching television, but that they are doing it simultaneously and that Tiffin is the one with the remote control. Kit is slouched down at one end of the couch, his muddy school shoes half untied, head propped up on his hand, gazing dully at the screen. Tiffin has traces of ketchup down his shirt and is kneeling up at the other end of the couch, transfixed by some violent cartoon, his eyes wide, mouth hovering open like a fish's. Neither one turns as I enter.

"Hello!" I exclaim.

Tiffin holds up a packet of Coco Pops and shakes it vaguely

TABITHA SUZUMA

in my direction, his gaze still fixed straight ahead. "We're allowed," he announces.

"Before dinner?" I query suspiciously, tossing my blazer onto the sofa and collapsing on top of it. "Tiffin, I don't think that's a very good—"

"This is dinner," he informs me, taking a large handful from the box and cramming it into his mouth, scattering the area around him. "Lochie said we could eat whatever we liked."

"What?"

"They've gone to the hospital." Kit rolls his head round to look at me with a long-suffering air. "And I have to stay down here with Tiffin and live off cereal for the foreseeable future."

I sit up slowly. "Lochie and Willa have gone to the hospital?" I ask, disbelief resonating in my voice.

"Yeah," comes Kit's reply.

"What the hell happened?" My voice rises and I jump up and start rummaging in my bag for my keys. Startled by my shout, both boys finally tear their eyes away from the screen.

"I bet it's nothing," Kit says bitterly. "I bet they're going to spend all night waiting in the ER, Willa will fall asleep, and by the time she wakes up, she'll be saying it doesn't even hurt anymore."

"What are you talking about?" Tiffin turns to him, his blue eyes wide and accusing. "Maybe she'll have to get an operation. Maybe they'll amputate her—"

"What happened?" I yell, frantic now.

"I dunno! She hurt her arm. I wasn't even down here!" Kit says defensively.

"I was," Tiffin announces importantly, shoving his whole arm into the cereal box. "She slipped off the counter and fell onto the floor and started screaming. When Lochie picked her up she screamed even more, so he carried her out into the street to get a taxi and she was still screaming—"

"Where have they gone?" I grab Kit by the arm and shake him. "St. Joseph's?"

"Ow—get off! Yes, that's what he said."

"Neither of you move!" I shout from the doorway. "Tiffin, you're not to go outside, do you hear me? Kit, can you promise you'll stay with Tiffin until I get back? And answer the phone as soon as it rings?"

Kit rolls his eyes dramatically. "Lochan's already been through all this—"

"Do you promise?"

"Yes!"

"And don't open the door to anyone, and if there's any problem, call my mobile!"

"Okay, okay!"

I run the whole way. It's a good two miles but the rush-hour traffic is such that taking a bus would be slower if not

    TABITHA SUZUMA

more torturous. Running helps activate the safety valve in my brain, forcing out visions of an injured, screaming Willa. If anything terrible has happened to that child, I will die—I know it. My love for her is like a violent pain in my chest, and the blood throbs in my head, a pounding hammer of guilt, once again forcing me to acknowledge that since my relationship with Lochan began—despite my recent efforts—I have still not been paying my little sister as much attention as before. I've rushed her through baths and bedtimes and stories; I've snapped at her at times when Tiffin was the culprit; I've declined request after request to play with her, citing housework or homework as an excuse, too wrapped up in keeping everything in order to give her a mere ten minutes of my time. Kit commands attention constantly with his volatility, Tiffin with his hyperactivity, leaving Willa by the wayside, drowned out by her brothers during dinner-table conversations. As her only sister, I used to play dolls and tea parties with her, dress her up, play with her hair. But these days I have been so preoccupied with other things that I even failed to register that she'd fallen out with her best friend, failed to recognize that she needed me—to listen to her stories, ask her about her day, and praise her for her almost impeccable behavior that, by its very nature, did not draw attention. The gash on her leg, for example: Not only was Willa stuck at school in pain all afternoon with no one to fetch her and comfort her, but—worse and more telling still—she didn't even think of saying anything to me about the incident until I happened to notice the huge bandage beneath the hole in her tights.

I am close to tears by the time I reach the hospital, and once inside, trying to get directions almost sends me over the edge. Eventually I locate Children's Outpatients and am told that Willa is fine but "resting" and that I will be able to see her as soon as she wakes. I am shown to a small room off a long corridor and informed that Willa's ward is just round the corner and that a doctor will come and speak to me shortly. As soon as the nurse disappears, I burst back out again.

Rounding a corner, I recognize, down at the far end of another blindingly white corridor, a familiar figure in front of the brightly painted doors of the children's ward. Head lowered, he is leaning forward on his hands, gripping the edge of a windowsill.

"Lochie!"

He whirls round as if struck, straightens up slowly, then approaches me rapidly, raising his hands as if in surrender.

"She's fine, she's fine, she's absolutely fine—they gave her a sedative and gas and air for the pain and were able to push the bone straight back in. I've just seen her and she's fast asleep, but she looks completely fine. After they X-rayed her the second time, the doctors said they were certain there'd be no long-term damage—she won't even need a plaster cast and her shoulder will be back to normal in a week or possibly even less! They said dislocated shoulders happen to children all the time, that it's really quite common, that they see it all the time and it's nothing to worry about!" He is speaking insanely fast, his eyes radiating a kind of frenzied optimism, looking at me with a frantic, almost pleading look as if expecting me to start jumping up and down in relief.

I stop dead, panting hard, brushing the stray wisps of hair back from my face, and stare at him.

"She dislocated her shoulder?" I gasp.

He flinches, as if stung by the words. "Yeah, but that's all! Nothing else! They've X-rayed her and everything and—"

"What happened?"

"She just fell off the kitchen counter!" He tries to touch me but I move out of the way. "Look, she's fine, Maya, I'm telling you! There's nothing broken—the bone just popped out of the shoulder socket. I know it sounds dramatic, but all they had to do was push it back in. They gave her gas and air so it wasn't too—too painful, and—and now she's just resting."

His manic demeanor and rapid-fire speech is faintly horrifying. His hair is on end, as if he has been running his fingers through it and tugging it repeatedly, his face white, his school shirt hanging loose over his trousers, clinging to his skin in damp patches.

"I want to see her—"

"No!" He catches me as I try to push past. "They want her to sleep off the sedative—they won't let you in until she wakes up—"

"I don't give a shit! She's my sister and she's hurt and so I'm going in to see her and no one can stop me!" I begin to shout.

But Lochan is forcibly restraining me and, to my astonishment, I suddenly find myself grappling with him in this long, bright, empty hospital corridor. For a moment I am almost tempted to kick him, but then I hear him gasp, "Don't make a scene—you mustn't make a scene. It'll just make it worse."

I fall back, breathing hard. "Make what worse? What are you talking about?"

He approaches me, his hands reaching for my shoulders, but I back away, refusing to be pacified by any more meaningless words of comfort. Lochan lets his arms fall with a hopeless, desperate look. "They want to see Mum. I told them that she was abroad on business, but they insisted on a number. So I gave them her mobile but it just went straight to voice mail—"

I pull my phone out. "I'll call her at Dave's. And I'll try the pub and Dave's mobile, too—"

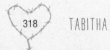

"No." Lochan holds his hand up in a gesture of defeat. "She's—she's not there. . . ."

I stare at him.

Lowering his arm, he swallows and walks slowly back toward the window. I notice that he's limping. "She's—she's gone away with him. Just for a holiday, apparently. Somewhere in Devon, but Dave's son doesn't seem to know where. He just said he thought—he thought they'd be back on Sunday."

I gape at him, horror coursing through my veins. "She's gone for the whole week?"

"Apparently. Luke didn't seem to know—or care. And her phone's been off for days. Either she forgot her charger or she's switched it off deliberately." Lochan goes back to lean against the windowsill, as if the weight of his body is too great for his legs to bear. "I've been trying to call her about the bills. Yesterday after school I went round, and that's when Luke told me. He's staying in his dad's flat with his girlfriend. I didn't want to worry you—"

"You had no right not to tell me!"

"I know. I'm sorry, but I figured there was nothing we could do. . . ."

"So what now?" I am no longer speaking in measured tones. A head pops out from a door farther down and I try to reel myself in. "Willa has to stay in the hospital until Mum comes to fetch her?" I hiss.

"No, no . . ." He puts out a reassuring hand and again I dodge it. I'm furious at him for trying to shush me, for keeping this from me, for treating me like one of the children and just repeating that everything is going to be all right.

Before I have the chance to quiz him any more, a short, balding doctor comes out through the double doors, introduces himself to me as Dr. Maguire, and shows us back into the small room. We each take a seat on a spongy, low-slung chair and, holding up large X-rays, the doctor shows us the before and after pictures, explains the procedure that took place and what to expect next. He is cheerful and reassuring, echoes most of what Lochan has told me already, and assures me that although Willa's shoulder will be sore for a few days and she will have to wear a sling, it should be back to normal in a week. He also informs us that she is now awake and eating dinner and that we can take her home as soon as she is ready.

We can take her home. I feel myself go limp. We all stand up and Lochan thanks Dr. Maguire, who smiles broadly, reiterates that we can take Willa home as soon as she's ready, and then asks if it would be all right to send Mrs. Leigh in now. Lochan puts his hand against the wall as if to steady himself and nods rapidly, chewing on his thumbnail as the doctor leaves.

"Mrs. Leigh?" I turn to Lochan with a questioni

He swings round and looks at me, breathing |
say anything. Okay? Just don't say anything." His voi
and urgent. "Let me do the talking—we can't risk contradict-
ing each other. If she asks you anything, just go along with the
usual business-trip story and tell her the truth—you had a late
class and didn't come home till after it had happened."

I gaze at Lochan across the small room in bewilderment. "I
thought you said they were fine about Mum."

"They are. It's—it's just procedure . . . for this type of
injury, they say. Apparently they have to file some kind of
report—" Before he can get any further, a knock sounds and a
large woman with a head of frizzy ginger hair enters.

"Hello there. The doctor told you I'd be coming in to have
a word? I'm Alison—from the Child Protection Agency." She
extends her hand toward Lochan.

A small sound escapes me. I turn it into a cough.

"Lochan Whitely. N-nice to meet you."

He knew!

I'm aware I'm being addressed. I take her podgy hand in
mine. For a moment I literally cannot speak. My mind has gone
blank and I've forgotten my own name. Then I force a smile,
introduce myself, and take a seat in the small triangle.

Alison is rummaging about in a large bag, pulling out a

folder and pen and various forms, chatting as she does so. She asks Lochan to confirm the situation with Mum, which he does in a surprisingly steady voice. She appears satisfied, scribbles a few things down, and then looks up from her notes with a broad, artificial smile.

"Well, I've already had a word with Willa about what happened. She's a delightful little girl, isn't she? She explained she was in the kitchen with you, Lochan, when she fell. And that, Maya, you were still at school, but your other two brothers were at home."

I look across at Lochan, willing him to make eye contact with me. But he seems to have deliberately turned away. "Yes."

Another of those fake smiles. "Okay, so in your own time, explain to me how the accident occurred."

I don't understand. This isn't even about Mum. And surely Lochan gave the details of the fall to the doctor in charge when he brought Willa in.

"R-right. Okay." Lochan leans forward, elbows on knees, as if desperate to tell this woman every detail. "I—I came into the kitchen and Willa was up on the counter where she's not allowed to be because it's—it's really quite high, and—and she was on tiptoe trying to reach a box of b-biscuits on the top shelf—" He is speaking in that manic, staccato way again, almost tripping over his words in his hurry to get them out. I can see the muscles in his arms vibrating, and he is scraping at the sore beneath his mouth so hard that it's starting to bleed.

Alison just nods, scribbles some more, looks up again expectantly.

"I t-told her to get down. She refused, saying her brothers had each eaten some and had then d-deliberately put the biscuits up there out of her reach." He is panting, staring at the form as if trying to read what's being recorded.

"Go on . . ."

"So I—I repeated what I'd just said—"

"What exactly did you say?" The woman's voice is sharper now.

"J-just—well, basically just: 'Willa, get down now.'"

"Was that spoken or shouted?"

He seems to be having trouble breathing, the air making a scraping noise at the back of his throat. "Um—well—well—the first time I was speaking quite loudly b-because I was worried to see her up there, and—and the second time, after she refused, I—I suppose, y-yes, I sort of shouted." He glances up at her, chewing the corner of his lip, the rise and fall of his chest rapid.

I can't believe this woman! Making Lochan feel guilty about shouting at his sister when she was doing something dangerous?

"And then?" The woman's eyes are very sharp. She seems particularly attentive now.

"Willa—she, well, she i-ignored me."

"And so what did you do?"

There is a terrible silence. *What did you do?* I repeat to myself, desperate to butt in but trapped by my promise to let Lochan do the talking, on top of the fact that I wasn't actually there. Does this Child Protection person ask the parent of every injured child brought into the hospital what it was the parent had done? Guilty until proven innocent? This is ridiculous! Children fall and hurt themselves all the time!

But Lochan isn't answering. I feel my heart start to pound. *Don't start getting stage fright now,* I beg with him in my head. *Don't make it look as if you have something to hide!*

Lochan is frowning and sighing and chewing his lip as if trying to remember, and with a shock I realize he is close to tears.

I press myself back into the chair and bite down hard to stop myself from intervening.

"I p-pulled her down." His chin quivers briefly. He doesn't look up.

"Could you explain exactly how you did that?"

"I went—I went over and g-grabbed her by the arm and then—and then I pulled her off the counter." His voice cracks and he raises his fist to his face, pressing his knuckles hard against his mouth.

Lochan, what the hell are you talking about? You would never deliberately hurt Willa—you know that as well as I do.

"You grabbed her arm and pulled her to the floor?" The woman arches her eyebrows.

Silence stretches out across the room. I can hear my own heartbeat. Finally Lochan lowers his fist from his mouth and takes a ragged breath. "I pulled her arm and—and—" He looks up at the corner of the ceiling, tears amalgamating in his eyes like translucent marbles. "I know I shouldn't have—I wasn't thinking—"

"Just tell me what happened."

"I p-pulled her arm and she slipped. She—she was wearing tights and her feet just slid off the counter's surface. I—I kept hold of her arm as she fell to try and stop her from hurting herself and that's when I felt this—this snap!" He squeezes his eyes shut for a moment, as if in terrible pain.

"So you were holding on to her arm when she hit the floor and the weight of her body pulled the bone out of the socket?"

"It was counterintuitive to let go of her as she fell. I—I thought I'd c-caught her, not—not wrenched her arm out of its socket. Jesus!" A tear glances off his cheek. He swipes at it rapidly. "I didn't think—"

"Lochie!"

His eyes meet mine this time. "It—it was an accident, Maya."

"I know!" I exclaim in soft outrage.

The damn woman is scribbling again. "Are you often left in charge of your siblings, Lochan?" she asks.

I recoil back into the chair. Lochan presses his fingers against his eyes and takes some steady breaths, trying to pull himself together. He shakes his head vehemently. "Only when our mother has to go away on business."

"And how often does that happen?"

"It—it depends. . . . Every couple of months or so . . ."

"And when she's away, I presume you have to fetch them from school, cook for them, help them with homework, entertain them, put them to bed—"

"We do it together," I say quickly.

The woman turns toward us both now. "That must be exhausting after a long school day—"

"They're good at entertaining themselves."

"But when they misbehave, you must have to discipline them."

"Not really," I say firmly. "They're pretty well-behaved."

"Have you ever hurt one of your siblings before?" the woman asks, turning toward Lochan.

TABITHA SUZUMA

He takes a breath. The fight with Kit flashes through my mind. "No!" I exclaim in outrage. "Never!"

In the cab on the way home, we are all three silent, spent, exhausted. Willa is curled up on Lochan's lap, her arm strapped up across her chest, the thumb of her other hand in her mouth. Her head rests against Lochan's neck, spots of light from passing cars floating over her golden hair. Lochan holds her tightly against him, staring blankly out the window, face pale and stunned, his eyes glazed, refusing to meet mine.

We arrive home to a tornado-hit kitchen, the front room's carpet embedded with crisp, biscuit, and cereal crumbs. To our amazement, however, Tiffin is actually in bed and Kit is still in the house, up in the attic, music pounding down through the ceiling. While Lochan gives a groggy Willa a drink and some Tylenol and puts her to bed, I climb up the ladder to let Kit know we're back.

"So has she broken her arm, or what?" Despite the nonchalant tone of his voice, I recognize a spark of worry in his eyes as he glances up at me from his DS. I push his legs to one side to make room on his mattress and sit down beside his sprawled-out figure.

"She hasn't actually broken anything." I explain about the dislocated shoulder.

"Yeah. Tiff said Loch lost his temper and pulled Willa off the kitchen counter." His face darkens suddenly.

I pull my knees to my chest and take a deep breath. "Kit, you know it was an accident. You know Lochan would never hurt Willa intentionally, don't you?" My voice is questioning, serious. I know the answer, I know he does too, but I need him to be honest with me for a moment and actually admit it.

Kit takes a breath, ready for a sarcastic retort, but then seems to hesitate as his gaze locks into mine. "Yeah," he confesses after a moment, a hint of defeat in his voice.

"I know you're angry," I say quietly, "about how things turned out with Mum and Dad, about Lochan and me always being the ones in charge—and Kit, you have every right to be . . . but you know what the alternative is."

His eyes have slid away, back to his DS, uncomfortable about the sudden change in conversation.

"If social services found out that Mum was no longer living at home, that we were on our own—"

"Yeah, yeah, I know," he interrupts gruffly, pounding the buttons of his games console viciously with his thumbs. "We'd be taken into care and split up and all that shit." His voice sounds fed up and angry, but I can sense the fear behind it.

"It's not going to happen, Kit," I reassure him quickly. "Lochan and I will make sure of that, I promise. But it does

TABITHA SUZUMA

mean we have to be careful, really careful, about what we say to other people. Even if it's just some mate at school. All it would take would be for him to mention it to his parents, or to another friend . . . all it would take is one call to social services—"

"Maya, I get it." His thumbs stop moving against the buttons and he looks up at me somberly, suddenly appearing much older than his thirteen years. "I won't tell anybody about Willa's arm—or anything else that could get us into trouble, okay? I promise."

CHAPTER TWENTY-ONE

Lochan

We keep Willa out of school for the rest of the week in order to avoid awkward questions, and I call in sick and stay at home with her. But by Monday she is bored, has lost the sling, and is eager to return to her friends. Mum returns from Devon, and when I finally track her down at Dave's for money, she shows scant interest in Willa's injury.

I am having trouble sleeping again. Whenever I ask Willa about her shoulder, she gives me this worried look and assures me that it's "all mended now." I know she reads the guilt on my face, but this only makes me feel worse.

The green glow of my digital alarm reads 2:43 when I get

up and creep out of my room and down the corridor. Released from the warmth of the duvet, I quickly start to shiver in my holey T-shirt and boxers. The creak of the bedroom door makes Maya stir and I wince, anxious not to wake her. Closing it softly behind me, I pad over to the wall opposite her bed, sliding down against it, my bare arms turning silver in the light of the moon. She continues to shift sleepily, nuzzling her face against the pillow, then abruptly raises herself on one elbow, pushing back her long curtain of hair.

"Lochie, is that you?" A startled, frightened whisper.

"Yeah—shh—sorry—go back to sleep!"

She struggles to sit up, rubbing sleep from her eyes. Finally her eyes focus on me and she shivers, pulling the duvet around her. "Are you trying to give me a heart attack? What on earth are you doing?"

"I'm sorry—I really didn't mean to wake you—"

"Well, you have now!" She gives me a sleepy smile and holds up the edge of the duvet.

I quickly shake my head. "No . . . I just—can I watch you sleep? I know that sounds weird but—but I can't sleep at the moment and it's doing my head in!" I give a sharp, painful laugh. "Watching you sleep makes me feel . . ." I inhale deeply. "I dunno . . . at peace . . . D'you remember, I used to do it when we were young."

She smiles in faint recollection. "Well, you're unlikely to get to sleep sitting there on the floor." She holds out a portion of duvet again.

"No, no, it's fine. I'll just stay here for a while and then go back to bed."

With a sigh of mock irritation, she gets out of bed, pads over, and pulls me up by the wrist. "Come on, get in. God, you're shaking."

"I'm just cold!" I snap, my voice coming out harsher than I intended.

"Well, come here, then!"

The warmth of her duvet envelops me. She slides onto my lap and the touch of her warm skin, her arms and legs wrapped around me, forces me to begin to relax. Hugging me tightly, she buries her face in my neck. "My God, you're an icicle."

I let out a strained laugh. "Sorry."

For a few moments we are both quiet. Her damp breath tickles my cheek. We lie down and I feel my body gently thaw against hers as she strokes the back of my head, running her fingers across my neck. . . . God, how I wish we could stay like this forever. Suddenly, for no reason, I feel close to tears.

"Tell me."

It's as if she can feel the pain through my skin. "Nothing. Just, you know, the usual crap."

I can tell she doesn't believe me. "Listen," she says. "Remember what Willa said the other day? We're the grown-ups. We've always shared the responsibilities. You don't have to start trying to shield me from reality now."

I press my mouth against her shoulder and close my eyes. I'm afraid of worrying her, afraid of telling her how torn up I feel inside.

"You think you can do the worrying for the both of us," she whispers. "But it doesn't work like that, Loch. Not in an equal relationship. And that's what ours is. That's what we've always had. Our relationship may be changing in some ways, but we can't possibly lose what we had before."

I exhale slowly. Everything she says makes sense. In every way imaginable she is so much wiser than me.

Blowing into my ear, she tickles me. "Hey, have you fallen asleep?"

I smile slightly. "No, I'm thinking."

"Of what, my love?"

A small aftershock runs through me. *My love.* That's who we've become. Two people in love.

"What happened with Willa . . ." I begin unsteadily. "That must have given you a fright."

"I think it gave us both a fright."

Unspoken words hover in the air between us.

"Maya, you know, I—I really did pull her arm quite hard. It's—it's no wonder she fell," I manage in a frantic rush.

She lifts her head from my chest and props it up on one hand, her face luminous in the moonlight. "Lochie, did you mean to pull her off the counter?"

"No."

"Did you mean to hurt her?"

"Course not."

"Did you mean to dislocate her shoulder?"

"No!"

"Okay," she says gently, stroking my face. "Then that train of thought leads nowhere. It was a complete accident. Don't let that stupid woman at the hospital make you doubt that for one tiny second!"

Tears of relief threaten to overwhelm me. I didn't think she blamed me, but I couldn't be sure. I take a deep breath. "But now social services has got us on its radar—Jesus!"

"Then we'll just have to keep beneath it, same as always." Maya pulls herself up onto her elbow, looking down at me. Her hair partly obscures her face and I cannot read her expression. "Lochie, you'll be eighteen next month. We've got this far. We can keep going! We can keep this family together, you and I. We're a good team; we're a great team. Together we're strong!"

I nod slowly against the pillow and reach up to stroke her

cheek. Maya circles my wrist with her hand and gently kisses each finger. My hand slides down her neck, her chest, comes to rest against her breast. . . . Suddenly I can feel my heart.

Maya is watching me intently, her eyes very bright in the shadows. I can hear my breath, hot and heavy, suddenly acutely aware that all that separates our two bodies is a cotton nightie, a thin T-shirt, and underwear. I run my hand down her ribs, across her stomach, toward her bare thigh. Maya leans forward. Taking the bottom of my T-shirt in her hands, she begins to raise it, slowly pulling it up and over my head. She then reaches down and pulls off her nightie. I emit a ragged gasp. Her body is perfectly white, in sharp contrast to her hair, which is almost fiery in the moonlight. Her lips are a dark pink, her cheeks lightly flushed, and her eyes bluer than the sea—watchful, uncertain. The colors and contrasts overwhelm me. My gaze travels down over her, taking in the upward curve of her breasts, the taut skin of her stomach, the long slender legs. I could stare at her forever. I can make out the ridge of her collarbone, the peaks of her hips. Her skin looks so smooth, I long to kiss it. I want to feel every part of her but my hands tighten against the sheet.

"We can touch each other," Maya whispers. "Just touch each other. There's no law against that."

Reaching out, she gently runs her finger up my stomach, across my chest, and into the curve of my neck; cupping my cheek in her hand, she leans forward to kiss me. I close my eyes and, with trembling hands, stroke her neck, her shoulders, her breasts. Circling her with my arms, I pull her gently back down against the pillows and slowly, tentatively, as if afraid of hurting her, begin to trace my fingers down her body. . . .

I awake with a start to find myself alone in Maya's bed, but the house around me is silent. A scrap of paper bearing my name is left beside me on the floor. After reading it, I fall back against the pillows, staring up at the cracked ceiling. Last night feels like a dream. I can't believe we spent it together, naked, our hands stroking each other's bodies—can't believe I actually felt her naked form press against mine. At first I was scared we might get carried away—might cross that final, forbidden barrier— but just touching each other was so incredible, so powerful, so thrilling, it took my breath away. I wanted more—of course I wanted more—but I knew that, for now, this would have to be enough.

I am jolted out of my reverie by the slam of the front door, the sound of a schoolbag being dropped to the floor, followed by softly creaking footsteps on the stairs. The bedroom door inches open, and I pull myself up against the headboard as Maya's face breaks into a smile. "You're awake!"

She bounds over to the window and throws open the curtains, and I rub my eyes against the bright morning light. I yawn and stretch, waving the note she left me.

"Maya, what were you thinking? We can't just skip school." The reproach in my voice fades as she jumps onto the bed beside me and gives me a cold kiss. "Eek, you're freezing."

She collapses beside me, the back of her head hitting the wall with a thud, squashing my legs with hers. "You didn't have anything important going on today, did you?"

"I don't think so. . . ."

"Good—well, me neither."

I take in her flushed face, the wisps of hair framing her face, her school uniform. "You pretended to the others you were going to school and then just came home again?"

"Yes—as soon as I saw Kit go through the gates, I turned back! You didn't think I was gonna give you the day off alone, did you?" She gives me a wicked grin. "Come on, you awake yet?"

Shaking my head, I raise my hand to my mouth and yawn again. "I don't think so. How come I didn't hear the alarm?"

"I turned it off."

"Why?"

"You were sleeping so deeply, Loch. You've been looking so knackered. I just couldn't bear to wake you. . . ."

I start to smile, blinking at her sleepily. "I'm not complaining."

"Really?" I watch her face light up. "We have the whole day to ourselves!" She gazes up at the ceiling in delight. "I'm going to get changed, and then I thought we could make pancakes and then we could go for a walk and then—"

"Wait, wait, wait. Come here first." I reach for her arm just as she is about to roll off the bed.

"What?"

"Come here!" Still squinting slightly against the light, I tug at her wrist. "Kiss me."

Maya laughs and obliges, sliding back down beside me. Slowly I unbutton her shirt and she wriggles out of her skirt. Ducking beneath the warmth of the duvet, I start tracing a line of kisses down her body. . . .

She is standing naked in front of the open door of her wardrobe when I return from the shower and it takes her a moment to notice me hovering in the doorway, watching her. She turns, meets my gaze, and blushes. She reaches out for the crumpled sheet at the end of her bed and wraps it round beneath her arms. The white material swirls around her feet, making me smile. I pull on my underwear and join her by the window, kissing her cheek. "I do."

She looks at me questioningly and then down at the sheet before breaking into giggles.

 TABITHA SUZUMA

"In sickness and in health?" she asks. "Till death do us part?"

I shake my head. "Way beyond that," I say. "Forever."

She takes my hands and leans in for a kiss. It hurts. Suddenly everything hurts and I don't know why.

"Look at the sky," she says, resting her head in the crook of my neck. "It's so blue."

And suddenly I do know: It's because everything is so beautiful, so wonderful, so utterly glorious—yet it cannot possibly last, and I want to preserve this moment for the rest of my life.

I wrap my arms around her and press my cheek against the top of her head, then notice the bracelet against her white wrist, the silver glinting in the morning sun. I reach down and touch it.

"Promise me you'll always keep it," I say, my voice unsteady suddenly.

"Of course," she replies instantly. "Why wouldn't I? I love it. It's the most beautiful thing I own."

"Promise me," I say again, running my fingers over the smooth metal. "Even if—even if things don't work out . . . You don't have to wear it. Just keep it hidden somewhere."

"Hey." She tilts her head so that I am forced to meet her eyes. "I promise. But things are going to work out. Look at us—they already have. You're about to be eighteen, and then the next month I'll be seventeen. We're nearly adults, Lochie, and once we are, no one will be able to stop us from doing what we want."

I lift my head, nod, and force a small smile. "Right."

I see her expression shift. She leans her forehead against my cheek and closes her eyes as if in pain. "You have to believe it, Lochie," she whispers. "We both have to believe it with all our might if we want to make it happen."

I swallow hard and grasp the tops of her arms. "I believe it!"

She opens her eyes and smiles. "So do I!"

This is the definition of happiness: a whole day stretching out ahead of me, beautiful in its emptiness and simplicity. No crowded classrooms, no packed corridors, no lonely breaks, no cafeteria lunch, no droning teachers, no relentless ticking clock, no counting down the minutes to the end of yet another dreary day . . . Instead we spend it in a kind of joyous delirium, trying to savor every moment, enjoy to the full our bubble of happiness before it bursts. We make pancakes and mess about with the strangest combinations of toppings: Maya wins Most Disgusting with her concoction of Marmite, cornflakes, and ketchup, which has me gagging over the bin. I win Most Artistic with frozen peas, red grapes, and Smarties on a bed of mayonnaise. We close the curtains in the front room and cuddle up on the sofa. Sometime in the early afternoon Maya falls asleep in my arms. I watch her in slumber, tracing my finger across the contours of her face, down her neck, over her smooth white shoulder, down the length of her arm, along each of her fingers. The sun pours in through the hastily drawn curtains; the clock on the mantelpiece ticks its relentless countdown, the thin needle making its way mercilessly round and round the face. I close my eyes and bury my face in Maya's hair, trying to shut out the sound, desperate to stop the precious time we have together from running through my fingers like sand.

When she wakes, it is just after three. In half an hour she will have to pick up Tiffin and Willa, while I clean up the mess in the kitchen and carefully remove any remaining items of clothing from her bedroom floor. I cup her flushed, sleepy face in my hands and start kissing her with a fervor bordering on hysteria. I feel angry and desperate.

"Lochie, listen to me," she tries to say between kisses. "Listen, my love—listen. We'll just start skipping school every couple of weeks!"

"I can't wait another whole fortnight—"

"What if we don't have to?" she says suddenly, eyes igniting. "We could spend every night together, like yesterday. Once we're sure Tiff and Willa are asleep, you can come and get into my bed—"

"Every night? What if one of them walks in? We can't do that!" But she has my attention.

"There's that rusty bolt at the bottom of my door, remember? We can just lock it! Kit always falls asleep plugged into his headphones. And the other two hardly ever wake up in the night anymore."

I chew on my thumbnail, thinking hard about the risks, desperately torn. I look up into Maya's bright eyes and remember last night, feeling her smooth naked body beneath my hands for the first time. "Okay!" I whisper with a smile.

"Lochie? Are you better, Lochie? Are you taking us to school tomorrow, Lochie?" Willa is all concern, climbing onto my lap as I sit sprawled out in front of the TV.

Tiffin's concern is more casual, but present nonetheless. "You got the flu or what?" he asks me in his growing East End accent, blowing the long fair hair out of his eyes. "Are you ill? You don't look ill. How long are you gonna be ill for, anyway?"

With a jolt, I realize that my taking a day off from school has thrown them. Previously I've gone in with the flu and even bronchitis, just because the kids had to be taken in, Kit had to be watched, social services had to be kept off our backs, so taking a day off wasn't usually an option. I realize too that they associate any kind of "serious" illness with Mum: Mum collapsing drunk on the doorstep, Mum retching over the toilet bowl, Mum lying passed out on

the kitchen floor. They aren't worried about my supposed headache—they are worried I will disappear.

"I've never felt better," I reassure them truthfully. "My headache's all gone. Why don't we all go and play outside together for a bit?"

It is amazing the difference a day off from school can make. Usually, by this time, I am dragged down with exhaustion, snappy and on edge, desperate to get the kids into bed so I can get a moment alone with Maya and a start on homework before I find myself falling asleep at my desk. Today, as the four of us set up a game of British bulldog, I feel almost weightless, as if the earth's gravity has dramatically decreased. So, as the sun begins to set on the mild March day, I find myself standing in the middle of the empty street, hands on knees, waiting for the three of them to come tearing toward me, hoping to make it to the opposite side without getting caught. Tiffin looks all ready for takeoff, one sneakered foot pressed back against the wall, his arms bent, hands clenched into fists, a look of fierce determination in his eyes. I know that on the first round, I have to give him a run for his money without actually catching him. Willa is receiving last-minute instructions from Maya, who, by the looks of things, is planning diversionary tactics to allow her to run straight across the road without getting caught.

"Come on!" Tiffin yells impatiently.

Maya straightens up, Willa hops up and down in excitement, and I count down, "Three, two, one, go!"

Nobody moves. I gallop sideways so that I'm directly facing Willa and she squeals in delighted terror, pressing herself back against the wall like a starfish, as if trying to push herself right through. Then Tiffin is off like a bullet, heading away from me at a sharp angle. Anticipating his move, I race toward him, blocking his trajectory. He hesitates, torn between the humiliation of running back to the safety of the wall and the risk of making a run for it. Boldly, he chooses the latter. I give chase immediately, but he's surprisingly fast for his size. He makes it to the other side by the skin of his teeth, face glowing pink with exertion, eyes triumphant.

Maya has used this diversion to send Willa on her way. She runs wildly toward Tiffin, so intent on reaching safety that she almost launches herself straight into my arms. I take a step back and growl in an attempt to send her off in a different direction. She freezes, a rabbit caught in headlights, her blue eyes huge with the thrill of fear. From either side of the street, the other two scream out instructions.

"Go back, go back!" Tiffin screeches.

"Go around him—dodge him!" Maya yells, confident in the knowledge that I'll only pretend to try and catch her.

TABITHA SUZUMA

Willa makes a move to my right. I lunge for her, my fingers brushing the hood of her coat, and with a squeal she hurls herself toward the wall, head-butting Tiffin in the stomach, who promptly doubles over with a dramatic yell.

Maya is now the only one left, dancing about on the other side of the street, making Tiffin and Willa laugh.

"Run—just run for it, Maya!" Tiffin screams helpfully.

"Go this way—no, this way!" Willa squeals, pointing wildly in all directions.

I flash Maya an evil grin to signal that I have every intention of catching her, and she bites back a smile, a hint of mischief in her eyes. Hands in pockets, I start sauntering toward her.

She goes for it. Catching me off guard, she sets off at an acute angle. I match her pace for pace and start laughing in anticipated triumph as we approach the boundary. Then, out of nowhere, she wrong-foots me and goes tearing back the opposite way. I hurl myself after her but it's no use. She makes it to the other wall, yelping in triumph.

In the next round I catch Tiffin, whose disappointment soon turns to glee as he finds himself in the role of predator. Ruthlessly, he goes straight for Willa and catches her within seconds of her leaving the safety of the wall, sending her flying. Bravely she picks herself up, briefly examines her scraped palms, and then dances about excitedly in the middle of the road, stretching her arms out as if hoping to block our path. As we surge toward her, Maya and I both try so hard to allow her to catch us that we end up colliding and she grabs us both, provoking much hysteria. Maya has just begun her turn when, in the distance, I make out a lone figure trailing down the road toward us and recognize Kit, dragging himself home dejectedly after an hour spent in detention for swearing at a teacher.

"Kit, Kit, we're playing British bulldog!" Tiffin yells excitedly. "Come and join in! Please! Lochie and the girls are all rubbish. I'm ruling this game!"

Kit stops at the gate. "You all look like a bunch of retards," he announces coldly.

"Well, come and liven up the game, then," I suggest. "You know, I could do with some competition. This game is piss easy for a runner like me."

Kit lowers his bag and I see him hesitate, torn between expressing the usual contempt for his family and the desire just to be a kid again.

"Unless you're worried I'll outrun you," I say, throwing down the gauntlet.

"Yeah, right, in your dreams," Kit sneers. He turns toward the front door but at the last minute pulls back. Abruptly, he takes off his blazer.

"Yay!"Tiffin screams.

"You can be on our team!"Willa screams.

"We don't have teams, you dumbhead!"Tiffin yells back.

Soon we are embroiled in yet another round. I am back in the middle and determined to chase Kit into the ground—without actually catching him, obviously. Typically, he is the last to peel himself off the wall after all the others have made it safely to the other side. He waits for what feels like an eternity, clearly trying to test my patience. I start wandering off, turning my back on him, even bending down to tie my shoelace, but he is wise to all my tricks. Only when I am a couple of meters away from him does he finally move, deliberately making it as difficult for himself as possible. He wrong-foots me, legs it sharp right, hesitates as I block him, then begins to back away. He gives me his cocky, mocking smile, but I can see the sharp determination in his eyes. I lunge for him. He dodges me by millimeters and sets off at a blinding sprint. I charge after him, intent on making up the short gap between us. I grab him by his shirt collar just as his hands slap the wall. When he turns to face me, his face is aglow with a delight I haven't seen in him for years.

We play on, well into the dark. Willa eventually collapses in exhaustion and goes to sit in the warmth of the hallway, watching us and yelling instructions through the open door. Maya is next to join her. I am left with Tiffin and Kit, and suddenly we're all playing for real. Tiffin's soccer skills come in handy, making him impossibly slippery to catch. Kit uses every trick in the book to distract me, and soon the two of them are ganging up on me, using each other as foils, locking me into the role of chaser. Finally, in exhaustion, I go for Kit like a demented bull. I catch him inches away from safety but he refuses to surrender, reaching out desperately for the wall and half dragging me along with him. We fall to the ground and I'm tearing at his shirt to stop him sliding out of my grasp while Tiffin is trying to use himself as a human chain between Kit and the wall.

"I won, I won!" Kit yells.

"No way! You have to touch the wall, you big cheat!"

"I touched it!"

"You didn't!"

"I touched Tiff's hand and he's touching the wall!"

"That doesn't count!"

I have Kit pinned to the ground and he screams to Tiffin for help. Tiffin bravely leaves the safety of the wall but immediately gets pulled down on top of us. "Got you both!" I cry.

"Cheater, cheater!" They deafen me with their yells.

Soon we can't move for laughter and exhaustion, Tiffin straddling my back and Kit, shaking with mirth, reaching out for a nearby twig and using that to touch the wall. We finally

peel ourselves off the road, filthy and battered. Kit's face is streaked with dirt and Tiffin's shirt collar torn as we limp inside, long after dinnertime, long after the homework hour. Once the boys have been persuaded to wash their hands, we collapse around the kitchen table with Maya and Willa, feasting on snacks and Nutella straight from the jar.

Kit tries to trip me as I get up to put the kettle on. "We should have a rematch," he informs me. "You need the practice."

And then he smiles.

CHAPTER TWENTY-TWO

Maya

Over the next few weeks a momentous change seems to occur. Suddenly everyone seems so much happier, so much more at ease. Kit starts behaving like a civilized human being. Lochan turns eighteen—we all go out to Burger King to celebrate, and Willa and I make a delicious, albeit lopsided cake. Mum neglects even to phone. Taking the odd day off from school allows Lochan and me time for us, time to tackle the mountain of things that needed doing long ago: trips to the doctor, the dentist, the hairdresser. Lochan helps Kit fix his bike and finally gets enough cash from Mum to buy new uniforms and pay some of the overdue bills. Together, we clean the house from top to bottom, devise a fresh set of house rules to encourage the kids to take on a few responsibilities of their own, and, most important of all, make time to do things as a family—to play in the park or sit around the kitchen table with a board game. Now that Lochan and I spend our nights together and skip school whenever things start to get too stressful again, time on our own is no longer so limited and having fun with the children becomes as important as looking after them.

Mum "checks in on us" from time to time, rarely staying more than a night or two, reluctantly handing us the cash that's supposed to get us through the week, resentfully pulling out her checkbook to pay the bills that Lochan thrusts at her. A lot of her anger stems from the fact that Lochan and I refuse to leave school and get jobs, but there is a deeper reason there too. She is still forced to support a family she is no longer a part of—has chosen to no longer be a part of. But apart from the financial side of things, none of us expects anything from her anymore, so no one is disappointed. Tiffin and Willa cease rushing to greet her, no longer beg for a few minutes of her time. Lochan is already starting to look for a job after his A-levels. At university, he insists, he will be able to work part-time and we won't have to keep begging Mum for money. As a family, we are now complete.

But I live for the night. Stroking Lochan, feeling every part of him, arousing him with just the touch of my hand, makes me long for more.

"D'you ever wonder what it would be like?" I ask him. "To actually . . ."

"All the time."

There is a long silence. He kisses me, his lashes tickling my cheek.

"Me too," I whisper.

"One day," he pants softly as I graze my fingers up his thigh. "Yes . . ."

Yet some nights we come so close. I feel the longing ache in my body and sense Lochan's frustration as keenly as my own. When he kisses me so hard it almost hurts and his body thrums against mine, desperate to go further, I begin to worry that by sharing a bed every night we are tormenting each other. But whenever we talk about it, we always agree we would far, far rather be together like this than go back to our separate rooms and not touch each other at all.

At school, as I gaze up at Lochan sitting alone on the steps at break time and he looks back down at me, the gulf between us seems enormous. We discreetly raise a hand in greeting and I count down the hours until I'll get to see him properly at home. Sitting on the low wall with Francie at my side, I often lose track of the conversation and sit there daydreaming about him, until one day, to my astonishment, I see that he is not alone.

"Oh my God, who's he talking to?" I cut Francie off mid-sentence.

Her eyes follow my gaze. "Looks like Declan, that new guy. His family just moved here from Ireland, I think. Apparently he's supersmart, applying for all these universities. . . . You must have seen him around!"

I haven't, but unlike Francie I don't spend most of my time ogling every older male pupil.

"Jesus!" I exclaim, surprise sounding in my voice. "Why d'you think they're talking?"

"They were having lunch together yesterday," Francie informs me.

I turn to stare at her. "Seriously?"

"Yeah. And when I passed Lochan in the corridor the other day, we kind of had a conversation." She opens her mouth wide.

"*What?*"

"Yeah! Instead of walking straight past me, pretending he hadn't seen me, he actually stopped and asked me how I was."

I feel an incredulous smile light up my face.

"So, you see, he *can* talk to people." Francie lets out a wistful sigh. "Maybe I can finally get him to go out with me."

I look back up at the steps again with a smile of delight. "Oh my God . . ." Declan is still there. He seems to be showing Lochan something on his mobile phone. I watch Lochan make a funny gesture in the air, and Declan laughs.

Still reeling with shock, I decide to take the plunge and ask Francie the question I'd been wanting to put to her for some time now.

"Hey, I've been wondering about something. . . . Do you—do you think that any two people, if they really and truly love each other, should be allowed to be together no matter who they are?" I ask.

Francie shoots me a look of amusement, sees that I'm serious, and narrows her eyes in thought. "Sure, why not?"

"What if their religion forbade it? If their parents were devastated or threatened to disown them or something—should they still go ahead anyway?"

"Sure," Francie answers with a shrug. "It's their lives, so they should be allowed to pick who they like. If the parents are crazy enough to try and stop them from seeing each other, they could run away, elope."

"What if it was something even more difficult?" I ask, thinking hard. "What if it was—I dunno—a teacher and a pupil?"

Francie's eyes widen and she suddenly grabs my arm. "No

way! Who the hell is it? Mr. Elliot? That guy in the IT department? The one with the tattoo?"

Laughing, I shake my head. "Not me, silly! I was just thinking hypothetically. Like we were talking about in history, about society having changed so much over the past half century . . ."

"Oh." Francie's face falls in disappointment.

I look at her with a snort. "Mr. Elliot? Are you kidding me? He's about sixty!"

"I think he's kind of sexy!"

I roll my eyes. "That's because you're crazy. But seriously, though. Hypothetically . . ."

Francie lets out a labored sigh. "Well, they should probably wait until the pupil was over the legal age limit, for starters—"

"But what if she was? What if she was sixteen and the guy was in his forties? Should they run away together? Would that be right?"

"Well, the guy would lose his job and the girl's parents would be worried sick, so they'd probably be better off keeping it secret for a few years. Then, by the time the girl was nineteen or so, it wouldn't even be a big deal anymore!" She shrugs. "I think it would be kinda cool to go out with a teacher. Just imagine—sitting in class, you could . . ."

I tune her out and inhale deeply, frustrated. There is

nothing, I suddenly realize, nothing that can compare to our situation.

"So nothing is taboo anymore?" I interrupt. "You're saying there are no two people who, if they love each other enough, should be forced apart?"

Francie thinks for a moment and then shrugs. "I guess not. Not here, anyway, thank God. We're lucky enough to live in a country that is pretty open-minded. As long as one person isn't forcing the other one, then I guess any love is allowed."

Any love. Francie isn't stupid. Yet the one kind of love that will never be allowed hasn't even crossed her mind. The one love so disgusting and taboo, it isn't even included in a conversation about illicit relationships.

The conversation haunts me over the following weeks. Although I have no intention of ever confiding our secret to anyone, I can't help wondering what Francie's reaction would be if she somehow found out. She is an intelligent, broad-minded person with a rebellious streak in her. Despite her bold declaration that no love is wrong, I strongly suspect that she would be as horrified as the next person if she knew of my relationship with Lochan. *But he's your brother!* I can hear her exclaim. *How could you ever do it with your brother? That's so gross! Oh God, Maya, you're sick, you're really sick. You need help.* And the strangest thing is that a part of me agrees. Part of me thinks: *Yes, if Kit were older and it were with him, then it would be totally gross.* The very idea is unthinkable; I don't even want to imagine it. It actually makes me feel physically sick. But how to get across to the outside world that Lochan and I are siblings only through a biological mishap? That we were never brother and sister in the real sense, but always partners, having to bring up a real family as we grew up ourselves? How to explain that Lochan has never felt like a brother but like something far, far closer than that—a soul mate, a best friend, part of the very fiber of my being? How to explain that this situation, the love we feel for each other—everything that to others may seem sick and twisted and disgusting—to us feels completely natural and wonderful and oh—so, so right?

At night, after kissing and cuddling and touching each other, we lie there and talk late into the night. We talk about anything and everything: how the kids are doing, funny anecdotes from school, how we feel about each other. And ever since I spotted him on the steps having a conversation, we talk about Lochan's newfound voice. Although he is keen to play it down, he does confess to having made a sort of friend in Declan, who initially approached Lochan because they both had offers from UCL. Speaking to anyone else is still something he avoids, but I'm overjoyed. The fact that he has made a connection with one person outside the family means that he can, that there will be others, and that once he goes to university he will finally meet people he has something in common with. And the night Lochan tells me he actually managed to stand up in front of his whole English class and read out loud one of his essays, I let out a squeal that has to be silenced by a pillow.

"Why?" I ask, gasping in delight. "How come? What happened? What changed?"

"I'd been thinking about—about what you said, that I should take one step at a time and that, well, mainly that you thought I could do it."

"What was it like?" I ask, struggling to keep my voice a whisper, looking into eyes that, even in the half light, sparkle with a gentle triumph.

"Horrible."

"Oh, Loch!"

"My hands were trembling and my voice was shaking and the words on the page suddenly turned into this mass of hieroglyphs, but somehow I got through it. And when I finished there were some people—and not just the girls—who actually clapped." He lets out a short exclamation of surprise.

"Well, of course they did! Your essays are completely amazing!" I reply.

"There was also this guy—a guy called Tyrese, who's

okay—and he came up to me after the bell and said something about the essay. I don't know what, exactly, because I was still deafened by terror"—he laughs—"but it must have been vaguely complimentary because he slapped me on the back."

"See?" I crow softly. "They were inspired by your essay! No wonder your teacher was so keen for you to read one out. Did you say anything back to Tyrese?"

"I think I said something along the lines of 'Oh-um-yeah-uh-cheers.'" Lochan lets out a derisive snort.

I laugh. "That's great! And next time you'll actually say something a little more coherent!"

Lochan smiles and turns on his side, propping his head up on his hand. "You know, recently, even when we're apart, I sometimes think that maybe I'm going to beat this thing, that one day I might be normal."

I kiss his nose. "You are normal, silly."

He doesn't respond but begins pensively rubbing a strand of my hair between his fingers. "Sometimes I wonder . . ." He trails off abruptly, suddenly examining my hair in great detail.

"Sometimes you wonder . . ." I tilt my head and kiss the corner of his mouth.

"What—what I'd do without you," he finishes in a whisper, gaze studiously avoiding mine.

"Go to sleep at a reasonable time, in a bed where you can actually roll over without falling out . . ."

He laughs softly into the night. "Oh yeah, an easier life in so many ways. Mum should never have got pregnant again so quickly after me. . . ."

His joke tails off uncomfortably and the laughter is sucked up into the darkness as the truth behind his words sinks in.

After a long silence Lochan suddenly says, "She certainly wasn't meant to have children, but, well, not that I really believe in fate or anything—but what if we were meant to have each other?"

I don't respond immediately, not quite sure what he's getting at.

"I guess what I'm trying to say is that maybe what seemed like a shitty situation for a bunch of abandoned kids actually, because of the way it happened, led to something really special."

I think about this for a moment. "Do you think, if we'd had conventional parents, or just parents, you and I would have fallen in love?"

Silence from him now. Moonlight illuminates the side of his face, a silvery-white glow washing across one half, leaving the other in shadow. He has that distant look in his eyes that either means his mind is on something else or he's giving my tentative question some very serious consideration.

"I've often wondered . . ." he begins quietly. I wait for him to continue. "Many people claim that the abused often go on to abuse, so for most psychologists, our mother's neglect—which is considered a form of abuse—would be linked directly to our 'abnormal' behavior, which they would interpret as abuse, too."

"Abuse?" I exclaim in astonishment. "But who would be abusing who? In abuse, there's an attacker and a victim. How could we be seen as both abusers and abusees?"

The blue-white glow of the moon casts just enough light for me to notice Lochan's expression turn from pensive to troubled.

"Maya, come on, think about it. I'd be automatically seen as the abuser and you the victim."

"Why?"

"How many cases of younger sisters sexually abusing older brothers have you read about? Come to think of it, how many female rapists and female pedophiles are there?"

"But that's crazy!" I exclaim. "I could have been the one to force you into a sexual relationship! Not physically, but by—I dunno—bribes, blackmail, threats, whatever! Are you saying that even if I'd abused you, people would still assume I was the victim just because I'm a girl and one year younger?"

Lochan nods slowly, his shaggy hair dark against the pillow. "Unless there was some really strong evidence to the contrary—an admission of guilt on your part, witnesses or something—then, yes."

"But that's so sexist, so unfair!"

"I agree, but people rely heavily on generalizations, and although it must sometimes happen the other way round, it's gotta be pretty rare. For a start, there's the physical aspect. . . . So it's not really all that surprising that in situations like this, guys are automatically assumed to be the abusers, especially if they're older."

I curl my legs up against Lochan's stomach and ruminate on this for a while. It all seems so wrong. But at the same time I'm aware that I'm guilty of the same prejudices—if I hear there's been a rape, or a child's been abducted, I immediately think male rapist, male pedophile.

"But what about if no one's being abused?" I ask suddenly. "What if it's one hundred percent consensual, like us?"

He exhales slowly. "I don't know. It would still be against the law. It's still incest. But there's not much info on it, because apparently it's something that very, very rarely happens. . . ."

We both stop talking for a while. So long, in fact, that I begin to think Lochie has fallen asleep. But when I turn my head on the pillow to check, I see his eyes are wide open, staring up at the ceiling, bright and intense.

"Lochie . . ." I roll onto my side and run my fingers down his bare arm. "When you said there's not much info on it, what did you mean? How do you know?"

He is chewing his lip again. Beside me, his body feels tense. He hesitates for a moment, then rolls back over to face me. "I—I did a bit of research on the Internet. . . . I just—I just . . ." He takes a deep breath before trying again. "I just wanted to know where we stood."

"With what?"

"With—with the law."

"To figure out a way of changing our names? Of living together?"

He rubs his lip, refusing to meet my gaze, looking increasingly agitated and uncomfortable.

"What?" I demand loudly, frightened now.

"To see what would happen if we got caught."

"Caught living together?" I ask incredulously.

"Caught—caught having a relationship—"

"Having sex?"

"Yes."

"By who?"

"The police."

I am finding it difficult to breathe suddenly, as if my windpipe is constricting. I sit up abruptly, hair falling down around my face.

"Look, Maya. It's not—I just wanted to check . . ." Lochan is pulling himself up against the headboard, struggling to find words to reassure me.

"Does that mean we can never—"

"No, no, not necessarily," he says quickly. "It just means that we can't until the kids are grown up and safe, and even then we have to be very, very careful."

"I knew it was officially illegal," I tell him desperately. "But pot's illegal, and so is speeding, and so is peeing in a public place. Anyway, how would the police even notice and why would they even care—it's not like we're hurting anyone or even ourselves!" I feel like I'm running out of breath but I'm determined to make my point. "And anyway, if we did somehow get caught, what the hell would the police do? Fine us?" I let out a harsh laugh. Why is Lochan trying to freak me out like this? Why is he acting so serious, as if we would be committing a real crime?

Half propped up against the headboard, Lochan stares at me. If it weren't for the stricken expression in his eyes, he would look quite comical, his hair all on end. His face radiates a mixture of fear and despair. "Maya . . ."

"Lochie, what? What's the matter?"

He breathes: "If we were found out, we'd be sent to prison."

CHAPTER TWENTY-THREE

Lochan

Thankfully we were too exhausted to talk about it much more that night. Before sleep overcame us, however, Maya wanted to know further details—what kind of sentence we could face, whether the law was different in other countries—but I could only repeat the little I had gleaned from my secret scouring of the Internet. There is actually precious little information to be found on consensual incest, though there is plenty on the nonconsensual kind, which seems to be the only type most people think exists. I have thoroughly searched for online testimonies but found only two that had actually made it into the public domain—neither of them in the UK and both between siblings who met again as adults after being separated at birth.

The topic only resurfaces briefly the following day before being dropped completely. Despite her initial reaction, Maya's shock and outrage seem to have been assuaged by my assurances that the only legal information I have found has been hypothetical—technically, yes, a couple accused of incest could face a jail sentence, but that would rarely happen in the case of two consenting adults. I am now legally an adult and Maya is close behind me, so we won't have to wait much longer. Police hardly go out searching for this kind of thing. And in the very unlikely event that some random person did find out, why on earth would they try and have us arrested or taken to court? Because they hated us? Wanted some kind of revenge? And unless we had biological children of our own— which would be insane—how on earth could anyone ever get enough proof to stand up in court? They would have to actually catch us in the act, and even then it would be their word against ours.

My main concern for the future is how to protect Kit, Tiffin, and Willa from being ostracized in the event of rumors about Maya and I living together and never having partners of our own. But by then they would have their own lives, and Maya and I would have hopefully moved away and, if necessary, changed

TABITHA SUZUMA

our names. Yes, we could simply change our names and live as openly and freely as any unmarried couple. No more hiding, no more locked doors. Freedom. And the right to love each other without persecution.

For the time being, though, Maya and I have to cram for exams. We are astonished when, out of the blue one day, Kit offers to take Tiffin and Willa to the movies to give us time to study. On another occasion he takes them to the park to play soccer. Roughly since that first game of British bulldog out in the street, he has stopped goading me, stopped slamming around the house, stopped winding up the kids, and stopped trying to undermine me all the time. He hasn't exactly become an angel overnight, but he no longer seems to feel threatened by my role in the family. It's almost as if he's accepted Maya and me as surrogate parents. I have no idea where it's all come from. Perhaps he has joined a nicer group of boys at school. Perhaps he is just growing up. But whatever the reason, I dare to believe Kit has truly begun to turn the corner.

He runs down to dinner one evening, triumphantly waving a piece of paper. "I'm going on a school trip when we have Easter! Nya-na, nya-nya-na!" He pulls a taunting face at the other two.

"Where?" Willa shrieks excitedly as if she were also included.

"Whoa! So not fair!" Tiffin exclaims, his face falling.

"Here, quick, quick, you've gotta sign it now!" Kit waves the sheet above my plate and thrusts a pen into my hand.

"I didn't realize your teacher was waiting for this on the doorstep!"

Kit pulls a face at me. "Very funny. Just sign it, will you?"

I scan the letter and balk at the price, quickly trying to work out where on earth we'll get the money from. Cancel the check for the phone bill that I only posted yesterday, eat baked beans for the next fortnight, pretend to Mum that we have no running water and need money for a plumber . . .

I forge our mother's signature. It saddens me a little to see how delirious with excitement Kit is about the trip—it's only an activity week on the Isle of Wight, but he has never been farther afield than Surrey.

"It's abroad!" he crows at Tiffin. "We have to take a boat! We're going to an island in the middle of the sea!"

I open my mouth, about to readjust Kit's vision of a desert island surrounded by palm trees in order to avoid terrible disappointment, when Maya catches my eye and subtly shakes her head. She's right. Kit won't be disappointed. Even rainy and cold, the muddy Isle of Wight will seem like paradise to him—and a million miles away from home.

"What are you going to do there?" Tiffin asks, slouching

down in his chair and prodding dejectedly at his chicken with his fork.

Kit throws himself down and kicks back, reading from the newly signed letter. "Canoeing, horse riding, rock climbing, orienteering"—his voice rises with mounting delight— "*camping?*" He returns the front legs of his chair to the floor with an astonished thud. "I didn't see that one. Yes! I've always wanted to go camping!"

"Me too!" Tiffin cries. "Why can't I go? Are you allowed to bring brothers?"

"Horse riding!" Willa's eyes are huge with disbelief.

"How come St. Luke's never takes us on trips?" Tiffin's lower lip quivers. "Life is so unfair."

I don't remember ever seeing Kit so excited. The only problem, though, is his fear of heights. It is something he has never admitted to, but there was that time—forever etched into my memory—when he fainted on the edge of the top diving board and dropped unconscious into the water. Then, only last year, he started feeling dizzy and fell while attempting to follow his friends across a high wall. He has never been rock climbing before, and knowing he would rather die than sit out and watch his classmates, I go to speak to Coach Wilson, the teacher in charge of the expedition, careful to ask for Kit not to be excluded, but for an adult to keep an eye on him. Still, I find myself worrying. Things with Kit are going so well, almost too well. I worry that the trip won't live up to his expectations; I worry even more that, with his daredevil nature, he may have an accident. Then I remember what Maya said to me about always thinking about the worst-case scenario and force myself to purge the worry from my mind.

By the end of term Maya and I are exhausted, clawing our way toward the Easter holidays. I can't believe that school will soon be a thing of the past. Apart from a few review classes after the holidays, all I have left are the actual exams. Naturally, they scare me a little, as my university place hangs in the balance, but beyond them lies the promise of a new life.

Time alone with Maya has been scant and I ache to have her to myself, even just for a day. But as soon as Kit leaves for his trip, the Easter holidays will be upon us, with last-minute studying to cram in around two weeks of child care. I feel as if we will never get the chance to be properly alone together. After being at school all day, entertaining children all evening, rushing through household chores, and then poring over textbooks for hours, there is rarely time for more than a few kisses before falling asleep in each other's arms. I miss those hours we once had at the end of each day; I miss stroking every part of her body, feeling her hands against mine, talking until we fell asleep.

And I bitterly, bitterly resent that, just because our relationship is considered wrong, all those hours of happiness we could have together are being stolen from us, and we are forced instead to sneak about, in constant fear of being caught.

I find myself desperate for even the little things—being able to hold her hand on the way to school, kissing her good-bye in the corridor before heading for our separate classes, having lunch together, spending break times snuggled up together on a bench or kissing passionately behind one of the buildings, running over and hugging when we meet at the gates after the final bell. All things that the other couples at Belmont take for granted. Their liaisons are looked upon with a mixture of awe and envy by the pupils who are still single, despite the fact that they rarely last for more than a few weeks before crumbling over some stupid fight or because a new, better-looking prospect comes along. I don't view those people with horror or disgust for being so shallow and fickle. So many superficial liaisons surround me, so many guys just looking for sex, for another conquest to add to their brag list before swiftly moving on. One might struggle to understand why anyone would embark on relationships that lack any real, meaningful emotion, yet nobody judges them for it. They are "young," "just having a good time," and sure, if that's what they want, why shouldn't they?

But then why is it so terrible for me to be with the girl I love? Everyone else is permitted to have what they want, express their love as they please, without fear of harassment, ostracism, persecution, or even the law. Even emotionally abusive, adulterous relationships are often tolerated, despite the harm they cause others. In our progressive, permissive society, all these harmful, unhealthy types of "love" are allowed—but not ours. I can think of no other kind of love that is so totally rejected, even though ours is so deep, passionate, caring, and strong that forcing us apart would cause us unimaginable pain. We are being punished by the world for just one simple reason: for having been produced by the same woman.

The anger and frustration chip away at me, even though I try to keep them at bay, even though I keep focusing on the day Maya and I will finally be free to live together openly, free to love each other like any other couple. Sometimes, worse than watching her at school from a distance is seeing her at home, too close to touch, together but apart, so near and yet so far. Having to yank back my hand as I instinctively reach for hers at the dinner table, trying to brush against her accidentally just for the small tingle of pleasure caused by the touch of her skin. Gazing at her face as she reads to Willa on the couch, yearning to feel her hair, her cheek, her

TABITHA SUZUMA

mouth. Even though I can't wait for the holidays to begin so I can spend every minute of the day with her, I know that this tiny but impenetrable distance between us will be torture.

And then, just days before the end of term, a miracle occurs. Maya gets off the phone one evening and returns to the dinner table to announce that Freddie and his little sister have invited both Tiffin and Willa for a sleepover that weekend. The timing could not be better—that same day, Kit will be leaving for the Isle of Wight. Two days—two whole days of uninterrupted time together. Two days of freedom . . . Surreptitiously, Maya shoots me a look of pure delight, and elation fills me like helium in a balloon. While Tiffin pretends to fall off his chair in enthusiasm and Willa drums her shoes against the underside of the table, I am ready to bounce off the walls and start dancing.

"Wow. So by Saturday all three of us will be gone," Kit comments almost pensively, looking first at Maya, then at me. "It'll just be you and Maya stuck at home."

I nod and shrug, struggling to keep the rush of joy from showing on my face.

We don't have a chance to celebrate until Maya finishes putting Tiffin and Willa to bed, but as soon as she does, she comes hurrying down to where I am squatting, Brillo pad in hand, scrubbing out the fridge.

"We have so earned this!" she whispers in near hysteria, grabbing me by the shoulders and giving me an excited shake. Straightening up, I laugh at the sight of her face, her eyes shining in excitement. I drop the Brillo pad and wipe my hands on my jeans as she slides her arms around my neck and pulls me gently toward her. Closing my eyes, I kiss her long and hard, pushing the hair away from her eyes. She reaches up to stroke my face and then pulls back sharply.

"What?" I ask in surprise. "They're all upstairs. . . ."

"I heard something." She is staring at the kitchen door, carelessly left ajar.

For a brief moment Maya and I look at each other in alarm. Then we recognize the distant beat of Kit's music and the sound of Tiffin and Willa arguing in their room above us. We begin to laugh.

"Christ, we're jumpy!" I exclaim softly.

"It'll be so great not to have to be like this for a bit," Maya breathes. "Even if it's just for a couple of days. The constant paranoia—worried about even touching hands!"

"Two days of freedom," I whisper with a smile, pulling her close.

As the big day approaches, I find myself counting down the hours. Kit will set off for school at the usual time; we're taking

Tiffin and Willa to their friends' house shortly after. Come ten o'clock Saturday morning, we will shed our meaningless labels of brother and sister and be free, finally free, from the ties that force us apart.

Friday evening, Kit is packed and ready, bags lined up carefully in the hall. Everyone is in a hyper mood and I realize we have forgotten to do the weekly shop and the kitchen is devoid of all food. To my astonishment, Kit volunteers to go down to the local supermarket and pick up something for dinner. However, my surprise soon turns to annoyance when he returns with a bag crammed full of crisps, biscuits, chocolate bars, sweets, and ice cream. But Maya just laughs. "It's the end of term—we may as well have a bit of a celebration!"

Reluctantly I agree and the evening soon turns into mayhem as we picnic on the carpet in front of the television. Tiffin's sugar levels go through the roof and he starts doing somersaults off the couch while Kit tries to provoke a crash landing by getting in the way. Willa wants to join in too, and I am sure someone is going to break their neck, but they are laughing so wholeheartedly at Kit's karate moves that I refrain from trying to calm them down. Then Kit has the bright idea of fetching his speakers from the attic and setting up a makeshift karaoke machine. Soon we are all squished up on the couch together, desperately trying to keep a straight face as Willa delivers a performance of "Mamma Mia," getting all the words mixed up yet singing with such gusto that I'm sure the neighbors are going to come knocking. Kit's rendition of "I Can Be" is actually quite impressive despite the foul language, and Tiffin leaps about the room, bouncing off the walls like a rubber ball.

By ten o'clock, an exhausted Willa has passed out fully clothed on the couch. I carry her up to bed while Maya manhandles a sugar-high Tiffin into the bathroom. I cross Kit in the corridor and stop.

"All ready for tomorrow? Got everything you need?"

"Yep!" he replies with a note of satisfaction, his eyes bright.

"Kit, thank you for this evening," I say. "You were—you were a good sport, you know."

For a moment he appears unsure how to respond to such praise. He looks embarrassed and then smiles. "Yeah, well, watch out. Entertainers usually charge for their services, you know."

I give him a friendly shove, and as he disappears up the ladder, a giant speaker under each arm, I realize that the five-year age gap between us doesn't feel like quite such a chasm anymore.

CHAPTER TWENTY-FOUR

Maya

Never before have I seen Kit quite so eager to go to school. *If only it were like this every day*, I think ruefully. After devouring his toast in three bites, downing his juice in two gulps, he grabs his packed lunch from Lochan and dashes out into the hallway to gather up the rest of his things. When he returns with his bags, I look at him in his new khaki jacket, bought especially for the occasion, at odds with the holey jeans he refuses to part with and the torn sweatshirt several sizes too big, and feel a pang. His sandy hair is uncombed and he looks pale from too many late nights—skinny, vulnerable, almost fragile.

"Did you remember to pack your mobile charger?" I ask him.

"Yeah, yeah."

"Remember to call us when you arrive, all right?" Lochan adds. "And, you know, maybe again at some point during the week, just to let us know how you're getting on."

"Yeah, yeah. Okay." He slings the strap of one bag across his chest, the other onto his shoulder.

"Have you got the money I gave you?" Lochan asks.

"No, I spent it."

Lochan's eyes widen.

Kit snorts with laughter. "You're all so gullible!"

"Very funny. Just don't spend it on cigarettes or you know you'll get sent straight home."

"Only if I'm caught! Right—I'm off!" he yells before Lochan can respond, banging his way down the hall.

"Bye-bye!" Willa calls after him. "I'll miss you!"

"Bring me back a present!" Tiffin yells optimistically.

"Have fun and be good!" Lochan shouts.

"And careful!" I add.

The door slams, shaking the walls. I look at the kitchen clock, catch Lochan's eye, and laugh. Half past eight—has to be some kind of record. *One down*, I think with growing anticipation, *two to go.*

After a forced breakfast, Tiffin starts bouncing around,

saying it doesn't matter if we're early, Freddie won't mind, we have to go! Willa takes refuge on my lap, picks at the dried cereal in her bowl, and debates whether spending the whole night at someone else's house is actually such a good idea after all. Especially given that she doesn't like the dark, that she sometimes has nightmares, that Susie might not share her toys, that four blocks away is actually quite far if you decide you need to come home in the middle of the night. Lochan turns from the sink to look at us with an expression of such horror that I can't help but laugh.

It doesn't take me long to remind Willa of the benefits of spending the night with a friend from school who not only has a garden and a dollhouse, but also, apparently, a new puppy. Willa perks up and suddenly decides her new plastic tea set will almost certainly come in useful and runs upstairs to add it to her bag of toys. As soon as she leaves the room, Lochan turns from the sink, up to his elbows in foam.

"What if she changes her mind?" he asks, stricken. "She's never been for a sleepover before. She could throw a wobbly in the middle of the night or decide she wants to go home as soon as it gets dark. We'd have to go and pick her up—"

I laugh. "Don't look so worried, my love! She won't. Tiffin will be there, she adores Susie, and there's a puppy, for chrissakes."

He shakes his head with a slow smile. "You'd better be right. If the phone rings, I'm unplugging it, I swear to God—"

"You'd do that to your five-year-old sister?" I gasp in mock outrage.

"For one whole night alone? Jesus, Maya, I'd sell her to the gypsies!"

Laughing, I go out to fetch something from the hall table. "Guess what I've got." Gleefully I hold out my closed fist.

Lochan gently takes my hand in his. Uncurls my fingers. "A key?"

"Mum's key. I slipped it off her key ring when she dropped by last weekend to pick up some clothes."

His face lights up. "Whoa, smart move!"

"I know! She's hardly likely to turn up, but now we know that even if she did, she wouldn't be able to get into the house!"

"Pity we can't lock her out forever!"

After dropping the kids off at Freddie's, I run like I used to when I was a child—wild and fast and free. My shoes splash through muddy puddles, spattering my bare legs with dirty spray, and old ladies, hunched under umbrellas, move hastily aside to let me pass, stopping to turn and stare as I go tearing by. The bland white sky unleashes hard, thick cords of rain, a freezing wind lashing the hard spikes against my face, making my skin sting. I am completely drenched, my coat flapping open, my shirt almost transparent, my hair dripping down my back. I continue running faster and faster. I feel as if I'm about to be caught by the wind, lifted up into the air like a kite, and sent dipping and swirling high above the treetops toward the distant horizon. I have never felt so alive, so brimming with freedom and joy.

Slamming into the kitchen, I raise my arms in the air. "Wow." I stare at him, happiness threatening to burst from me like a stream of effervescent bubbles. "I can't believe it. I literally can't believe it. I thought this moment would never come."

Lochan starts to laugh.

"What?"

"You look like a drowned rat."

"Thanks!"

"Come here!" He darts toward me around the kitchen table and grabs me by the wrist. "Kiss me!"

I laugh and tilt my head up as he raises his warm hands to my face.

"Ugh, you're freezing." He kisses me softly and then a little harder. I'm aware of my hair dripping all over him.

"Let me get changed, then!"

I turn and run upstairs to my room. As I retrieve my towel from beneath a pile of clothes, Lochan comes in and leaps onto my bed, then turns round to sit with his knees drawn up, his back to the wall. I rub my hair and dry my face, then peel off my soaked skirt. I grapple with the top button of my shirt with one hand, bending over to rummage for a pair of jeans with the other. Unable to find them, I realize that my button is stuck. With a sigh of annoyance, I stop and pick at it with my nails.

I'm aware of Lochan getting up from the bed and coming over. "Jeez, you're even more useless than Tiffin!"

"It's because it's wet! I think this stupid shirt shrank in the rain or something."

"Hold on, hold on . . ." His warm hands brush against mine, tugging gently at the sodden material. Shivering, I drop my arms by my sides and feel his bangs tickle my forehead as he leans toward me, head lowered, breath warm against my neck. His eyes are narrowed in concentration as, beneath his insistent fingers, the button finally starts to loosen. He continues to fiddle with it, his head still bent, and I can feel his breath quickening, heat radiating from his cheeks. The top button comes undone, and without looking up, he starts unfastening the next.

I am standing very still, acutely aware that neither of us has spoken for several minutes. A strange hum seems to fill the air like an unspoken thought hanging between us. Lochan is intent on undoing my shirt but seems to be having trouble, his hands unsteady. I watch his face carefully, wondering if we are sharing the same thought. When he gets to the third button, my shirt flaps open, revealing the top of my bra. I hear Lochan's breath quicken as he continues to work his way downward in silence, concentrating on his task. The edge of his hand brushes against the top of my breast; he is undoing the last button now and I'm aware of the rapid rise and fall of my own chest, the touch of his fingers through the thin, wet fabric raising gooseflesh all over my skin. My shirt falls open and he slides it off my shoulders, letting it fall to the carpet. Reaching for my bra, he suddenly stops, one hand hovering above my breasts, and from that one moment of hesitation I know.

"It's okay," I whisper, my voice suddenly weak. "I want to."

His eyes dart nervously to mine, the blood hot in his cheeks, his expression a mixture of fear and longing. "Really?"

"Yes!"

Tears and laughter swirl together inside me. I stroke my cheek against his gently, so gently that his skin feels like the wings of a butterfly. I close my eyes and move my lips lightly across his face, barely touching, so that my whole mouth begins to tingle. He closes his eyes too, takes a long, deep breath, and lets it out very slowly. My lips follow a path down his neck, into the hollow beneath his collarbone. His fingers tighten around mine and he lets out a small gasp. Raising my head, I softly kiss the corner of his mouth before moving away across his face. His mouth follows mine and I tease him, refusing to allow our lips to meet, until his breathing quickens and he releases my hand to cup my cheek and coax my mouth toward his. We finally start to kiss—soft, gentle, fluttery kisses. Shivers of pleasure run through my whole body and his hand trembles against my cheek. His breathing deepens—he wants to kiss me harder—but I resist, trying to draw this out for as long as I can. He touches my face, runs his fingers over my cheek, and we continue our small, feathery kisses, skin against skin, so warm, so familiar, so gentle, until he reaches up behind my back and unhooks my bra.

He strokes my breasts with quivering fingers, circling my nipples, sending nervous shivers of excitement through me. Eyes fixed, brow narrowed in concentration, he seems to be holding his breath. Then suddenly he emits a small sound, the air exiting his lungs in a rush. Tentatively I reach for the bottom of his T-shirt. When he doesn't protest, I pull it gently up and over his head. As he reappears, hair ruffled, he brushes his fingertips across my skin, kissing my breasts. I unbutton his jeans and he inhales sharply, his body immediately contracting beneath my touch. His breath is hot, fast, and damp against my cheek and he reaches for my mouth, kissing me harder still. As he draws me toward him, a strong tremor runs through his body and into mine. His arms tightly encircle me, and the warmth of his chest pressed against me makes me gasp. He is kissing my neck, my shoulders, my nipples, breaking off to take in small gulps of air, his hands on my breasts, my stomach, inside my knickers, pushing them down my legs. I slide them off and step out of them, then reach for his boxers and pull them down. He kicks them from around his ankles and then we are standing together, naked together for the first time in the bright light of day.

How amazing to be together like this with the door open, the window open, the curtains fluttering in the breeze! The rain clouds have passed and the sun has come out and everything in my room seems white and bright. Lochan reaches instinctively for the door handle and then stops himself, laughing. And suddenly it's as if all the laughter and happiness in the world is right here, right here between us in this room. Our love, our first taste of freedom—even the sun seems to be beaming down its approval—and I finally feel that everything between us is going to be all right. We won't have to hide forever—people will accept, people will have to accept. When they see how much we love each other, when they realize we were always destined to be together, when they understand how happy we are—how could they possibly reject us? All our struggles were so we could reach this point, this exquisite moment—finally holding each other, touching each other, kissing each other, without fear of being caught, without guilt or shame—sharing our bodies, our beings, every part of our souls.

He follows me onto the bed, lying down beside me and continuing to kiss me, stroking my nipples with his fingertips, licking my neck. I touch his penis but he pulls my hand away, breathing hard.

"Wait—" He stares at me, his taut body thrumming against me like a live wire. "Maya, are—are you sure?"

I nod slowly, a touch of fear creeping into me. "Will it hurt?"

"If it hurts, we'll—we'll just stop. All you have to do is say stop. I'll be really careful—I will, I promise. . . ."

I smile at the fervor in his voice. "It's all right. I trust you, Lochie."

"But only if you're sure . . ." His hands are like vices round my wrists, still trying to prevent me from touching him.

I take a deep breath, as if preparing to launch myself into a void. "I'm sure."

Our eyes lock together, sealing a silent agreement with our gaze, and in his face I see reflected my own fear and longing.

"Do you have some—"

"Yes." He raises himself quickly off the bed and disappears from the room.

Moments later, he returns with one in his hand. A panicky

TABITHA SUZUMA

flutter rises in my chest. Without a word, Lochan sits down with his back to me and starts fiddling with the shiny purple wrapper. Lying against the pillows, I pull the duvet over me. My heart is slamming against my ribs. I can't believe we're actually going to do this. I watch the smooth white curve of his spine, the sharp angles of his shoulder blades, his rib cage rapidly expanding and contracting, the muscles in his arms tightening as his hands fumble between his legs. I notice that he is trembling.

Finally he turns back toward me, his breathing shallow and rapid. I lean in for a kiss and we lie back down on the bed, his mouth fierce and urgent against mine. This time he is on top of me, propped up on his elbows, rubbing his face against my cheek. I run my hands up and down his stomach and feel him shudder. Tentatively I move my legs apart and draw up my knees. I feel it prod my thigh.

"Farther up," I whisper.

He has stopped kissing me now, his face inches above mine, concentration etched between his brows as he shifts slightly, trying to find the right place. After several near misses, he leans over to one side and reaches down to try and guide it in. His hand knocks against my leg. "Help me," he whispers.

I reach down and, after what seems an eternity, get it to the right place. I withdraw my hand and immediately feel myself tense. Lochan presses against me; I wince in anticipation: *This is never going to fit.* For a moment nothing happens. Then I feel him begin to push his way inside me.

I inhale sharply. Lochan's face hovers above mine, staring down at me, his breath rapid and labored. His eyes are wide, green irises flecked with blue. I can make out each individual eyelash, the cracks in his lips, the sweat beading on his forehead. And I can feel him inside me, his body trembling with the desire to go further.

"Are you all right?" he asks shakily.

I nod.

"Can—can I keep going?"

Another nod. It hurts, but that's not important right now. I want him, want to hold him, want to feel him inside me. He begins to push farther. A sharp stab makes me flinch, but then suddenly he is all the way in. We are as close as two people can be. Two bodies, blended into one . . .

Lochan is still staring down at me, an urgent look in his eyes, emitting ragged little gasps. He begins to move slowly back and forth, his elbows sunk into the mattress, clutching at the sheet on either side of my head.

"Kiss me," I breathe.

He lowers his face toward mine, lips brushing my cheek, my nose, then slowly making their way toward my mouth. He

kisses me gently, very gently, breathing hard now. The pain between my legs starts to fade as he continues to move inside me, and I feel another sensation, one that makes my whole body quiver. I run the backs of my hands gently down his chest and stomach, into the depressions between his hips and then up the sides, urging him with my hands to move a little faster. He does, pressing his lips together and holding his breath, the flush on his face deepening, spreading down to his neck and across his chest. Sweat glistens on his forehead and cheeks, a small drop running down his face, then falling onto mine. As he moves, his bangs brush against my forehead. I hear the sound of my own breath, small puffs of air escaping my mouth, mingling with his. I never want this to stop—this fear mixed with ecstasy, my whole being humming with longing, the press of his body against mine. The feel of him inside me, moving against me, making me shiver with excitement. I tilt my head up for another kiss and his lips descend over mine, harder this time. Scrunching up his eyes, he breaks away and holds his breath for a few seconds, then lets it out in a rush. Suddenly he opens his eyes again, his look desperate and urgent.

"It's okay," I reassure him quickly.

"I can't—" The words catch in his throat and I feel him tremble against me.

"That's okay!"

With a small gasp, his movements begin to quicken. "Sorry!"

I feel him twitch inside me, his pelvic bone digging into mine. Suddenly he seems locked in his own world. He closes his eyes and his jagged gasps tear at the air, his body growing tighter and tighter, his hands tearing at the sheets. Then, with a deep, sharp inhalation, he presses himself hard into me, again and again, shuddering violently with a series of small, wild sounds.

Once he is still, the full weight of his body presses down on me and he collapses against my neck. He is holding me very tightly, his arms pressing against mine, his fingers digging into my shoulders, his body still twitching. Exhaling slowly into the cool air of the room, I run my hand over his damp hair, across his neck and down his back, feeling his heart pound violently against my own. I kiss his shoulder, the only part of him I can reach, and stare up in astonishment at the familiar faded blue ceiling.

Reality has been altered, or at least my perception of it has dramatically changed. Everything feels different, looks different. . . . For a few moments I am not even sure who I am anymore. This boy, this man, lying in my arms has become a part of me. We have a new identity together: two parts of a whole. In the last few minutes, everything between us changed forever. I saw Lochie as no one had ever seen him, felt him inside me, sensed him at his most vulnerable, opened myself up to him in turn. In those few minutes I took him inside me, became a part of him, as close as two separate beings could ever be.

He slowly raises his head from my shoulder and looks down at me with a worried gaze. "Are you okay?" he pants softly.

I nod, smiling. "Yes."

He heaves a sigh of relief and presses his mouth against my neck, the sweat running between us. He kisses me between ragged breaths, and when I catch sight of the wild, flushed look on his face, I begin to laugh. Gazing down at me, he starts laughing too, and his whole being seems to radiate joy. And all at once I think: This whole time, my whole life, that harsh, stony path was leading up to this one point. I followed it blindly, stumbling along the way, scraped and weary, without any idea of where it was leading, without ever realizing that with every step I was approaching the light at the end of a very long, dark tunnel. And now that I've reached it, now that I'm here, I want to catch it in my hand, hold on to it forever to look back on—the point at which my new life really began. Everything I ever wanted, right here, right now, all captured in this one moment. The laughter, the joy, the enormity of the love between us. This is the dawn of happiness. It all begins now.

Then, from the doorway, comes a shattering scream.

CHAPTER TWENTY-FIVE

Lochan

Never in my life have I heard such a terrible sound. A scream of pure horror, of undiluted hatred and fury and rage. And it keeps coming, rising louder and louder, closer and closer, blocking out the sun, sucking out everything: the love, the warmth, the music, the joy. Tearing at the brilliant light all around us, slashing against our naked bodies, ripping the smiles from our faces, the breath from our lungs.

Maya grabs hold of me in fright, arms wrapped around me, gripping me tightly, face pressed against my chest, as if imploring her body to merge into mine. For a moment I cannot react, simply clutching her to me, intent only on protecting her, shielding her body with my own. Then I hear the sobs—the shrieking, hysterical sobs, the screeching accusations, the demented wails. I force my head up and see, framed in the open door, our mother.

As soon as her horrified eyes make contact with mine, she launches herself at us, grabbing me by the hair and yanking back my head with astonishing force. Her fists pound against me, her long nails cutting into my arms, my shoulders, my back. I don't even try to push her off. My arms circle Maya's head; my body presses down over hers, acting as a human shield between her and this madwoman, desperately trying to protect Maya from the attack.

She cries out in terror beneath me, trying to bury herself in the mattress, pulling me down against her with all her might. But then the shrieks begin to coalesce into words, perforating my frozen brain, and I hear: "Get off her! Get off her! You monster! You evil, twisted monster! Get off my baby! Get off! Get off! Get off!"

I will not move, will not let go of Maya even as I continue to be yanked by the hair and half dragged from the bed. Maya, suddenly realizing that the intruder is our mother, starts struggling to free herself from my grasp.

"No! Mum! Leave him! Leave him! He didn't do anything! What are you doing? You're hurting him! Don't hurt him! Don't hurt him! Don't hurt him!"

She is screaming at her now, sobbing in terror, pulling herself out from beneath me, trying to reach over and fight Mum off, but I won't let them touch, won't let the monster reach her. When I see a clawed hand descend toward Maya's face, I swing my arm wildly, making contact with Mum's shoulder. She staggers back and there is a thud, the sound of books tumbling from shelves, and she is gone, her wails echoing all the way down to the floor below.

I leap from the bed, hurl myself at the bedroom door, and slam it shut, shooting the bolt across.

"Quick!" I yell at Maya, grabbing knickers and a T-shirt from her clothes pile and tossing them over. "Put them on. She'll come back with Dave or someone. The lock's not strong enough—"

Maya is sitting in the middle of the bed, sheet clutched to her chest, hair wild and tangled, face white with shock and wet with tears.

"She can't do anything to us," she says desperately, her voice rising. "She can't do anything, she can't do anything!"

"It's all right, Maya. It's all right, it's all right. Just please put these on. She's going to be back!"

I can only find my underwear—the rest of my stuff must be buried beneath the heap of fallen books.

Maya pulls on her clothes, leaps up, and runs over to the open window. "We can climb out," she gasps. "We can jump—"

I yank her back, forcing her to sit down on the bed. "Listen to me. We can't run away—they'd catch us anyway, and think, Maya, think! What about the others? We can't just abandon them. We're going to wait here, okay? No one's going to hurt you, I promise. Mum's just being hysterical. And she wasn't trying to attack you, she was trying to rescue you. From me." I am fighting for breath.

"I don't care!" Maya is shouting again, tears coursing down her cheeks. "Look what she did to you, Lochie! Your back is bleeding! I can't believe she hurt you like that! She was pulling out your hair! She—she—"

"Shh, sweetheart, shh . . ." Turning to face her on the edge of the bed, I clasp the tops of her arms in an attempt to hold her still. "Maya, you've got to calm down. You've got to listen to me. No one's going to hurt us, d'you understand? They just want to rescue you—"

"From what?" she sobs. "From whom? They can't take me away from you! They can't, Lochie, they can't!"

More yelling. We both freeze at the sound, this time coming from the street. I am the first to reach the window. Mum is pacing up and down in front of the house, shouting and screaming into her mobile phone.

"You've got to come now!" she's sobbing. "Oh God, please hurry! He's already punched me, and now he's bolted himself in with her! When I went in, he tried to suffocate her! I think he's going to kill her!"

Curious neighbors are popping their heads out of windows and doors, some already hurrying across the street toward her. I feel myself break out in a cold sweat and my legs threaten to give way.

"She's calling Dave," Maya shouts, trying to pull away as I drag her from the window. "He's going to break the door down. He's going to beat you up! I've got to go down and explain everything! I've got to tell them you haven't done anything wrong!"

"Don't, Maya, don't. You can't! It won't make any difference! You have to stay here and listen. I have to talk to you."

Suddenly I know what I must do. I know that there is only one solution, only one way left to save Maya and the kids from harm. But she won't listen, struggling and kicking her bare feet against my legs as I lock my arms around her to stop her from running to the door. I force her back down on the edge of the bed, pinning her against me.

"Maya, you have to listen. I—I think I have a plan, but you've got to listen or it won't work. Please, sweetheart. I'm begging you!"

Maya stops struggling. "Okay, Lochie, okay," she whimpers. "Tell me, I'm listening. I'll do it. I'll do whatever you want."

 TABITHA SUZUMA

Still gripping her, I stare at her terrified, wild-eyed face and breathe deeply in a frantic effort to organize my thoughts, calm myself, hold back the mounting tears that will only terrify her further. I prepare to grab her should she make a run for the door.

"Mum isn't calling Dave," I explain, my voice shaking hard. "She's calling the police."

Maya freezes, her blue eyes wide with shock. Tears hang on her lashes; the color is gone from her face. The silence in the room is broken only by her frantic gasps.

"It's all right," I say firmly, struggling to keep my voice steady. "In fact, it's a good thing. The police will sort this out. They'll calm Mum down. They'll take me away for questioning, but it will only be—"

"But it's against the law." Maya's voice is quiet with horror. "What just happened. We'll be arrested because we've broken the law."

I take another deep breath, my lungs cracking under the strain, my throat threatening to close up completely. If I break down, it's all over. I'll frighten her so much that she'll stop listening to me and will never agree to what I'm about to suggest. I have to convince her that this is the best way, the only way.

"Maya, you've got to listen—we have to go through this fast; they could be here any minute." I stop to catch my breath again. Despite the terror in her eyes, she just nods, waiting for me to continue.

"Okay. First you've got to remember that being arrested does not mean going to prison. We won't be going to prison because we're only teenagers. But listen to me now: This is very, very important. If we both get arrested, we'll be kept in for questioning. That could take a few days. Willa and Tiffin will come back to find us gone. Mum will probably be drunk, and even if she's not, social services will be called in by the police and all three kids will be taken away because of what we've done. Just imagine Willa, imagine Tiffin, imagine how terrified they'll be. Willa was worried—" My voice quavers and I break off for a moment. "W-Willa was worried about spending just one night away!" Tears force their way into my eyes like knives. "D'you understand? D'you understand what will happen to them if we both get arrested?"

Maya shakes her head at me in silent horror, mute with shock, fresh tears filling her eyes.

"There is a way," I carry on desperately. "There's a way we can prevent all that. They won't take them away if there's one of us here to look after them and cover for Mum. D'you get it, Maya?" My voice begins to rise. "One of us has to stay. It has to be you—"

"No!" Maya's cry slices straight through my heart. I tighten my grip on her wrists as she begins to pull away. "No! No!"

"Maya, if they're taken away by social services, neither of us will ever see them again until they're adults! They'll be scarred for life! If you let me go, there's a good chance I'll be out in a few days." I stare at her, desperately hoping she trusts me enough to believe this lie.

"You stay!" Maya looks at me, her eyes imploring. "You stay and *I'll* go! I'm not scared. Please, Lochie. Let's do it that way!"

I shake my head in desperation. "It won't work!" I say frantically. "Remember that conversation we had a few weeks ago? No one will believe us if we say it was you who forced me. And if we tell them it was consensual, they'll arrest us both! We have to do it like this. Don't you understand? Think, Maya, think! You know there are no other options! If one of us is to stay behind, it has to be you!"

Maya's whole body crumples forward as the reality hits her. She falls toward me but I cannot take her in my arms, not yet.

"Please, Maya," I beg her. "Tell me you'll do it. Tell me now, right now. Otherwise I'll go crazy not knowing—not knowing whether you and the others are safe or not. I won't be able to take it. You've got to do it. For me. For us. It's our only chance to ever be together as a family again."

She hangs her head, her beautiful amber hair hiding her face from view.

"Maya—"A frantic sound escapes me and I give her a shake. "Maya!"

She nods silently, without looking up.

"You'll do it?" I ask.

"I'll do it," she whispers.

Several seconds pass and she doesn't move. With shaky hands, I wipe the sweat from my face. Then, suddenly, Maya raises her head with a strangled sob and holds out her arms for comfort. I can't do it. I simply can't. With a sharp shake of the head, I move away from her, straining my ears for the sound of a siren. A low murmur of voices rises from beneath us—no doubt concerned neighbors, rushing in to comfort our mother. Denied the hug she so desperately needs, Maya seeks comfort instead from a pillow drawn up against her chest. Rocking back and forth, she appears to be in a state of complete shock.

"There's one more thing . . ." I turn to her, realizing suddenly. "We—we have to get our stories straight. Otherwise they'll hold me for longer and you'll be pulled in repeatedly for questioning and things will get much worse—"

Maya closes her eyes as if to shut me out.

"We haven't got time to make anything up," I say, my voice catching on every word. "We'll—we'll just have to tell it exactly how it was. E-everything that happened, how it first started, how long it's been . . . If our stories don't match up, they could arrest you, too. So you've got to tell the truth, Maya, d'you understand? Everything—every detail they ask you for!" I take a frantic breath. "The only thing we're going to add is that—is that I forced you. I forced you into everything we did, Maya. D'you hear me?"

I'm losing control again, the words shaking like the air around me. "The first time we kissed, I said you had to go along with it, or—or I'd beat you. I swore that if you told anyone, I'd kill you. You were terrified. You really believed I was capable of it, and so from then on, every time I—I wanted you, you—you just did what I asked."

She looks up at me in horror, silent tears spilling down her cheeks. "They'll send you to prison!"

"No." I shake my head, struggling to sound as convincing as possible. "You'll simply say you don't want to press charges. If there's no accuser, there'll be no court case. I'll be out in a few days!" I stare at her, silently imploring her to believe me.

She frowns and shakes her head slowly, as if desperately trying to comprehend. "But that doesn't make sense. . . ."

"Trust me." I'm breathing too fast. "Most sexual abuse cases are never taken to court because the victims are too afraid or ashamed to press charges. So you'll just say you don't want to press charges, either. . . . But, Maya"—I reach out and grip her arm—"you must never, ever say this was consensual. You must never, ever admit to taking part in this freely. I forced you. Whatever they ask, whatever they say, I threatened you. D'you understand?"

A stunned nod.

Unconvinced, I grab her roughly by the arms. "I don't believe you! Tell me what happened! What did I do to you?"

She looks up at me, bottom lip quivering, eyes glistening. "You raped me," she replies, and presses her hands to her mouth to muffle a scream.

We huddle together beneath the duvet one last time. She is curled in toward me, cheek resting against my chest, shaking in shock. I hold her tightly, staring up at the ceiling, terrified I will start crying, terrified she will see just how afraid I am, terrified she will suddenly realize that even though she won't press charges, there's someone else who will.

"I d-don't understand," Maya gasps. "How could this happen? Why did Mum come back today of all days? How the hell did she get in without her key?"

I'm too stressed to even think about that, or care. The only thing that matters is that we've been caught. Reported to the police. I never really thought it would actually come to this.

"It must have been a neighbor. We weren't careful enough with the curtains." Maya shakes with a silent sob. "You've still

got time. Lochie, I just don't understand! Why won't you run?" Her voice rises in anguish.

Because then I won't be around to tell my version of the story. The version I want the police to hear. The version that absolves you of all wrongdoing. If I run, they could arrest you instead. And if we both go, we expose ourselves as accomplices and it's all over.

I say nothing, just hold her tighter in the hope that she will trust me.

The sound of the siren makes us both start. Maya jackknifes from the bed and tries to leap for the door. I force her back and she starts to cry.

"No, Lochie, no! Please! Let me go downstairs and explain. It looks so much worse like this!"

I need it to look worse. I need it to look as bad as it can. From now on I have to think like a rapist, act like a rapist. Prove I've been holding Maya against her will.

Sounds of slamming car doors rise from the street below. Mum's hysterical voice starts up again.

The front door bangs. Heavy treads in the hallway. Maya screws up her eyes and clings to me, sobbing silently.

"It'll be all right," I whisper desperately in her ear. "This is just protocol. They'll only arrest me so they can question me. When you tell them you don't want to press charges, they'll just let me go."

I hold her tightly, stroking her hair, hoping that one day she'll understand, that one day she'll forgive me for lying. Careful not to think, careful not to panic, careful not to waver. Loud voices from below—Mum's, mainly. The sound of multiple footsteps on the stairs.

"Let go of me," I whisper urgently.

She doesn't respond, still pressed up against me, her head buried against my shoulder, arms wound tightly around my neck.

"Maya, let go of me, now!" I try to unhook her arms. She won't let go. She won't let go!

The thuds against the door make us both jump violently. The noise is followed by a sharp, authoritative voice: "This is the police. Open the door."

I'm sorry, but I've just raped my sister and am holding her here against her will. I cannot be so obliging.

They give me a warning. Then the first strike is heard. Maya lets out a terrified scream. She still won't let go of me. It's vital I turn her round so that when they get in, they find me grasping her with her back to me, arms pinned by her sides. Another crack. The wood around the bolt splinters. Just one more strike and they will be in.

I push Maya away from me with all my strength. I look into her eyes—her beautiful blue eyes—and feel the tears surge. "I

404   TABITHA SUZUMA

love you," I whisper. "I'm so sorry!" Then I raise my right hand and strike her hard across the face.

Her scream fills the room seconds before the lock breaks and the door crashes open. The doorway is suddenly crowded with dark uniforms and crackling radios. My arm circles Maya's arms and waist, pinning her back against me. Beneath the hand clapped over her mouth, I feel a reassuring trickle of blood.

When they order me to let go of her and step away from the bed, I cannot move. I need to cooperate, but physically I can't. I am frozen in fear. I am terrified that if I uncover Maya's mouth, she will start to tell them the truth. I'm terrified that once they take Maya away, I will never see her again.

They ask me to put my hands up. I begin to loosen my grip on Maya. *No*, I'm screaming inside. *Don't leave me, don't go! You are my love, my life! Without you, I am nothing, I have nothing. If I lose you, I lose everything.* I raise my hands very slowly, fighting to keep them in the air, fighting against the overwhelming urge to take Maya back into my arms, kiss her one last time. A female officer cautiously approaches as if Maya were a wild animal, about to take flight, and coaxes her out of the bed. She lets out a small, muffled sob, but I hear her take a deep breath and hold it. Someone wraps a blanket around her. They are trying to usher her from the room.

"No!" she screams. Bursting into a sudden volley of broken

sobs, she turns frantically back toward me, blood staining her lower lip. Lips that once touched me so gently, lips I know so well, love so much, lips I could never have imagined hurting. But now, with her cut lip and tearstained face, she looks so shocked and battered that even if she were to lose her resolve and tell the truth, I'm almost confident she would not be believed. Her eyes meet mine, but under the officers' watchful gaze I'm unable to give her the slightest sign of reassurance. *Go, my love,* I beg her with my gaze. *Follow the plan. Do this. Do this for me.*

As she turns, her face crumples and I fight against the urge to cry out her name.

As soon as Maya is out of the way, the two male officers descend upon me. Each grabbing me by an arm, they instruct me to stand up slowly. I do so, tensing every muscle and clenching my teeth in an effort to stop shaking. A thickset officer with small eyes and a puffy face smirks as I get up from the bed and the sheet falls away and I'm left standing in my boxers. "Don't think we need to frisk this one," he says, chuckling.

I can hear the sound of Maya crying downstairs. "What are they going to do to him? What are they going to do to him?" she keeps shouting.

The reply is repeated over and over by a soothing female

voice. "Don't worry. You're safe now. He won't be able to hurt you again."

"Have you got some clothes?" the other officer asks me. He looks not much older than me. *How long has he been in the police force?* I wonder. Has he ever been involved in a crime as disgusting as this?

"In my b-bedroom . . ."

The young officer follows me to my room and watches me get dressed, his radio sputtering into the silence. I feel his eyes on my back, on my body, full of disgust. I can't seem to find anything clean. For some irrational reason, I feel the need to wear something that's freshly washed. The only thing at hand is my school uniform. I sense the man's impatience in the doorway behind me but I am so desperate to cover my body that I can't even think straight, can't remember where I keep my things. Finally I pull on a T-shirt and jeans, shoving my bare feet into my trainers before realizing that my T-shirt is inside out.

The bulky officer joins us in the room. They seem far too big for this confined space. I'm painfully aware of my unmade bed, the socks and underwear that litter the carpet. The broken curtain rail, the old chipped desk, the peeling walls. I feel ashamed of it all. I glance at the small family snapshot still tacked to the wall above my bed and suddenly wish I could take it with me. Something, anything, to remind me of them all.

The older officer asks me some basic questions: name, date of birth, nationality. . . . My voice still manages to shake despite all my efforts to keep it steady. The more I try not to stammer, the worse it gets. When my mind goes blank and I can't even remember my own birthday, they stare me down, as if they think I'm deliberately withholding this information. I strain for the sound of Maya's voice but can hear nothing. What have they done to her? Where have they taken her?

"Lochan Whitely," the officer states in a flat, mechanical tone as he handcuffs me. "An allegation has been made to the police that you raped your sixteen-year-old sister a short time ago. I am arresting you for breach of section twenty-five of the Sexual Offenses Act for engaging in sexual activity with a child family member."

The accusation hits me like a fist in my stomach. This makes me sound like more than a rapist: a pedophile. And Maya, a child? She hasn't been one for years. And she isn't below the age of consent! But of course, I realize suddenly, even just two weeks shy of her seventeenth birthday, she is still considered a child in the eyes of the law. At eighteen, however, I am an adult. Thirteen months. Might as well be thirteen years . . . The officer is now reading me my rights. "You do not have to say anything. But it may harm your defense if you do not mention when questioned something which you later rely on in court.

TABITHA SUZUMA

Anything you do say may be given in evidence." His voice is deliberate, heavy with authority; his face a mask—blank, cold, devoid of all expression. But this is not some cop show. This is real. I have committed a real crime.

The young officer informs me they will now take me outside to the "transport vehicle." The corridor is too narrow for the three of us. The big officer leads the way, his tread heavy and slow. The other grips me tightly just above the elbow. I've been able to hide the fear until now, but as we approach the staircase, I suddenly feel a surge of panic begin to rise. Stupidly, it's triggered by nothing more than the need to pee. But suddenly I realize I'm desperate to go and have no idea when I'm next going to get the chance. After hours of questioning, locked up in some cell, in front of a whole bunch of other prisoners? I stumble to a halt at the top of the stairs.

"Keep moving!" I feel the press of a firm hand between my shoulder blades.

"Can I—can I please just use the bathroom before I go?" My voice comes out frightened and frantic. I feel my face burn, and as soon as the words are out of my mouth, I wish I could take them back. I sound pathetic.

They exchange glances. The thickset man sighs and nods. They let me into the bathroom. The younger officer stays in the open doorway.

The cuffs don't make it easy. I feel the man's presence fill the small room. Shuffling round so I have my back to him, I struggle to unbutton my jeans. Sweat prickles across my neck and down my back, trapping the T-shirt against my skin. The muscles in my knees seem to vibrate. I close my eyes and try to relax, but I need to go so badly it's impossible. I can't. I just can't. Not like this.

"We haven't got all day." The voice behind me makes me flinch. I button up and flush the empty toilet. Turning round, I'm too embarrassed to even raise my head.

As we shuffle our way down the narrow stairs, the young officer says in a gentler tone, "The station's not far. You'll have some privacy there."

His words throw me. A small hint of kindness, a note of reassurance, despite the terrible thing I've done. I feel my facade begin to slip. Breathing deeply, I bite my lip hard. Just in case Maya sees me, it's imperative I make it out of the house without falling apart.

Voices rise and fall from the kitchen. The door is firmly shut. So that's where they've taken her. I hope to God they are still treating her as the victim, comforting her rather than bombarding her with questions. I have to grit my teeth, clench every muscle in my body, to prevent myself from running to her, hugging her, kissing her one last time.

I notice a pink skipping rope hanging over the banister. A

 TABITHA SUZUMA

single Jelly Baby from last night remains on the carpet. Small shoes are scattered over the rack by the front door. Willa's white sandals and the lace-up trainers she has finally learned to tie—all so tiny. Tiffin's scuffed school shoes, his much-prized soccer boots, his gloves and "lucky" ball. Above them their school blazers hang discarded, empty, like ghosts of their real selves. I want them back; I want my children back. I miss them, the pain like a hole in my heart. They were so excited to go that I didn't even have time to hug them. I never got to say good-bye.

Just as I am being jolted past the open door of the front room, a movement catches my eye and makes me stop. I turn my head toward a figure in the armchair and, to my astonishment, find Kit. He is sitting, white-faced and immobile, beside a woman police officer, his carefully packed Isle of Wight bags lying carelessly discarded at his feet. As he slowly turns toward me, I stare at him, uncomprehending. I am pushed from behind, told to "move it." I stumble against the door frame, my eyes begging Kit for some kind of explanation.

"Why are you here?" I can't believe he is witnessing this. I can't believe they somehow got hold of him before he left, involving him, too. *He's only thirteen, for chrissakes!* I want to scream. He should be on the trip of his life, not watching his brother get arrested for sexually abusing his sister. I want to kick at them in fury, force them to let him go.

His eyes leave my face, traveling down to the cuffs circling my wrists, then to the police officers trying to drag me away. His face is pale, stricken.

"You told him!" he shouts suddenly, making me jump.

I stare at him, stunned. "What?"

"Coach Wilson! You told him about the heights thing!" Suddenly he is screaming at me, his face distorted with fury. "As soon as I got to school, he took me off the rock-climbing list in front of the whole class! Everyone laughed at me, even my friends! You ruined what was going to be the best week of my life!"

Forcing myself to keep breathing, I feel my heart start to pound. "It was you?" I gasp. "You knew? About Maya and me? You knew?"

He nods wordlessly.

"Mr. Whitely, you need to come with us right now!"

The comment about Maya and me being left home alone, the sound of the door while we were kissing in the kitchen . . . Why on earth didn't he confront us? Why wait until now before telling?

Because he didn't want to be taken into care. Because he never intended to tell.

For some strange reason I am desperate for him to know that I never asked for him to be taken off the rock-climbing list, never dreamed he might be humiliated in front of his friends, never meant to ruin his first trip ever, the most exciting week of his life. But the

TABITHA SUZUMA

officers are shouting at me, pushing me out of the front door with considerable force now, banging my shoulders against the walls, dragging me toward the waiting police car. I twist and turn my head, frantically trying to call back to him over my shoulder.

The neighbors have come out in full force, congregating en masse around the waiting police car, watching with fascination as I am pushed down into the backseat. The belt is drawn across me and the door beside me slams. The large officer gets into the front, his radio still crepitating; the younger one gets into the back, beside me. The neighbors are closing in now like a slow wave, leaning, peering, pointing, their mouths opening and closing with silent questions.

Suddenly there is a violent thud against the door at my side. I whip my head round in time to see Kit, pummeling frantically at the window.

"I'm sorry!" he screams, the sound heavily muffled by the reinforced glass. "Lochie, I'm sorry, I'm sorry, I'm sorry! I didn't think about what would happen—I never thought she'd call the police!" He is crying hard, in a way he hasn't done for years, tears lashing his cheeks. His body convulses with violent sobs as he punches at the window in a frenzied bid to free me. "Come back!" he screams. "Come back!"

I wrestle with the locked door, desperate to tell him it's okay, that I will be back soon—even though I am well aware this isn't true. More than anything, though, I want to tell him it's okay, that I know he never intended for it to come to this, that I understand he simply lashed out in hurt and anger and bitter disappointment. I want to let him know that of course I forgive him, that absolutely none of this was his fault, that I love him, that I always have, despite everything. . . .

A neighbor drags him off and the car begins to pull away from the curb. As we pick up speed, I turn my head for one last look and, through the back window, see Kit sprinting after us, his long legs pounding the sidewalk, the familiar look of single-minded determination on his face—the same determination he showed during all those soccer, catch, and British bulldog games we used to play. . . . Somehow he keeps pace with the car until we reach the end of the narrow street, until we accelerate out onto the main road. Frantically craning my head to keep him in sight, I see him finally stumble to a halt, his hands by his sides: defeated, crying.

You don't let Kit lose! I want to shout at the officers. You never let any of them lose! Even when giving them a run for their money, you always, always let them catch you in the end.

He stands there, staring at the car as if willing us back, and I watch him rapidly shrink as the space between us grows. Soon my little brother is just a tiny speck in the distance—and then I can no longer see him at all.

TABITHA SUZUMA

CHAPTER TWENTY-SIX

Lochan

We stop in a large car park full of different kinds of police vehicles. Once again I am taken firmly by the arm and pulled out. Pain from my bladder makes me wince as I stand, the breeze against my bare arms causing me to shiver. After crossing the tarmac, I am led through some kind of back entrance, along a short corridor, and through a door labeled CHARGE ROOM. Another uniformed officer sits behind a tall desk. The two officers at my side address him as "Sergeant" and inform him of my offense, but to my great relief he barely looks at me, mechanically tapping my details into his computer. The charge is read out to me yet again, and when

I am asked if I understand it, my nod is not accepted. The question is repeated and I'm forced to use my voice.

"Yes." This time I only manage a whisper. Away from the house and the danger of further upsetting Maya, I can feel myself losing strength: succumbing to the shock, the horror, the blind panic of the situation.

More questions follow. Again I am asked to repeat my name, address, date of birth. I struggle to reply; my brain seems to be slowly shutting down. When asked my occupation, I hesitate. "I—I don't have one."

"Are you on unemployment benefit?"

"No. I'm—I'm still at school."

The sergeant looks up at me then. My face burns beneath his penetrating gaze.

Questions about my health follow, and my mental state is also questioned—no doubt they think only a psychopath would be capable of such a crime. I am asked if I want a lawyer and respond immediately with a shake of the head. The last thing I need is someone else to be involved, to hear about all the terrible things I've done. Anyway, I am trying to prove my guilt, not my innocence.

After being uncuffed, I am told to hand over my possessions. Fortunately I have none and feel relieved I didn't take the photo from my room. Perhaps Maya will remember it and keep it safe. But I can't help hoping she'll cut off the two adults at either end of the bench and just keep the five children sandwiched in the middle. Because, ultimately, that was the family we became. In the end we were the ones who loved each other, who struggled and fought to stay together. And it was enough, more than enough.

They ask me to empty my pockets, remove the laces from my shoes. Again the tremor in my hands betrays me, and as I kneel between the suited legs on the dirty linoleum, I sense the officers' impatience, their contempt. The shoelaces are placed in an envelope and I have to sign for them, which strikes me as absurd. A body search follows, and at the touch of the officer's hands running over me, up and down my legs, I start to shake violently, holding on to the edge of the desk to steady myself.

In a small anteroom, I am seated on a chair. My photo is taken, a cotton swab scraped around the inside of my mouth. As my fingers are pressed one by one against an ink pad and then down onto a marked piece of card, I am overcome by a feeling of complete detachment. I am a mere object to these people. I am barely human anymore.

I am thankful when I am finally pushed into a cell and the heavy door slams shut behind me. To my relief the cell is empty—small and claustrophobic, containing nothing more than a narrow bed built into the wall. There is a barred window near the ceiling, but the light that fills the room is purely artificial, harsh and overly bright. Graffiti and what looks like feces smear the walls. The stench is foul—far worse than the most disgusting of public urinals—and I have to breathe through my mouth to avoid gagging.

It takes me forever to relax enough to empty my bladder into the metal toilet. Now, finally away from their watchful eyes, I cannot stop trembling. I fear that an officer will burst in at any moment, am acutely aware of the small window in the door, the flap just beneath it. How do I know I am not being watched right this minute? Normally I am not this prudish, but after being pulled out of bed in my underwear, frog-marched seminaked to my bedroom by two policemen, forced to dress in front of them, I wish there were some way of covering myself up forever. Ever since hearing the horrific charge, I have been feeling acutely ashamed of my whole body, of what it has done—of what others believe it has done.

Flushing the toilet, I return to the thick metal door and press my ear against it. Shouts echo down the corridor, drunken swearing, a wail that goes on and on, but they seem to be coming from some way away. If I keep my back to the door, then even if an officer peers at me through the window, at least he won't be able to see my face.

No sooner have I ascertained that I finally have some degree

TABITHA SUZUMA

of privacy than the safety valve in my mind that had kept me functioning until now opens, as if by force, and the images and memories flood in. I make a sudden dash for the bed, but my knees give way before I reach it. I sink down on the concrete floor and dig my nails into the thick plastic sheet sewn onto the mattress. I pull at it so violently, I'm scared it might rip. Doubling over, I press my face hard against the stinking bed, muffling my nose and mouth as much as I can. The gut-wrenching sobs tear at my whole body, threatening to split me apart with their force. The whole mattress shakes, my rib cage shuddering against the hard bed frame, and I am choking, suffocating, depriving myself of oxygen but unable to raise my head to draw breath for fear of making a sound. Crying has never hurt so much. I want to crawl under the bed in case someone looks in and sees me like this, but the space is far too small. I cannot even remove the bedsheet in order to cover myself—there is simply nowhere to hide.

I hear Kit's anguished cries, see his fists pound against the window, his skinny frame racing to keep up with the car, his whole body crumpling as he realizes he is powerless to rescue me. I think of Tiffin and Willa playing at Freddie and Susie's, running round the house with their friends in excitement, oblivious of what awaits them on their return. Will they be told what I have done? Will they be questioned about me too—

asked about all the cuddles, the bath times, the bedtimes, being tickled, the rough-and-tumble games we used to play? Will they be brainwashed into thinking I abused them? And in years to come, if we ever get the chance to meet again as adults, will they even want to see me? Tiffin will have vague memories of me, but Willa will have known me for only the first five years of her life—what, if any, memories will she retain?

Finally, too weak to keep her from my thoughts any longer, I think of Maya. Maya, Maya, Maya. I choke her name into my hands, hoping that the sound of her name will bring me some comfort. I never, ever should have taken such a terrible risk with her happiness. For her sake, for the children's sakes, I should never have allowed our relationship to develop. I cannot regret it for myself—there is nothing I wouldn't have endured just for the few months we had together. But I never thought about the danger to her, the horror she would be forced to undergo.

I am terrified of what they might be doing to her right now—bombarding her with questions she will struggle to answer, torn between protecting me by telling the truth and accusing me of rape to enable her to protect the children. How could I have put her in such a position? How could I have asked her to make such a choice?

The clash and crash of keys and metal locks jolts through

my body, startling me into confused, panicked consciousness. An officer orders me to get up, informs me I'm being taken to the interview room. Before I can get my body to respond I am seized by the arm and jerked to my feet. I pull away for a moment, desperate to get my thoughts in order—all I need is a moment to clear my head, remember what it is I have to say. This could be my only chance and I have to get it right, all of it, make sure there isn't the slightest discrepancy between Maya's story and my own.

I am cuffed once again and led down several long, brightly lit corridors. I have no idea how long it's been since I was shoved into the cell. Time has ceased to exist: There are no windows and I cannot tell what time of day or night it is. I feel dizzy with pain and fear—one wrong word, one wrong move, and I could mess it all up, let something slip that would some-how implicate Maya in this, too.

Much like my cell, the interview room is harshly lit, bright fluorescent light turning the whole room an eerie yellow. It isn't much bigger than the cell, but now the stench of urine is replaced by sweat and stale air. The walls are bare and the floor carpeted. The only furniture is a narrow table and three chairs. Two officers are seated on the far side: a man and a woman. The man looks to be in his early forties, with a nar-row face and close-cropped hair. The hardness behind the eyes, the grave expression, the set of the jaw, all suggest that he has seen this many times before, has been breaking criminals down for years—he looks sharp and shrewd, and there is something tough and intimidating about him. The woman, on the other hand, looks older and more ordinary, with scraped-back hair and a world-weary expression, but her eyes also have that sharp gaze. Both officers look as if they have been well trained in the art of manipulating, threatening, cajoling, or even lying to get what they want from their suspects. Even in my confused, hazy state, I immediately sense that they are good at what they do.

I am directed to the gray plastic chair placed opposite them, less than half a meter away from the edge of the table and backed up against the wall behind me. We may as well all be in a cage together: The table is not very wide and it all feels far too close for comfort. I am acutely aware of my clammy face, the hair sticking to my forehead, the thin fabric of my T-shirt cling-ing to my skin, the sweat patches visible on the material. I feel dirty and disgusting, the taste of bile in my throat, sour blood in my mouth, and despite the officers' impassive expressions, their revulsion is almost tangible in this small, enclosed space.

The man hasn't looked up since I was brought in, but keeps scribbling away in a file. When he does raise his eyes, I feel myself flinch and automatically try to scrape my chair back, but it does not budge.

 TABITHA SUZUMA

"This interview is going to be recorded and videoed." Eyes like small gray pebbles bear into mine. "Do you have a problem with that?"

As if I have a choice. "No." I notice a discreet camera in the corner of the room, trained on my face. Fresh sweat breaks out across my forehead.

The man flicks the switch of some kind of recording device and reads out a case number, followed by the date and time. He goes on to state, "Present is myself, Detective Inspector Sutton. To my right, Detective Inspector Kaye. Opposite us, the suspect. Would you identify yourself, please?" Who exactly is he speaking to? Other police officers, truth analysts, the judge and jury? Will this interview be played in court? Will my own descriptions of my heinous crime be played back to my family? Will Maya be forced to listen to me stutter and stumble my way through this interrogation and then be asked to confirm whether I've been telling the truth?

Don't think about that now, for chrissakes. Stop thinking about that now—the only two things you should be focusing on right now are your demeanor and your words. Everything that comes out of your mouth must be completely and utterly convincing.

"Lochan Whi—" I clear my throat; my voice is weak and uneven. "Lochan Whitely."

The next few questions are the usual: Date of birth?

Nationality? Address? Detective Sutton barely looks up, either jotting things down in his file or fast-forwarding through my notes, his eyes flicking rapidly from side to side.

"Do you know why you're here?" His eyes meet mine very suddenly, making me start.

I nod. Then I swallow. "Yes."

Pen poised, he continues to look at me, as if waiting for me to continue. "For—for sexually abusing my sister," I say, my voice strained but steady.

The words hang in the air like small red puncture wounds. I feel the atmosphere thicken, tighten. Even though the interrogating officers have it all written down in front of them, my actually saying the words aloud, in the presence of both a video camera and a voice recorder, makes it all suddenly unalterable. I barely feel as if I'm lying anymore. Perhaps there is no one universal truth. Consensual incest to me, sexual abuse of a child family member to them. Perhaps both labels are correct.

And then the questions begin.

At first it's all background stuff. The tedious, endless minutiae: where I was born, the members of my family, everyone's dates of birth, the details surrounding our father, my relationship with him, with my siblings, with my mother. I stick to the truth as much as possible, even telling them about our mother's late shifts at the restaurant, her relationship with Dave. I am careful to omit the parts that I hope Mum and Kit will have the sense to gloss over too: her drinking problem, the fights over money, the move to Dave's house, and finally the almost total abandonment of her family. Instead, I tell them that she has only recently started working late shifts and that I babysit in the evenings, but only once the children are in bed. So far, so good. Not an ideal family setup, but one that just about fits within the bounds of normality. And then, after they have been given every little detail, from the number of rooms in our house to our respective schools, our grades, and our extracurricular activities, the question is finally asked:

"When was the first time you had any kind of sexual contact with Maya?" The officer's gaze is direct and his voice as expressionless as before, but he suddenly seems to be watching me carefully, waiting for the slightest shift in my expression.

Silence thickens the air, draining it of oxygen, and I am aware of the sound of my own rapid breathing, my lungs automatically crying out for more air. I'm aware, too, of the sweat running down the sides of my face and I'm certain he can see the fear in my eyes. I am exhausted and in pain and desperate for the toilet again, but clearly the interview has a long time yet to run.

"When—when you say 'sexual contact,' do you mean, like—like, feelings, or when we first—I mean, I first t-touched her, or—"

"The first time you had any inappropriate exposure or contact." His voice has hardened, his jaw tightened, and the words shoot out of his mouth like small bullets.

Fighting my way through the fog and panic, I try to come up with the correct answer. It is vital I get all this right so it will match up exactly with Maya's account. Sexual contact—but what exactly does that mean? That first kiss the night of her date? Or before that, when we were dancing?

"Would you answer the question!" The temperature is rising. He thinks I'm stalling in order to try to exonerate myself, when in reality it's the opposite.

"I—I'm not sure of the exact date. It m-must have been November sometime. Y-yes, November—" Or was it October? Oh God, I am messing this up already.

"Tell me what happened."

"Okay. She—she came home from a date with a guy from school. We—we got into an argument because I was giving her the third degree. I was worried—I mean, angry. I wanted to know if she'd slept with him. I got upset—"

"What do you mean by 'upset'?"

No. Please.

"I started—I began to cry. . . ." Like I'm going to do now, just at the memory of the pain I felt on that night. Turning my head toward the wall, I bite down hard, but the pain of my teeth cutting into my tongue doesn't work any longer. No amount of physical pain can cover up the mental agony. Five minutes into the interrogation and already I'm falling apart. It's hopeless; everything's hopeless; I'm hopeless; I'm going to fail Maya, fail them all.

"Then what happened?"

I try every trick in the book to keep the tears at bay, but nothing works. The pressure mounts, and I see from Sutton's expression that he thinks I am stalling for time, pretending to feel remorse, lying.

"Then what happened?" This time, his voice is raised.

I flinch. "I said to her—I tried to—I said she had to—I forced her to—"

I can't get the words out, even though I'm desperate to, wishing I could scream them from the rooftops. It's like being forced up in front of the class again, the words clogging up my throat, my face burning with shame. Except this time I'm not being asked to read out an essay, I'm being interrogated about the most intimate and personal details of my life, all those tender moments spent with Maya, all those precious times that have made the past three months the happiest I've ever known. Yet now they are being smeared across our family like the feces in the cell—putrid, foul, horrific abuse, myself as perpetrator, forcing my younger sister into revolting sexual acts against her will.

"Lochan, I strongly suggest you stop wasting our time and start to cooperate. As I'm sure you're aware, in the UK, the maximum sentence for rape is life imprisonment. Now, if you cooperate and show remorse for what you've done, that sentence will almost certainly be reduced, perhaps even to as little as seven years. But if you lie or try to deny anything, we will find out anyway and a judge will be far less lenient."

Again I try to answer, again I fail. I see myself through their eyes—the sick, screwed-up, pathetic sex addict, reduced to abusing a younger sister he once played with, his own flesh and blood.

"Lochan . . ." The female detective is leaning toward me, clasped hands stretched out across the table. "I can see you feel bad about what happened. And that's good. It means you're beginning to take responsibility for your actions. Perhaps you didn't really believe that having a sexual relationship with your sister would harm her, perhaps you never meant it when you threatened to kill her; but you need to tell us exactly what happened, exactly what you did, what you said. If you try to gloss over things or leave things out or stall or lie, then things are going to get much, much worse for you."

Taking a deep breath, I nod, trying hard to show them that I'm willing to cooperate, that they don't have to keep up this Good Cop, Bad Cop charade in order for me to confess. All I need is the strength to pull myself together, hold back the tears, and find the right words to describe all the things I forced Maya to do to me, all the things I forced her to endure.

"Lochan, do you have a nickname?"

Detective Kaye is still doing her pally stuff, where she pretends to comfort and befriend me in the hope that I will trust her enough to relax, calm down, believe she is trying to actually help rather than to extract a confession.

"Loch—" I blurt. "Lochie—" No, oh no. Only my family calls me that. Only my family!

"Lochie, listen to me now. If you cooperate with us today, if you tell us everything that happened, it will make a big difference to the outcome of all this. We're all human. We all make mistakes, right? You're only eighteen, I'm sure you didn't realize the severity of what you were doing, and a judge will take that into consideration."

Yeah, right. How stupid do you think I am? I'm eighteen and I'll be tried as an adult. Save your manipulating lies for the ones who are really trying to conceal their actions.

I nod and dry my eyes on my sleeve. Tearing at my hair with cuffed hands raised above my head, I begin to talk.

The lies are the easy part—forcing Maya to stay home from school, getting into bed with her every night, repeating the same threat, again and again, whenever she begged me to leave her alone. It's when I have to tell them the truth that I flounder—it's our truth, our innermost secrets, our most intimate times, the precious little details of our brief, idyllic moments together. Those are the parts that make me stammer and shake. But I force myself to continue, even when I can't hold back the tears any longer, even when they start spilling down my cheeks and my voice starts to shake with repressed sobs, even when I feel their looks of revulsion merge with ones of pity.

They want to know every little detail. The time on the bed, our first night together. What I did, what she did, what I said, what she said. How I felt . . . How I responded . . . How my body responded . . . I tell them the truth, and someone reaches into my chest and slowly starts splitting me apart. When we finally reach this morning's events, when it comes to what they refer to as "penetration," I want to die to stop the pain. They ask me if I used protection; they ask me if Maya cried out; they ask me how long it lasted. . . . It hurts so much, feels so utterly humiliating, so completely degrading, that I feel sick.

The interrogation seems to go on for hours. It feels like the middle of the night and we have been shut up in this tiny, airless room for all eternity. They take turns popping out for coffee or snacks. They offer me water, which I decline. Eventually I am so wrung out that all I can do is suck on my middle two fingers like I used to as a small child and slump sideways against the wall, my voice completely hoarse, face sticky with congealed sweat and tears. Through a thick haze, I hear them inform me that I will be escorted back to my cell and that the interview will continue tomorrow.

The tape is switched off and another officer comes to collect me, but for a few moments I can't even get to my feet. Detective Sutton—who, for the most part, has remained cold and impassive—sighs and shakes his head with a look bordering on pity. "You know, Lochan, I've been in this job for years and I can tell that you're feeling remorse for what you've done. But I'm afraid it's all rather too late. Not only are you charged with committing a very serious crime, but your threats appear to have left your sister so terrified, she has signed a statement swearing that your sexual relationship together was fully consensual and instigated by her."

All the air exits my body. My exhaustion evaporates. Suddenly only the thudding of my horrified heartbeat fills the air. She told them the truth? She told them the truth?

"A signed statement—but that's void now, right? Now that I've admitted everything, told you exactly what happened. You know she only said those things because I told her to, because I said I'd have her killed if I ended up in prison. So no one believes her, do they? Not now I've confessed!" My cracked, dried-up voice is shaking hard, but I must stay calm. Showing remorse is one thing, but I have to somehow disguise the extent of my horror and disbelief.

"That'll depend on how the judge sees it."

"The judge?" I'm shouting now, my voice verging on hysteria. "But Maya's not the one being accused of rape!"

"No, but even consensual incest is against the law. Under section sixty-five of the Sexual Offenses Act, your sister could be tried for 'consenting to penetration by an adult relative,' which carries a sentence of up to two years in prison."

I stare at him. Speechless. Stunned. It cannot be. It cannot be.

The detective sighs and tosses the file back onto the table in a sudden gesture of weariness. "So unless she retracts her statement, your sister now faces arrest too."

Why, Maya, my love? Why, why, why?

Collapsed on the floor, half propped up against the metal door, I stare blindly at the opposite wall. My whole body hurts from lying completely motionless for what must be several hours now. I no longer have the strength to continue banging my head back against the door in a desperate, frenzied attempt to think of a way of somehow getting Maya to retract her statement. After shouting over and over, pleading with the guards to

TABITHA SUZUMA

let me call home, I eventually lose my voice completely. Maya and I will never be allowed to contact each other again—at least not until I've served out my sentence which, according to that interrogation officer, could be more than a decade from now!

My mind is falling apart and I can barely think, but as far as I understand it, the fact is that unless Maya retracts her statement, she will be arrested just as I was, possibly even in front of Tiffin and Willa. With no one to look after them, no one to cover for our mother's drinking and neglect, all three children will doubtlessly be taken into care. And Maya will be brought to the police station, subjected to the same humiliations, the same interrogations, and accused, just as I was, of committing a sexual crime. Even with my word against hers, there will be little I can do. If I continue to insist I am the abuser, they will immediately question why I am suddenly so desperate to absolve Maya of all wrongdoing—especially after having both repeatedly abused and threatened to kill her should she tell anyone. I will be cornered, powerless to protect her, for the more I insist that Maya is innocent and I am the guilty one, the more likely they will be to believe Maya's confession. It won't take them long to figure out that I'm taking the blame to protect her, that I'm lying because I love her, and that I would never abuse, threaten, or harm her in any way. And of course there's Kit—the only real witness. Even Tiffin and Willa, if they are questioned, will insist that never once did Maya ever appear afraid of me—that she was always smiling at me, laughing with me, touching my hand, even hugging me. And so they will realize that Maya is as complicit in this crime as I am.

Whatever I try to do now is hopeless, especially as any attempts to catch Maya out will fail as she will be the one telling the truth. She'll easily be able to explain away the blow to her lip as my last desperate attempt to make it look as if I was abusing her.

Maya will be brought to court and sentenced to two years in prison. She will start off her adult life behind bars, separated not only from me, but from Kit, Tiffin, and Willa, who love her so much. Even after serving out her prison sentence, she will emerge emotionally scarred and stuck with a criminal record for the rest of her life. Denied all access to her other siblings for her crime, she will find herself utterly alone in the world, ostracized by her friends, while I remain locked up, serving out a considerably longer sentence because I'll have been tried as an adult. The thought of all this is, quite simply, more than I can bear. And I know that, unless I can somehow get through to her, the stubborn, passionate Maya who loves me so much will not capitulate. She has made her choice. How I wish I could tell her that I would rather be locked away for life than put her through any of that. . . .

TABITHA SUZUMA

No use sitting here falling apart. None of this can happen. I will not let it. Yet despite thinking and thinking for hours on end, lashing out sporadically against the cold concrete around me in utter frustration, I cannot come up with any way to get Maya to change her mind.

I'm beginning to realize that nothing will make Maya retract her statement and accuse me of rape. She'll have had time now to realize that, by doing so, she will send me to prison. If I'd run, as she initially suggested, if by some miracle I'd managed to avoid getting caught, she would have lied in a heartbeat for the sake of the children. But knowing that I am sitting here, locked in a prison cell, the rest of my life dependent on her accusation or confession, she will never capitulate. I realize this now with earth-shattering certainty. She loves me too much. She loves me too much. I so wanted her love, all of it. I got my wish . . . and now we are both paying the price. How stupid I was to ever ask her to do this, I realize, to expect her to sacrifice my freedom for hers. My happiness meant everything to her, as much as hers did to me. Had the situation been reversed, would I have even considered falsely accusing Maya in order to avoid a punishment of my own?

Yet still the regret gnaws away at me. If I'd run when I had had the chance, if I'd left and somehow escaped arrest, Maya would not have confessed. Nothing would have been gained by telling the truth; it would have only hurt the children. She would have never confessed if I hadn't been caught. . . .

My gaze travels slowly up the wall to the small window in the corner, just below the ceiling. And suddenly the answer is right there in front of me. If I want Maya to retract her confession, then I must not be here to receive a sentence. I must not be trapped in a cell facing jail time. I must leave.

Unpicking the threads of the sheet sewn onto the mattress soon causes my hands to stiffen and my fingers to go numb. I keep track of the time between guard checks, counting rhythmically to myself beneath my breath as I carefully, methodically, sever the seams. Whoever designed these cells has done a good job of ensuring their security. The small window is so high off the ground that it would require a three-meter ladder to reach it. It is also barred, of course, but the bars stick out at the top. With an accurate throw, I feel confident that I can lasso a loop over the spiked bars so that the knotted strips of torn sheet hang down just low enough for me to reach, like those ropes we used to climb in gym. I was good at that, I remember, always the first to the top. If I can achieve a similar result this time, I will reach the window, that small patch of sunlight, my gateway to freedom. It's a crazy plan, I know. A desperate one. But I am desperate. There are no options left. I have to go. I have to disappear.

The bars covering the glass show signs of rust and don't

look that strong. So long as they don't break before I actually reach the window, this could work.

Six hundred and twenty-three counts since the last steps were heard outside my cell door. Once I am ready, I'll have ten minutes or so to pull this off. I've read about people managing to do this before—it doesn't just happen on cop shows. It is possible. It has to be.

After finally working my way round the entire edge of the plastic sheet, I give it a small tug and feel it shift under me, no longer attached to the mattress beneath. Positioning it in front of me, I use my teeth to make the first tear and begin to rip, bit by bit. By my rough calculations, three strips of sheet tied together should be just about long enough. The material is tough and my hands are aching, but I can't risk just yanking at the sheet for fear of the sound of tearing being overheard. My nails are torn, my fingertips a bleeding mess, by the time the material is separated into three equal pieces. But now all I have to do is wait for the guard to pass.

The footsteps begin to approach, and suddenly I am shaking. Shaking so hard I can hardly think. I can't go through with it. I'm too much of a coward, too damn scared. My plan is ridiculous—I am going to get caught; I am going to fail. The bars look too loose. What if they break before I reach the window?

The footsteps begin to recede and I immediately start tying the strips together. The knots have to be tight, really tight—enough to take my full weight. Sweat pours off me, running into my eyes, blurring my vision. I have to hurry, hurry, hurry, but my hands won't stop shaking. My body screams at me to stop, back down. My mind forces me to keep going. I have never been this afraid.

I miss. I keep missing. Despite the weight of the plastic material and the heavy knotted loop at the end, I cannot get it to catch on one of the spikes. I made the loop too small. I overestimated my ability to hit a target while panicking with unsteady hands. Finally, in mad desperation, I hurl it right up to the ceiling, and to my astonishment, the loop comes down to catch on a single outer spike, the knotted strips of sheet hanging down against the wall like a thick rope. I stare at it for a moment in total shock; it's there, waiting to be climbed, my path to freedom. Heart pounding, I reach up to grasp the material as high as I can. Pulling myself up with my arms, I raise my legs, draw up my knees, cross my ankles to trap the material between my feet and begin to climb.

Reaching the top takes far longer than I'd anticipated. My palms are sweaty, my fingers weak from all the unpicking and tearing, and unlike school climbing ropes, the strips of sheet have almost no grip. As soon as I reach the top, I hook my arms

 TABITHA SUZUMA

round the bars, my feet scrabbling for a foothold against the bumpy, chipped wall. The toe of my shoe finds a small protrusion, and thanks to the grip of my trainers, I am able to cling on. Now for the moment of truth. Have the bars been loosened by my climb? Will a final violent downward pull cause them to break away from the wall?

I haven't time to inspect the rust around the fastenings now. Like a rock climber on a cliff's edge, I cling to the bars with my hands and to the wall with my feet, every muscle in my body straining against the pull of gravity. If they catch me now, it's all over. But still I hesitate. Will the bars break? Will they break? For one brief moment I feel the golden light of the dying sun touch my face through the dirty window. Beyond it lies freedom. Shut up in this airless box, I am able to catch a glimpse of the outdoors, the wind shaking the green trees in the distance. The thick glass is like an invisible wall, sealing me off from everything that is real and alive and necessary. At what point do you give up—decide enough is enough? There is only one answer, really. *Never.*

The time has come. If I fail, they will hear me and either keep me under surveillance or transfer me to a more secure cell, so I'm acutely aware that this is my one and only chance. A terrified sob threatens to escape me. I'm losing it—someone will hear. But I don't want to do this. I'm so afraid. So very afraid.

With my left arm still hooked over the bars, taking almost the full weight of my body—metal cutting into flesh, digging into bone—I release one hand to reach for the sheet hanging down below me. And then I realize this is it. The guard will be back down the corridor any minute now. I have no excuses anymore. It's time for me to set us all free. Despite the terror, the blinding white terror, I slip a second loop over my head. Tighten the noose. A harsh sob breaks the still air. And then I let go.

Willa's big blue eyes, Willa's dimple-cheeked smile. Tiffin's shaggy blond mane, Tiffin's cheeky grin. Kit's yells of excitement, Kit's glow of pride. Maya's face, Maya's kisses, Maya's love.

Maya, Maya, Maya . . .

up at a familiar ceiling, my bed a cold tomb in which I now lie alone. The tranquilizers have long been binned, the threat of hospitalization dropped now that I'm managing to eat and drink again, now that I've regained my voice, found a way of making my muscles contract and then relax in order to be able to move, stand, function. Things are almost back to normal: Mum has stopped trying to force-feed me, Dave has stopped covering for her to the authorities, and both have drifted back across town together after restoring some kind of order in the house and putting on a convincing show for social services. I have returned to the familiar role of care provider, except that nothing is familiar to me anymore, least of all myself.

A basic routine has resumed: getting up, showering, dressing, shopping, cooking, cleaning the house, trying to keep Tiffin and Willa and even Kit as busy as possible. They cling to me like limpets—most nights all four of us end up together in what used to be our mother's bed. Even Kit has regressed to a frightened child, although his valiant efforts to help and support me make my heart ache. As we huddle together beneath the duvet in the big double bed, sometimes they want to talk; mostly they want to cry and I comfort them as best I can, even though I know nothing can ever be enough—no words can ever make up for what happened, for what I put them through.

During the day there is so much to do: speak to their

teachers about returning to school, go to our sessions with the counselor, check in with the social worker, make sure the kids are clean, fed, and healthy. . . . I am forced to keep a checklist, remind myself what I'm supposed to be doing at each point during the day—when to get up, when to have meals, when to start bedtime. I have to break down each chore into little steps; otherwise I find myself standing in the middle of the kitchen with a saucepan in one hand, completely overwhelmed, lost, with no idea why I'm standing there or what I'm supposed to do next. I start sentences I cannot finish, ask Kit to do me a favor and then forget what it was. He tries to help me, tries to take over and do everything, but then I worry that he is doing too much, that he, too, will have some sort of breakdown, and so I beg him to stop. But at the same time I realize he needs to keep busy and feel he is helping and that I need him to help too.

Since the day it happened, the day the news came, every minute has been agony in its simplest, strongest form, like forcing my hand into a furnace and counting down the seconds, knowing they will never end, wondering how I can possibly endure another one, and then another after that, astonished that despite the torture I keep breathing, I keep moving, even though I know by doing so the pain will never go away. But I kept my hand in life's furnace for a single reason only—the children. I covered for our mother; I lied for our mother; I even told the children exactly what to say before social services arrived—but that was when I still had the arrogance, the ridiculous, shameful arrogance, to believe that they would still be better off with me than taken away and placed in care.

Now I know different. Even though I have slowly reestablished some sort of routine, some semblance of calm, I have turned into a robot and can barely look after myself, let alone three traumatized children. They deserve a proper home with a proper family who will keep them together and be able to counsel and support them. They deserve to start afresh—embark on a new life where the people who care for them follow society's norms, where loved ones don't leave, or fall apart, or die. They deserve so much better. No doubt they always have.

I do honestly believe all this now. It took me a few days to convince myself fully, but eventually I realized that I had no choice: There was actually no decision to make, no option but to accept the facts. I do not have the strength to continue like this; I cannot go on another day. The only way to cope with such crushing guilt is to convince myself that, for their own sakes, the children will be better off elsewhere. I will not allow myself to think that I, too, am abandoning them.

My reflection hasn't changed. I'm not sure how long I've been standing here, but I'm aware that some time has passed

because I am starting to feel very cold again. This is a familiar sign that I have ground to a halt, come to the end of the current step and forgotten how to make the transition to the next. But maybe this time my delay is deliberate. The next step will be the hardest of all.

The dress I bought for the occasion is actually quite pretty without being too formal. The navy jacket makes it look suitably smart. Blue because it is Lochan's favorite color. Was Lochan's favorite color. I bite my lip and blood wells up on the surface. Crying is apparently good for the children—someone told me that, I don't remember who—but I've learned that for me, as with everything I do now, there is no point to it. Nothing can relieve the pain. Not crying, laughing, screaming, begging. Nothing can change the past. Nothing can bring him back. The dead remain dead.

Lochan would have laughed at my clothes. He never saw me so poshly dressed. He would have joked that I looked like a city banker. But then he would have stopped laughing and told me that actually I looked beautiful. He would have chuckled at the sight of Kit in such a smart suit, suddenly seeming so much older than his thirteen years. He would have teased us for buying Tiffin a suit, too, but would have liked the brightly colored soccer-ball tie, Tiffin's own personal touch. He would have struggled to laugh at Willa's choice of outfit, though. I think the sight of her in her treasured violet "princess dress" that we got her for Christmas would have brought him close to tears.

It has taken so long—nearly a month because of the autopsy, the inquest, and all the rest—but finally the time has come. Our mother decided not to attend, so it will just be the four of us in the pretty church up on Millwood Hill—its cool, shady interior empty, echoey, and quiet. Just the four of us and the coffin. Reverend Dawes will think Lochan Whitely had no friends, but he'll be wrong—he had me, he had all of us. . . . He will think Lochan wasn't loved, but he was, more deeply than most people are in a lifetime. . . .

After the short service we will return home and comfort one another. After a while I will go upstairs and write the letters— one to each of them, explaining why, telling them how much I love them, that I'm so, so very sorry. Reassuring them that they will be well looked after by another family, trying to convince them, as I did myself, that they will be much better off without me, much better off starting over. Then the rest will be easy— selfish but easy—because it has been carefully planned for over a week now. Obviously I can't possibly remain in the house for the children to find, so I will go to my refuge in Ashmoore Park, the place I called paradise, which I once shared with Lochan. Except this time I shall not return.

The kitchen knife I've been keeping beneath the stack of

 TABITHA SUZUMA

papers in my desk drawer will be hidden beneath my coat. I will lie down on the damp grass, stare up at the star-studded sky, and then raise the knife. I know exactly what to do so that it will be over quickly, so quickly—the same way I hope it was for Lochan. Lochie. The boy I once loved. The boy I still love. The boy I will continue to love, even when my part in this world is over too. He sacrificed his life to spare me a prison sentence. He thought I could look after the children. He thought I was the strong one—strong enough to go on without him. He thought he knew me. But he was wrong.

Willa bursts into the room, making me start. Kit has brushed her long, golden hair, wiped her face and hands clean after breakfast. Her baby face is still so sweet and trusting; it pains me to look at her. I wonder whether, when she is my age, she will still look like me. I hope someone will show her a picture. I hope someone will let her know how much she was loved—by Lochan, by me—even though she won't be able to remember it for herself. Out of the three of them, she is the most likely to make a full recovery, the most likely to forget, and I hope she does. Perhaps, if they allow her to keep at least one photo, some part of it will jog her memory. Perhaps she will remember a game we used to play or the funny voices I used to do for the different characters in her books at bedtime.

She hesitates in the doorway, unsure whether to advance or retreat, clearly desperate to tell me something but afraid to do so.

"What is it, my darling? You look so beautiful in your dress. Are you ready to go?"

She stares at me, unblinking, as if trying to gauge my reaction, then slowly shakes her head, her big eyes filling with tears.

I kneel down and hold out my arms and she launches herself into them, her small hands pressed against her eyes.

"I d-don't want to—I don't want to go! I don't! I don't want to go say good-bye to Lochie!"

I pull her close, her small body sobbing softly against mine, and kiss her wet cheek, stroke her hair, rock her back and forth against me.

"I know you don't, Willa. I don't want to either. None of us does. But we need to—we need to say good-bye. It doesn't mean we can't visit his grave in the churchyard; it doesn't mean we can't still think about him and talk about him whenever we want."

"But I don't want to go, Maya!" she cries, her sobbing voice almost pleading. "I'm not going to say good-bye. I don't want him to go! I don't, I don't, I don't!" She starts to struggle against me, trying to pull away, desperate to escape the ordeal, the finality of it all.

TABITHA SUZUMA

I wrap my arms tightly around her and attempt to hold her still. "Willa, listen to me, listen to me. Lochie wants you to come and say good-bye to him. He really wants that a lot. He loves you so much—you know that. You're his favorite little girl in the whole world. He knows you're very sad and very angry right now, but he really hopes one day you won't feel so bad anymore."

Her struggles become more halfhearted, her body weakening as her tears increase.

"W-what else does he want?"

Frantically I try to come up with something. *For you to someday find a way to forgive him. For you to forget the pain he caused you even if it means you have to forget him. For you to go on to live a life of unimaginable joy . . .*

"Well—he always loved your drawings, remember? I'm sure he'd really like it if you made him something. Maybe a card with a special picture. You could write a message inside if you want to—or otherwise just your name. We'll cover it in special transparent plastic, so that even if it rains, it won't get wet. And then you could take it to him when you go and visit his grave."

"But if he's asleep forever and ever, how will he even know it's there? How will he even see it?"

Taking a deep breath, I close my eyes. "I don't know, Willa.

I honestly don't know. But he might—he might see it; he might know. So, just in case he does . . ."

"O-okay." She draws back slightly, her face still pink and tearstained, but with a tiny glimmer of hope in her eyes. "I think he will see it, Maya," she tells me, as if begging me to agree. "I think he will. Don't you?"

I nod slowly, biting down hard. "I think he will too."

Willa gives a small gulp and a sniff, but I can tell her mind is already on the work of art she is going to create. She leaves my arms and moves off toward the door but then, as if suddenly remembering something, turns back.

"So what about you, then?"

I feel myself tense. "What d'you mean?"

"What about you?" she repeats. "What are you going to give him?"

"Oh—maybe some flowers or something. I'm not artistic like you. I don't think he'd want one of my drawings."

Willa gives me a long look. "I don't think Lochie would want you to give him flowers. I think he'd want you to do something special-er."

Turning away from her abruptly, I walk over to the window and peer up at the cloudless sky, pretending to check for rain. "Tell you what—why don't you go and start making the card? I'll be down in a minute and then we can all set off

TABITHA SUZUMA

together. And remember, on the way home we're going to have cakes at—"

"That's not fair!" Willa shouts suddenly. "Lochie loves you! He wants you to do something for him too!"

She runs out of the room and I hear the familiar sound of her feet thudding down the stairs. Anxiously I follow her to the end of the corridor, but when I hear her ask Kit to help her find the felt-tips, I relax.

I return to my room. Back to the mirror I can't seem to leave. If I keep looking at myself, I can persuade myself I'm still here, at least for today. I have to be here today, for the children, for Lochie. I have to turn off the mechanical switch just for these next few hours. I have to let myself feel, just for now, just for the funeral. But now that my mind is thawing, coming back to life, the pain begins to rise again, and Willa's words won't leave me alone. Why did she get so angry? Does she somehow sense that I've given up? Does she think that because Lochie's gone, I no longer care what he might have wanted from us, for us?

I suddenly grip the sides of the mirror for support. I am on dangerous ground—this is a train of thought I cannot afford to follow. Willa loved Lochan as much as I did, yet she is not hiding behind an anesthetic; she is hurting as much as I am, yet she is finding ways to cope, even though she's only five. Right now she isn't thinking about herself and her own grief, but about Lochie, about what she can do for him. The least I can do is ask myself the same question: If Lochie could see me now, what would he be asking for?

But of course I know the answer already. I've known the answer all along. Which is why I've carefully avoided thinking about it until now . . . I watch the eyes of the girl in the mirror fill with tears. *No, Lochie,* I tell him desperately. *No! Please, please. You can't ask me for that—you can't. I can't do it, not without you. It's too hard. It's too hard. It's too painful! I loved you too much!*

Can a person as kind as Lochie ever be loved too much? Was our love really destined to cause so much unhappiness, so much destruction and despair? In the end, was it wrong after all? If I am still here, doesn't that mean I have the chance to keep our love alive? Doesn't that mean I still have the opportunity to make something good come out of all this, rather than unending tragedy?

He gave up his life to rescue mine, to rescue the children's. That was what he wanted; that was his choice; that was the price he was willing to pay for me to continue living, for me to have a life worth living. If I die too, his ultimate sacrifice will have been in vain.

I sway forward so that my forehead presses against the cold glass. I close my eyes and start to cry, silent tears tracking down

452   TABITHA SUZUMA

my cheeks. *Lochie, I can go to prison for you. I can die for you. But the one thing I know you want, I can't do. I can't go on living for you.*

"Maya, we need to leave. We're going to be late!" Kit's voice calls up from the hall. They're all waiting, waiting to say good-bye, to take the first step toward letting go. If I am to live, I will have to start letting go too. Let go of Lochie. How can I possibly ever do that?

I look at my face one more time. I look into the eyes Lochie used to call as blue as the ocean. Just a few moments ago I told myself that he never really knew me if he thought, even for a second, that I could survive without him. But what if I'm the one who is wrong? Lochie died to save us, to save the family, to save me. He wouldn't have done that if he'd thought, even for a moment, that I wasn't strong enough to go on without him. Perhaps, just perhaps, at the end of the day, he is right and I am wrong. Perhaps I never knew myself as well as he knew me.

I walk slowly toward my desk and pull open the drawer. I slide my hand under the piles of paper and close my fingers around the knife's handle. I pick it up, its sharp edge glinting in the sun. I hold it under my jacket and go downstairs. In the kitchen, I open the cutlery drawer and place it right at the very back, out of sight. Then I push the drawer firmly closed.

A violent sob escapes me. As I press the back of my wrist against my mouth, my lips meet the cool silver. Lochan's present to me. Now it's my turn. Closing my eyes against the tears, I take a long, deep breath and whisper, "Okay, I'll try. That's all I can promise you right now, Lochie, but I'll try."

As we leave the house, everyone is fussing and squabbling. Willa has lost her butterfly clip; Tiffin claims his tie is choking him; Kit complains that Willa's moaning will make us all late. . . . We file out through the broken gate and onto the street, all dressed up in the smartest clothes we have ever owned. Willa and Tiffin both want to hold my hand. Kit hangs back. I suggest he take Willa's so that we can swing her between us. He obliges, and as we launch her high into the air, the wind whips back her long dress, revealing a pair of bright pink knickers. As she clamors for us to do it again, Kit's eyes meet mine with an amused smile.

We walk down the middle of the road holding hands, the sidewalk far too narrow for all four of us together. A warm breeze brushes across our faces, carrying the smell of honeysuckle from a front garden. The midday sun beams down from a bright blue sky, the light shimmering between the leaves, scattering us with golden confetti.

"Hey!" Tiffin exclaims, his voice ringing with surprise. "It's nearly summer!"